Thirsty Boots

by

Mackay Roberts

Thirsty Boots

© 2018 by Mackay Roberts

To contact the author:

mackayrobertsauthor@gmail.com

 HACKMATACK
PRESS

East Concord, NH 03301

ISBN: 978-1981846351

Editor's Note

Thanks so much for taking a look at this novel by Mackay Roberts. It's a powerful and moving story of young adults coming of age. These characters, who come from diverse backgrounds, face the tumultuous complexities of the modern world, while discovering the inner person that makes them unique. They find friends, make choices, suffer consequences, and seek direction for the future. This rollicking novel is set in the late 1960s, a time of political turmoil, cultural unrest, civil disobedience, street protests, and foreign wars – much like the present age we are living in here in America.

This is a pre-publication version of the novel. It is sent out to early readers and reviewers before the final editing and typesetting are completed. Please forgive any typos, misspellings, or other errors in the text. Hopefully, these will be cleaned up before release. Feel free to note any problems with the text by sending me an email at the address below.

If you have words of praise or of critique, feel free to jot an email to the publishing house. (hackmatackpress@gmail.com)

Thanks for reading this early copy. I hope you enjoy it.

Jennifer Cruz, Senior Editor

HACKMATACK
PRESS

"The answer my friend, is blowin' in the wind,
The answer is blowin' in the wind."

~ Bob Dylan

Prologue

Rob Bachmann   August, 1969

Woodstock blew me away! Not until I arrived at Woodstock, did I realize I'd already been on an amazing journey, which had changed my life forever!

When my friends and I left Harrisburg, we were on a lark to finish summer and kickoff our senior year at Carlisle College. Driving through the Catskill Mountains, we found ourselves swept up in a wave of people heading to Yasgur's Farm. The swelling streams of raw humanity were mind boggling.

Colorful currents of people and vehicles were everywhere. Psychedelic school buses, old cars, new cars, vans, motor homes, funny European Peugeots and Volvos, trucks hauling trailers, and tiny sports cars. The roads were jammed, overwhelmed by a tidal wave of America's youth. Long hairs in bell bottoms and leather vests mingled with straights in jeans and button-down shirts, girls in pleated wool skirts and penny loafers. Groovy chicks in granny dresses, peasant blouses and bare feet walked alongside a group of nuns in black and white habits. Whoa! What an eclectic assemblage of the next generation!

Arriving early, we set up camp on the edge of a hayfield behind the stage, which was still being built. The noise of screaming saws and pounding hammers filled the air. The crowds swelled; eventually traffic had come to a complete stop. People then abandoned their vehicles and hiked into the scene with just the clothes on their backs. Many sat in the grassy bowl-shaped field in front of the stage still being constructed. There was no music, but 50,000 young people sprawled on the lawn waiting for something to happen.

In a way we were all waiting for something to happen. The Woodstock experience was an allegory for my generation--those of us who came of age in the tumultuous '60s. It was the era of sex, drugs, and rock & roll – the answer to all of life's questions! Our formative years had been spent in a world coming apart; actually exploding at the seams! Nuclear war and communist menace, segregation and civil rights, poverty and the military industrial complex, urban riots, campus protests, political upheaval, Vietnam and the anti-war movement, free love and free sex, flower power and hippies, drugs and dropping out. What a mess! As a generation, we had so many questions and too few answers.

That first evening, I found myself sitting around a campfire with my friends, wondering. We came from many different backgrounds before we cam together in college. Between us we've seen the good, bad, and the ugly. We hailed from happy loving homes, broken homes, strict religious homes, mean & hateful families, and even passive indifference. We grew up with materialism, poverty, and middle-class security. Unfortunately, many of us endured way too much physical, emotional, and sexual abuse.

Yet we were all looking for life's answers. Although from vastly different backgrounds, we shared the turmoil and tumult of the world in which we were raised. After reaching college, we were asking questions like: "Who am I? What makes me special? How can I connect to others, find belonging, build community? What's my purpose? How can I relate to the rest of the universe? Is there more to life than what I've seen so far?"

Not all of us made this trip. Randi, Nikki, Gary, Doug, Faith, Frank, and Linda were sitting around the fire with me enjoying this crazy experience. Jack was still in the hospital broken and hurting. Frenchie and Arty had serious jobs for the summer, the kind that pay real money and they expect you to show up for work. Billy, of course, was off hobnobbing in his White House internship.

By the time we reached Woodstock, we could see Woodstock was a metaphor for life itself. Finally, a little light at the end of the pilgrimage we started three years ago. It has not been an easy trip. Hopes and dreams have been shattered. People we love have died. Some were innocent victims; others ruined their lives with bad choices. Tragedy struck close friends and irreversibly altered the future – sometimes for better, sometimes for worse.

Yet, we made friends we will keep for a lifetime. We learned a lot – not just information, but wisdom and truth. Most of us indulged in new experiences, met wise mentors, tasted worlds we never knew existed, had deep conversations, and great laughs. By the time we got to Woodstock, like most of our generation, we were seeking to set our souls free, to find a path for life, to sing a song of celebration, and to find the stardust which gets us back to the garden. It was a time of new beginnings--of new life.

At this point, I have faith our lives will never be the same. The journey isn't over, but I know there's no going back. I have no idea how it's going to turn out, but I'm committed to pressing on until I find whatever it is I'm looking for. My course is set. I'm headed for a brave new world!

The music at Woodstock was incredible. The people were even more impressive than the music. The rain came and went, technical glitches slowed the process, yet the magic of wonderful music played on. Mud was everywhere, lines were long, supplies were hard to come by, and the toilets overflowed. But the community was astonishing. People cared for one another, offered a helping hand and shared whatever they had. Individuals pitched in and helped each other in kind and thoughtful ways. In a just few days, 500,000 total strangers became Woodstock Nation.

My life journey did not begin with Woodstock, but it marks a turning point in my story. The best place to start a story is at the beginning. Maybe not at the inception of birth as this story is not about my life. It is about my finding life, which is an altogether different tale. Perhaps I should begin at the end of my childhood, when I launched out into the great quest for life, on the adventure which every person must face if they are to find *home*. Before I left for college, I was already a long way from home.

Year One

1

Rob Bachmann   August, 1966

Slumped dejectedly on my bed, I was overwhelmed with grief. Sitting on the old baby blue bedspread, nervously plucking the little blue tassels covering the faded material. The bed was a simple rectangular box made out of ½ inch plywood. No box spring, just a lumpy secondhand mattress, dropped straight on the plywood base. Like most of the furnishings in my room, the bed was built by my father as a weekend project. My dresser, a small closet with sliding doors, the narrow cubby for my sports gear – all built by Fritz Bachmann. In fact, Dad built the house, a two story colonial at 418 Ferry Road, in the small town of New Britain in Bucks County, Pennsylvania. He designed it, drew up the blueprints, made a 3-D model, and was the general contractor. The family moved in when I was 4, and Dad spent a decade of weekends working on home improvement projects to finish the house.

I grew up in this room. Spent much of my lifetime retreating here, being lonely here, often hiding here. Now I'm preparing to leave this room, my home, my life as I have known it. Open on the floor, in front of the bed sits my beat-up green Army footlocker which I carted off to Ressica Falls Boy Scout Camp each summer of my teen years. Blue jeans, t-shirts, BVDs, a pair of dress shoes, and the few good clothes I own are neatly folded and stowed in the footlocker. Extra socks, swim gear, my toiletry kit and other odds and ends are stuffed into the denim laundry bag leaning against the night stand.

Everything I want to take to college is packed, yet all I can do is to sit and stare at the wall and feel the pain. The aguish begins in my guts, swells through my throat and bursts out of my eyes as wet tears running down my cheeks. God, I can't believe I'm still crying! The misery rears up, wrapping around my chest, crushing my lungs, making me feel I will never be able to take another breath of air for the sheer agony lancing through my being. Only then does the pain radiate upward into my brain where I can see it and recognize it for what is.

All I can do is stare. I feel frozen in time. "I wonder what day is it, anyway?" I'm having trouble sorting it out. "I still can't believe the sun keeps coming up each morning," More vacant staring. "How would I know what day it is?" For what seems like hours, I have been stuck in this position, stupidly staring in silence at my dull gray bedroom walls. Nothing to see there. Nothing but a tattered old poster of a prancing Mick Jagger and a smaller framed photo of Joan Baez at the Newport Folk Festival. Finally, a light goes on in my exhausted brain. "It must be Tuesday," I say aloud to the wall. Tomorrow I leave for freshman orientation at Carlisle, and last Saturday was the funeral. Shaking my head, I still can't get up. I'm so confused, disoriented. Do I even want to leave for college now? I don't know. I can't think straight. Really, I haven't been able to think at all since we got the news.

The service took place in the small chapel at the Longenecker Funeral Home on Main Street in New Britain. It's the same place we had Mom's funeral when I was twelve. Remembering that day and her service makes me wonder at how little emotion or regret I experienced when she died. At the time, rather than the agonizing pain now consuming me, all I felt was a sense of relief. Mom might be gone, but at least the eternal bickering between my parents would stop. I remember six years earlier, when I sat on the hard chapel pew with Dad, my older brother Teddy, and Molly, my little sister. At the time I simply felt numb. The process seemed so weird. Sort of heartless. Stripped of emotion. There she was, up in the front of the funeral home in a box. People got up and said this and said that, and yet no one ever mentioned her name. It was so cold and remote. Remembering makes me snort. I swear I've seen dairy cows buried with more ceremony and feeling.

When Mom died things actually did get better. The fighting stopped. Ted tried to fill in for Mom with Molly and me. Dad just retreated into stony silence; not much different from before her death. Ted meant well, but he never had the personality to be a caregiver. A typical first-born son, Ted was always self righteous, rigid, obsessed with his own sense of importance and a constant need to be perfect. Always "Ted," never "Teddy." I called him Teddy anyway, but not to his face. My big brother was never warm and fuzzy. Honestly, he was a bit of an ass. No wonder I often felt like an orphan.

But this death was so unexpected! I never saw it coming, did not even think it was a possibility. It blew me away. I've never been one for touchy feely sharing and hugging. Guess I'm reserved and I like to keep to myself. Rarely will I volunteer what I'm thinking or feeling. I'll bet if you asked them, my closest friends would describe me as remote. It isn't that I never think or feel - I spend a great deal of time thinking, learning, evaluating, and contemplating. But I find it difficult to share what's on my mind with other people. When Ted died, I had absolutely no idea what to think, to feel, and I had nothing to say. It just staggered me into total silence.

The funeral last Saturday had been horrific. Ted had always been the bright light of hope in the Bachmann family. The shining star, the best, the most admired. He loved school and excelled at everything. An honor student, a three sport athlete, my brother made Eagle Scout at sixteen. While he shone at school, what Teddy dearly loved was building stuff in Dad's workshop and reading books about old Civil War battles. Ted, two years older than me, had enrolled at Bucknell College and majored in engineering. At the end of his second year, however, Ted dropped out of college to join the Marines, to "fight for America!" as he put it, in the war now heating up in Vietnam.

After ten weeks of boot camp at Paris Island, Ted came home for a few days of leave to visit the family. Then, at the beginning of August, three weeks ago, he shipped out to Vietnam. Ted was dead within a week. His platoon landed at Khe Sanh in Quang Tri Province and was assigned to a Marine fire base in the Northern Highlands of Vietnam. But it was not the Viet Cong who killed him. Running a routine patrol out in the jungles with his squad, Ted tripped on a vine across a jungle path, fell sprawling and was shot by the accidental discharge of his M-16. A week later he was back home. In a box. The featured attraction of another Bachmann family funeral down at the Longenecker Home. The raw and fiery pain inside me burns and burns. All I can do is sit, shake my head and groan.

There is simply no way to get my head around this tragedy. It feels like I have run full speed, headfirst, into a brick wall and knocked myself unconscious. When I come to, I am dazed, confused, bruised. I hurt all over, don't know what happened, and am so disoriented I have no idea what to do next. Yet, it isn't just the funeral crushing me. It isn't only my brother's sudden death which freezes the blood in my veins. It isn't the thought that Teddy will never come home and be part of my life. There is something altogether different weighing on my heart and my spirit.

Three weeks ago, when Ted was home on leave, we had a chat one afternoon. "Come on down to the picnic table," Teddy said, "So we can have a little time together before I leave." Together we walked across the backyard to the old picnic table under the willow tree and sat. After Mom's death, this is where Teddy often brought me for pep talks, and to give me some room to ask questions and to process my feelings. Whenever Ted was trying to play the nurturing role in my life, he would call me "Sport." That day he began, "Sport, I feel I need to share something with you before I head off to Vietnam…" For ten long minutes we sat together on the weathered benches while Ted shared the most agonizingly painful story I have ever heard. It was a story about the Bachmann's, about my family. It was a story of murder, lies, betrayal and it was a black family secret Ted said no one else could ever know. After swearing me to secrecy, we got up and went back to the house.

Teddy got on the bus the next morning, rode to Philadelphia, flew off to the war and is now buried and gone. Not only was Ted ripped out of my life, he abandoned me with this family secret. He's gone and I'm still here holding a secret that's festering in my heart. I'm not sure how much of my grief comes from my brother's unexpected death, how much is from the awful story Ted bestowed on me, and how much is the sense of betrayal and abandonment at being left alone with this evil knowledge. Altogether, it's as if an atom bomb has been dropped on our house. My home's been destroyed. My family is gone. Everything about my life as I have lived it until now is in complete ruins.

It reminds me of when I was ten and the Findleys' house burned down. The Findleys were close neighbors and friends who lived in one of our street's original farmhouses. One October evening, something went awry in the mechanical systems and the house caught fire. Fortunately, the family was out. But by the time the volunteer firemen got there, the home was fully engulfed in flames. Our family and other neighbors gathered on the street and watched as the house burned to the ground. In the morning there was nothing left but smoldering ruins and ashes. The remains were bulldozed into the basement and covered with dirt. What was once a home is now nothing but a vacant lot full of weeds.

This thought makes me contemplate my own home, my life, and what I used to think of as my family. It is all gone. Destroyed. Blown to smithereens. Just like the Findleys' house. Nothing to save. Time to walk away. Sitting on my bed, swamped in misery, my guts churn with anguish. This feels like its killing me. Still, I have no desire to talk to anyone about the pain in my heart. It hurts so bad, but I can't share it. Better to wall myself off, marinate in misery, be crushed by my grief, and remain isolated with my wounds. Better to grow a heart of stone than live with this suffering. What good would talking do? And I can't talk about the family secret. Since Teddy told me, I've been having nightmares. Now this happens. Today, it feels like my life will always be one never ending nightmare.

Finally, after a few hours, I realize I just have to get up. Pacing around the room, walking though the stuff on the floor, my brain begins to work. Finally, a thought. Out loud I mutter, "I've got to move on. I've got to get out of here. I certainly can't stay here any longer. I'm all done. I need a fresh start." With those words, I knelt down and finished packing my things in the footlocker and the denim sack. It's funny; when I was a kid, I was always running away from home. It seemed like a good solution to my wretched home life. Now, it feels like an even better idea. Laughing, I muttered, "Who says you're never too old to run away from home?" I had already arranged for my cousin, Carl, to give me a ride to college in the morning. I've decided. That's what I'll do. Go to college. It will be a start. Something new. I'll try to resurrect my life there. It's as good as any other plan. With that thought, I finished packing.

Early Wednesday morning, when Carl Bachmann pulled up to my house in his restored 1958 Ford pickup, I was wandering aimlessly around the front yard. My footlocker and laundry bag are lined up neatly by the driveway. Carl steps out of the truck, which looks as if it has been primped for an art show. The glossy black paint and bright chrome work gleam with a high wax finish and loving care. Seeing this beauty, I had to laugh and tease my cousin. "You would never know you live on one of the last working hog farms in Bucks County by looking at your wheels! How do you keep your ride so clean?"

"It's called wash and wax, Cousin. I realize it's something you've never heard about, but maybe this fancy college will teach you how that works." Carl sneered back at me as I laughed and smiled in return.

"Point well made and taken," I reply. "Guess I've never wasted much love on my transportation."

Carl hooted, "That's an understatement!"

I tossed my battered footlocker and laundry bag in the Ford and climbed into the passenger seat.

Carl commented, "You're packing pretty light to go off to college for a year, aren't you?"

"Hey, that's all I own," I replied. "I don't plan on coming back. It may sound crazy, but at this point, I can't see returning to New Britain even to visit. I'm all done here. I have no idea where I'm headed but it's not going to bring me back here. Don't know what college will be like, but I'm hoping I can make a new start." Carl just stared at me in amazement as he absorbed this unexpected announcement.

Riding west on the Pennsylvania Turnpike, we entertained each other swapping old stories from our misspent youth and our days at Central Bucks High. While the old war stories played on, I kept thinking along different lines. Honestly, I can hardly wait to move on from these old memories and find something better to call my life. I keep chewing over the fact I'm finally leaving home. Wahoooo!!! After all those years running away as a kid, I'm actually, really, leaving home! For two hours, I keep mulling this over. In a way, it gives me a sense of perverse pleasure. Carl keeps rattling on about the good old days. Maybe that's his version of home, I think, but it's not mine. I know where I come from. I am a Bachmann, founders of Bachmann's Pretzels. I was raised in New Britain, a small village outside Doylestown, PA, the home of Bachmann Pretzels. But I can assure you, that place and those people are not my home.

I never saw the campus before the day we arrived. Carlisle is only two hours away from New Britain, but I didn't bother to look at it. The pictures in the catalog and brochures were good enough for me. I mean, how bad could it be? It wasn't like I was going to Utah or Florida. This is Pennsylvania! As Carl pulled in the front gates and drove up though the streets of the campus, all I can do is stare in amazement. From the air, the campus must look like a cross section of a large, old oak tree with expanding concentric circles of architectural styles. In the center are majestic gray limestone buildings from the early 1800's. Around these is a layering of modest brick structures built after the Civil War. Outside these two earlier layers stands the radically modern buildings of concrete, steel, and glass built after WWII.

What pulls all these discordant designs into a unified whole is the landscaping and Mother Nature herself. Groves of mature trees appear throughout the campus. Shade is provided by tall oaks, maples, beech, hemlock, and hickory trees. Wide, green lawns are scattered all through the grounds. A couple dozen Adirondack chairs are placed in small clusters across the central lawn to encourage conversation and relationships. Perennial gardens provide swaths of color along with bright displays of annuals along the walkways. Asphalt paths connect the buildings for dry footing in inclement weather and park benches are scattered along these walks so passersby might sit and enjoy the beauty, reflect, rest, or have a chat with a friend. It is amazing! It actually takes my breath away.

"Okay," I was finally able to say to my cousin, who was also agog. "I am impressed! You know, I never visited, so I had no idea how beautiful it would be."

Carl grunted, "You're not kidding. I've always thought Bucks County would be the most beautiful place I ever laid eyes on. I think I shortchanged myself with that assumption. I may need to reconsider how long I go to Bucks County Community College." After a pause Carl asked, "Rob, when we loaded up at your house, you said you would not be coming back. Did you really mean that?"

I managed a shrug, "It's hard to explain. When I was growing up in Upper Bucks, I never thought about living anywhere else. I love the woods, the fields, the farms, and the wildlife. I can't get enough of the Delaware River, the trout streams and bass ponds. It is such a rich, fertile land. When I was fifteen, I could picture myself sitting at the Miss Britain Diner at age 65, having lived my entire life in town. And I was ok with that."

"Now I feel like a sailor whose ship has sunk. Or a cowboy whose horse dropped dead in the desert. The whole world I grew up in feels lifeless to me now. What's the point of standing around waiting for something to rise from the ashes? It's over. If I can't find a new life somewhere else, I won't have a life. I don't want the old life. It's done. It's dead."

"Well, ok, man. If you say so." Carl paused. "Hey, I gotta take off. Give me a call or drop me a line, and let me know how you're doing. If you want to go rabbit or pheasant hunting this fall, let me know. I'll come get you, and you can stay at our house."

"Thanks, Carl. And thanks for the ride. Be seeing you…."

Standing outside my dorm, I watched Carl drive off. It has been a long day already. The first chapter of my life is quietly closing. A new chapter is beginning. I wandered through campus, looking for the bookstore. I found the Student Center; one of big limestone monstrosities at the center of campus. Next to it is the Campus Bookstore. Of the 490 freshmen on campus this first day of Orientation, it looks like 80% are distributed equally between these two buildings. I got in the Bookstore line to pick up the required texts for my classes starting Monday.

The guy in front of me in line stands about 5' 10", but he has the shoulders of a much larger man. Broad shoulders, a big short neck, and well-defined biceps. He turns around and smiles at me.

Sticking out his hand, he says, "Gary Robbins."

I shook his hand. "Hi, I'm Rob Bachmann. Are you a jock?"

Gary laughs. "Heck no, I'm a hockey player."

"Ahh…that explains a lot. Where are you from, Gary?"

"Good question. I'm not sure how to answer." Robbins pauses, "I live in Richmond, but I am most definitely not **from** there. Or better yet, my family lives in Richmond, but I'm not from there. It's a long story. Where are you from, cowboy?"

I was to learn Gary loved to call everyone by weird, affectionate, pet names he makes up on the spot. "Hey Rob Bob, what's cooking?" Definitely a funny guy. Gary is glib, maybe even articulate… for a hockey player. Right from the start I pegged Robbins as a people person. He likes people. He is energized by people. Whenever he can, he seeks out face time.

"I'm from Doylestown in Eastern Pennsylvania. Well, actually, New Britain is a few miles outside Doylestown. It's all the way across Pennsylvania. Just before you hit the Delaware River and Jersey."

We stood in line waiting to get our books, and talked about sports. Gary laughed that I had spotted him as an athlete. He talked about hockey – most of which went right over my head. In Upper Bucks County, the only hockey we ever see are pick-up games on frozen ponds during an especially cold winter.

I told Gary about the love of my athletic life – pole vaulting. I have varsity experience in a number of track events: 440, the mile relay, shotput, discus, and javelin, but my sweet spot is the pole vault. I lettered in soccer for four years, but I only have eyes for the vault. My senior year I went to the PA State Track Meet and cleared 12 feet, which is college level jumping. From the glazed look in his eyes, I suspect Robbins knows as much about the pole vault as I do about hockey. Zip!

"Whoa. Get a load of her!" Gary exclaimed. We've collected our books and walked out to the patio between the Bookstore and Lane Hall, the student center. Gary is staring at a long, leggy blonde just joining the line still streaming into the Bookstore. "Isn't she pretty? But not very happy."

Gary's observations are spot on. Those are exactly the thoughts going through my brain when I clamp eyes on this striking blonde. Very good looking and not at all cheerful.

"Aren't you going to say anything?" Robbins presses.

Looking at this flaxen haired beauty is giving me brain freeze. "I am speechless. Stupefied. I have no words for this, Hockey Boy. Sorry," is all I can get out. Even my eyelids began to get hot. I'm afraid I'll get scorched eyeballs or my eyes will explode if I keep staring at this babe too long.

This lovely woman was spectacular! Exquisite! On the tall and elegant side of 5' 10", she was wearing a canary yellow summer dress covered with small blue flowers – modest, flattering, and quite feminine. It suggests she might be from a conservative Christian family from somewhere in the Deep South. Her wardrobe is perfect for the heat of the last week of August in south-central Pennsylvania. She managed to look elegant, and prim while sparkling like a tall flute of champagne.

As she walked along with the other students, the sundress made her figure come alive. Yow! Just the way it flows over the curves of her ripe body, it hangs, no, dances over her tight little ass as she walks; it jounces and accentuates her lovely chest. She is poetry in motion. I still couldn't think of a thing to say.

"HEY, SUNSHINE," yelled Robbins. So inappropriate! But that was Gary. He scooted over next to her in the bookstore line, "Are you new here? I'm Gary Robbins. What's your name?"

The blonde turned and looked at him like he was a misbehaving pooch about to pee on her leg. She just starred for a minute. I thought "this is not going to end well." Then her face broke into a big grin. "Faith McFadden, freshman," she said offering her hand.

"Welcome!" replied Gary shaking the proffered hand. He jogged back to where I was waiting.

McFadden has thick blonde hair shot full of strawberry blonde highlights. Windblown and a little crazy, she has pushed it back on her head with a pair of sunglasses. Her face is wide with high cheekbones and a sprinkling of freckles over her nose and under the eyes. The neat waist was cinched with a narrow white belt.

9

Her legs were shapely and hard – she is definitely fit. From the back, when she walks, it looks as if her legs go all the way up to her shoulder blades. These statuesque legs finish with clean, neat feet, slid into flat sandals. But, again, there is that worried, unhappy, look on her face. Closer examination reveals a set of small vertical wrinkle lines above her nose between her eyebrows. These may have been from stress, anxiety, or fear. I wondered if they are always there. A simple smile would have been enough to win the day and transform her into a real beauty. But after that brief grin for Gary, the smile is nowhere in sight.

2

"All this pain,
I wonder if I will find my way.
I wonder if my life could really change
at all..."
~ Michael & Lisa Gungor

Faith McFadden   August, 1966

If you had told me three months ago that I would be going up North to college, I'd have laughed out loud. Ludicrous! Now here I stand, on a warm humid August morning, by the side of Fish Fever Lane waiting for my ride to college. Early morning sunshine filters through the massive green branches of the live oaks overhead, dances through the hanging garlands of gray Spanish moss, and falls to the ground painting a pattern of moving light in front of my feet. Fish Fever Lane is not the best neighborhood on St Simons Island (SSI), where I was born and raised. In fact, if you scour all 98 square miles of this barrier island off the coast of Georgia, you'd be hard pressed to find a crummier neighborhood than mine.

My father, Mickey McFadden, a hard-core redneck, cracker and devoted racist, would hate to hear me say it, but our street is so poor it's actually in the colored section of town. The street – well, even that term may be an exaggeration – the street is an alley of packed sand weaving between old oak trees stretching off into the palmetto swamp in the center of the island. At one end is Hazel's Café, a negro diner / grocery store, built of old weathered clapboard which has not seen a coat of paint in decades. It does have a classic red tin Coca Cola sign which dresses up the view from Demere Road. At the other end of my street is a cluster of ancient slave cabins, which are still inhabited by some of the poorest black folks on the Island. In the middle of this run down, depressing street sits the McFadden homestead.

I am so embarrassed and ashamed of where I live. It's not just that our neighborhood is run down, full of trash and abandoned vehicles. It's dirty, overgrown with weeds and kudzu vines, and all the houses look neglected, unloved. On the whole, St Simons is beautiful, and people come from all over the world to visit and to live here. Miles of white sand beaches, towering stands of ancient live oaks, seabirds and wildlife, the green marshes of Glynn, palm trees and tropical breezes, sunsets which go on forever. But where I live is the unwashed stinky armpit of SSI. Our house is just like those on the rest of the street. Small, cramped, falling apart, surrounded by a yard full of junk. In church they tell me it's no great sin to be poor. It may not be a sin, but it feels awful to me. In my case, my family is both dirt poor and crazy! This makes for a double burden of shame and embarrassment.

11

From where I'm standing, I can still hear screaming from inside my house. Since I announced I had won a full scholarship to Carlisle College, my parents have been going crazy. My father can't believe I would disobey him and go off to a Yankee college. For three weeks he's been braying, "You are a whore! You are an adulteress! You are in rebellion from God. When you disobey me, you disobey God Almighty! If you dare cross the Mason-Dixon Line, God will strike you dead for your sin and disobedience! If you leave here and commit this sin, I will close my heart to you, close my door, and you may never return! You will be dead to me!"

Meanwhile, my mother shrieks at him and claws at his face when she can get near him. "Mickey, please, please, control yourself! You will burst a blood vessel, you will have a stroke, and you will hurt yourself. If you drop dead, who will provide for the girls and me?" Always the practical one, my mother. In her way, she is trying to make peace. I'm afraid she swallows most of my father's right wing, fundamentalist religious beliefs, but she is also the one who holds our dysfunctional family together against the raving madman who calls himself my father.

While this rage-aholic war continued between my parents, my younger sisters, Hope and Charity have also been crying their eyes out. For the last three weeks, the girls have been petrified I would go off to college and leave them defenseless in this home of religious nutters. But what can I do? I can't protect them. I have absolutely no influence over my parents or my home life. No matter how much my sisters sob and blubber. My hands are tied. There's nothing I can do to help them. Inside, all I want to do is cry. Instead, I clench my jaw, grind my teeth, and stare straight ahead.

This is my only chance. I have to get out of here and find a better way to live. For three weeks this cacophony of rage, screaming and tears has overwhelmed my life. I'm so sick of my family! I am so mad God stuck me with this crazy assed bunch of lunatics! What did I ever do to him to deserve this! My chest is filled with raw festering anger, just like everyone else in the house behind me. All I want to do is get away, leave it behind. So I stand on the edge of the sandy lane with my battered Navy duffle bag and two old cardboard suitcases, waiting for Pat and Kris Rouseau to show up.

A tiny, dark blue station wagon rounded the corner by Hazel's Café and eased down the street. The 1962 Corvair pulled up in front of my dumpy, little house. Jumping out of the undersized car, Pat and Kris both gave me big hugs. "Faith, I'm so glad you're ready! It's a long drive." says Kris. We silently ignore the screaming coming from the house behind me.

Pat asks, "This all you have?" as he loaded my stuff into the trunk of his car.

"That's it. Thanks so much, you guys, for giving me a ride to college. I appreciate it more than I know how to say." We settled into the Corvair and Pat pointed the car north, off the Island. I'm on my way! To Carlisle College and to a new life! Bye-bye, fruitcakes!

As we drove up I-95, I'm thinking about how much I owe these dear friends. For the past two years, the Rousseau's have been my youth group leaders at the Free

Will Bible Baptist End Times Ministries, the church in Brunswick my family attends. Not everyone there is crazy, or as crazy as my father. Dad is probably the most unhinged fundamentalist in the congregation. The Rousseau's are at the other end of the spectrum. They seem normal. I'm pretty sure they buy into the Baptist theology and the Pentecostal belief in spiritual gifts. Yet they have always been loving, unfailingly kind, and gentle to my sisters and me. In that, they are just the opposite of my nutcase parents.

In fact, they are the only reason I am going to college at all. Pat Rouseau was originally from Connecticut and he graduated from Carlisle College a few years ago. He was the one who encouraged me to apply. Pat's Uncle Ned is the Dean of Admissions at Carlisle. I'm pretty sure Pat pulled some strings with his uncle to get me accepted and to win the scholarship. I owe them my acceptance, my scholarship, and what little sanity I have left. With that pleasant thought, I stretched out on the cramped back seat of the Corvair and tried to get comfortable. I'm feeling calmer, realizing that at the end of this journey, I will be in a new place, beginning a new life. Hopefully, my new life will turn out to be more like Pat & Kris and less like my crazy family back on SSI.

By the time we arrived at Carlisle College, all I wanted to do is get out of the car! And scream! I'm 5' 10" and I have pretty long legs. That consumer nutcase, Ralph Nader, says the Chevy Corvair is unsafe at any speed. And I'm here to tell you, it's uncomfortable for any length of time, too, no matter what speed it's going. Don't get me wrong, I'm extremely grateful to Pat & Kris, for being willing to spend three days hauling me to Carlisle College. I had no idea Pennsylvania is that far from St. Simons! Right now my butt is sore, but eventually, I think I'll be glad I'm this far from home. I came here to get a fresh start, to meet new people and to see new places. So far, everything is going according to plan.

"Where to begin?" Kris asks. "Maybe find the freshman check-in and get your dorm assignment?"

"Why don't you gals go do that?" replies Pat. "I want to go find Uncle Ned and let him know we're here. We're planning on having lunch with him so you can meet him. Kris and I are staying at his house tonight before we head back home in the morning."

"I will be glad to meet your Uncle," I added. "Without his help, I'd be signing up for Glynn County Community College back in Brunswick, and waitressing at Coconut Willie's on the island. Please tell him how grateful I am for his getting me accepted and for the scholarship!" I turned to Kris, "Let's go see if we can get this expedition underway!"

We stood in a long line to check into my dorm and register for classes. As I was to discover, Freshman Orientation consists of a lot of standing in long lines, waiting in large groups, and being shuffled around between various venues, where we then get to do more waiting. As we waited, Kris amused me by telling stories about her time at the University of Georgia, the largest college in Georgia with over 18,000 students. UGA, in Athens, is ten times the size of Carlisle, so when she told horror stories about trying to get a required freshman class in a huge room with thousands of students milling about, 650 registration tables, each representing a different course, and with too few staff and volunteers, it made my situation seem manageable.

Kris continued to make me laugh, talking about the dining services, how big her dorm was, and the constant midnight "snipe hunts" for "Uga," the live bulldog who served as the University mascot. She says, "As a UGA freshman, we all had to wear little beanies for the first two weeks, so upperclassmen could pick on us and make us do stupid hazing pranks. It was dumb and annoying!"

"Man, that is such a turn off," I exclaimed. "I've been bullied enough in my life, and that's all that is – being bullied! When the strong take advantage of the weak and pick on them, make fun of them, push them around…That really frosts my cookies! I sure hope they don't try anything like that around here."

"You know, I never thought of it at the time," said Kris, "but I guess you're right. When I went to college we just did what we were told. If someone said, 'This is a UGA tradition,' no one questioned whether it was a tradition worth keeping. I don't think we realized, as young adults, we should be making our own decisions, not letting others make our choices. Maybe I'm not sensitive to things like bullying because I never went through it. How about you, Faith, have you had much experience with bullies?"

We continued walking toward the Bookstore while I wondered how to respond, but then I blurted out, "Do you really want to know?"

"Yes, you can tell me anything. You know I'm on your side, Faith." Kris responded.

"Kris, you're in our church, so you know about my family. We're very religious! My parents say they joined the Free Will Bible Baptists because they are 'not lukewarm about what they believe.' My home was filled with rules and regulations-- many of them quite specific. Dad would shout at us, 'Sugar is the tool of the devil!' We were not allowed to have ice cream, cookies, or candy. In fact, he said no to anything that was tasty or fun. If you were hungry, my parents would say, 'eat a slice of wheat bread.' Every single rule, everything he was against, everything he criticized us for doing, had some basis in the Bible or with the Lord, according to Dad.

"Mom had her own set of rules. Unfortunately, they were different from Dad's. Mom's religious rules say the only people who are saved are people chosen by God to be saved. God selects those who are predestined for salvation. The rest of us he condemns to hell. And there's very little the individual can do about it. Growing up, all these conflicting rules were used to bully us. To control us. There is something broken in my Dad, but I don't know what it is. Whatever it is has made everything else in our family broken. I'm not sure if my mother was broken before she married Dad, but she sure is now."

"Oh, honey, that's so hard," Kris responded.

"Our home was a house ruled by shame, fear, and guilt. No matter how hard my sisters and I tried to do our best, we were criticized for falling short. If we pleased one parent's rules, we offended the other parent. I always felt humiliated I was not doing better at living a 'good Christian life.' When something went wrong, they always blamed one of the children. With my parents, it is always somebody else's fault – they never make any mistakes. I've never heard my parents say, 'I was wrong, I'm sorry.'"

I settled into silence. Kris looked troubled. Finally, she said, "I hear what you are saying. I have long thought there are too many Christians in the South and not enough followers of Jesus." After a long, thoughtful pause, she said, "Your family situation sounds tough. Like a living hell. Thanks for having the courage to share with me." Kris paused then added, "I don't have any answers, but I will pray for you. And I'll look out for Hope and Charity when I get home."

Eventually, we arrived at the Bookstore. There I snagged twelve overpriced text books for the first semester. We headed away from the center of campus towards my new dorm, Allison Hall. The walkways wind between large gray stone buildings and grassy lawns. Along the paths, flowerbeds are filled with a profusion of black-eyed Susan's, chrysanthemums, cone flowers and other bright annuals. We walked past turn of the century homes which have been renovated and are now used for college offices. These buildings are lovely. I would give anything to live in a house like that. And to think they are simply occupied by desks and file cabinets. What a waste!

Allison Hall is a brick structure in the middle ring of campus buildings. Three stories tall, or more accurately, two and a half stories. The ground floor is buried four feet deep with the windowsills level with the lawn. As you enter the front door, you go down half a flight of steps to get to the first floor or you can go up half a flight of steps to reach the second floor. The third floor, which, of course, is where my room is located, is another full flight above.

Kris looked at me and laughed. "I don't know what you expected, but college life can be hierarchical. Seniors get first pick of everything and freshmen get what's left after everybody else chooses. Freshmen are always in the furthest dorm from meals and classes, and always on the highest floor in dorms without elevators. It's the way it is in every college. Don't worry, you'll feel better about it when you're a senior."

"I honestly don't know what I anticipated," I replied. "It actually looks like a pretty nice dorm to me, and walking up and down those stairs and back and forth across campus will keep me from having to work out so much." I laughed, "I'll have buns of steel without even trying!"

"At a girl!" Kris responded. "Let the workout begin!" We grabbed my luggage and hiked up the stairs to my room.

I stuck my head around the door frame and I saw my new roommate had already arrived. "Hi, I'm Faith McFadden, and I think I'm your roommate." I said.

"Hey, great to meet you Faith. I'm Randi Fox. I'm from Philly. How about you, where do you come from?"

"St. Simons, Georgia."

"Georgia, wow, that's a haul from here. How long did it take you to get here?"

"We left the island at six am yesterday and got to campus about ten this morning. Of course, we stopped overnight, so I don't know – maybe fifteen hours of driving. This is my friend Kris. She and her husband Pat drove me here."

Kris stuck out her hand, "Hi Randi, nice to meet you."

Randi Fox was petite, maybe 5' 4". She had abundant auburn hair, and appeared to have a happy disposition. Her face kept breaking into a sunny smile. My first impressions left me confused. Style wise, Randi looks conservative, well put together – the Big City Girl. But she has this impish little gleam in her eyes which makes me wonder if she likes to bust loose. What she is really like? Only time will tell.

We started to unpack and settle into our room. Then I noticed all of Randi's clothes are neatly ironed and folded. It freaked me out! Even her underwear is ironed and folded! She seems like a meticulous housekeeper; organizing everything as she puts it in her dresser drawers and closet. Everything is perfect, crisp, and structured. I am not exactly a neat freak. OK, I'm a slob! It's not that I'm dirty, just creative in my organizational scheme. Ha, ha! Alright, I am a messy. Maybe I'm a visual organizer and I need to see what stuff I have available to wear? Or I need to see my stuff to remember I have it? I don't know, but I began to worry about how compatible we will be.

Just as I start to think about our future harmony, Randi looked over at me and asked, "How tall are you, Faith?" Randi, as I was to learn, is that kind of girl. She just blurts out whatever is on her mind, and yet, somehow, it doesn't sound offensive.

"I'm 5' 10"? Why?"

Randi laughed. "You are really tall, and you have long legs. Your legs are as high as my waist! That's crazy! I'm going to call you Legs!" She laughed again. When Randi smiled, it was like someone just turned on all the lights in the room. Her grin is infectious. Without saying a word, her smile tells you she is happy to see you, thinks you are a fascinating person, and just being with you for these few minutes makes today a great day. I began to think this rooming situation might work out after all.

As we unpacked, the conversation warmed up. I'm not sure I've ever met anyone like Randi. She says exactly what she thinks. People don't do that in the South. I find myself wondering if Randi is a "namer." With one shrewd hunch she seems to put her finger on something that makes a person special or unique. And when she names it, it sounds like a compliment, not a judgment. She is amazing!

It didn't take long to unpack and organize my few possessions. Kris and I headed back to campus to meet Pat and Uncle Ned for lunch. Walking down West High Street on the edge of campus, I saw a restaurant across the street. It looked like a student hang out. "Chilly Dawgs," reads the big sign across the front of the store. Kris and I looked at each other and burst out laughing. "A sign of home,"

Kris says with a smile. "I hope those ain't cold Georgia bull dawgs they're eating in there. Damn Yankees!" We both laughed again. Two southern gals enjoying a joke most of my new classmates will never get.

That may have been the moment it hit me. The truth was sinking in. I've left home, and I'm never going to be the same person. Bob Dylan is singing a song on the radio warning people that, 'the times they are a changing...' That's certainly true for me. I feel like I've arrived at Carlisle from a place of broken promises, of constant disappointment, with a deep aching loneliness in my soul. In my heart, I really believe there is something better out there. I just have to keep looking until I find it.

We sat down to eat lunch on the patio next to the Musselman Dining Center. While it sits in the center of campus where most buildings are old limestone monoliths, the main eatery is itself a modern building. Faced with flat slabs of gray rock, it has high glass walls all across the front of the structure. The patio, on the west side, is paved with the gray slates and covered with round black iron tables and chairs for dining in good weather. The sunny, breezy day was perfect for the patio.

There I met Pat's uncle. Dean Rouseau was tall and lean, almost thin. Dressed in a blue and white pinstriped Oxford shirt with a red paisley tie, he looked elegant and dapper even in the late summer heat. "Faith," the Dean said, "I am so happy to finally meet you. Patrick has told me so much about you. We're delighted to have you here at Carlisle. We don't get many students from Georgia and we're pleased to have you join our community. I think you are the first freshman we've recruited from St. Simons since I've been at the college."

As we ate, Dean Rouseau plied me with questions about St. Simons Island. He seemed curious about the way of life on a coastal barrier island. I wondered if he has been thinking we all live in shacks on the beach and work on shrimp trawlers. I tried to give him some details and a few colorful anecdotes. As we finished our meal and prepared to leave, a trim athletic student with sandy brown hair stopped by our table.

"Excuse me, I hate to interrupt." Addressing me he said, "I'm Gary Robbins. I met you earlier today in the bookstore line."

"I have not forgotten the experience," I quipped.

Gary laughed. "Oops, sorry about that. Sometimes I just get carried away. Are you by any chance the freshman from St. Simons?"

I wasn't sure what to think of this new salvo. "Yes, I'm from St. Simons. Why do you ask?"

Gary laughed a warm friendly laugh. "No. I'm not just being nosey. Although, I admit, I'm pretty nosey," he added with a chuckle. "I've actually been to St. Simons! My family owns a cottage on Sea Island, the next island over. It's a beautiful place. No, the reason I interrupted you is I want introduce you to a classmate from New Hampshire. Several of us are having a little debate about which member of the freshman class came the furthest. You and Jack are definitely in the running and perhaps together you can help us settle the question. May I borrow her?" he asked the table. "I want to introduce her to Jack Flynn, the guy from New Hampshire."

"Sure, go ahead," replied the Dean. "Just send her back undamaged."

Everyone laughed and I trotted off with Gary to join a group of students at a nearby table. As Gary and I walked across the patio, I saw a dark haired fellow in the middle of a group of students gathered around the table. As we approached, he stood up to greet me, and I realized he is dressed all in black. From head to toe. Tall, dark, and handsome! Yow, this guy was an eyeful!

Gary made the introductions. "Faith, this is Jack Flynn. He is from New Hampshire. Jack, this is Faith McFadden. She is from Georgia. St. Simons Island, to be precise."

I'm afraid while I shook Jack's hand, I also stared, more like gawked, at the rest of him. His long lean legs were encased in black peg leg jeans ending in black, hand tooled cowboy boots. The jeans were cinched tight around his lean waist by a narrow black leather belt with a small silver cowboy buckle. He was wearing a black long sleeve shirt. Flynn's full jet black hair leaped off the front of his head, flows down over his ears, and after brushing his shoulders, curved up at the back of his neck like an overextended ducktail. I'll bet this head of hair causes many of the women in his life to have severe bouts of envy. Yummy. Whew! This man is a looker!

As I shook his hand, Jack broke into a big grin. "Hi, Faith, nice to meet you," he murmured. He has a warm smile and a mischievous twinkle in his eye. With a laugh he added, "I hear you and I are in the running for the most far out student of the Class of 1970. Well, you know what I mean – from furthest away." The group around the table laughed.

A first glance gives the impression Jack might be austere, reserved, perhaps severe. That was wrong! His glowing smile easily convinced me Jack Flynn likes people, or at least that he likes me. As we chatted, it was clear his laughter comes easily. He was quick with a clever come back, enjoys conversation, and doesn't take himself too seriously. I could really go for a guy like this. Hmmm...

Meanwhile, Gary prattled on as I continued to stare at Jack Flynn. Gary was saying, "I've been to St. Simons, and it is a tropical delight. It's one of the barrier islands off the southern coast of the state – almost as far south as the Florida line. Is that further from here than New Hampshire?"

I laughed at Robbins. "I wouldn't know. I've never been to New Hampshire. In fact, I've never traveled much outside Georgia and Florida until I got in the car to come here. Now that was a trip that was far out! I thought we would never arrive! Where exactly in New Hampshire are you from?"

"Well, it's an itty bitty little town, you never heard of. Promise not to laugh?"

"I promise," I replied. Staring up at Flynn, I thought, here's another thing I like about this guy. He's tall. I have to look up to see into his eyes.

Jack smiled at me, "So you say... OK, here goes...my hometown is Effingham."

There was a moment of stunned silence around the table, and then everyone roared with laughter. I couldn't contain myself – I cracked up. When I finally got myself under control, I said, "You're from F-ingham? Sure you are... Tell me you're just teasing us."

"No, I am not making it up." Jack insisted. "It is spelled e-f-f-i-n-g-h-a-m. The town was named by a colonial settler after the Earl of Effingham, back in merry old England."

Everyone around the table laughed some more. "Fuckin A!" exclaimed Arty Swaboda, a freshman from Pittsburgh. "Oops, I'm sorry. I meant Fuckingham! Ha Ha!"

Flynn grinned. You could tell he has heard it all before. "OK, Faith, so how far out are you? How far is St. Simons from Carlisle?"

I wrinkled my nose and paused to think. "I'm not sure what it is in miles. I never looked for fear I would chicken out. But we left the island yesterday at six am and drove until six pm. We drove another three hours this morning. So, a total of fifteen hours to get here. How about you?"

Flynn laughed. "I have you beat in hours on the road. But I took the bus. My Dad drove me to the bus station in Concord. I waited a while and got the bus to Boston. I waited some more before the Peter Pan bus went to New York City. Then I took a bus to Philly and from there, another bus to Harrisburg. My cousin Matt picked me up in Harrisburg and drove me to his house in Newville so I could recover. Total elapsed time? Seventeen hours. But actual travel time, maybe twelve hours. You may have me beat." Jack laughed, "So how's your butt? Still a little sore? Mine is killing me!"

I chuckled. I like this guy! He's different, with his monochromatic wardrobe, and being from F-ingham. But I think he's a cool guy. Anyone who can make me laugh is good medicine for what ails me. So good looking, too. I think I could fall for a guy like this. But there's something about his eyes... He looks a little wild. Maybe he's insecure or anxious. If so, I can relate to that too.

3

"One day Alice came to a fork in the road
And she saw a Cheshire cat in a tree.
"Which way do I take?" She asked.
His response was a question.
"Where do you want to go?"
"I don't know," Alice answered.
"Then," said the cat, "it doesn't matter."
~ Lewis Carroll

Jack Flynn   August, 1966

A few days earlier I had gotten off the Concord Bus at the main bus terminal in Boston. My Dad drove me into Concord, before first light. An hour and change later, here I am in the big city! First impressions? This place stinks! The whole terminal reeks with a powerful, pungent aroma. It smells like hot pretzels, body odor, rotting garbage, exhaust fumes, cigarette smoke, sweat and emotions - anxiety, fear, loss, loneliness, sadness. Can you smell sadness? I think you can.

The terminal is an old building, large with dark woodwork, benches everywhere and a worn gray linoleum floor. At the moment, the place is mobbed with people of all types, sizes and descriptions. Maybe it smells because it's old. Been here too long, serviced too many people, and seen too much heartache. The trash cans overflow, the place looks dirty, and I get the sense the maintenance standards aren't high. I suppose this is the bottom tier of the transportation industry in America.

Riding the bus for four hours from Boston to New York gave me plenty of time to think. I find myself overwhelmed with my own sadness. I don't know if the sadness from the people around me, at the bus station and on the bus, is contagious, but the longer I sit and contemplate what is happening to me, the sadder I become. None of this was my idea! Pack up and go off to college in some strange place hundreds of miles from my home, my family and all the people and places I love. The more I think about the whole sorry mess, the more miserable I feel.

Growing up in the Lakes Region of New Hampshire, I enjoyed a warm loving home, a large extended family, and a relaxed lifestyle in an area of incredible natural beauty. Throughout my childhood, my reoccurring thought was always, "What's not to like, about my life?" In 1937 my grandfather, Patrick Flynn, built a little ice cream stand on the shores of Province Lake. It has grown into a full-service restaurant and a lakeside resort which provides jobs for most of our family and a solid economic foundation. I have 11 aunts and uncles, and 28 first cousins. Most of those relatives live in the small town of Effingham or nearby.

I was a pretty happy kid growing up. There were some bumps in the road, but I came through in good shape, until the past few years. To be honest, I've never been crazy about the family business. Like everyone else in our family, I put in my time working there, but I just can't see myself spending my life hawking ice cream cones. I like mechanical things better than people. Building go-carts, working on dirt bikes, tinkering with old motors, and things like that. In high school, I spent my free time restoring old cars in the barn behind our house. My senior year, I bought a '57 Jaguar sedan and a beat up '63 Triumph TR-3. Within a few months I was able to transform these wrecks into vintage classics and resell them for a nice profit. While I was busy working on this project, I kept thinking this could be what I might do for work when I graduated. Meanwhile, trouble was brewing and I never saw it coming.

Let me give you a little advice about taking a bus trip. Just like real estate, it's all about location, location, location! Where you sit on the bus really matters. If you sit in the back, you are close to the bathroom. So, the good news: you're close to the john if you need to go. The bad news: the further towards the back of the bus you sit, the reek of urine and human waste from the rolling outhouse gets worse. I'm sitting in the back. As the bus rumbles south on Interstate 95, I keep thinking about my cousin Ronnie Bucksport and smelling the odors from the lavatory. It's like shoving my head in the toilet and its going to go on for hours. This stinks! The whole deal with Ronnie really stinks!

Ronnie is a distant cousin on my mother's side. After graduating from high school, Ronnie set himself up as a drug dealer. The secret to his success was his ability to launder all the dirty cash coming in from his network of drug sales. Ronnie created a string of retail tourist businesses, and dabbled in residential real estate. Sales from his legitimate businesses were able to wash huge amounts of drug cash. Bucksport won the drug wars with clever accounting. By the time he was thirty five, he was the largest drug wholesaler in Maine and New Hampshire.

Let me be perfectly clear: I have never liked Cousin Ronnie. Never even given him the time of day. But my family thinks I am…well, they think I'm too easily influenced by the people around me. That my strongly held opinion on any subject depends on the last person I talk to. I think that's harsh! I hope it's not true. Alright, I admit I'm not very clear on what I want to do with my life. Don't want to work at the restaurant. I think I'd like to fix and flip cars, but the elders don't think that's a real job. Somehow, my Dad, Granddad and uncles got the idea that I would get lured into Ronnie's drug business and end up spending my life in state prison.

When Ronnie started to cruise through Effingham in his lipstick red '65 Corvette, the Flynn men went ballistic. They gathered together like wild bison bulls, circling to protect a young calf from vicious wolves. I suppose I should be grateful to have a family who has my back, but these councils of war never included me. I don't know if I'm that amiable, eager to please, or if I really am tolerant of flaws in others. But I feel I should be able to defend myself. Or at least have a voice in my fate. Nope! Without the least bit of discussion from me, they decided the best way to protect me was to get me out of town, to get me well beyond the reach of cousin Ronnie and his drug dealing ways.

Now here I am, on the bus ride from hell, carrying me away from my home, my family, and everything I love. I feel like a refugee. I've been excommunicated from my own life. I'm like the proverbial scapegoat – everyone's piled the blame on me and I get kicked out of the tribe to wander in the wilderness. I haven't done anything wrong, yet here I am being shipped off to a strange land and a strange people with no idea what the next four years of my life will hold.

I've never seen anything like the people on the bus or in the cities I rode thorough on the way to Carlisle. And I have no desire to see anything like those places or people again. I think I rode through the reeking armpit of America. I'll admit, once you get west of Philadelphia, the countryside gets pretty. In some ways it reminds me of New England. But otherwise, it is too much city and too many weird people for my taste. Finally, I was rescued from seventeen hours of this never ending nightmare when my cousin Matt LeBoufe picked me up at the bus station in Harrisburg.

One of the reasons I was sent to Carlisle College is my Aunt Maddy and Uncle Leroy live in nearby Newville. I guess they are supposed to keep an eye on me. The LeBoufe's oldest, Matt, has just finished a four year hitch with the US Army, and is enrolling as a freshman at the college. We will be in the same class. Bleary eyed from lack of sleep, I stumbled off the bus in a fog of fatigue, weariness, sore joints, and aching muscles. I am grateful to have survived. Matt was standing in front of the waiting crowd smiling at me as I alighted.

"Hey Matt, what's shakin?" I offered.

Matt grinned back at me. "Good to see you, Jack. How was your trip…you look like shit!" He laughed. "Long ride?"

"Yeah, a long ride in the nuthouse. You would not believe half of what I've seen in the last eighteen hours."

I had not laid eyes on Matt for a number of years. When he graduated from high school in 1962, he decided the only way he would be able to afford college (being one of six kids) was to pay for it himself. The week after graduation, Matt enlisted for a four year stint in the Army. He spent three years in the Signal Corps stateside, and a year stationed in Vietnam. When his four years were up, he was discharged as a full Sergeant and took advantage of the GI Bill to attend Carlisle College; Matt would be the only twenty three year old freshman in our class.

I looked Matt over. He looks much older than my peers. Matt is not short, but he is stocky. He looks a bit like a fireplug. What my Mom would call husky. LeBoufe is not fat, just sturdily built. His appearance makes him look strong and solid. Reliable. The kind of guy you want to have next to you in a tight spot. His face is round, his is head is round, and all this roundness is crowned by strawberry blonde hair. Matt has a big smile and a booming laugh. What really sets him apart, however, is a big red handlebar mustache flowing out from his lips, off the sides of his face and curving up in a graceful arch to two pointy tips. It is magnificent! Matt is quite vain about his masterful 6-inch 'stash, waxes it frequently, and constantly twirls the ends.

We piled into his brand new, canary yellow Volkswagen Beetle and headed for Newville. As we drove along I asked, "When did you get out of the service, Matt?"

"July 1st. I enlisted June 15th four years ago and they make you stay until the first of the following month, once your enlistment is up."

"So how was it, you know, the Army?"

"Not bad. Basic training at Fort Dix was good. Because I enlisted for four years, I got to choose the Army Signal Corps. Even so, everybody has to do basic training and infantry combat training." LeBoufe went on, "With the way things are going in Vietnam, they think everyone will end up over there, and no matter what your job, you better be able to fight. The Gooks are everywhere – crawling out of the window vents, and popping out of the water drains. There really is no front – it's the front no matter where you are, the minute you step off the plane."

"Wow that sounds rough, "I replied.

"No shit," said Matt. "If you ever get a chance to join the service – run like hell! Actually, the service stateside wasn't too bad. A bit boring, and full of mind numbing regulations, and loads of repetition. But other than being a snooze, it was pretty easy work to earn a full ride though college." Matt continued, "But Vietnam – that is a different kettle of fish. It's a total cock-up!"

"What do you mean?"

"Everything is a mess, no one knows what's going on, and no one knows why we are over there. We have been fighting – for some damn reason – since 1954. First the French, and now the US. It could easily keep going another ten years. It is a madhouse!" Matt sighed, "It's just like Shakespeare said, 'a tale told by an idiot, full of sound and fury, signifying nothing.' If you are counting on the government to sort this out, or to provide leadership, I'm afraid you're wasting your time. Here's my prediction: each year we will send more men and equipment and each year we will make less progress. When it's all said and done, ten percent of the boys we send over will be killed, twenty percent will be wounded, and thirty percent will come home hopelessly addicted to drugs."

After a long pause, Matt added, "I think I was able to survive with my soul intact and for that I'm grateful. I was fortunate enough to be stationed in Saigon running radio systems. Those poor Marines stationed up in the firebases in the Northern provinces, they are the guys who, if they survive, will relive Vietnam as a waking nightmare for the rest of their lives. It's so sad…"

We spent the next two days relaxing at the LeBoufe's. We slept in, took long walks along Big Spring Creek, and played lawn games with Matt's younger brothers and sisters. By the time we loaded up to leave for college, I had recovered from the ordeal of my bus ride. I think I'm feeling a little more positive about this whole college experience, although I still have plenty of worries.

By the time I checked into my dorm in Rhodes Hall, got my books, and had lunch with some other students, I felt overwhelmed. Meeting new people is always an uncomfortable experience for me. It's exhausting. The other students seem nice, especially Faith McFadden. Faith is a knockout! She is beautiful, blonde, tall, willowy, graceful, and dressed in bright vibrant colors. Me, well I'm no fashion plate. My style is severe and simple: dressed from head to toe in black. Even my hair and eyebrows are black. Guess I'm her opposite.

My sister Meghan says I always look like I'm on my way to a funeral. Matt claims my weedy black ensembles make me look like a young, hip, male version of Whistler's Mother. I don't know what kind of first impression I make. When people meet me, I'm afraid I give them the feeling of being dark, brooding, severe, and foreboding. Like Whistler's Mother.

By the time lunch was over, I was beginning to miss home again. Inside I felt lonely, homesick, and overwhelmed by all the new experiences. Mom tells me I'm shy and I can struggle with meeting new people. I don't know about that, but I do know when I spend too much time with too many people, I get over stimulated, and can get uncomfortable. The solution is simple. I need space. I need nature. After lunch I decided to walk around to the back of campus where I found a gravel path headed away from all the action. The path wandered across fields to a 30-acre pond surrounded by mature trees. I followed a trail through the woods, around the water, flushing several wood ducks, and a Great Blue Heron.

Eventually, I felt relief seeping in. Nature and solitude help me deal with all the people and the newness. Still, I find myself thinking about home. I miss Mom, I still miss Maggie and she's been gone for three years. I miss Meghan, my older sister, and she left home to get married four years ago. She's probably pushing her kids around Wolfeboro right now, enjoying the perfect late summer weather.

It makes me wonder what things could have been like if I had been allowed to stay home? Would I have been happy? Would Ronnie have sucked me into his evil empire? These thoughts keep thrashing around in my head. It's like getting a thorn stuck in your finger. You can't see it well enough to pull it out, but you can feel it working around under the skin, poking and disturbing you. It's as if there's this thorn of a thought in my brain, poking, prodding, just making me uncomfortable, making me wonder, making me ask, "What if?"

Later that afternoon, I found myself sitting with almost 500 freshmen in the Main Auditorium of Carlisle College. A large, well lit hall with row after row of tiered padded blue seating, dropping down in elevation until it reached the foot of the stage. This platform wrapped around the front and formed the stage for theatrical productions. Right now it is set up with several rows of seated campus dignitaries waiting to address the incoming freshman and transfer students. A procession of officials welcomed us and offered bits of information and guidance for our time at the college. Finally, the Dean of Students shuffled to the podium. A large man, his overall appearance was… rumpled. Rumpled navy blue suit, rumpled white shirt, and even his tie was askew. The little bit of hair on his balding head was disheveled.

The guy sitting next to me leaned over and whispered, "Clearly he did not get the job because of his fashion sense or his good looks." I looked at my neighbor. A tall fellow with broad shoulders and auburn hair. Big fluffy reddish-brown hair hanging over his shirt collar. A smile is plastered across a face full of friendly freckles.

I replied, "You're right. Let's hope he got the job because he's good at what he is supposed to do."

My neighbor stuck out his hand in introduction, "Rob Bachmann."

"Jack Flynn," I replied. We both settled down to listen.

"Ladies and gentlemen, I am Dean Benchoff, the Dean of Students. Allow me to welcome each of you to the Carlisle College Class of 1970."

A cheer went up from the crowd. As it died down, Benchoff continued. "Almost a century and a half ago, this college was founded by many of the same men who signed the Declaration of Independence, who fought the American Revolution, and who founded this great nation of ours. Since 1823, this college has built a rich history. Today, each of you becomes a part of this ongoing tradition."

The Dean paused briefly. "Carlisle College was founded by the big thinkers of its day. People whose thoughts changed the course of an empire and created a new nation, now the most powerful nation on earth – by asking big questions, by thinking big!" Benchoff took a breath. "This is the proud tradition you in the Class of 1970 now join. As a result of your time here, you will have the opportunity to change the world. We on the faculty and staff want to challenge you to live up to your potential, to live up to the history of Carlisle, and to Ask Big Questions!"

"Today," intoned the Dean, "you are entering a new phase of your life. Most of you are beginning the adventure of adulthood. Some have overcome enormous challenges to arrive at this point. For others, your college experience will represent the first challenge you have faced in life. For all of you, there will be plenty of challenge in the days ahead during your time at Carlisle.

"A number of you will fail to succeed academically. Others will not master the balance of self discipline and self control required to manage studies and a social life. Some will choose to abuse alcohol, drugs, or other substances and will end up in the hospital or worse, rather than in a graduation ceremony.

"A few will manage to flaunt the rules to the point you will be expelled. Others, I am sorry to say, will make poor relational choices, which will lead to problems. In spite of all the challenges which lay ahead, I want you to remember there is always hope. As Winston Churchill famously said, 'Never give up!'

"Let me point out that with adulthood comes both rights and responsibilities. Among your rights are the many extraordinary opportunities you will enjoy here at the college. You get to make choices. This is a weighty opportunity. It does not matter where you're from, who your people are, whether you are rich or poor, whether you have assets or not, nor how much education your parents had. *You are the pioneer of your own life.* You are now becoming the captain of your own ship, of your own destiny. The choices you make here over the next few years will shape your future life in profound ways. Nothing in your past need limit you. I urge you – focus on making good choices for yourself."

As the Dean talked, I found myself wondering if the Flynn elders called him about me. It sounds as if Benchoff had written this speech for me. It certainly speaks to my situation.

The Dean continued, "While here at the college, you will meet people. This alone, may have more impact on your life outcomes than your academic studies. Make an effort to meet as many people as you can. Get to know them. Find out what makes them tick. Mix it up – don't just hang out with people like yourself or people you're comfortable with."

"As of today," he added, "you are now part of the family. The Carlisle College family. Ask your professors for help. Find people who can mentor you. Ask staff for help. Ask fellow students for aid. We are here to help you succeed, but you will have to reach out to get the most out of your experience."

"Let me conclude by challenging each of you to Ask Big Questions during this year. Who am I and what makes me significant? Is there something that gives meaning to my life? What am I passionate about? Is there a way to find community, to connect with others, to provide a sense of belonging? Is there more to life than what I can see and touch?"

"A famous teacher once said, "Ask and it will be given to you; seek and you will find; knock and the door will be opened to you." This is deep wisdom, which I have found to be true in my own life. I encourage you to adopt the same philosophy for your time here at Carlisle. If ever there is anything I can do to encourage you on your journey, or that our faculty and staff can do, please don't hesitate to ask." With these words, Dean Benchoff folded his notes, and walked back to his seat.

The audience was quiet for a moment and then broke into steady applause. I leaned over and whispered to Rob, "What did you think?"

He laughed, "Pretty cool! The Dean delivers the pep talk better than he dresses. My guess is he's the real deal - in spite of his appearance."

Bachmann's own appearance was intriguing. He was wearing a blue oxford cloth button-down dress shirt over a pair of well worn Levi jeans. The jeans were held up by an army surplus khaki belt with a plain brass clasp in front. Peaking out from under his jeans was a pair of handmade Indian moccasins. Not the kind you buy in the store with hard rubber soles. The kind you actually cut out of cowhide and stitch, layer by layer, into custom footwear which actually fits your unique feet and lifestyle.

Rob asked me, "What did you think of the Dean?"

I chuckled, "Pretty impressive. He may have been giving that speech for a year or two. I heard he is crazy about fishing, Knows all the hot spots for miles around. Maybe we can ask him to 'help' us by sharing some fishing tips?"

Rob replied, "Do you like to fish? So do I. What kind of fishing do you do?"

"Any kind you can think of - chucking worms, fly fishing, and I'll even use dynamite if it's necessary. I'm not a purist – more of a pragmatist," I affirmed.

"Oh, and I like to hunt and trap too! We should definitely get Benchoff to 'mentor us.' The Dean is supposed to know where to catch huge trout."

We both cracked up, then Bachmann turned and introduced me to his other neighbor. "This is Billy Harrison, my roommate. He's from York." Harrison reached across to shake my hand and said, "Red Lion, actually. It's a suburb of York. Much better football team. Much better everything, but that's just my opinion."

Billy was medium height, medium build, with a mane of bright blonde hair. The face was grinning like an imp. It was hard to know what Billy was thinking, but he looked happy about something. Harrison was as expressive as most New Hampshire men are reserved. He laughed again. He sure was happy.

"Well, if you guys are up for it, let's go to dinner," I suggested. We headed out.

During the first week of classes, Carlisle enjoyed gorgeous early fall weather. Bluebird skies and cool temperatures in the morning, which pushed close to the 80° mark by mid-afternoon. Every afternoon the quad in the middle of campus was covered by students enjoying the balmy weather. Some sat in the clusters of Adirondack chairs and talked. Others parked themselves under tall shade trees reading for pleasure or for class. That Wednesday afternoon I was hanging out on the Quad, lounging on a bench, reviewing some class materials and doing some people watching. The scent of fresh cut grass wafted through the air. A few yellow leaves floated down, gently landing on the bright green grass. The flower beds were still filled with color, some red shrubs and a lot of dark blue blooms I didn't recognize.

An attractive brunette nonchalantly strolled into this scene and made herself at home. She was wearing jeans and a light blue cashmere sweater. She reached into her bag and pulled out a plaid blanket and flipped it out on the lawn. Then she kicked off her shoes, rolled her jeans above her knees, seeking some sun. She lay on the blanket, stretching to get comfortable, and soaking up the sunshine. She looked like a cat in a puddle of sunlight on the dining room floor.

This one is new. She's not somebody I met during orientation. I'd be happy to change that. As this thought went through my mind, I saw Billy Harrison walking across the Quad. Billy always seems to be 'on.' Like he's a comedian on stage in front of an audience. Unless he is addicted to uppers, there is something about his personality that makes him feel the need to attract attention and to please people. My hunch is that he is a showboat, the class clown. Of course, that's what my parents think about me, that I'm a people pleaser, just in a quieter sort of way.

I waved at Billy and he came over to where I was sitting.

"Hey Jack, what's cooking?" Billy asked.

"Not much," I replied. "Just catching some fresh air and checking out the chicks. How's it going for you?"

"Pretty slow, but it's early yet. And there are a lot of good lookin' babes, don't you think?"

"No doubt," I shot back. "Speaking of which, do you have any idea who that brunette is in the blue sweater?"

"The gal on the plaid blanket?" asked Billy. "Yeah, I think its Nikki somebody from State College. Don't know much about her. Think she's interesting?"

"I do," I replied. "I'll have to find out more."

"Well, I'm on my way to class. See ya!" Billy ambled off.

"Thanks for the tip and have a good day."

I am finding this chick intriguing. She gives off an air of calm, cool, and collected. Unlike many people our age, this woman appears comfortable inside her own skin. She has pretty dark brown hair, almost black. It's naturally curly and she has tried to restrain it by tying it back in a sort of a wild ponytail. Her forehead is high with clear skin, and her light blue eyes match her pale blue sweater. Eventually, she rolls over, reaches into her bag and pulls out a paperback book which she begins to read. Moments later, she reaches into the bag and pulls out a full-size dictionary, which she proceeds to refer to occasionally as she reads. This is a woman who is curious, eager to learn, and who does not want to miss any chance to gain knowledge. I wonder what makes somebody like her tick?

Later on, a group of students gathered around the mysterious Nikki in blue. I am fascinated to watch how she interacts with them. Engaging with the kids clustered around her blanket, I can see her eyes sparkle; as she leans into the conversation, and waits eagerly to catch the punch line of someone's story. When the line is delivered, she rips out a booming laugh. Wow, what a great laugh! Here's a woman I want to know better. I made a note to look her up in the *Freshman Viewbook*.

That evening, sitting in the dorm TV room, I looked up Nikki in blue. When I found her listing and photo, I broke out in hearty laughter. In fact, I laughed until I cried. The guys scattered around the lounge stared at me as if had I lost my marbles. But they can't see what I am looking at. Wow! Unbelievable! Nikki's Viewbook photo shows her standing on a pier sticking out into a lake. You can tell it's somewhere up North by the rocky shoreline surrounded by thick stands of spruce and fir. It's a big lake – in the background behind Nikki there are whitecaps blowing across the picture.

Nikki is standing on this dock, in a howling wind, dressed in jeans and a heavy red and black checked wool jacket. It's the kind of jacket you expect to see on an L.L. Bean catalog cover, worn by a grizzled old Northwoods deer guide. Her hair is blowing away from her head in the same direction as the whitecaps. Clamped in her hand, proudly centered in the picture is a four-pound smallmouth bass. She has this huge trophy fish, big drooping belly, shoved into the camera lens, and her grin is maniacal with enthusiasm about this great catch. Even her free hand is pointing at the bass as if to say, "See this? Am I not the hottest chick ever?"

Funny or what? What a hoot! As I said, this is one interesting woman.

4

"Ninety-five percent of success is showing up."
~ *Woody Allen*

Nikki Clausen   September, 1966

College life is a pleasant surprise. Not that I'm unfamiliar with the college scene. I grew up in State College, a little burg in the middle of Pennsylvania. While a small town, State College is a pretty big deal to residents of Pennsylvania, as it is the home of Penn State University. Dad is a history professor at Penn State. Mom teaches music at the Bellefonte Area High School. With both parents immersed in education, I grew up knowing all about the academy.

The college sits in a bowl formed by the seven mountains around it. The "Seven Sisters" as these peaks are called, protect a wide fertile valley filled with bucolic farms, small villages, and numerous cottage industries. The land is filled with trees, flowers, songbirds and wildlife. The valley is crisscrossed by a dozen trout streams. Little wonder the locals' nickname for this place is "Happy Valley." This is the kind of countryside that could make you believe there is a God.

By my senior year, I was torn. I love the Valley and all the rich outdoor opportunities I've enjoyed here. And I love learning. As a teen, I spent hours reading and studying. I like to reflect on what I'm learning. I can wander in the fields and woods for days on end thinking about lots of things. Yet I just can't see myself at Penn State. The college is huge! Massive. Over 40,000 students. Much too big for me. The whole thought overwhelms my senses. Honestly, I feel claustrophobic just thinking about taking classes there and being swallowed up by the madding crowds of coeds. I'm pretty sure I wouldn't learn much in such an educational factory. Even more, my soul cringes at having to live in such a big city, even if it is a city of learning. No, thank you!

Carlisle College is exactly what I've been looking for. I've been here two weeks and I just love it! I love the campus, I love the students, and I love the size of my classes. It all seems so manageable. Plenty of nature and outdoor adventures close to campus. I feel like Goldilocks with the three bears. Too big, too small, and just right. This place is just right in every way. It fits me perfectly. After two weeks, the only thing I miss from home is Willy. No, Willy's not my boyfriend; he's my worn out old Bassett Hound. I shared my childhood with Willy. Guess he's my best friend. He knows all of my deep dark secrets and yet, he never squeals. I adore Willy. But other than the dog – not a twinge of homesickness.

Lovely Indian summer weather continued into the second week of classes. Thursday afternoon I had no classes, so I headed for the Quad and parked myself in a bright red Adirondack chair to catch some sun and do a little reading for Psychology class. I am amazed looking at the variety of students scattered on the grassy lawn and drifting though the green space.

The Quad is like an old patchwork quilt with bits of this and squares of that. Flowerbeds with clumps of red, white and yellow mums. Purple Lavender flowers here and there. Big black walnut trees are already shedding yellow leaves and dropping green nut hulls on the lawn.

So much variety in people and attire! More daring girls were lying out in bathing suits. Some of their suits cover a lot less than I would be comfortable showing. Others are sunning in hot pants and halter tops. My mom always says leave a little bit to the imagination. Guys are tossing around Frisbees and footballs. You can tell who the serious students are; they all have their clothes on and are sitting and reading, or talking in little clusters.

Across this hodgepodge of color, strides a tall, lean guy dressed in black. Black shirt, black jeans, black cowboy belt, black cowboy boots. Wow! He's a looker. He walks right up to me and points at the chair next to mine.

"This pew taken?" he asks.

"No, cowboy, make yourself at home," I respond.

He plopped down and said, "You are not by any chance Nikki Clausen, are you?"

I laughed, "Good guess! Got it in one."

"Hi, I'm Jack Flynn. Nice to meet you.

"It's nice to meet you, Jack." I answered. "So really, how did you know my name? Is my photo up on the Wanted Posters in the Post Office already?"

It was Jack's turn to laugh. "Not exactly. I saw your fish photo in the Viewbook. What a hoot! Does this mean you like to fish?"

"You bet it does! I'm crazy for all things outdoors. How about you, do you fish?"

"I love it. I'm from New Hampshire," he replied.

"Wicked cool!" I exclaimed. We both burst out laughing. 'Wicked' is a kind of insider joke in NH and Maine. It means something is wonderful or good. When we finally stopped hooting, I continued, "I spent a couple summers working as a counselor at Camp Kehonka, a girls' camp, on Lake Winnipesaukee. That's where my Viewbook picture was taken. The smallmouth was 24 inches long and weighed just over four and a half pounds."

"I grew up thirty minutes northeast of Wolfeboro."

"Where exactly?" I queried.

"Effingham"

"No shit! I've *been* to Effingham!" I exclaimed.

"Really? I can hardly believe that. New Hampshire is so small, and my town is tiny." said Jack.

"Yeah, every summer, the camp staffers would mount a day trip and drive up to Effingham to get t-shirts from the Master Baiter shop."

Jack roared with laughter. "Are you making this up? That is so funny. You have been to my home town and your only purpose was to shop at the Master Baiter? Not that there are too many places to shop in Effingham." He grinned, "Believe it or not, I worked at the bait shop three years during high school. Maybe I waited on you and your friends?"

Now I was laughing so hard, I had tears streaming down my face. "Incredible! Absolutely incredible! The expedition to Effingham was one of the staff highlights every summer. It was something we could do that was naughty, but it wasn't illegal or anything. And man, did those shirts cause a commotion when we wore them home!"

Jack asked, "Did you get ice cream on your way through town?"

"We stopped for lunch and ice cream. It was a long day. Wait, Flynn's Family Restaurant?"

"Yup, that's my family's restaurant. And the Resort next door. Three generations."

"Whoa…If I had paid attention, I could have met you years ago." I laughed. "Of course, I'm not sure I would have been too interested in a guy selling Master Baiter t-shirts. Did they make you wear one?"

"Only when we were working in the store. Okay, now that you know all about me and have been to my hometown, and caught the best smallmouth in the lake, tell me about you?"

"I'm a typical small-town girl. So normal, I border on boring. I grew up in State College, where my Dad teaches history at Penn State. Dad grew up in Stowe, Vermont, and my mom was raised in southern France. Her parents were Presbyterian missionaries. State College is pretty big. But I was raised in Pleasant Gap, a village 11 miles outside State College. Probably fewer than 1,000 residents."

"Hey, that's smaller than Effingham. We topped 1,400 in the 1960 Census!" said Jack with a laugh.

I went on, "I'm an only child, but I know everybody in our neighborhood and in the village. Growing up they were like one big extended family to me. Half the adults in the neighborhood were my Aunt or Uncle. Not actually related, but we were close as families. The kids went on hikes together, rode bikes, went camping, went fishing, and shared all of Happy Valley with each other. The mountains in central Pennsylvania would remind you of New Hampshire. Tons of outdoor stuff to do, although our bait shops just sell bait. Ha, ha!"

Jack laughed at my little joke.

"My Uncle Butch is probably the best outdoors man I know," I continued. "He fishes, hunts, traps, camps, knows woodcraft, survival skills, and how to live off the land in the wild…. Eat maggots mostly. Ha, ha!" Jack laughed along with me.

"No, seriously, he sent snapshots to school of himself holding up big blanket beavers, strings of mink, bunches of red fox, and even a 50 lb coyote he trapped. I think Uncle Butch is afraid a liberal arts college like Carlisle will be filled with 'liberals.' So he gave me these snapshots, and told me to put them up on my door so I could attract the right kind of man."

Jack chuckled again. "Well, we should go fishing. I'm told the trout fishing here is world class. If it's a little slow, then maybe you could teach me how to eat maggots!"

Just then an athletic looking guy with broad shoulders and a happy smile came bouncing across the Quad. He looked like Tigger in a Winnie the Pooh cartoon in his eagerness to join us....Boing! Boing! Boing!

"Whoa, Nellie," he cried. "You guys are having entirely too much fun! What are you laughing about? I'm sure Dean Benchoff has some kind of rule against excessive laughter. I'm Gary Robbins. If I promise not to tattle, can I join you?"

This guy cracked me up. I laughed again, long and hard. "Sure, Tigger, drag up a chair."

Gary got another Adirondack chair and slid it into our circle. "Thanks; you guys just looked like you were having so much fun; I had to check it out."

"Gary, I'm Jack Flynn. I met you quickly at lunch the first day of orientation."

"That's right," replied Gary. "I remember. You and Faith: the Far Out Twins! Ha Ha," he continued, laughing. "You're the guy from New Hampshire, right?"

"That's me," said Jack. "And this is Nikki Clausen, who hails from State College. She has actually been in my hometown and has the most interesting photo in this year's Viewbook."

Jack and I introduced ourselves, and then I asked the newcomer, "So tell us about Gary? Where are you from?"

"Ah, Stump the Stars...I like that game. Not sure how to answer where, so I'll try the first question. Hi, I'm Gary Robbins and I Love Hockey! Love, love, love hockey. And on weekends, I adore hockey."

"No really, where are you from," I insisted. "How can we make snap judgments about you if we don't know where you're from?"

"Good point. Okay, here's the deal. My family lives in Richmond. When the college sends bills 'home' they send them to Richmond. But even though I was born and raised there, I've never felt like I am *from* there. I honestly don't feel like one of them. Like the Jim Morrison song. 'People are strange, when you're a stranger, people look ugly when you're alone.'"

I interrupted, "You don't sound like you're from the South. I can understand everything you are saying. Where is your accent?"

Gary continued, "Thanks, I guess. Growing up, I was pretty much convinced I had been kidnapped, or exchanged at birth with some other family. Like the Prince and the Pauper. I have nothing in common with my parents, their friends, or the

32

kids in Richmond. I listen to them and it sounds like psychobabble. They are speaking in tongues. I have no idea why they say what they say, or feel what they feel, let alone why they do what they do. I am baffled by their views and values. I've wanted to run away from home since I was three years old.

"Actually," Robbins continued, "my first vivid childhood memory is of running away from home. I was about four and I got up early on a Saturday morning. I packed my little book bag with some extra socks, lunch, canteen, my teddy bear and other necessities and snuck out the back door. I went down the street to a neighborhood park and hid in the woods. At lunch time, I realized no one had found me yet. In fact, no one came to look.

"So I hid my pack in the woods and went home for lunch. We all sat down to eat, my parents and me. Halfway through the meal, Hazel, our maid, came in and announced Freddy Wiebel was here from next door. Freddy was ten years old. A constant "do-gooder." I even think he was a Cub Scout, or something.

"Freddy came in dragging my satchel announcing, 'I found Gary's stuff in the woods in the back of the park, Mr. & Mrs. Robbins, so I brought it home for you.' No one said a thing. My parents just stared at me with puzzled expressions." After a long pause, Gary finished his story. "That Freddy; what a rotten little shit!"

Twenty yards away two girls lay sunning on a beach blanket listening to a radio. I perked up when I heard Chubby Checker come on. Unable to control myself, I hopped up and shouted, "Hey, Turn that up! I love that song!" I began jumping and jiving and dancing all around the chairs. As the music rose in volume, I sang along … "Come on baby, let's do the Twist; Come on baby, let's do the Twist."

Gyrating all over the lawn, my black curly hair came loose and was waving wildly around my head like Medusa' snakes. I put my arms up and kept waving them while I was shaking my rear end. "Around, and around, and around…" I sang and kept shaking my booty. By this point, everyone was laughing and clapping along. I could not believe no one else had joined me dancing. "COME ON!" I shouted. "How can you NOT dance?" I kept spinning, waving, and shaking to the beat, while the crowd shouted encouragement.

When the song came to an end, I was at the limits of my energy. I sang, "Gonna twista, twista, twista, …Til we twist the house down!" With that, I collapsed, exhausted, in the grass. A moment of stunned silence greeted this exhibition. After a bit of heavy breathing, I lifted my head from the grass and said, "Did I mention I like to dance? Hi, I'm Nikki Clausen, and I like to dance."

Jack and Gary both laughed. "Ok, I think we have that down," said Gary.

The two girls from the blanket with the radio came over. "That was great." said the short one. "I'm Randi Fox. This is my roommate, Faith McFadden. We live in Allison." The second girl was tall.

Jack Flynn stepped in, "I know Faith. We met the first day of orientation. At lunch. We two have been voted 'Most Far Out' for the Class of 1970."

Faith smiled and laughed, "That's right," and stuck out her hand to shake Jack's.

Jack explained his cryptic comment had to do with how far away their home towns are from the college. Then he made the introductions around our growing circle.

While everyone got acquainted, I found myself thinking what an odd couple these two roommates are. They remind me of Mutt & Jeff, the famous cartoon strip in the Sunday paper about two mismatched characters and their adventures. Mutt was really short, while Jeff was really tall.

Randi, a stunning redhead, is short. Petite, light of frame, lithe - like a gymnast. Her coppery hair hangs down over her shoulders, stopping alongside her shoulder blades. A quick smile, and a jaunty angle to her head perched on her neck. Her most endearing feature, however, is a light dusting of freckles – all over. This one was going to break a lot of boys' hearts during her college career.

Faith is a long, tall blonde. She looks like a Norse goddess. While Randi is short, Faith is very tall, and statuesque. A natural blonde, her incredibly long legs stuck out of short cut off denim jeans. Visually, she is the very opposite of her roommate.

After introductions, Randi said, "I'm Jewish and my Mom in Philadelphia sent me a care package for Rosh Hashanah, the Jewish New Year. She sent challah, and an apple honey spice cake. Would you like some?" She held out a pair of foil wrapped packets.

Faith said, "Yes, please do. Both are wonderful and we were sitting over there stuffing our piggy little faces before Nikki put on her dance recital."

As the delicious food went around our circle, Gary asked, "When is Rosh Hashanah?"

"This year it's September twenty fourth and twenty fifth. It's always two days, in the fall. We call it the Feast of Trumpets. Basically, the holiday is to commemorate the forming of Adam & Eve, and they blow trumpets made of rams' horns and feast a lot. It is really like a birthday party for the human race."

"That's cool," I responded. "It sounds very upbeat. I guess I always think of religion as a downer. You know, sin, punishment, weeping, gnashing of teeth, burning in hell – that sort of thing. I guess I don't know very much about religion."

Faith laughed. "It sounds like you've been to my home church! Your descriptions are spot on, although a little bit too positive." She laughed again, but it was rueful laughter.

A pair of guys approached our circle. Both were medium height, medium build, medium weight, but one had dark hair and Slavic facial features and the other had a square head, a cherubic smile and bright blonde hair. The blonde said, "Hi, I'm Billy Harrison. I know Jack, we've met before."

Jack smiled and said, "Yeah, I remember you Billy." Jack shook Billy's hand. "You're from Red Lion, not York".

Billy said, "This is my friend Arty Swaboda. He is from Pittsburgh, but don't hold that against him. He was born there against his will. Nobody gave him any say in the matter."

Arty laughed. "I'm sure if I had had a vote, I would have been born in Red Lion." We all laughed and made more introductions.

Billy looked around the group, "We're both in Wood Hall, on the other side of the Quad. Some guys in our dorm told us there's going to be a kegger Friday night at Carbon Creek State Park, fifteen minutes from here. It's up the road, in the foothills of the Tuscarora Mountains."

Arty chimed in, "Yeah, you guys are more than welcome to come. We're going to organize rides from Wood Hall at eight Friday night. Bring $5 to cover the beer. There's an upper classman named Skeeter something, who is of age and he'll go get the kegs."

"I've seen him around," said Gary. "My roomy is a second year engineering student and he and Skeeter are friends. You've probably seen him – he drives a silver Chevy El Camino."

Randi asked, "What's an El Camino?"

Jack laughed, "It's like a family car gets married to a pickup truck, and the El Camino is their baby." He laughed some more. "It's this new kind of car which has the front end of a sedan, with all the comforts of a nice car, but it has the back end of a pickup truck. Cargo bed, tail gate, the whole bit. Kinda low and mean like a racing machine, but room in the back for a load of fence posts or a stack of hay bales."

"Or a bunch of beer kegs," piped up Arty. "Anyway, this guy Skeeter agreed to get the beer in his El Camino. Who wants to come?"

"OK…" I spoke up, "I know this is going to sound crazy, but I was thinking of organizing a night fishing trip on Friday. I already went to see Dean Benchoff to pick his brains about good fishing spots. He told me how to get to this place on White Pine Creek which is deep and slow and has holdover trout, some smallmouth bass, and big catfish."

"Wait," asked Arty. "You want to give up going to a kegger to go fishing in the dark? That sounds kinda dumb to me."

"No, no, it's not in the dark." I shot back. "We go there before it gets dark. We build a big campfire, bring a Coleman lantern, and camp chairs and blankets. We set up, throw out lines and sit there shooting the breeze while we wait for a bite. Roast marshmallows, drink some beers. It will be fun."

"Gee," said Billy, "I'll have to think about that one." He paused a beat. "I guess I'll go to the kegger," and laughed uproariously at his own little joke.

"Fuckin A!" exclaimed Arty. "We don't fish where I come from. Have you ever seen the Allegheny River? It still occasionally catches fire and the Fire Department has to come down and make sure it doesn't burn stuff on the shoreline. You can put me down for the kegger."

Jack laughed at Arty's comment. "I want to go fishing. I haven't been fishing for weeks, not since I arrived at this joint. I'd love to come. I'm craving some fishing time. You know who else you should ask, is that guy over there." Jack pointed to a tall lanky guy sitting across the Quad on one of the low stone walls wrapped around the perimeter. "His name is Rob Bachmann and I happen to know he likes to fish. He suggested we should suck up to the Dean and learn about some of his fishing spots."

I looked where Jack was pointing and saw a handsome guy with a muscular build and dusty auburn hair, kind of wavy and perhaps a bit too long, sitting relaxed and at ease on a stone wall. Bachmann had an easy smile and seemed unperturbed, self composed. Not arrogant or stuck up – but confident in himself. Many of my new classmates, well let's say they look like they come from somewhere west of Punxsutawney, and Carlisle is their first taste of the big time. Bachmann was dressed in clean jeans, a blue Penn State T-shirt, and black Chuck Taylors. Rob looks like he'd fit in with almost any group on campus. Even his smile reflects a degree of ironic amusement at the discomfort everyone around him is feeling with this new scene. It doesn't appear he is worried about making friends or fitting in.

"Hey, I've met him too," injected Gary. "He's a pole-vaulter. And he's a cool guy. I met him the first day. Want me to invite him over?"

"Sure," I said.

"HEY, BACHMANN!" yelled Gary at the top of his lungs. "WE NEED YOU OVER HERE! GET YOUR SWEET CHEEKS IN GEAR NOW!!!!"

"Gee, that was friendly," laughed Billy and Randi.

Bachmann's head jerked up, he looked in our direction, squinted for a minute, his freckled face breaking into a smile when he saw Gary waving at him. Rob unfolded himself off the wall and ambled over to the group. Addressing Gary, he said, "Hey hockey boy, what's up? Billy? You behaving? Jack – the fishing man! What's up brother?"

"Rob, we have a fishing proposition to make, but first let me introduce the group." Gary proceeded around with introductions to Randi, Faith, Arty, and me.

"So here's the deal," Jack began "Nikki over here is a very competitive fisherperson and she's already got the drop on us with Benchoff. She's been sucking up to the Dean and got a hot location for a night fishing spot. Wants to mount an expedition this Friday night. Any interest? Or you can go to a kegger up at Carbon Creek State Park with your roommate here and Arty?"

"Night fishing?" Rob asked me. "For what exactly?"

"It's a big creek, a deep hole in a bend. Holdover trout, smallmouth bass, and big catfish," I responded.

"Where do I sign up? That sounds great." replied Rob.

"Can I make a confession?" Gary piped up. "I have never gone fishing. Ever. In my life. There it is. Shameful, I know, but I have to tell it like it is. But it sounds like fun, particularly the night fishing version. Could I come? I don't have any equipment, but I might learn something by watching y'all."

Jack laughed. "No problemo, cowboy. I bet we can tackle you up. Nikki, how many spare rods do you have?"

"Three or four." I replied.

"Rob, how about you?" Jack asked.

"Five or six."

"Hey man, I guess we have you covered. Anybody else want to join in?"

Randi Fox spoke up, "I'm going home to Devon this weekend. Not only is it Rosh Hashanah, but it's my Mom's birthday."

Faith had been sitting quietly. "Well, I don't have too much experience stumbling around in the woods in the dark. I certainly don't know how to fish, but I do know how to party and drink. I worked as a waitress at Coconut Willie's, the party spot on St Simons, for three years in high school, so I guess I'll go with the kegger." Addressing Billy and Arty she said, "See you guys tomorrow night at eight."

Just as our little crowd began to disperse and drift off in different directions, a white guy with a big afro came running up. "Hey, there's a fire! It's in one of those brick dorms near Lincoln!" he panted.

Randi looked at Faith and exclaimed, "Holy Crap! That's where our dorm is!" She turned and asked afro boy, "Is it bad?"

"Well, you can see flames and smoke pouring up the side of the building. And a bunch of fire trucks just pulled up!"

Without another word, we all wheeled around and broke in a run for the Lincoln Ave side of campus.

5

"Many men go fishing all their lives
without knowing it is not fish they are after."
~ Henry David Thoreau

Rob Bachmann   September, 1966

We tore across the lawn, Faith and Randi looking sick with apprehension. When we got closer to the rising plume of smoke, it was clear it wasn't Allison burning, but Conklin Hall, a men's dorm next door. Both girls looked somewhat relieved, but still concerned for the people in Conklin. When we arrived on the scene, I could see billows of thick black smoke rising up above the back of the dorm. Gary said, "There's Andy, my roommate, and Skeeter. Let's find out what they know." We slid over to join a cluster of gawking students.

"Hey guys, what the hell is goin' on?" Gary blurted.

Andy Sergeant dead panned, "Looks like a fire to me."

Skeeter Stetson, a senior, laughed. "Holy Smoke, Batman! You ain't kidding!" He laughed some more. He strikes me as the kinda guy who is amused by much in his experience.

Fire was billowing out of one of the rooms on the back of the third floor of the red brick dorm. It tore up the brick facade and engulfed the fire escape. Just then a battered 1960 Chevy Impala raced through the smoke and skidded to a halt in front of the scene. The Impala was painted a faded lime green, with a small red emergency light stuck on the roof. I noticed a set of deer antlers wired onto the hood where the car's hood ornament should be. It wasn't a great rack, maybe eight points. It was wide, perhaps sixteen inches across, but it had little tines – three or four inches high. A squatty little deer rack. But there it was – a trophy, proudly displayed on the front of the sick green hood.

Skeeter leaned over, "Now watch this." The driver's door creaked open and out clambered a round, middle age man dressed in a campus security uniform. He was dumpy, looked like he'd been sleeping in his clothes, and had trouble getting his limbs organized.

"That, my new friends," Stetson explained, "is Deputy Dawg, one half of our illustrious Carlisle College security force. The Chief of Security is Junior Starrett. Junior works mornings but he takes the college's one police cruiser home with him when he clocks out. Deputy Dawg works the evenings, but he has to drive his own car. That's what you're looking at. The flasher is for emergencies."

Deputy Dawg, straightened himself up, tugged on his clothes to clear the wrinkles out of his uniform coat, and looked around to see how he might take charge. This could be his fifteen minutes of fame. He strode over to the firemen to assert his authority. Just then the crowd let out a collective gasp, followed by the sound of a terrific, "Kurrrump!" A huge explosion erupted from the dorm and a fireball lit the scene. "Kaawoosh!" then "BOOM!" The crowd and the firemen backpedaled away from the flames. You could hear metal projectiles tearing through the trees. Fortunately, most of the firemen were off to the side with Deputy Dawg trying to get organized.

The blast came straight out from Conklin Hall and blew metal railings and other bits of shrapnel directly towards the street. The fire escape, as it was blown to bits by the exploding fireball, became a killing machine. Thankfully, there was nothing much in its path or the damage would have been much worse. Afterwards, chunks of steel railings were found impaled in several maple and oak trees, like spears hurled from the hands of an angry god. The rest of the scrap metal was driven harmlessly into the lawn and flowerbeds. Miraculously, there were no injuries. The explosion blew out the flames, so neither the fire brigade nor Deputy Dawg got to perform any heroics in putting out the blaze. Both left the scene disappointed and unrequited.

Later, Skeeter told us, "I heard the fire was deliberately set. Some freshman, in Conklin Hall, who was unhappy at school, got a five gallon can of gasoline, took the cap off, and placed it in the middle of the fire escape. He piled all the plastic trash bags on the gas can. He lit the trash to give himself time to get away before it blew. Unbelievable! He's lucky nobody was killed when that sucker went off. Imagine, four weeks at Carlisle and he wants to blow himself and everybody else to Kingdom come?"

After dinner on Friday night, Jack and I drove up to Nikki's dorm in a battered blue Ford panel van. Nikki was standing on the slate gray front steps waiting.

"Hey you guys, where'd you get the wheels?" Nikki asked as she approached. It was a weary and worn out Econoline van, which had obviously traveled a lot of miles, had some interesting adventures and was wearing a few bumps and bruises to prove it. A vehicle with character.

"Borrowed it from my new buddy Doug Novaksky," Jack answered. "He's in my dorm, Rhodes Hall. Doug's from North Jersey, the nice part of Jersey. His story is a lot like mine. Multi-generational tourist business up in the mountains where all the folks from Jersey drive up to vacation, by the Delaware River and the Poconos. Hot Dog Johnny's is famous for frosty root beer, two dozen kinds of hotdogs, and French fries which are hot, crispy and melt in your mouth. Well, at least that's the story Doug tells. Hot Dog Johnny's is paying Doug's way through college.

"Unfortunately, Doug is not in love with the hot dog business. He tells me he's in love with rock music. Claims his high school garage band is so good they were ready to become the next Buddy Holly or Yardbirds. When he mentioned this to his parents, they went ballistic. His folks sent him off to college with instructions to come to his senses by the time he graduates. Doug's van started out earning a living in the family hot dog business, and then served as the road bus for Doug's rock band. Now it's our passport to fine fishing. Let's get going!"

We added Nikki's gear to the already large pile of beach chairs, blankets, snacks, fire gear, and fishing tackle in the blue van. When this Ford van was originally built there were only two seats in the front and cargo space took up the rest. Fortunately, during the garage band phase, a bench seat had been bolted in behind the driver chairs, providing seating for five people plus lots of luggage room.

"Where's Gary?' inquired Nikki.

"I told him to meet us here at 6:30." I explained. "What time is it now?"

"A little past 6:30," said Nikki. "Let's give him a few minutes....Wait, here he comes." We all looked up as Gary came tearing around the corner of Steiner Hall at a full gallop.

"Sorry I'm late," he gasped. "I got held up at dinner, then went to the dorm to get a sweatshirt. Thanks for not abandoning me! OK," he yelled, "let's get this show on the road!"

We left campus on the long drive which passes the old stone College Chapel and crosses a little bridge before connecting to Lincoln Ave. The bridge and chapel are built from the warm brown fieldstone common to this area. Very pretty. The bridge, which crosses the Antietam Creek, is short, but high for its length, so if you hit it with any speed it acts as a giant speed bump. Done correctly, it can give the impression of being on a roller coaster. We whoop-dee-dooed right off campus.

The countryside we rode through is showing signs of fall. Trees are beginning to display red, yellow, orange, and brown leaves. Walnut trees around the farm houses have lost their yellow leaves and left them blowing in the yards. Corn fields are turning a shade of pale tan indicating the end of the growing season. After following Nikki's directions for twenty minutes, Jack turned the van onto a gravel pull out bordering White Pine Creek. He parked next to a line of tall, shag bark hickory trees and we tumbled out. Jack, Gary and I hauled all the gear down to the creek, while Nikki gathered firewood for the evening. She soon had a nice campfire burning in a ring of rocks down by the stream. Before long, we were situated, with baited lines in the water and settled in to relax and wait.

I leaned back and proceeded to ignore my rod as soon as it was rigged. It's grand to be parked by a stream which might produce fish. I love the chill feel of the air as evening sets in, the crisp smell of fall leaves, and the wood smoke rising from our fire. The riffle above the pool gurgled and thumped. Across the water I can hear turkeys settle into their evening roost. The daytime sounds of the woods grew quiet, and the night sounds turned up their volume. Crickets, cicadas, and other insects sang in chorus. Bullfrogs joined in with the bass from the creek bank. A lonely owl hooted deep in the woods. "Who cares if we catch fish," I said. "This is great." Twilight settled through the trees and the night sky grew dark.

Nikki asked, "Have you heard anything else about the Conklin fire?"

"Holy Crap!" exclaimed Gary. "Stetson was right; the fire was set by a freshman, a guy named Ronnie Reynolds. He rooms with Frank Spinelli, a guy from Ridgewood, New Jersey."

Jack spoke up, "One of the RAs in Conklin told me Ronnie has been having trouble adjusting. He was homesick and a kid on his floor has been picking on him. The RA said Ronnie's family moved from Ohio to Minnesota in high school and he lost all his friends. Now he's in a new place, again, and he doesn't know anybody. Plus this bully's been doing a number on him. A jerk named Ratso Ramsey."

"Ratso Ramsey! Holy Dog Doo," exploded Gary. "I *know* him. He's from Richmond and he is a stinky little weasel if there ever was one!"

"Wait, I've heard his name," I jumped in. "Isn't he the kid with the Thunderbird convertible, who won't eat at the dining hall?"

"That's the guy," said Nikki. "He lives in Conklin, drives a shiny new black T-Bird with red leather upholstery, and rides up to Mom's Hoagies or over to Chilly Dawgs for lunch and dinner every day. He claims dining hall food isn't fit for human consumption. He's apparently loaded – rolling in money."

Gary chimed in, "I went to school with him until I was fourteen. We were at St Christopher's, a boys' school for the upper crust in Richmond. His name is actually Craig Ramsey and he's from one of the wealthiest banking families in the South. He never liked his name so he made up a nickname, 'Alfie.' A few months after he got to St Chris the other boys started calling him 'Ratso.'

"You know how nicknames start and how they stick? It's an appropriate handle. Everyone decided this guy was a nasty little rodent, and not to be trusted. He does look a lot like a rat. Long skinny body, a pointy head, sunken cheekbones. One look in his eyes tells the story. He would rather pee on your shoe than say hello. He comes from money but has no social graces. Instead he has a chip on his shoulder and a full-time grudge against the world. As far as I can tell, he actually likes to be called Ratso."

Gary went on. "It's easy to see why he's a twisted bully. His family is very high brow, snooty, and hung up on their wealth and position. But Ratso has an older brother, Franklin Agnew Ramsey, IV. La dee da! Frank Ramsey is heir to the family business and all the attention is on him. He is always cheered, encouraged, and praised. Ratso is simply ignored. He's the doofus little brother. The family clown, loafer, slacker, the dunce. He was not so much disrespected as overlooked."

Nikki chimed in, "I can see where that might make you resentful, but that's still no excuse for picking on a guy like Ronnie who is unhappy and having trouble."

Just then Jack's rod tip started to twitch. He leaned down and opened the bail so his line could slide out. Slowly it did. Picking up the rod he clicked the reel in gear and lifted firmly.

"Hey, I got one," he exclaimed as he fought to gain line against his bucking rod. We could see flashes of yellow and brown by the light of the fire. We all cheered encouragement and advice as Jack worked a big brown trout up to the bank. He carefully slipped a net under his prize and laid it on the grass.

"What *is* that?" asked Gary.

Nikki spoke up, "That is a brown trout and a very good one at that."

Jack stretched his tape measure along the brownie and declared, "sixteen inches!" He gently returned the net into the water and released the trout. "It's really too big to eat. If they are much over twelve inches, they won't fit in the frying pan and are hard to cook. I'll let him go to make more babies."

"OK then," laughed Nikki, "First fish, biggest fish, and most fish – all the prizes belong to Jack, so far," she chuckled. "The rest of us better get to work."

"Not likely," I replied. "I'm not here to work. I'm here to fish. Pass me a marshmallow and a beer."

After a few moments of quiet, listening to the night noises and the crackle of the fire, Nikki asked, "Do you think your history determines who you become? Like Ronnie Reynolds or Ratso – is our future determined by our past? Does your history shape your future?"

Gary volunteered, "I wonder about that – a lot. I grew up an only child in a wealthy home. My family's business makes cough syrup, and stuff like that. My parents and grandparents are big deals in Richmond. The unstated assumption is that when I grow up, I'll return to Richmond and take their place in the business and in society. My parents rarely talk to me, so they have no idea what I'm thinking. I have no interest in inheriting their cozy world. I've always felt like an outsider in their culture."

He continued, "Richmond is a mess. Its history is about segregation, racism, and a headlong effort to separate the 'haves' from the 'have nots.' Growing up, the only black people I ever saw were gardeners, maids, cooks, or wait staff at the country club. I could never figure out why white adults talked to blacks the way they did. When I was fourteen, I saw television footage of police attacking crowds of Negros with dogs, fire hoses, and guns in Birmingham, and I was shocked people could treat others that way. White people attacked black neighborhoods and the police joined the attackers. I saw cops wade into crowds of peaceful protesters indiscriminately slashing and smashing people in the face...well I don't have words for what I felt. Something inside me told me this is terribly wrong. I knew then the culture my family and friends are all a part of is something horrible.

"I called my grandparents on Long Island. I've spent my summers with them since I was ten. We're close, not like I am with my parents. I simply asked them to help me. I needed to get out before I became like my family. Granddad got on the phone and convinced my parents to send me to Stony Brook, a boarding school near them. I spent the last four years at Stony Brook or at my grandparents. I think it saved my life. That's what I mean when I say I am not from Richmond."

Jack threw a few more sticks on the fire. It blazed up lighting the faces around the campfire. "I don't know what to say, Gary, except that sounds tough." Jack continued, "I like my family a lot, although I am not sure how crazy I am about the family business. I love the outdoors and nature in New Hampshire, but obviously," he said pointing to our surroundings, "there are plenty of places you can find nature. My family is really tight, very supportive, and very loyal. They might be workaholics, which is not a positive, but that may be the nature of a family business."

Jack continued, "I spent plenty of time working around the restaurant as a kid, but never particularly enjoyed it. My older sister Meghan opted out of the family business early – when she was a senior in high school. She got herself knocked up, married her boyfriend, and moved out of town to be near to his family in Wolfeboro. My little sister Maggie and I were sort of best friends. We enjoyed hanging around our family's farm. Maggie did every kind of agricultural project imaginable. I like shop projects and ended up restoring old British sports cars.

"Neither of us was drawn to the family business nor were we crazy about living in Effingham – in the middle of nowhere. It's not the end of the world, but you sure can see it from there. But Maggie and I loved hanging out at home. We had a big rambling old farm house, the barn, the pastures, the woods. Everything we needed was right there. I don't think either of us wanted anything more from the world.

"When Maggie was twelve she caught spinal meningitis at school. She came home one afternoon with a headache and a fever. She was dead in three days." Jack paused. He was visibly choked up. Tears leaking down his cheeks. He whispered, "Losing Maggie was like having my heart ripped out. For a year I was surprised every time the sun rose. I didn't understand how it could, when she was gone. The last three years of high school were sad – like someone took the color out of the world and left me in a land of black and white and gray. Maggie's death tore the heart out of my life. I hope I can find a fresh start."

We sat for a while digesting what Gary and Jack had shared. The night noises made a pleasant racket as we stared into the dancing flames of the fire. The marshmallows and drinks kept going around. Every time someone threw wood on the fire it blazed up with light. Gary's rod was at the end of the line of poles. Things were pretty quiet in the fishing department. His rod, like ours, was resting in the crotch of a forked stick shoved in the mud bank. All of a sudden there was a 'thunk' and Gary's rod bounced up in the air and off the stick. We turned and watched as the rod started dragging down the bank straight towards the water. Nikki was up in a flash after the rod. She grabbed the handle just as the rod slid into the creek. "Holy Shit, you have a monster on this!" she shouted at Gary. "Get your sweet cheeks over here and learn how to land the Big One."

Gary was beside himself. "What do I do?" he yelled as Nikki passed him the rod.

"Hang on tight," replied Nikki. "Keep your rod tip up and let your tackle do the fighting."

"What's that screaming sound, and how come my line is going out not in?"

"That's the drag. It keeps the big ones from bustin' your line. Here, let's adjust the drag a little. There you go. When he pulls off line, don't reel, just let him run. When he stops, start reeling in. Rod tip up."

Gary fought the fish, with Nikki coaching him, for ten minutes before Jack netted the beautiful catfish.

"Wow, that puppy is big!" exclaimed Jack. "It's got to weigh over five pounds." He pulled out his tape to measure the pale gray trophy. "Twenty three inches long. Whoa!"

Gary asked, "Do I have to throw it back? It's the first fish I've ever caught."

I laughed, "Well you sure started with a bang! No, I wouldn't throw it back. Here's my advice. Let's take it back to school, get some pictures of you with this beauty and then we'll clean it, filet it, and have a catfish fry back at the dorm. There's enough meat on that bad boy to feed all of us and a couple friends. Saturday night fish fry, that's my advice."

"And catfish is delicious," chimed in Jack. "In New Hampshire we call them hornpout, and a good one might be 12-inches long. That is the biggest one I've ever seen in my life! Way to go, Gary!"

"I'll take your advice. Let's eat it! But first I want pictures to prove what a manly man I'm becoming."

Jack slipped the catfish onto a stringer and put the fish back in the water, to keep it fresh until we return to campus. We settled back in our camp chairs and launched into a round of fish tales by the more experienced fishers in our group. After a while, we settled into companionable silence once more. There is something about gazing into the flames of a campfire…

Eventually, I spoke up. "Nikki, I keep thinking about your question about whether our past determines our future. I think that cuts to the heart of a lot of issues in life. I confess, I'm German – Pennsylvania Dutch actually, and we're not into sharing our feelings. I've spent most of my life pretending that I don't have feelings, or trying to suppress any I stumbled across. But let me give it a shot."

After a minute I continued, "My childhood home was not a happy place, like yours, Jack. My favorite daydream as a kid – and I thought about this constantly – was that the Russians had nuked the USA, and I was the only person left alive. Loved it! When I got older, my career ambition was to grow up to become a hermit and a poacher--to live off the land and be completely independent and self-supporting." I laughed. "I guess you can see a theme here. My parents fought and bickered constantly. My brother Ted, sister Molly, and I were simply pawns in their war.

"It's funny, Gary, you talked about feeling like an alien in Richmond. I always felt like a stranger in my family, like maybe I was an orphan and I had a better family somewhere else. I just did not fit. And I was sure if I squinted just right, there in a flash, the answer would appear. I would see the light and I could begin to find my way home – to the home where I really belonged.

"When I was twelve, my mother died in an accident. You'd expect it would have a major impact on me, but it didn't. I never really knew her. She was just the crazy screaming woman engaged in the Bachmann's Hundred Years War with my father. When she died, there was not as much background noise, less bickering, and no screaming and shouting matches between my folks." For a long minute I sat in silence. "When I look at my life today," I continued, "I realize there is no going back. My family life, my home – such as it was, my history; they're all gone. Like someone dropped a bomb on my house and it all got blown to hell. There's nothing left but a smoking crater where I once used to live. I never had much of a past. And the past I had is gone. I'll have to find my own way to the future."

We sat in silence for a while longer. As I watched the flickering flames of our campfire, I can hear a scratching sound coming from the dark behind us. Then we heard bottles clinking in the cooler. Jack looked at me, then Nikki, then Gary. "If we're all sitting here by the fire" he asked, "Then who is rooting around in the beer?"

"Or what," I added.

We turned and pointed our flashlights at the cooler. The lid was up and something dark and furry was digging in the ice and beer. "Probably a raccoon," said Nikki. "Uncle Butch says they like beer."

Jack eased out of his chair and slowly circled back towards the cooler with his flashlight leading the way. "If it's a coon, we can get a rock and brain it." He kept circling then suddenly stopped. "Hold off on the rocks for a bit. In fact, you might want to stay still. This raccoon has a big wide white stripe down the middle of his back and his behind is pointed right at my face. I don't think he knows I'm here, but I'd sure hate to startle him."

"It's a skunk," Nikki stage whispered to Gary.

"And it's busy eating our night crawlers," Jack continued. "Should I arm wrestle him for the rest? Ha ha!...just kidding! He can have them all," he finished as he resumed his seat by the fire.

"Well, friends, I guess Mr. Skunk has put the finish on our evening" I said. "No bait, no more fishing. Let's give him a few minutes to finish the worms then we can douse the fire and head back to campus."

"I'm sorry to see the evening end," Nikki replied. "It was great. But give Skunky as much time and space as he wants. Then I'm ready to pack it in as well."

In short order we loaded up Novaksky's old blue van and rolled back toward campus with our lone catfish resting on ice.

6

*"The greatest danger for most of us is not that our aim is too
high and we miss it,
but that it is too low and we reach it."*
~ *Michelangelo*

Faith McFadden   September, 1966

On Friday night I was excited to go to the kegger. Coming to Carlisle, I hoped to
turn over new leaf in life. Ever since I was a kid, I've felt pressured by people. My
parents always forcing me to conform to their religious beliefs. Folks at church do
the same. In high school, classmates used peer pressure to try to get me to be like
them. Working at Coconut Willie's, I felt leaned on by customers and staff to
conform to the morals of the party set at the bar. It feels like I've always been under
pressure from someone to be somebody else. I've never been allowed to be myself
or to figure out who I am, or who I want to be.

When I was fourteen I developed a coping strategy - I simply lied to everyone. I
told my parents whatever they wanted to believe - whatever made them happy. At
church, I played the 'good Christian girl' and no one asked any more questions. I
told my peers at school they were all swell. That seemed to satisfy them. I sucked
up to the party set at Willie's, and told them what they wanted to hear.

The downside of this strategy is I find I am always lying. I lie as easily as I
breathe. It's gotten to the point, when I open my mouth, the first thing that pops out
is a big fat lie. Even I don't know what the truth is anymore. I need a fresh start. I
want to meet new people. People who don't know me, and who have not been
subjected to all my lies. I need new friends. This kegger sounds like a great
opportunity to get a fresh start.

At ten minutes to eight, I walked over to Wood Hall, not far from my dorm. A
bunch of students gathered in a loose knot on the edge of the parking lot. Half a
dozen cars were idling nearby. As I walked up, a squatty gray Dodge Dart pulled
up with its windows down and the Four Tops blasting from its oversize speakers.
"Sugar pie, honey bunch..."

"Yo, Faith, what's up?" shouted Arty Swoboda from the driver's side window.
"Can we offer you a ride?"

Billy Harrison popped up on the far side of the car, scooting out of the window
until his butt was perched on the sill. The radio blasted, "I can't help myself, I'm a
fool in love you see," as Billy lip synced the words to me. Then he said, "Come on
Faith, ride with us. It'll be fun."

"Ok." The back door swung open and I hopped in. Arty and Billy were in the front. A cute brunette was sitting on the far side of the back seat. She had dark brown hair, medium length, with bangs cut straight across her black eyebrows. Wearing jeans, a white T-shirt, with a well worn blue denim jacket, this chick looks adorable. Billy introduced us. "Faith this is Delilah Brown. She's also a freshman. Delilah, this is Faith McFadden. She's from some little island off the coast of Georgia."

I stuck out my hand, "St Simons Island, near Brunswick."

Delilah replied, "I'm from Baltimore - like Billy is from York, PA." I laughed. Good one! As we shook hands, Delilah smiled, "I'm actually from Dayton, Maryland, a small town west of Baltimore. It's dreadfully rural, but there's only one big city in the state – Baltimore, so we tend to say we are 'from' Baltimore. My dad is the pastor of the Methodist Church in Dayton."

As Arty drove north away from Carlisle, we chatted amiably and enjoyed the ride. Delilah is very pretty, has big brown eyes, a vivacious smile and a charming manner. I'll bet the boys flock to her like flies to honey. I don't know what it is, but from that first conversation I had mixed feelings about Delilah. Watching her flirt with Arty and Billy in the front seat made me wonder if she was the kind of girl you can trust? Or is there something else going on under that precocious exterior? After a few minutes Swoboda said to Billy, "Billy, swap seats with Faith. I want to get to know her better."

"Sure," answered Billy. Without hesitation he turned around to dive head first into the back seat. Delilah and I laughed, even though his pile up of arms and legs between us made it crowded. It seemed like the logical thing to do was go over the seat to take Billy's old spot. So, I did.

"Faith, tell me about yourself," began Arty.

"Like what kind of stuff?" I rebutted.

"McFadden. What's that, Irish?"

"My dad is Irish. His people came over to work building the railroads in the 1870s. Potato famine Irish. Mom is half Scots-Irish and half Creek Indian. She grew up on the edge of the Okefenokee Swamp in South Georgia. What kind of name is Swoboda?" I returned.

"Czech." said Arty. "My grandfather came over from what is now Czechoslovakia to work in the steel mills in Pittsburgh. His family settled in Homestead, east of the city and the location of one of U.S. Steel's big plants. My grandfather worked in the mill. Dad still works there. There's no way I want to do what they do. Its tough, brutal work. Assuming I graduate, I'll be the first one in my family to finish college. I'm interested in engineering or accounting. If I end up at US Steel, I want to be in management and not out on the shop floor. What are you interested in studying?"

I paused while I considered Arty's question. "I don't really know. My reasons for coming to Carlisle are complicated. I've always been told what I should do by a lot of other people. My goal right now is to be completely open. To try a lot of things and see what appeals to me. See what captures my interest and imagination."

We drove down a small dirt road, winding through the closed campground in the State Park. We eventually arrived at the back of the campground and pulled up next to a silver El Camino and several other cars. We piled out of Arty's Dodge Dart and found ourselves joining a diverse group of college kids walking up a trail away from the cars. The trail was narrow, and carpeted with pine needles and fallen leaves. Delilah, who was walking next to me, grabbed my arm and said, "I'm afraid of the dark. Can I hold your arm?"

I laughed, "Sure," but I pulled out my flashlight and shone it ahead on the trail. "I may not be used to stumbling around in the woods at night, but I'm not afraid of the dark. Back on St Simons, I would often sneak out at night and get in trouble. I've always found a flashlight is the key to not getting caught or getting into too much trouble."

Delilah laughed. "Good to know I ended up with a pro at staying out of trouble."

"Did you say your Dad is a pastor?"

Delilah replied with a hesitant, "Yeeess… Why do you ask?"

"In the church I grew up in, the pastor's family never got into trouble. His kids always had to be perfect, or at least to give that impression."

Delilah laughed. "Did that ever make you wonder what was really going on?" She hesitated a beat then continued, "I have to agree with you about the expectations. As a pastor's kid, my parents put a lot of pressure on me to at least to pretend to be perfect – though we all know nobody is. I often feel like I'm forced to live like Dr. Jekyll and Mr. Hyde. I'm one person at home and in church and a completely different person in the real world."

"That sounds like a bummer, but I can relate. I grew up in a strict fundamentalist church and I know what you mean."

Delilah and I followed the trail and came into a clearing in the forest. In the middle of the space a big bonfire was burning brightly. Ten feet back from the fire large dry logs had been dragged up to serve as seats. Off to the right stood three steel beer kegs. One was set up on rocks with flat stones in front as a table to serve the plastic cups of beer. The other kegs were in reserve for later in the evening.

Skeeter Stetson was circulating through the students collecting five bucks per person to cover the cost of the beer. He seems like a naturally funny guy. Almost every person he talks with breaks out laughing at his clever remarks. Someone had a big black transistor radio and it's blasting out rock tunes from the underground rock station out of Harrisburg. WMHR is the best contemporary rock station in the Cumberland Valley. They play a lot of new music and all the old standards as well. Just now the radio is belting out *Gloria*, and kids are shouting out the lyrics along with the radio. Knots of students dance as the firelight flickers in weird shapes over the gathered throng. It's like watching a small mob ebb and flow according to the music playing moment by moment.

I got a cup of beer and drifted over to a log a bit further away from the crush – on the other side of the fire. A tall, dark, handsome guy sat next to me on the log.

"Frank Spinelli," he said sticking out his hand in greeting.

"Get Out!" I exclaimed. "I've heard people talking about you."

Frank began to blush. You could see it right up in the roots of his hair on his forehead. It bloomed on his cheeks as well. This is embarrassing.

"No, no," I explained, "it was all good. Everyone had nothing but good things to say."

Frank looked relieved. "That's nice to hear. You had me going there for a minute. I'm Italian, in case you can't tell, and sometimes people pick on me because of my heritage."

"No sweat," I said. "I know a fair bit about discrimination. I'm from Georgia and my Dad is a cracker, - what southerners call a redneck who is lower than poor white trash. Our family is so poor, we live in the Negro section of town. Talk about embarrassing! Even the blacks are embarrassed for us. My Mom is half Creek Indian. When 'good Christian people' call you and your sisters 'half breeds' you know you are not about to be invited to many social functions on the island."

"Really, your Mom is half Indian?" asked Frank. "That is so cool."

"My mother's father, Henry Morningstar, is a full-blooded Creek and Chief of the tribes around the Okefenokee Swamp in Southern Georgia." I added.

"Wow that is super neat," said Frank. "My family came to America from Sicily, in Italy. My great grandfather was a member of the mob in New York City. I have no idea what he actually did, but his second son, my grandfather Gino, decided he didn't want to join the family business. When he graduated from high school, he left New York City and moved to Fort Lee, New Jersey.

"He opened a tailor shop and added a cleaning business. He never got rich, or drove a big Cadillac like his brothers and cousins who stayed in the mob. But he encouraged his two boys to get a good education and an honest job. Dad went to Princeton on a scholarship and graduated from Harvard Medical School. He's a heart surgeon. Uncle Vince is a lawyer and works in some big job for the State of New Jersey in Trenton. Dad bought a house in Ridgewood, which is a very snooty bedroom community outside New York. That's where I was raised. Kids in school would rag me because I'm Italian."

Frank seems a little sensitive for a guy who is so good looking. With some trepidation I asked, "Is it true you room with the guy who set Conklin Hall on fire?"

"Ah, yes." said Frank. "Now that is absolutely true." He laughed, "Poor Ronnie. I'm guessing Ronnie has issues he is dealing with. Long story short, Ronnie is due at the Dean's Court on Monday morning and he'll probably be expelled for setting the fire. He's already been charged by the cops with arson, property damage, and endangering others. His parents are flying in from Minneapolis over the weekend and will probably end up taking him home."

"What happened to that guy Ratso?" I queried. "Did he get into any trouble? Is he here, at the kegger?"

"It's a bitch, but just what you would expect," Frank sighed. "Ratso got off scot free and no he is not here. He was invited, but he claims keggers are too low class for anybody like him. I hope no one talks to him for the rest of his college career. What a creep!"

Frank wandered off to get another beer from the brew station. I relaxed, enjoying the scene, nursing my first beer. I have no interest in getting wasted, I just want to meet people and have fun. Watching all the people is entertainment enough. I can see Delilah working the crowd. Interesting, she only seems to be talking to guys? And she is making a big hit. When she turns her beautiful brown eyes on a guy, bats her eyelashes, and leans in to murmur something, you can just see the guy's lights go on. Delilah has sex appeal and she has it in abundance.

The radio blasts out hits like *California Dreamin'* by the Mamas and Papas and *Paint It Black* by the Stones. Neither of these are good dance tunes. But when *The Mashed Potato* comes on, people let out a big cheer and start grinding out the Mashed Potato dance and laughing and screaming. It looks like some of these kids are pretty wasted already and we've only been out here for an hour. Just then a tall guy with a flat top sat down next to me on the log.

"You're Faith, right?"

"Yup."

"Hi, I'm Andy Sergeant. I met you at the fire at Conklin yesterday."

"I remember. You're Gary Robbin's roommate. You're a sophomore, right?"

"You got it."

"Gary seems like a sweet kid; what's he really like?"

Andy laughed. "Well, he might surprise you. You know he's a hockey player?"

"Yes...but...,"

"Like most hockey players, he chews tobacco. It is so gross! He walks around our room and all over the dorm carrying a soda can, spitting tobacco juice into it. When we have visitation hours, come check out our room. There are half empty soda cans on every window sill and ledge filled with slimy, stinky tobacco juice."

"That's incredible! Hard to imagine," I replied, laughing at the thought.

Andy continued, "I have no idea what it's like in the South; I've never been further south than South Jersey. But here, most athletes chew tobacco. Baseball players, football players, and hockey players.

"What else can you tell me?" I inquired.

"Well that is the only bad news on Gary. In spite of the chew, he is a decent guy. Did you know he is a Lynch? As in the Wall Street firm Merrill and Lynch? Yup, his mother's dad is J. Edmund Lynch, partner in the big investment firm. His father's family runs Robbins Pharmaceuticals in Richmond. You would never know it from looking at him, but his family is loaded.

"In fact, as soon as I found out about his family, I forgot about it. It seems so not like him. He is a decent caring human being. My dad was the first person in our family to finish college. He worked his way through Drexel at night and became an electrical engineer. Our family and friends are normal everyday folks. We're happy to have a roof over our heads and food on the table. Gary doesn't seem any different from the people I hang out with at home. I could bring him to my house and he'd fit right in."

"That's an amazing story," I replied. "I would think you could easily pick out somebody from great wealth at a college like Carlisle. Most of the kids here seem to be hopeful of going someplace in life, but they don't seem entitled, like they come from some place special."

"I would guess you could pick out super rich kids too," Andy agreed. "Like that creep Ratso Ramsey. But maybe he stands out because he is a creep, and not because he comes from money? It's funny, you can tell Gary is not comfortable with his family's wealth. He keeps talking about 'Not being from Richmond,' as if it's some sort of black mark on his character."

Just then Billy plunked down on my other side. He appeared to have a good buzz on and was heading for the place where the drinker starts to slur his words. Which, of course, normally comes before he loses all judgment, starts a brawl, or passes out cold? "Hey Faith, how's it going?"

"I'm having a great time," I replied. "How about you, Billy?"

"Couldn't be better! Hey Andy, how's it hanging?"

Andy laughed. "I'm doing fine. Maybe I'll go get another brew." He wandered away.

Billy then leaned in, "Can I ask you a question?"

"Well, you can ask. I'm not sure if I will answer, but I'll consider your application."

Billy laughed at me. "It's like this," he began. "You are a very bright and observant young lady. I can see that. I've been watching you since school began. You notice a lot and I bet you have a good idea which way the wind is blowing."

OK, I thought, this is going to be a weird conversation. Very flattering, but what's he after? I wonder where this guy is going with this line of bullshit.

Billy continued, "I want you to know how glad I am we are both in the Class of 1970. My feeling is this class and the people in it have a lot of potential to do well and to make the world a better place."

Alright then, I thought. Wonder what he's up to? I feel I'm being manipulated, like when I was walking up the trail with Delilah. Why do I feel he's had this exact conversation with everyone here?

Billy went on. "My point is, I think…, I feel…, I want to serve our class, to help out and make a difference. I was thinking of running for Class President or for Student Government. If I did, would you support me? Would you work on my election campaign?"

51

So there it is. The hidden agenda. And I just thought Billy might be a little drunk and confused. No, instead, he is political! "Honestly, Billy, I guess I'm not very political. It's ok with me if you run, but I don't think I want to invest myself in a campaign. I'm just not sure how much good it does." I flashed him my big megawatt smile. "Good luck and all that. Let me know how you make out."

We lapsed into silence. Oops, guess that was the wrong thing to say. As we sat there staring at the flames, Skeeter approached and offered me another cup of beer. "Thanks," I said. "I needed that. How has your night been going?"

Skeeter laughed. "So good, so far. You're Faith, right?" Turning towards Billy, he said, "and you live in Wood Hall, right?"

Billy stuck out his hand. "Billy Harrison. I met you at the Conklin Dorm fire." Billy jumped up. "Hey, there goes Delilah. Maybe I'll try my question on her. See you guys around."

Skeeter laughed. "Do you know how you say that in Philly? 'You'se guys.' Ha ha! What a hoot!"

"In the South we'd say 'Y'all.'" We both started laughing. "I heard your El Camino is a mongrel."

"What do you mean?" Skeeter seemed a bit offended.

"You know, a half breed. The illegitimate offspring of a farm truck and a street racer. Is that true?"

Skeeter cracked up. "OK, if you put it that way, I guess it is true."

"Do you live on a farm?" I asked.

"Well, not exactly. My family is Stetson, as in the cowboy hat. The hat came from the Wild West but believe it or not, the corporate headquarters is in Center City Philadelphia. My great-great grandfather, John Stetson created the cowboy hat in the West and the plant that makes cowboy hats is still in Texas. But the company makes lots of different kinds of hats and is headquartered in Philly. My dad is the VP of Marketing and we live in the suburbs. Our home used to be a farm. We own about fifteen acres, but it really is more of an estate than a farm. Dad commutes on the train into Center City to work."

"So, why the need for the El Camino? It's not like you are working on a ranch."

"Ahh, but I like it. It's a really cool vehicle. Comfortable enough to take a girl on a date, but you can use it to haul gear, or kegs, or even a half dozen friends. Want to go for a ride? I can give you a ride back to campus and you can see just how cool the El Camino is."

I thought, why not? "Sure," I replied, "I'd like that."

I saw Billy and Delilah walking towards the woods. The two of them looked like they had formed a mutual admiration society. Odd, but I get the same vibe from both Billy and Delilah. Hiking up to the party, I felt like she was playing me. Trying to suck me into her orbit in some sympathetic way. Billy was doing the same, but his agenda was political not personal like Delilah. Won't they make an interesting pair? "Billy," I shouted. He turned. "Tell Arty I got a ride back with Skeeter and not to wait for me."

"Okie dokie," Billy yelled back. He and Delilah waved to us as they disappeared into the dark forest.

Skeeter and I left the party and hiked down the trail to where the cars were parked. This time it was me grabbing for Skeeter's arm in the dark. I confess, I never mentioned my flashlight, I just clung tightly to his strong, well-developed bicep. I kind of like this guy. He is at least three inches taller than me, which is always an issue if you're a tall woman. He was dressed in long Wrangler jeans with a red checked cowboy shirt, with the little metal buttons on the pockets, and fancy trim. This cowboy looks good! He is good looking too, with sandy hair and a big straight smile.

On top of that he has his own wheels and is a senior. Not bad for a freshman girl from No Where, Georgia. Skeeter is also funny. I suspected as much, watching him work the crowd at the kegger. As we walked out, he kept up a steady chatter of funny stories about previous keggers and college life in general. After my weird talk with Billy, I needed a break. Politics, ambition, and manipulation - too depressing.

Skeeter makes me laugh. It feels good. I need more of that. We arrived at the bottom of the trail. I could still hear the laughing and shouting from the party up on the mountain. And I smell the wood smoke from the fire drift down the slope. It's a great time to be out and to be alive.

Skeeter gave me a tour of the El Camino before we climbed in. I have to admit – it is a sweet ride. A pretty vehicle, with all the classic Chevy good looks. Lots of silver and chrome on the outside. Skeeter opened my door and helped me in. A gentleman! How nice. He climbed in and I slid into the middle so I could sit close to him. We drove down off the mountain and Stetson kept up a steady stream of funny stories, which had me laughing. He's patting my knee with his free hand and stroking the skin on the nape of my neck as his arm rests on the back of the seat. I'm getting the impression he likes me.

I am certainly interested in him. He kept telling me funny stories about a place called Grandpa's Grinder. According to Stetson, it's the hang out in Carlisle which serves booze to under-age college kids. The establishment has a big white fiberglass chicken mounted on the roof of the building – ten feet tall, according to Skeeter. It's to advertise their fried chicken specials, but the college kids are always stealing it, or dressing it up for Halloween or Easter or using it for some hilarious prank.

"I'll take you there, you'll like it. The food is great, you can get a drink, and you'll meet the most interesting people there, both college people and townies!"

We arrived back in front of my dorm. Skeeter turned off the El Camino and pulled me into him. He gives me a kiss. At first his kiss was gentle, then a little more exploratory. Soon we were playing a little tongue game as we make out. It's nice. But then his hand started to slide up my waist and on to my chest.

"Whoa, big boy." I cautioned. "Let's not get carried away. This is not even our first date. Your El Camino is great, but don't think we are going to make it here in front of my dorm."

He laughed, "Oops, sorry, I got carried away. I certainly meant no disrespect."

I pulled his hand off my waist, "Come with me for a minute."

We climbed out of the car and I took him by the hand. I led him into the shrubbery by the dorm and around to the back of the building. I don't know if he thought he was going to get lucky or what, but he followed willingly. I sat him down on a bench set amidst the flower beds, "This is one of my favorite places to come at night. Look up there between the trees." I pointed. "I like to sit on this bench and look at the stars. On clear nights, they are so crisp and sharp. The sky is immense. I don't know much about stars or the universe, but this gives me a totally different perspective on life." For the next few minutes we just sat; holding hands and gazing at the beautiful night sky.

Finally, I felt its time to call it a night. He gave me a gentle good-bye kiss, and walked me to the door. I fell into a peaceful sleep…something which seldom happens. If I had any idea of the hell about to break lose in our lives in the next few hours, I probably would not have slept a wink.

7

"Life is difficult."

~ Scott Peck

Jack Flynn   September, 1966

When I woke at seven Saturday morning, I felt better than I have in a while. Our fishing trip was a great success. I love being outdoors! Sitting by a fire and rapping with new friends was wicked neat! I went to breakfast in a good mood, but it didn't last long. Rob came up to me in a panic.

"Billy never came home from the kegger last night. I can't imagine where he could be. I'm afraid he is a bit of a boozer. I'd hate to think he got smashed, and wandered off into the woods and got hurt. What if he is out there bleeding to death?"

"Stay calm, Rob. There are lots explanations which don't involve death or dismemberment. Let's go talk to your RA." We left the Dining Hall to find Mac Graham. Mac got his fellow RAs to search the dorm, but they found no sign of Billy. He used the hall phone to call Dean Benchoff. When he came back he said, "The Dean says there's another person missing who was at the kegger."

"Holy crap!" exclaimed Rob. "How does he know about the kegger?"

Mac laughed. "One thing you will soon learn is there is little at Carlisle College Benchoff does not know about. If it involves students and their well being, he knows. He has spies everywhere. I'll bet he can give you a complete list of everybody at last night's kegger right now. The Dean is like Santa Claus. He knows who has been naughty and nice; he knows who is sleeping with whom; and I'll bet he even knows who bought the kegs last night."

Graham continued, "Dean says there's a freshman, Delilah Brown, who didn't come home. Benchoff is calling out the campus search team. We can help them look. He will meet us out front in ten minutes."

A few minutes later, Benchoff came strolling up the sidewalk dressed in his fishing outfit. Khaki slacks, shirt, fly fishing vest bulging with pockets, fly boxes, and fishing gear. I felt bad we pulled him away from his morning's fishing. Mac filled him in on what we knew.

"Ok, I'd like you to go round up any volunteers you can find for a campus wide search. We need to get Campus Security involved and we will meet here in ten minutes."

Rob, Mac and Linda Pence, Delilah's roommate, ran off to find anyone who would help. I stood with the Dean while he waited patiently for Junior Starrett, the head of Campus Security. Finally he roared up in a white Ford Crown Vic with the

Carlisle College seal on each front door. Spewing gravel and loosing a cloud of dust in his haste, the Chief jumped out of the Vic and hustled over to the Dean.

"Yes, Sir," Junior offered, throwing the Dean a snappy military salute.

Benchoff organized the volunteers and instructed the teams to investigate every building on campus. "Chief, I want you to manage the teams and get every building on campus searched. Call Officer Noble and have him get down here in case we have to look in town." Officer Noble was apparently Deputy Dawg's real name. Who knew?

"Yes, Sir!" snapped Junior. He jumped in his cop car and tore off with siren blaring and lights flashing.

Benchoff laughed. "I'll bet today will be his best day all year!"

Rob, Nikki, Gary, Faith, Andy Sergeant, and Skeeter were in my crew as we spread out over campus searching buildings. An hour later we assembled back in front of Wood to touch base.

Nikki said, "We searched five buildings without any luck. There could easily be 50 buildings on campus!"

"You got that right," chimed in Gary.

"Not to worry," Skeeter said. "We've done this before. Benchoff has lots of experience with the process. He starts with the campus search. Last year we had a couple of students go missing, just like Billy and Delilah. Turns out these two were a couple in love and very horny, so they had got in the habit of going up to the chem lab to boff each other's brains out late at night. They figured no one could see them because of the lab benches built into the floor and who would go into a chem lab if they didn't have too? This ploy worked great until a janitor accidentally locked the door on them one Friday night. That's just where we found them when we did the campus search the next morning."

"Ha, ha, I guess the joke was on them," laughed Rob.

Andy added, "If the campus search doesn't work, they explore town, and last but not least, they organize search and rescue teams to go out and scour the woods where the kegger was."

The volunteers collected together in front of Wood Hall. No one had seen the missing pair. The Dean addressed the group. "Thank you all for your help. Now we'll send our professionals in to help the police and local authorities to search town."

"Where will you look?" asked Gary.

Benchoff replied, "Try not to worry. These aren't the first students we've had go missing. We'll check the local hospitals – you'd be amazed at the drugs kids ingest from time to time. Sometimes people are in accidents and get injured. Then there are the motels - coeds have been known to stop in for some Friday night physical exercise and lose track of time." Students throughout the group of onlookers sniggered. Benchoff continued, "And the local jails – you know, all the usual places one looks for college students. Oh, and we will check in with Dr. Long. If nothing turns up, we'll search the mountainside in Carbon Creek State Park this afternoon."

We decided to go to the Dining Hall to hang out and wait for news. Didn't seem like there was much more we could do. Besides, it was almost lunchtime.

As we walked over to Musselman, Faith asked, "Who is Dr. Long?"

Andy and Skeeter busted up laughing. Andy replied, "Dr. Long holds the distinction of being the weirdest professor on campus. Probably. He teaches Philosophy, has a doctorate from Columbia, and has been at Carlisle for over 30 years. Dr. Long has a place out in the country, a beat up old farm. He invites students out to his 'country house' to enjoy his hospitality. The good Dr. entertains by introducing students to various kinds of illegal drugs. And more of his libertarian views of life. You know, like Timothy Leary? 'Turn on, tune in, drop out?' I don't know if he sells drugs, but he creates new users out of his student guests. You can get anything you want at Dr. Long's. Mary Jane, uppers, downers, meth, heroin, LSD – you name it; he's got it. That's probably why they check there for missing students."

Skeeter interrupted, "Have you seen the two Great Danes romping on campus? You know the ones that run all over and occasionally hump on the front lawn?"

Faith and Nikki cracked up. "Yep," said Nikki, "I've seen them at play. I wondered if that was a biology experiment gone rogue." Everybody laughed.

Skeeter added, "Percy and Venus, the Great Danes, belong to Dr. Long. And he drives a purple Cadillac funeral hearse to college. You know, the big high fins? Front bumper covered with chrome and looks like Dolly Parton's hooters? And all in a beautiful plumb purple paint job. Can't miss it."

We all looked at each other. No one spoke, but Skeeter grinned. "He's a genuine whack job."

When we got to the Dining Hall, everyone got in line, picked out their lunch choices and settled down at one of the long tables. Most of the furniture in Musselman is standard issue institutional dining hall stuff – long rectangular tables with stackable seats. That's where we sat to eat our meal. But in the front corner of the hall are five large round wood tables which each hold 8 people. At these tables and along the outside walls are spread roughly fifty old fashioned wood and leather club chairs. I don't know if they came out of the old library, or if they were donated by an alum when he closed his law offices. Deep burgundy leather, with soft padding held in place with brass upholstery tacks, the wood framed chairs have wrap around back and arm supports and look comfortable.

Most kids never sit in this section, because it is different. I guess nobody wants to be odd. But seeing as we were going to be waiting, and those leather chairs looked so comfortable, we all got up and shifted over to the club chair corner. The other nice thing about this area is it is right up front by the windows. From here you can see everyone going in or out of the Dining Hall. You can also look out and see everything going on outside. Rob suggested if Benchoff decided to search the mountain, we will be able to see what was going on.

After we got comfortable in the club section, Nikki asked, "Have any of you ever been lost?" This bold question was followed by a long minute of silence.

Finally, Rob spoke up. "I've been lost. In the woods. A couple times. I can tell you it was no fun."

I asked, "How did you respond?"

"I panicked," Rob laughed. We all joined him in his laughter. "But then I realized, I've felt alone most of my life, so it was just a different kind of alone. In fact, much like other day. No big deal."

For a long time no one spoke. My guess is this topic makes everyone feel awkward. Gary broke the silence, "Well, I can relate to that. Not being lost. I've never been lost, in the literal sense. I've actually spent most of my life trying to run away from home. I guess that's a way to volunteer to be lost. But living in my home, I felt lost and abandoned. I love that phrase Ritchie Havens uses – 'like a motherless child.' That's how it felt to be in my home. Lost, but still at home. Weird."

Gary is an interesting guy. He's so open and honest about his experiences and how he feels. It's like he is in touch with his feelings, and yet he is not a wuss. He's a manly kind of guy.

Nikki followed up by asking, "If you got lost, who would come looking for you?"

"Ouch!" said Faith. "I'm pretty sure if I got lost, no one would come looking for me. At least not back home on St. Simons."

"I'm thinking my entire clan would turn out to beat the brush for me if I got lost." I said. "It's just the way they are. We may bicker a lot inside the family, but we stick together against any outside threat."

Gary smiled. "As I told you, I used to run away all the time and no one ever noticed. They either never figured out I was gone or they just couldn't be bothered to come and look for me."

We settled in and made ourselves comfortable as we waited to see what happened next. Nikki, looking intently out the window, commented, "There are people beginning to gather out there. I can see some Boy Scouts, and Andy is out there with his ROTC buddies. Looks like some locals are coming out to help to search. That's really cool! Deputy Dawg and Junior are both out there and some people I don't recognize. Benchoff was right when he said this place is a community! I am blown away by the number of folks out there who will give up a Saturday afternoon to look for two strangers."

Just then my cousin Matt came in and walked over to our group. I greeted him warmly, "Hey, Matt, glad you could join the party!"

"Who's Matt?" said Skeeter. "This fine looking young man with the handlebar mustache is none other than Frenchie LeBoufe, leader of the Adams Hall Marauders!"

"Frenchie? That's what you call him?"

"It's his nickname earned fair and square in the bowels of Adams Hall. We can't tell you specifics. You know the code: 'What happens in Adams stays in Adams!' But let me assure you Frenchie earned his name with some pretty outlandish practical jokes. Thanks to the US Army, Frenchie has forgotten more about communal life than most of us will ever know."

Throughout this speech, Matt grinned and laughed. I can tell he thinks it's funny and is glad to be accepted by his dorm mates.

Matt winked at me, "Hey Jack, just wait until you get a nickname. They come out of the blue and stick like glue. Not much you can do about it. Because we are blood relatives, you may call me Matt, but I'm afraid the rest of these goons are going to call me Frenchie."

He laughed again. "I saw it happen in the Army. Sometimes community life produces deep truth about a person which others recognize and the nickname sticks. Like that poor putts Ratso Ramsey. There's a personal tag that will probably stick for life. It cuts to the core of who he is as a person. Ouch!

Matt changed the subject. "Dean Benchoff told me to come and get you. If you want to join the search up at Carbon Creek, we're getting ready to go."

8

"We have nothing to fear but fear itself."
~ Franklin Delano Roosevelt

Nikki Clausen   September, 1966

Our group piled out of Musselman and headed towards the gathering throng. The Dean had rounded up about fifty college students, volunteer firemen, campus ROTC students and a local Boy Scout troop to help in the search. As this crew of volunteers prepared to board buses to ride up to the State Park, Benchoff looked at Jack, Rob, and me and crooked his finger at us, indicating he wanted us to come over. As we trotted up, I noticed the Dean in conversation with a heavyset gentleman, in a black shirt and clerical collar, sporting long white hair and a bushy beard. He looked a lot like Santa Claus.

"Father X," began Benchoff. "Let me introduce Nikki Clausen, Rob Bachmann, and Jack Flynn. Friends, this is Father Francis Xavier, a Catholic priest who served as a missionary in Southeast Alaska for forty years. Father X knows more about woodcraft, camping, outdoors skills, the natural world, and outdoor living than almost anyone you're going to meet in your lifetime."

"Dean, you make me blush," retorted Father X.

"Just the unvarnished truth," replied the Dean. "These three are standouts from the freshman class, the Class of 1970, who I have my eye on because of their love of the outdoors."

Father X stuck out his hand saying "Howdy" to each of us. Laughing, and looking right at Jack, he turned to the Dean and said, "I was afraid you were making the connection so Jack and I could trade fashion notes." Jack blushed to the roots of his hair. Everyone laughed. I admit, with the twin black shirts, I see the joke.

Benchoff laughed his rich booming guffaw. Addressing the three of us, he went on, "Father X is a fount of knowledge about outdoor things in general, but also in field & stream opportunities close to the college. He lives, simply enough, in a small cabin out behind the Tuscarora Mountains Outfitters store on West High Street. Father X is here today with members of the Tuscarora Hiking Club. The three of you should make an effort to get to know the Father. He's the kind of guy who can offer a great deal of wisdom and knowledge you might find interesting and helpful."

The Park Rangers and State Police organized us into teams to search the mountainside. Apparently they have experience trolling the woods for missing college students and have the drill down pat. The Head Ranger explained, "These hills were mined for white clay and phosphorous at the beginning of the 20th century leaving behind pits on many slopes. These old mine pits are ten to twenty feet deep and perhaps the same in width. The sides are steep, almost vertical. If you tumble into one, unless you get lucky, you will not be able to climb out on your own. If you tumble into one without warning, it would be easy to break an arm or leg or get badly injured." At this point, the crowd grew silent. You could hear a few gasps among the student volunteers at this last remark. We were worried about Billy and Delilah.

Benchoff spoke up. "Becoming lost is a fairly common experience. It happens in lots of settings and can happen to anyone. Many of you have already been lost in your life. Children get lost at the circus, or at a supermarket. Hikers lose the trail. The good news is that most of the time when someone gets lost it turns out okay. This is no solace to the lost person. They're in a predicament. It can be frightening."

The Dean paused. "So our goal is to get out there today and relieve our friends' suffering as quickly as we can. Be careful and look out for each other."

We began the difficult process of combing the forested hillsides eager to find Billy and Delilah and hoping to not fall into a mine pit ourselves. At least that's what was going through my head. We were organized into lines of searchers at ten yard intervals. We headed off into the undergrowth shouting, "Billy, Delilah. Can you hear us?"

It was late September and the leaves were turning brilliant shades of red, orange, yellow, and brown. The oak trees remained stubbornly green as did the evergreens. It was picturesque. As we walked, leaves rained down from limbs above. Any stray breeze encouraged a shower of leaves. I could smell the rich damp tang of dying, decaying leaves. It overwhelmed my senses. I always feel so nostalgic in the fall. As we walked along I kept thinking, "I'd sure hate to be the one stranded in a pit with a broken leg in late September." Of course, it had only gone down to forty eight degrees the night before, but sixteen hours lost, without water, and potentially with injuries, does not sound like much fun to me. I've never been lost myself, but I can imagine the pain and anguish it causes the victim. Nobody would volunteer for this experience. It made me glad to be part of the rescue party rather than a victim.

Finally, after ninety minutes, we heard the screech of whistles and blasts from an air horn above us on the mountain. These are the signals we were to use if we found anyone. Our team drifted uphill towards the sound and joined a knot of people chattering excitedly. "Frenchie found them," exclaimed Faith as I walked up. "Both of them! They were in a pit but they are both alright, no serious injuries." I spotted Billy and Delilah, wrapped in grey wool blankets by the firemen walking them back to the parking area. Our crew followed them down the trail.

When we got back to campus, a group of us gathered in Musselman. It was only three pm, but we all felt a need to debrief from our traumatic experience. Gary offered to go out and get pizza. We settled into our new spot, up in the club chair section, and chatted while he made the run down to Mom's Hoagies. Several other student searchers joined us at the club table. I introduced myself to a young black man sitting next to me. "Hi, I'm Nikki Clausen. I don't think I've met you yet?" I offered.

"Bunny Washington," he said, sticking out his hand. "I live in Conklin. I'm a freshman."

"So am I. A freshman, I mean. Is your name really Bunny?"

He laughed. "Actually, the name on my birth certificate is Parker Cederick Washington. In my neighborhood, the poorer the family, the more the inclination to give the baby a big fancy name. Where I grew up in East Harlem, we were all poor; so there were a lot of fancy pants names." Bunny laughed again. "But when my Grandma first saw me she said, 'Ain't he the cutest little bunny?' Washington laughed some more. "Well, you know nicknames. It stuck."

Bunny was tall with a medium build. His skin was a light chocolate brown, like a glass of Swiss Miss. His black curly hair was cut in a short Afro hairstyle. He was well dressed. Olive green slacks, pale green polo shirt, and a brown sweater. Compared to many of my college peers, he looks like he actually cares about his appearance.

"Forgive me for being nosey." I said. "I'm told I can be very blunt, but I'm curious. I really can't help myself," I continued. "You look like you're a long way from East Harlem."

Bunny roared with laughter! "You got that right, sister," he gasped, wiping tears from his eyes. He had trouble controlling his mirth. "That is so true. It's a long story. But the short version is I spent my last three years of high school at Lenox Academy in Lenox, Mass. It's a private boy's boarding school. They brought in a dozen students from the ghetto to add racial diversity to the student body. I got a full ride from East Harlem which is pretty much how I ended up at Carlisle with all you pretty white people."

Washington laughed again, and smiled at everyone sitting around the table. Some of us might have been uncomfortable, but I didn't sense any bitterness from Bunny. I'll bet he thought it was funny. "OK, but how do you get from NYC to crashing around in the undergrowth of South-central PA?" was my follow up. "I have trouble seeing you feeling at home in the woods. Sorry. I told you I was tactless."

"No, no, it's ok. I admire your frankness." replied Bunny. "Lenox was a hard place to fit in. Most of the boys came from society. Daddy was the CEO of a big company. Or a celebrity. The notion of blending a dozen inner city black kids into this student body, was crazy. But Lenox had a second campus, a wilderness education center in the Green Mountain National Forest up in Vermont. It offered biology, botany, physical sciences, wildlife studies and outdoor classes." Bunny paused for a beat to think.

"Once I discovered The Meadows, I spent every semester I could up in Vermont. There, everyone was an equal. As a poor kid from Harlem I had about as much woods knowledge as a rich kid from some swanky Upper East Side address. We both had zip – no knowledge at all. In fact, I loved the Meadows because you were judged not by your skin color or your net worth but on who could start a fire the fastest in a pouring rain storm. Competence in the outdoors gave me social status I could never have achieved any other way. Now I feel comfortable in the woods. I not only know how to bust through jungles of rhododendron and mountain laurel, I can identify both species. "

"Why do you dress so slick?" I blurted. I know, most people would never dream of asking such intrusive questions, but there I go, just blundering along. Guess I've always been too outspoken.

"That's easy." Bunny replied. "I worked as a fashion model in NYC last summer. Most of my decent clothes are outfits I got to keep after a shoot. I don't have access to a car and haven't had time to find Goodwill or a thrift store so I can dress like the rest of the guys."

That really got Jack going. "Ha ha!...that's funny, although, pretty true. Except for you and me, most of the guys at Carlisle dress like they've been shopping in a missionary barrel." Bunny was beginning to make us all relax and feel comfortable.

Just then Gary came in the front door carrying a stack of boxes. Inside each was a large Sicilian pizza with various toppings. Instead of being round, pizzas in the Cumberland Valley are made in rectangles. Cut into squares instead of narrow triangles. But still yummy, even with the weird shape.

As we dug into the pizza, Rob remarked, "I'm struck by how people react to being alone."

"Or how they feel about asking for help," I added. "Apparently, Billy didn't feel phased by being lost."

Rob suggested, "That could be the aplomb of the walking drunk."

"What do you mean?" I asked.

"You know, when a drunk has an accident or falls down a flight of steps? Often being drunk is a protection. They are so relaxed they never get hurt in a fall. Too loose. As Billy's roommate, I have to admit he drinks a lot and comes home drunk almost every weekend."

"What about Delilah?" asked Gary.

Linda Pence, Delilah's roommate spoke up. "I think she was upset by the experience. When we got back to the dorm, she didn't want to talk about it. She just took a shower and went to bed."

"What do you know about Delilah?" Gary probed.

"Her dad is the Pastor of a small, conservative church in Maryland. She was raised in a Christian home and she talks about that stuff a lot. My family are Chreasters."

Jack snorted. "Chreasters? What's that? I never heard of that. I was raised Catholic. Well, sort of."

Linda laughed, "No, it's not a religion or a denomination. Chreasters are people who only go to church on Christmas and Easter. My family just went to the nearest Methodist Church. Delilah's family and church take their religion far more seriously. Delilah's always quoting Bible verses at me."

Gary hesitated and said, "I hate to say this, but from the perspective of a guy, she may come from a Christian family, but Delilah Brown oozes sex. She may have been raised in church, but when I see her on campus, it's like she has this flashing billboard that says, 'I'm easy. Let's go for a tumble in the hay.'"

I was astonished at this comment. "Really? I don't get that at all."

Rob said, "That's because you're a woman. Delilah's advertising billboard is only targeted at the male gender. I doubt many women can see it. Am I right?"

The guys in our group all nodded agreement. Andy said, "When I see her walk by it's like the heat is pouring off her. I would be frightened to be alone with her in a room. Unless I wanted to get laid. Pardon my French ladies. I would be very reluctant to go to prayer meeting with Miss Brown for fear she would end up preying on me. Like a human praying mantis."

Skeeter interjected, "One of the firemen who pulled them out of the pit said there was a blanket and two used condoms in there." That brought on a moment of thoughtful silence.

Linda volunteered, "When I walk with Delilah I can see what you are talking about. I don't really know what it is, but she sends out invisible signals to every guy in sight. Girls don't seem to notice her. Sort of like a dog whistle. You don't hear a sound, but you can sure see the dogs react."

Linda went on. "I don't know what the deal is with Delilah and men. But I do think she cares a lot about being seen to be Christian. My guess is she was embarrassed to be seen in public messing around with Billy Harrison. Not because she's embarrassed by Billy. He's cute! But because her family would be embarrassed by such behavior. It's not the sex that bothers her. It's that people might perceive her as being fast and loose. If you ask me, she was embarrassed at being discovered, not at having sex."

With that insight, we finished our pizza and headed in our different directions.

9

"The unexamined life is not worth living."
~ Socrates

Faith McFadden   October, 1966

Fall in Pennsylvania is spectacular! On St. Simons, the weather is always warm and moderate. It may be somewhat boring, actually. October in the Cumberland Valley is amazing! Mornings dawn with a crisp bite in the air. Trees are covered in awe inspiring palates of color. Outside our window is a dogwood tree with deep red leaves. Campus is covered with bright red Norway maples, brilliant orange and yellow sugar maples, yellow hickory and walnut trees. Wow!

After the dorm fire, the kegger, and the mountain rescue, my life began to settle into more predictable patterns. My classes are interesting, especially Theater and Political Science. Theater is fun. It's is a way of telling a story. It is a means to imagine different outcomes to real life problems. You can create new scenarios for how a person's life turns out. I guess my propensity for lying is a plus in Theater. My professor thinks I'm a creative spirit. I don't think he has any idea I'm just a compulsive liar.

College life is not bad. Get a good night's sleep, eat breakfast, go to class, study, do papers, hang at the library, more classes, dinner, study, then bed. Periodically, I take a break, usually in the mid-afternoon, to do something fun. The one positive thing which came out of Billy and Delilah's getting lost up on the mountain is our Koffee Klatch.

After that traumatic Saturday in September, a bunch of us started hanging out in the Club Section of Musselman on a regular basis. Different students drift into that comfortable seating section to enjoy a morning break where we can chat and refresh. We have regulars, but it is an open group where folks can come and go according to their schedules or level of interest. Jack Flynn, Nikki, Rob, Gary Robbins and I are the most frequent participants. We enjoy the opportunity to talk, catch up on the news, or delve into deep philosophical questions of life. The five of us came up with the name 'the Koffee Klatch.' Billy, his pal Arty Swoboda, Skeeter Stetson, Frank Spinelli, Bunny Washington, and Andy Sergeant show up regularly. Linda Pence, Randi Fox, and Frenchie LeBoufe pop in occasionally.

The chairs are comfortable, the food and drink good. The fellowship is better. Most of us come by for coffee or tea a little after 10am. Nikki, however, is addicted to TAB, the new diet drink by Coca Cola. If you come at seven am for breakfast, Nikki will be sucking back a TAB. At Koffee Klatch – same thing – drinking TAB. Lunch – more TAB. All afternoon – more TAB. At nine at night she is having the last TAB of the day. So, she's an addict. She might be addicted to worst substances, I suppose.

The real attraction is the chance to talk together and experience community. No matter how deep the conversation, it feels safe to share in Koffee Klatch. Safe people are always hard to find. Those of us thinking about who we are, where we've come from, and where we want to go in life need safe friends we can talk with, ask questions, and debate viewpoints.

For example, one morning Gary asked, "I know we don't have to declare a major until next year, but how do you think about what you might want to do in life, let alone pick a major for college?"

"Tough question!" exclaimed Nikki. "I've been wondering about that. I'm not sure I want to replicate my parents' lives. Not that there's anything wrong with the way I was raised, but it always felt a little repressed, stifling, protected. My parents are both so…predictable. Steady, practical, prosaic."

Jack laughed. "Prosaic – that's a good one. I can just see me accusing my family of being prosaic!"

Gary laughed too. "OK, I'll bite. What is prosaic?"

Nikki giggled, "There I go again. It means to be commonplace, ordinary, and conventional. My parents would think it a high compliment. Only in 'Nikki World' is it considered bad." Taking another sip of her TAB, she gave a toast. "Up with adventure, the challenging, the new, the daring and different! Down with the prosaic!"

Randi jumped in. "Why do we have to do what our parents did? Why can't we make our own choices? My parents don't care what I do as long as I grow up to be an observant Jew. Carry on the traditions. Marry a Jewish boy, have a Jewish home, keep the Sabbath, produce Jewish kids, celebrate all the Jewish holidays. I'm not ashamed of my Jewish heritage. But the foundation of the Jewish faith is in a special relationship with God. As far as I can tell, my maternal grandfather in Los Angeles is the last person in my family who actually believes in God. Not my other grandparents, not my parents or their siblings. None of them believe in God. They want to be observant Jews but skip the faith in God part. I'm confused! How can I be in a relationship with God in my practices, but not in my beliefs?"

"Wait a minute," Arty protested. "That all sounds so airy fairy. What does your parents' life have to do with what you decide to do with your life? I think the answer to Gary's question is simple. Follow the Almighty Dollar. You figure out where the money is. Then you find the best way to get there, land a good job, work hard, get promoted, become a company man, make a good living, and retire on Easy Street. For me, the best company I could possible work for is US Steel. If I can get into management, I'll make a good living, have great benefits, and live in a good neighborhood. That kind of job will allow me to enjoy the good suburban life. Nice house, nice car, nice schools, and nice vacations."

"But what if you don't like the work?" asked Gary.

"Tough shit," Arty replied. "Go for the money and enjoy your life outside of work. I may not be able to get through engineering; then I'll switch to accounting or general business. I just want to get in the door at Big Steel and get my ticket punched. The rest will work itself out."

Jack interjected, "My folks would say family is the highest value in life. Granddad Flynn says the family is bound together by ties of blood and marriage. Your first and only allegiance should be to the family. Whatever is good for the family should determine your actions in life. I don't think he would accept that an individual could have a design or destiny which falls outside the family or clan."

"That, my friend, is the philosophy of the Sicilian mob families in New York," ventured Frank. "They expect everyone to march lockstep with what the Don requires of them. But my Grandfather showed you can break away from that, and find another life for yourself and your family."

"None of us gets to pick our family." Rob said. "Our family experience influences us – sometime for good, sometimes not. But the essence of adulthood is that we get to make choices. Reject the bad things from your history. Adopt new things. It doesn't matter if your past is really bad, say Hitler was your dad. Or if it's just boring, or doesn't feel like a fit for you. We get to make choices about where we go and who we become in life."

After a pause, I made a contribution. "That's an intriguing idea, Rob. I'm afraid my instinct is to reject everything my parents stand for. My last few years at home were about rejection and rebellion. I don't like my parent's constant controlling behavior so my reaction is to reject them and everything about them. That doesn't let me sort out the good from the bad and make my own choices."

After a bit of quiet space, Gary spoke. "An idea I learned in Psychology is that we are all influenced by our family of origin and how we are raised. Some have good situations, some bad. And we can react in positive ways or in negative ways. So our nurture could be negative –say you grow up in an orphanage – but you can still make good choices. It can make you bitter or it can make you better. You can grow from it or you can let it crush and destroy your life."

"Interesting you should put it that way," said Jack. "I read a book by Viktor Frankl, who was a young medical resident sent to the concentration camp at Auschwitz with his family. He saw his entire family killed. Frankl went on to study his and others' experience of horrific suffering. He concluded that even in affliction, life has meaning. In the opportunity to seek meaning and to make the choices we can, Frankl concludes we can redeem almost any painful or negative situation."

"Wow, that's heavy, man," said Gary. "Yet, somehow, it gives me hope. Thanks for opening up and talking. It helps me a lot."

Not every conversation at Koffee Klatch involves such heavy subjects. One morning Jack and Rob were waxing eloquent about one of their favorite topics – trout fishing! Those two guys are over the top about any outdoor sport you can think of, especially about trout. Nikki, always poking fun at the two of them asked, "Have either of you figured out how to catch any of Benchoff's big trout yet?"

"Ho, Ho, Ho wouldn't you like to know, Miss Clausen?" Rob chortled. "Yes we have! Last Tuesday Jack and I caught twelve of the biggest trout you ever saw in less than sixty minutes up on the LeTort."

Jack sniggered along with his fishing buddy. "It was unbelievable! The best trout fishing I've ever had. But it wasn't the Dean who helped us score such a great success. You'll laugh, but do you remember Father Xavier, the priest Benchoff introduced us to? Hard to believe a guy who looks like Santa Claus could be so knowledgeable about fishing, but there it is. You will have to turn your conniving charms on Father X if you ever hope to get up to speed on the fishing."

"OK," Rob confessed. "We were actually planning on fishing for big spawning browns in the Yellow Breeches. We went into Tuscarora Mountain Outfitters (TMO) to get some flies and ran into Father X. He lives out back and works a little at TMO tying flies. He talked us into fishing the LeTort instead and convinced us to fish just one fly – the Wooly Worm. Ugliest fly you ever saw."

Jack picked up the story. "What followed was the best hour of fishing I've ever had in my life. Using Father X's ugly little non-descript fly, we caught a 13-inch brook trout, three big rainbows and eight huge brown trout. The smallest brown was eighteen inches long. The largest was twenty inches and weighed six pounds."

"Sweet!" exclaimed Nikki! "That's just great."

Rob broke out in a big grin and laughed. "Unbelievable! I've never caught so many trout or such big trout in a single outing. Thank you, Father X!"

10

Faith McFadden   October, 1966

I've never had a group of friends before. My peers at church were so worried about following the rules. They were critical and judgmental. I couldn't trust them. The girls in public school thought I was a right wing fundamentalist nutcase and didn't want to be friends. Koffee Klatch lets me hear what other students are thinking, without having to say much. Sometimes the conversations are heavy, but usually there's a lot of fun and laughter. Nikki and Skeeter are hilarious. They have a way of putting a twist on things which makes us all laugh. Their witty comebacks are a hoot. Gary is always saying stupid, but funny things too, and Rob spins a great yarn, he's a natural story teller.

Since the Carbon Creek kegger, Skeeter has been paying attention to me. Last Tuesday Randi and I were on the Quad catching some sun. Skeeter strolled up. "Hey girls, how are you'se guys doin'?"

Randi, who is from Philly, got the intended joke and cracked up. "Aren't you the Philly guy?" she replied. "If you really wanted to teach Faith about Philadelphia culture, you'd bring us cheese steaks, hoagies, and some Tastykake Krimpets!"

Skeeter plunked down on the blanket next to me. "How I wish I could get you a Tastykake. But we're too far from home for that. Past the Main Line, or West Chester, Tastykakes cease to exist."

"What's the Main Line?" I asked.

"It's the western suburbs of Philadelphia, where Randi lives. Radnor, Lower Marion, Gladwyne, Devon, Wayne." Skeeter replied.

"What's a Tastykake?" I asked.

Randi and Skeeter laughed. "Just the nectar of the gods and the best food ever created by the hand of man." Skeeter chortled.

"What he said," added Randi, still laughing hard.

"Be more helpful. What are you talking about?" I inquired.

Randi spoke first. "Tastykakes are baked treats made in Philadelphia. Tastykake Krimpets, my favorites, are sponge cake with butterscotch frosting. Koffee Kakes are just what they sound like--a one-serving coffee cake. Juniors have cake covered by chocolate icing, and there's a coconut version."

Skeeter interrupted Randi and exclaimed, "They have different pies: lemon, blueberry, apple, custard, and Kandy Kakes - little round cakes with peanut butter draped over and all wrapped in chocolate.

"You really can't get them anywhere but in Philly?" I asked.

"That's it. If you want to say you have lived life to the full, you must come to Philly and have a Philly cheese steak, a hoagie, and some Tastykakes." finished Stetson. After a pause he continued, "I'll tell you a secret though. You can't get a Tastykake or a hoagie out here, but...you can get a genuine Philly cheese steak. Right here in Carlisle!"

Randi's eyes lit up "No! Not really?"

"It's true. The guy who runs Grandpa's Grinder is from Philly. When he bought Grandpa's, he taught his cooks how to make genuine Philly cheese steaks. It's the real deal," Stetson looked pleased with himself.

We sat for a while and listened as Randi told us stories about growing up on the Main Line. Then Skeeter turned to me, "They are showing the new Clint Eastwood movie on campus on Friday night. It's a cowboy flick: *The Good, the Bad, and the Ugly*. Would you like to go with me?"

I thought for a minute. "I like westerns. Sure, I'll go with you. What should I wear?"

"Oh, just casual dress. We could go out for a bite afterwards, -- maybe Chilly Dawgs."

"Sounds like fun. Thanks." I responded.

"I'll pick you up at your dorm at seven. See you then." Skeeter got up and gathered up his books. "See you 'round Randi," he said with a grin in her direction, and he walked off.

Randi and I sat for a minute watching Stetson's back disappear across the Quad. Then she turned to me with a big grin on her face and said, "I told you he is sweet on you."

Friday night Skeeter arrived at my dorm to pick me up. He entered the visitor's lounge wearing a soft tan buckskin jacket with eight inch fringes around the bottom, across his shoulders and down the middle of each sleeve. "Wow, what a great looking jacket!" was all I could say.

Skeeter laughed. "What about the rest of my outfit," he said with a deadpan face.

Under his buckskin jacket, he was wearing a blue checked cowboy shirt on top of skinny wrangler blue jeans tucked into tan leather cowboy boots. I laughed, "You go together, cowboy. Where did you get such great duds?"

Looking pleased, Skeeter grinned, "The last time Granddad went out to the hat factory in Texas, I gave him my sizes and asked him to get me a few items from a local cowboy store. One that sells Stetson hats, of course. Granddad was happy to oblige." He laughed with pleasure at himself. "I thought it only appropriate when taking a beautiful girl to a cowboy movie."

Skeeter is such a bullshitter, but appealing. A charming rogue, that's what Skeeter Stetson is. I put my arm in his and let him walk me outside to his El Camino. As he opened the passenger door I said, "You know, the movie is only a five-minute walk from here?"

Skeeter grinned and said, "Yes, I know, but when you have an El Camino, why would you miss the chance to drive around campus and be seen with the prettiest girl in Carlisle?"

I laughed as he handed me into his car. Skeeter came around and slid in next to me. We took off. Sure enough, he spent the next 25 minutes driving a circuitous route around campus waving at everybody. Finally, we pulled into the parking lot behind the Auditorium. Always the gentleman, Skeeter jumped out to open my door. Arm in arm we strolled into the theater to watch the film.

Ninety minutes later, Clint Eastwood vindicated and victorious, the film came to an end. Thank God! It was pretty grim. "Wow!" I laughed. "As a theater student, I thought that was bad."

Skeeter laughed with me. "What happened to Rawhide and Rowdy Yates? It was awful. Clint Eastwood must have been hard up for money." We both chuckled at the pain.

"How about a bite to eat?" Skeeter suggested as we got back in the El Camino.

"That would be nice, but let me suggest we take the short way and skip the scenic drive? I'm actually hungry and I'm afraid if you take the campus tour again, I will be gnawing on your buckskin fringes." As I said this, I slid over next to Stetson, wrapping my left arm around his right arm. My fingers kept fondling his fringes while he tried to avoid my distractions, driving with his left hand.

It took four minutes to get to Chilly Dawgs. The place is non-descript, but it has a great location – right across from campus. Skeeter and I walked up to the counter and read the menu on the back wall. The aroma of fresh baked bread wafting out from the kitchen was enticing.

"Everything here is great. Best hot dog in the Valley and you can have it dressed two dozen different ways. The hamburgers are handmade, plump, juicy and to die for. The fries are crisp, hot and melt in your mouth. They can make you a salad if you want, but I usually get a medium hot Italian sausage pizza with a large chocolate shake." After a little more banter with the guy at the counter, we placed our order.

"I'll have a chilly cheese dog with an order of fries and a Cherry Coke." I added, "Might as well try the house specialty." Skeeter had his usual order.

I have to laugh at Skeeter. He is such a goofy guy. Crinkly around the edges, but sweet at the center in spite of his fancy clothes, his fancy El Camino and his Daddy's fancy estate. You can tell he has a way with people. I could see the counter guy likes and admires him. Have to admit, he's growing on me.

We sat in a booth while we waited for our food. I continued the conversation, "As long as I'm getting to know you, I'd be interested in what your real name is and how you came to be called Skeeter?"

Stetson just laughed. "A fair question. My real name is Stanley Baldwin Stetson. Talk about stuffy, boring and pretentious, huh? Baldwin is a family name from my mother's side, her maiden family name. Stanley is my Granddad's first name.

"OK, but that still doesn't tell me how you got from Stanley to Skeeter."

"I've noticed wealthy or successful families often give their children names that would sound good for an investment banker. Stanley Baldwin Stetson. Or names that look good on a law firm office building. 'Parker, Parker and Snodgrass.' But when they get the kid home, they discover everyone, including the kid, hates his name. It's not what you want to call a human being. So they give him a nickname. Chip, Mitt, Winky, Beanie, Alphie, Binky. What foolishness!'

Skeeter paused. "I was born Stanley Stetson. Which nobody much liked after I got home from the hospital. For years my Dad called me, 'The boy.' My mom called me 'sweetie pie.' Thank God she never used that outside of the house. When I was in first grade, I discovered baseball and I was good at it. I played on a school team. One day, when I was seven, my mother came to watch a game. She saw me scampering around the bases and said, "Look at Stanley go! He scoots around the bases like a water skater on the pond. Just look at him skeeter along!" That was it. After that everyone started calling me Skeeter. First my family, then friends and eventually, everybody.

"A year later, when I was eight years old, my Mom woke up dead one morning. What I mean is she went to bed fine and the next morning she was lying in bed dead. The doctors said she had a brain aneurism. I guess a blood vessel broke in her brain while she was asleep, and it killed her. I think because Skeeter was Mom's pet name for me, no one had the heart to change it. Somehow my name makes me think of her, as if I still have a little bit of her with me."

"That is so sad..." I responded. "I don't know what to say. I've never had anyone close to me die."

Skeeter picked up the conversation. "We got through it. Dad was hit hard by Mom's death. I guess if your spouse is sixty, you've thought about it – having your mate die. Age and death seem to go together. When your wife is thirty-two, and you have an eight-year old son, you don't sit around making contingency plans in case your wife dies. For a while, he was a mess and I was even more of a mess.

"Mom's baby sister, Sukie, had just graduated from Swarthmore College. She came out to help. Dad had a housekeeper, but it's not the same as family. Sukie is the aunt I've known all my life. I was comfortable with her. Somehow there was this dynamic, where Sukie could love her lost sister by loving Dad and me. I've never questioned her love for me. She is there for me 100%.

"Anyway, after three years, Dad sat me down and told me he and Sukie were in love and wanted to get married. He asked me how I would feel about it, which I thought was decent of him. I was eleven when they married. Sometimes it's hard to explain our family relationships, but Sukie is technically both my aunt and my stepmom. She let's me call her Sukie, but I prefer to call her Mom."

After Skeeter's story, I was feeling pretty tender towards him. We finished our food and got back in the El Camino and drove to campus. He parked in a patch of dark shadows at the rear of my parking lot. We sat in the El Camino kissing and cuddling for a while. Eventually, Skeeter hands kept drifting up to my breasts. Then he slipped a hand up my back and unhooked my bra. Very nice. I admit, I was enjoying the process. But I didn't want it to get out of hand.

"Hey cowboy," I finally spoke up. "You might take a few deep breaths and get control of yourself. You're not going to make it with me on the front seat. It is just not something I'm prepared to do."

"So sorry." He muttered. "I guess I got carried away by my passion." Regrouping quickly, he said, "Let's go look at stars!" He jumped up and we reorganized our clothes. Skeeter reached behind the seat and pulled out a large wool blanket. "I have a blanket. Perhaps we could go out behind your dorm and look at the stars?" Charming, but still a rogue.

Holding hands, we strolled out behind the Allison and found a soft grassy spot without any overhanging trees blocking the view of the sky. I spent the next hour lying back gazing up at the stars. They amaze me. Knowing the universe is so vast, how can you not consider the possibility there is a God or that there's life on other planets or in different solar systems?

Skeeter kept kissing me and fondling every part of my body he could reach. He kept his hands outside my clothes, so I let him have his fun. One of the things I've noticed about being physically mature is that guys can't seem to keep their hands off me. When I was twelve, I looked like I was sixteen and I attracted a lot of attention from high school boys. When I was sixteen, I looked like I was twenty. Working at Coconut Willie's, I wasn't old enough to serve liquor, but I could pass. Willie wasn't careful about the details of the law.

An older guy in the kitchen, Larry Bennett, was sweet on me, even though he was nineteen and out of high school. When I was sixteen, Larry asked me to stay late and help him clean up the kitchen. Before I really knew what was going on, Larry and I were back in the prep kitchen making out. The next thing I know, my jeans and panties are around my ankles, my t-shirt and bra up around my neck and good old Larry has me up on the stainless steel prep table and he is popping my cherry.

Finally, I turned to Skeeter, "It's getting late. Probably time to call it a night."

"Aww. Really?"

"Really. You can see me again sometime if you want," I said, planting a soft lingering kiss on his lips.

"I want. How about I take you to dinner tomorrow night? I'd like to introduce you to Grandpa's Grinder. I think you'll like it. Much nicer than Chilly Dawgs."

"Sure, that would be fine."

73

"I'll pick you up at six." With a kiss on the steps, my first date with Skeeter Stetson came to an end.

I fretted about what to wear on my date. I don't own much in the way of nice 'going on a date' clothes. I settled on a red taffeta dress I picked up at Goodwill for eight bucks. It's pretty with a flared flouncy skirt which hits the top of my knees. The waist is elastic, gathered together, and tight. The scooped neck line shows plenty of cleavage. Anticipating a great evening, I wore my best black bra and panties.

As Skeeter escorted me to the car he said, "Wow! That's quite the dress. You look really nice in it."

"I read a research paper which said red is a provocative color," I laughed. "Do you think that's true?"

"Definitely," was all he could murmur in reply.

Grandpa's Grinder is in a sprawling one-story building. The building wasn't much, but the chicken was out of sight! Better than promised. Over the front door, perched on the roof is an enormous white fiberglass chicken. It's twelve feet high, with bright yellow legs and beak and a snazzy red comb.

"OK, I am duly impressed! That is one heck of a chicken! We have nothing to rival that on St Simons Island and I'm sure I have never seen anything quite so…chickenesque."

Skeeter laughed. "It's astonishing, isn't it?

Inside Grandpa's I was hit by the music. It's loud. Cowboy music. West Texas Honky Tonk. The kind of music you expect to encourage line dancing. Sure enough, a bunch of folks in the next room in their Saturday night cowboy and cowgirl best, were doing a line dance to the music. Skeeter was dressed in denim. Denim jeans on top of cowboy boots, a white ironed button down Oxford shirt, and a blue jean jacket over that. He looked nice. I was proud to be sitting with him.

Skeeter ordered Philly cheese steaks for both of us. I added a salad, and he ordered fries. We each had a Yuengling beer, a local brew of some renown. Since 1829, according to the bottle. Skeeter told me Grandpa's is pretty loose about checking ages, so if you looked anywhere near 21, no one was going to hassle you. Exactly the way it is at Coconut Willie's.

After we finished eating, we enjoyed a second beer and got up to dance when the live band started about 8. It was a cowboy band, of course, and they launched their set with a rousing version of the theme song from *Rawhide*. I can tell you that went over a lot better than the Clint Eastwood movie from the night before. Pretty soon, it got louder and rowdier in the restaurant. We could hardly hear each other without shouting, so Skeeter suggested we leave.

As he put me in the car, Skeeter said, "How'd you like to do a little star watching?"

"That would be great. It looks clear enough to really see some stars," I answered.

"Let me take you to a place with less ambient light than campus. We'll be able to see better."

"OK." I said as I snuggled up to Skeeter's right thigh. I was feeling very good. Mellow and happy. It may have been the beers, but I think it was just being with Skeeter. He drove to the back of campus behind the athletic fields in a dark patch by big clump of lilacs bushes.

As we hopped out he said, "Now I want you to trust me, OK?"

"You bet," was my only reply. Skeeter pulled a folded tan canvas tarp out of the back of his truck, a rolled up sleeping bag, and a big four cell flashlight.

"Here, I want you to carry the sleeping bag." Skeeter told me. "It's light. Made with goose down so it packs small but is really warm. I'll take the tarp and flashlight. Hold my arm so you don't lose the trail."

I squeezed Stetson's hard bicep and pressed my breast into him. It was a clear night, a little cold, almost crisp as we walked along the trail to a large patch of woods. We came out along the edge of a pond. You could see the moon shining through trees and onto the water. It looked like a spotlight shining down the length of the pond. It was breathtakingly beautiful. Skeeter led me to a little glade in the woods with a thick stand of tall grass and an unobstructed view of the pond, the moon, and the night sky. He laid down the canvas on the meadow grass, and then unzipped the sleeping bag on top. "This is a double bag – made for two people to share." Skeeter explained. We climbed onto the bag and found our nest in the grass incredibly soft. We lay there watching the stars and snuggling together. Finally, he pulled the top of the bag over us for warmth.

OK, I'll admit it. I was wet between my legs before we left the parking lot. I'm attracted to Skeeter and want to be with him. Inside our warm down cocoon, he kept up his chatter and little jokes as we gently undressed each other. Then he slowly and smoothly had his way with me and I with him. As I said before, he is a charming rogue.

Later, as we lay entwined together gazing at the stars, I found myself marveling at the beauty of the stars, the gentleness of this man, and the wonder of love.

11

"A friend is a present which you give yourself."
~ *Robert Louis Stevenson*

Jack Flynn   October, 1966

One morning Rob and I got into a conversation about plans for the Thanksgiving break. I guess I was worried about what I would do. I miss my family and wish I could go home and see them. "Plans for Thanksgiving?" Rob asked. "It's only the middle of October! We're getting into small game season, pheasant and quail is yet to come, then turkey and deer, and trout will hit until Christmas. Don't worry about Thanksgiving! I say, live a day at a time. Enjoy today, it may be the last you'll have."

"I guess you have a point. Its five weeks until Thanksgiving and there are more important things to worry about – like where should we hunt opening day of pheasant season? Every time I hear a rooster cackle, it sends shivers up my spine. At the same time Rob, I can't help feeling your outlook on life is bleak. 'Enjoy today. It may be the last you'll have.' Did you come up with that hitchhiking? It makes you sound fatalistic. 'First, you're born. Life's a bitch. Then you die.' Is that Nietzsche's influence?"

Rob laughed and said, "Nietzsche is on the reading list for Philosophy class, but I haven't got there yet. I think my outlook comes from experience. I always thought my dysfunctional family was 'normal' but it was the only family I knew. How was I to know it could be different?" Rob went on, "Now I realize my family was a nightmare. Full of strife and fighting. Except for my Gram, there was no warmth or human affection in our family. Even the family you have can be torn out of your hands in an instant and leave you with nothing. After my mother died I spent years wondering if having a bad family is actually better than having no family at all? I don't know."

This is one of the reasons Rob is fast becoming my best friend. We can get into philosophical conversations. More than anyone I know, Rob is honest about what he's feeling and thinking. Many people just don't think about life and what it means, who they are, where they are headed and is it really where they want to go? Rob is not only thinking, he's willing to talk about it.

A week later, I asked Rob if he wanted to go into Tuscarora Mountain Outfitters on Saturday to pick up more ammunition for the opening of pheasant season. "I don't know about you," I said, "but I'm low on shells. I used all my high brass sixes on ducks and shot up a lot of low brass loads on squirrels."

Rob laughed, "If you didn't shoot five shells to kill a squirrel and ten shells to polish off a duck, you might be in better shape." He chortled again and I had to laugh with him. It's true, I'm not a great shot, but I still love to hunt.

We made plans to meet Saturday morning after breakfast to go into TMO. Saturday dawned wet and windy. After a hot breakfast and a couple cups of coffee, we drove into town. The parking lot at TMO was crowded. It could have been guys getting ready for next week's opener. Or maybe just nothing better to do on a rainy Saturday morning.

Rob and I headed straight back to the gun department to buy shotgun shells. He shoots a 12 gauge Spanish side by side double barrel shotgun while I have a 16 gauge Ithaca Sweet Sixteen pump. When we each found the right ammo, we paid at the register. Rob suggested, "We ought to look up Father X and see if he has tips about places to hunt pheasants. He steered us right on the Wooly Worm and the trout."

"You got that right," I replied. "There's no way we would have figured that out on our own."

Rob hooted, "Maybe, it's ok to ask for help? As a man there's so much which makes me resist asking anybody for help – even with directions. I want others to think me competent. I want to feel I'm competent. Only sissies ask for directions. Or help."

"Our culture reinforces that bias," he added. "Think about the John Wayne movies, Daniel Boone, the Marlboro Man. All these male images show the individual, isolated and proud, the loner."

"Think about Ronnie Reynolds," I added. "What if he had asked for help instead of firebombing Conklin Hall? He'd still be in school, adjusting, learning, and probably getting along. Instead he'll spend the next year in and out of court, paying restitution, having to get counseling, maybe end up in the juvenile farm, or having to live at home with his parents bitching at him for pulling such a stupid prank."

After a long, pause, Rob said, "I never thought of it that way. A black mark on his record, a year in hell - all because he didn't ask for help. Let's not go there. Come on; let's go find Father X."

We walked around behind the store to the twenty by twenty foot frame building where Father X lives. It looks like a storage shed, except for the metal chimney poking out of the roof. A steady plume of white smoke was drifting up and away from the shack. Rob knocked, footsteps approached, and the door creaked open. When Father X saw us, his eyes lit up and he said, "Jack, Rob, what a nice surprise! Come on in and get out of the rain." We did as instructed and entered his humble home.

His cabin was small but cozy. Across the back wall stood a bed, wash stand, a chair, and a wardrobe. A kitchen counter with sink, cabinets and a Coleman gas stove plus a small dining table takes up the next wall. The rest of the space has a motley collection of furniture - a sofa, chairs, and lamps, nestled around an old Swedish Jotul wood stove which radiated warmth into the room. The priest was wearing baggy blue jeans, a black clerical shirt, topped by a lumpy gray wool sweater. His feet were shoved into worn sheepskin slippers – he was the perfect picture of comfort. Father invited us to take a seat.

After offering coffee from the big pot on the back corner of the stove, Father X said, "I'm so glad you guys stopped by. What brings you out this way?"

I jumped in. "We came in to buy more shells for the pheasant opener next Saturday, but thought we might ask you if you had any favorite places to hunt small game?"

"Ahh, that I do, young man," mused the Father. "If I was able to hunt pheasant and quail, I would head west out of town on Newville Road. Five miles out, look for an ice cream stand on your left called the Big Spring Creamery. Turn left on Kerrsville Road. The first two farms on your right are where you want to hunt. Good Mennonite families, the Alderfers and the Burkholders, live there. Knock on the door and ask permission. I'm sure you'll be welcome. They're generous families."

Rob and I both exclaimed, "Thanks so much."

Rob asked, "I hope you don't mind my asking, but how is it you can no longer hunt?"

After loading fragrant tobacco into his pipe and getting it going with a match and some strong puffs, the Father began to speak. "I was born and raised in Brooklyn, New York. All of my childhood, I had a longing for nature. I wanted to see big trees, big forests, raging rivers, complex ecosystems and meadows of wildflowers. I read of such things, saw pictures, but could hardly get there from Brooklyn. When I went to seminary and became a priest, I asked to be assigned to a rural, remote, and underserved area. They sent me to St Pat's here in Carlisle." He laughed uproariously with his rich booming voice.

"I guess if you compare Carlisle to Manhattan, you might think Carlisle is the boonies. Folks in New York City think anything north of Rockland County is New England. Most don't actually believe there is anything west of New Jersey." The Father chuckled again and took another pull on his pipe. "I lived and worked here for five years. It wasn't what I had in mind, but I reveled in the Valley. Farms, fields, woods, streams, and wildlife everywhere." He paused again. "Every year, I asked to be sent to some place which was actually rural, remote and underserved. I guess my superiors got tired of my whining. After five years, I was posted to Sitka, a small coastal village in Southeast Alaska. Just what I was hoping for!"

"Wow, that's neat," Rob and I both exclaimed. It was easy for us to identify the Father's love of nature and desire to be immersed in it. Who wouldn't jump at the chance to live in Alaska? I leaned over to Rob, "I told you its ok to ask for help!" All three of us had a laugh at that.

Father X continued his story. "I served with an Indian tribe, the Tlingits, who live up and down the coast of the Alaska Panhandle. I worked and lived among the Tlingit for forty years and loved every minute of it. Two years ago I was diagnosed with a heart problem. Two leaky valves. It slowed me down. The doctor said it was dangerous and I would drop dead in a hurry without surgery. So now I am back stateside waiting for my turn in the OR. I have the energy to eat cookies, but not hunt pheasants." He hooted with laughter at his own joke.

"Can I ask you another question, Father?" I paused as he smiled encouragement. "I was raised Roman Catholic, but we never talked much about what that means, and I certainly never had a relationship with any of the priests at church. Last spring there was an article in Time Magazine – 'Is God Dead?'"

Rob interrupted, "I saw that! It was just before trout season opened."

Father X laughed, "I guess we know where your priorities lie!"

"Well, what I mean to say is when I was a kid we went to mass at least once a month. But I can't say I've ever heard my family talk about God. Like is he real? Our religious practice focused on traditions. We go to church to 'do mass.' That's it. Kind of like taking your family car through the car wash. You do it every Sunday, whether the car needs it or not. It's just a way to take care of your ride. A habit, a tradition. Still, I don't hear anyone talk about the reality of God. Do they assume it? If so, what does his existence mean? Or doesn't it matter?"

"Interesting questions," said our host. "How about you Rob?"

"I confess, I was raised without much influence from church. My parents became Quakers when they married, but by the time my brothers and I arrived, they didn't practice anything. I don't think I went to church a half dozen times from the age of four to eighteen. I was raised in blissful ignorance of religion."

Rob paused. "Essentially, I know nothing about religion or spiritual things. Yet, I often find myself wondering if there isn't something more to life, which I'm not yet seeing? I feel there is a bigger, better something out there. If I just squint harder or squeeze my eyes partially closed, I might see it shimmering on the horizon, like a mirage in the desert. I hear the explanations of life from adults around me...they sound hollow. Mom was religious, but I can't say I ever figured out what her faith was in. Maybe in religious feeling itself? I'm not sure the existence of God would matter to her. Dad is a strong, self-made man. He believes you get out of life what you invest in it in hard work and personal sweat."

Rob took a breath. "When they ask what I believe in Philosophy class, I say I'm agnostic. Don't know if there is a God or not but I can't prove it either way. I'm acquainted with people who go to church, but I never hear them talk about a living God. So is God real? When they talk about faith, it sounds like belonging to 4-H, or the Grange, or a Friday night bowling league. Church sounds like a country club for folks who are interested in religion, like my Mom."

"Hmmm," said Father X, after a bit of silence. "This is troublesome. So if you believe in God and practice a religion and it turns out there is no God or he died...?"

"You are up the proverbial creek without a paddle," concluded Rob.

"Likewise, if you assume there is no God and live based on that conviction and it turns out he really does exist...?" continued the Father.

"Again," said Rob, "you're screwed, if you will forgive my French!"

Father X laughed. "What a conundrum! It may be that figuring out if there is a God, might be a very important thing to do in life. What do you think?"

Xavier stood up and put a couple logs on the fire. Then he said, "Every thinking adult asks these kind of questions. 'Who am I? What makes me special? How can I connect to others, find belonging, even community? What is my purpose? How can I relate to the rest of the universe? Every culture, tribe, and people group looks to make a connection between humans and a higher power, a creator, a God. What we call religion. The search is common to mankind, but the answers and opinions vary widely."

Father X paused to sip his coffee. "However, all these religious opinions contradict each other. Most offer different explanations, beliefs and practices. I have heard well meaning folks say, 'All religions lead to God. They're just different paths which lead to the same place.' But they contradict one another – they can't all be true." Father X laughed. "When you leave here, what would you think if I told you, 'It doesn't matter what road you take. Take any road you like – they will all lead you to Wood Hall.'"

Rob snorted, "I'd say, 'Not bloody likely!'"

"Exactly," said the priest. "Do all roads lead from TMO to your dorm? Do all religions lead to God?" Not likely! Use your own judgment. You must develop your critical thinking skills. Don't let others tell you what to think. Don't believe everything you hear or read. Don't let some slick college professor railroad you into something which makes no sense at all." He paused and then was silent.

After some more quiet, I asked, "Let me guess. You're not going to tell us what you think, are you?"

He smiled an enigmatic smile. "Perhaps later, but for now let me leave you boys with a question.

"What makes you think the sun will rise tomorrow morning? When you watch the ocean tide go out, what makes you think it will come back in? As fall turns to winter, the days get short, the nights get long. Cold and dark seep over all the earth…what makes you believe spring will eventually return, renew the land and bring a new season of life?"

The Father paused and gave us a moment to consider these questions. Then he said, "Would either of you be willing to bet these things will not happen? The morning sun, the rising tide, the blessing of spring? I don't think you would. Why not?"

With that, the priest stood and said, "I'm a bit tired. I think I'd better take a wee nap. Let me know how you make out next Saturday with the pheasants." He gave us each a hand shake, a pat on the back and ushered us out of his warm camp into the cold steady rain with lots to reflect on.

12

"The great thing in this world is not so much where we stand,
as in what direction we are moving."
~ *Oliver Wendell Holmes*

Nikki Clausen   November, 1966

October faded into November, as colorful leaves fell off the trees, puddled on the ground, and blew away. In place of the vibrant colors of the previous month, November dressed our campus with austere silhouettes of winter hardwoods. The dark outlines against the gray sky reflected their own inner beauty. Stark, barren, and yet hauntingly beautiful.

Cold weather moved in. It was too brisk to spend much time outdoors. I improvised by getting to know people and making new friends. One Tuesday I ate breakfast with Snowden McAllister. I knew her slightly from Art History class, and we were becoming friends. After our meal we sat chatting for nearly an hour. She sipped herbal tea, and I had my usual TAB.

Snowden is a pretty girl, about 5' 7", with honey blonde hair, a natural red blush to her cheeks and tiny hint of freckles. Her hair is almost always in a pony tail. Loose strands hang out and dangle by her face giving her an appealing look. When she smiles she has a fabulous dimple on her right cheek. Occasionally I see her wear a dress, but her normal attire is blue jeans and a white T-shirt. Snowden has been tagged with the nick name 'Snow White' almost since the day she arrived. But she handles it gracefully. The only thing I know about her is that she loves art.

"Snow, tell me a little bit about your story," I asked.

"I was born and raised in Bethesda, Maryland. Our town is in Maryland, but it's actually a suburb of Washington DC. Washington is famous for three things: traffic, humidity, and politics. Bethesda is a bedroom community. People live and work in DC, but at night they head home to sleep in Bethesda. My house is twenty minutes from downtown. Of course, traffic in Washington is always a beast. Stop and go, stand still traffic congestion at almost any hour of any day."

"Wow! I've got nothing like that in Happy Valley," I replied. "Maybe that's why we're so happy? On game days, when the Penn State football team is playing in Beaver Stadium, traffic in State College slows down but you just have to leave yourself a little more time. What do your parents do?"

"Dad is an IRS tax lawyer." Snowden smiled. "Yup, he doesn't have many friends." She laughed at her joke. "He's rigid, highly structured, and likes to pigeon hole everything. He's always been high control. Whenever we see him, he's criticizing Mom or me. Fortunately, we see very little of Dad because he works long hours. He even goes in on weekends.

"Mom is a full-time homemaker. Truthfully? She's kind of bland, and worries a lot about dusting and polishing the furniture. Scrubs the kitchen floor everyday. Sweeps leaves off the driveway. She is busy with civic groups, plays bridge, is in a reading club, the Garden Club and volunteers at the hospital. She aspires to be a regular June Cleaver, just like the Beaver's Mom."

"My problem - I am nothing like either of them. We have little in common. I got interested in art in middle school and it continues to fire my imagination. Art makes me feel I can express all the inner feelings I'm struggling with. A picture is worth a thousand words, if you ask me."

"Wow! You are different from your folks. I suppose I freak out my parents as well. They call me 'Science Girl.' Most of the things I enjoy – fishing, camping, hiking, botany, wildlife, astronomy –are just off their radar. They never discourage me, but they don't see what I see in science. When we argue, I always ask for empirical evidence – you know, like a science experiment. They think I should just accept their view because they are older and wiser."

"My Dad would like the way you think. 'Prove it!' he's always saying. Damn lawyers!" Snow laughed. "My parents are always picking on me. He and Mom have no place for creativity, free expression, whimsy – anything that makes for good art. They're freaked out I have decided to major in fine art. We're so different. They just don't know what to do with me."

Snowden paused for a long time and added, "I just want to figure out who I am. I want to be accepted for being a unique person. Eventually, I want to belong and be loved, I suppose."

"Aww, honey, that's what we all want. Deep in our hearts we want to know 'what makes me unique? What makes me special? Will anybody love me and accept me for who I truly am, or will I have to go through life pretending to be someone else, in order to be accepted by others?'"

Just then Snowden's head whipsawed at the clock up on the wall. "Yikes!" she exclaimed. "I have a nine thirty appointment with a pottery wheel at the studio and four minutes to get there. Thanks for the good chat." McAllister popped up, pulled on her Harvard sweatshirt, and bolted for the door.

"Bye, Snow White," I hollered after her with a laugh.

On the following Friday Koffee Klatch was just Spinelli, Bunny Washington, and me. With hunting season open, we saw less of Rob and Jack. If there was any daylight, they were out hunting or trapping. Those two guys are crazy! The only time we see them at Koffee Klatch is if it is flooding, snowing, or freezing and the wind is blowing sideways at 25 miles an hour.

Frank asked Bunny, "I was raised on the west side of the Hudson River across from New York City. The typical suburban life. What was it like growing up in the city?"

Bunny thought for a minute. "Long story short? My Mama was raised on a dirt poor farm in eastern Virginia. Nothing but hard work, more hard work, and plenty of grinding poverty. When she got sick of it she moved to NYC to live with a cousin. She had two kids while having an affair with a married man, bounced around for a while, and met a streetcar conductor, Jake Washington, who turned out to be my daddy. She is vague about family details. I often feel there's a lot my mother hasn't told me. Eventually, she had eight kids by three or four men. I'm the youngest.

"Mama strayed a lot. My older sisters had to raise us. Too many people, too many issues, and Mama constantly having dramas. Daddy switched careers and went into dealing drugs. He left before I got to school. I always wondered why he loved dealing drugs more than he loved me. My overwhelming memory from childhood was the dread of being left behind. My childhood was consumed with a perpetual fear of being abandoned by the people who provided for me."

I spoke up. "Wow that's hard. Your home life sounds draining. Just surviving would suck all the energy out of you. How did you get to the prep school in Massachusetts?"

"Ahh, well that is an interesting story," said Bunny.

Just then Robbins came bouncing up in his usual effervescent mode. "Hey Sweet Cheeks, how are y'all doing?" he said to me. Everyone laughed.

Frank said, "Oh I thought he was talking to Bunny." That cracked us up. What goof-offs!

Bunny chuckled. "As I was saying… growing up in Harlem wasn't bad. My family was a mess, but everything else was pretty good. I never experienced racism – not until I went to Lennox Academy. Everybody in my hood and in my world was black. So, no problemo. The schools were good; there were lots of public services. I went to the Boys Club, where I had a mentor who got me into sports. He helped when things got crappy at home. I suppose I was both a trouble maker and a leader. Mrs. Jackson, who ran the Boys & Girls Club, called me in one day and asked me if I would be interested in going to a private boarding school in New England, Lennox Academy."

Bunny waited a beat. "After hearing about my home life, it should be no surprise I jumped at the chance to get away. I received a full scholarship for the last three years of high school. I also got to pick seven kids from my neighborhood to go with me to Lennox.

"How did that work out for you?" I asked with some trepidation.

"The first white boy who called me a nigger got a pair of black eyes, a bloody nose, and a cut up lip. I beat the kid to a pulp. I expected to get kicked out. But at Lennox, the rule was you could break a rule once, but only once. They gave me another chance, and I got to stay. Looking back, I'm not sure the mean kids were racist. They didn't attack me because of my color. They attacked me because I was different. It made them feel fearful and insecure. When I think about it, I suspect it was really because they were haves and I was a have not. They probably picked on any full scholarship kid the same way. Not because of skin color, but because of social station."

Frank interjected, "You sound like you're talking about Ratso Ramsey."

"If you understood Ratso's home life, you wouldn't be surprised," Gary commented. "Ratso lives in his older brother's shadow. Frank, the heir to the family throne, gets a fully restored, supercharged '48 MG Roadster. Ratso gets a stock '64 Thunderbird. Frank goes to Yale. Ratso's at Carlisle. He always gets the leftovers."

Spinelli said, "That is so outside my experience. My dad is a surgeon, which in the world of doctors, is to be top dog. He makes big money, but in Jersey everyone treats us like normal people. My one neighbor is an electrical engineer. The neighbor on the other side hangs wallpaper. There are lots of smart kids in my high school. I bet seven out of the top ten kids in my graduating class are from average families."

I said, "I can relate to that. State College is littered with smart people. Driving down the street you never know who's wealthy, who's successful, who's famous, and who's normal. Saturday morning everyone is in The Diner on College Avenue scarfing down the famous sticky buns. The folks in the next booth could be dairy farmers, a dean at the University, a guy who owns a big electronics company, a local mechanic, or a wealthy socialite from New York City. There's is no way to tell. And we like it that way."

"Gary, forgive me if this is painful, but when you talk about Richmond, it sounds like there is still segregation? I thought the Civil-Rights Act put an end to all that?"

"That's something I find most Yankees don't understand. In Richmond, and most of the South, the Civil War is not over. They call it 'The War of Northern Aggression' and they are still mad as hell. Trying to fight back. Richmond, and most of the South, is still segregated! I'll bet that surprises you?"

"Really?" said Frank. "I thought Martin Luther King and President Johnson got rid of segregation."

Gary explained. "Richmond was the capital of the Confederacy. Guys like Ratso Ramsey are still pissed off. He thinks he should be living on the family plantation down on the Rappahannock River. His family owned thousands of acres of land and a thousand slaves. He thinks he should be living a rich planter's life with nigras to wait on him.

"When the Feds banned segregated public schools in 1960, whites across the South fought back. They just closed all the public schools and opened private, 'Christian' schools for the whites. White flight academies. The blacks got no education. Later the public schools were reopened for blacks and a few poor whites. Most schools today are still segregated.

"In Richmond, whites moved across nearby county lines. Suburban schools are 95 % white. Richmond city schools are 95% black. City leaders put Interstate 95 through the middle of the best black middle class neighborhoods and destroyed them. Now the interstate is used to keep blacks out of downtown, where the whites work and to force blacks to live in the projects in the East End. Wherever you go in the city, there's segregation. Maybe Bunny is right, maybe the whites are afraid of people who are different. Maybe it's the 'Haves' being afraid of the 'Have Nots.' I am so grateful to be out of there."

"I'm blown away." I responded. "I had no idea this is still going on today. It's completely outside my experience." A sad, uncomfortable, quiet fell on our group.

Bunny finally commented, "I think Gary's right. When you see injustice, you cannot just turn a blind eye and pretend it isn't happening. You have to name it for what it is. You can try to fix it, or you leave it behind, vote with your feet and refuse to participate." With that sobering comment, we broke up to head our individual ways.

Monday, November 21^{st,} dawned bright and clear. It was cold. Hard frost lay on the ground. I had an early final exam, but made it to Musselman by ten fifteen. The group was a buzz. Jack and Rob were there. Gary, Frank, Frenchie, Faith, and Linda Pence rounded out the group. I got my Tab and joined them.

"What's up, Buttercup?!" exclaimed Gary. Such a clown.

"Not much. Just finished my English final. What is everybody so excited about?"

"Have you heard the news about Snow White?" Frank asked.

"No. What's up with Snow?"

"She's gone missing. Disappeared. Vanished without a trace."

For a moment, I sat in stunned silence. I was astonished. "Disappeared how? When?" I asked.

Linda Pence shared, "Snow went into Harrisburg with girls from Winn Hall Saturday, to shop the hippie boutiques on 2nd Street. They took the College shuttle bus in at one pm."

Rob explained. "It's like Samson Street in Philly. Like Rittenhouse Square. It's where all the hip people hang out. Mod clothing, leather shops, record shops, head shops and that sort of thing."

"OK. I have the idea. Go on, Linda." I said.

"Snow went in with a bunch of girls from our dorm." continued Linda. "They came home at different times and lost track of Snow. Some stayed to eat dinner. Bands were playing live music. Anyway, the last bus came at 11 pm and everyone just assumed Snow went home earlier."

Faith picked up the narrative. "No one noticed she wasn't back – she's in a single. Some girls stopped by to get her for lunch on Sunday and discovered she was missing. It took a few hours to figure out she never came back from Harrisburg."

"That's awful!" I exclaimed. "What are they doing about it?"

Frenchie spoke, "They did a campus search this morning. Found nothing. Harrisburg police started combing the bars and other places on 2nd Street. I expect they'll do more of that."

"Will they search around here?" Rob asked.

Frenchie said, "I think so. I heard they are bringing in the National Guard and asking for volunteers this afternoon to do sweeps through the fields and woods around campus. Snow may have come back, but been disoriented by something she consumed in town. If she got off the bus and wandered off, she could still be out there. Some of your hippies pass out weird drugs and might snare an innocent like Snowden."

Jack asked, "I wonder what could have happened to her?"

"The possibilities are bad, really bad, and truly awful," said Frenchie. "In the Army we often got called out on searches. Sometimes we found them. Sometimes we found nothing. Sometimes we found a body."

We talked a bit longer. Those of us without a final exam joined the search. We scoured the fields, the woods, the pond and even the orchards surrounding campus without any signs of Snowden.

The next day was the last day before Thanksgiving vacation. As soon as anyone's last final took place, people bailed out. By mid afternoon cars and trucks were streaming off campus headed back home for the holiday. I felt sad to leave school without any resolution about Snowden, but what else can we do? The Dining Hall is due to close up at six and by eight the campus will be deserted.

I have invited Gary Robbins to come home with me for the Thanksgiving break. He was one of those students who didn't have a place to go. In Gary's case, he didn't want to go home to Richmond and he couldn't find a ride to Long Island. Or perhaps, he was angling for an invitation from me? I don't know. I am happy to bring him home. My parents will be cool with that and it will be fun to show him my hometown. We left campus about two pm after one last status check on Snowden.

13

"Home is the definition of God."
~ Emily Dickinson

Rob Bachmann   Thanksgiving Break, 1966

In October, when Jack was fretting about Thanksgiving break, I told him to take a chill pill. It never pays to worry too far ahead or to worry about things you can't control. What's the worst that could happen? You camp out in the dorms, and walk into town to rustle up some food. Who knows, maybe Dean Benchoff might invite you home? How cool would that be? If you ask me, Jack worries too much.

It turned out fine. Frenchie LeBoufe invited Jack and me to come home for Thanksgiving with his family. I was excited. I'm enjoying learning about other people's families. I had no idea there were so many different ways to 'do family,' all of which seemed much better than my experience.

Late Tuesday afternoon, Jack and I piled into Frenchie's canary yellow VW Beetle for the ride to Newville. We hopped on I-81 and zipped along for thirty minutes before we got off at the Newville exit. We were in the middle of nowhere. All I see are large dairy farms. Cows and barns every direction you look. It reminds me of Peace Valley in Bucks County where my mother grew up. As we cruised up a two lane road, we crested a hill and there is the village. It consists of a main street with four or five parallel side streets running over the crown of the hill. Newville is laid out like the criss-crossed pie crust on a blueberry pie. A perfectly neat lattice of streets and houses draped over a hill

On the outskirts is a railroad track which splits the properties holding the Newville Building Supply, from the Cumberland County Grain Depot. The lumber yard is operated by Frenchie's dad, Leroy LeBoufe. The feed silos across the tracks are used by local farmers to store harvested grain or to ship it to market. We drove up the east side of town, where Frenchie turned into East Big Spring Avenue, a short cul-de-sac with a dozen homes.

The LeBoufe homestead is a neat two story Cape sheathed in white clapboard accented with black shutters. A typical Cape design with dormers, but you can see rooms and additions have been added over the years to accommodate a growing family. Frenchie explained, "Dad built the house himself. With the help of all his contractor buddies who buy materials from the lumber yard. It started out as a simple house. When I was young, every weekend we did a new home improvement project. Adding a porch, pouring concrete sidewalks, laying linoleum, adding bedrooms, framing in a porch so it could be used as a bedroom. I don't know if you know this Rob, but I have five younger brothers and sisters."

As he talked, Frenchie pulled the VW into the large gravel driveway between the house and the barn / garage. He honked once and a boiling cyclone of humanity piled out of the side door of the Cape.

Jack laughed, "And here are the rest of my crazy LeBoufe cousins. Don't worry, they won't bite. Well, most of them won't bite…most of the time."

"Hey you guys, simmer down," yelled Frenchie. "You'll scare my friend."

I was surrounded by chattering kids of various ages. Plus yipping beagles and a tired old yellow Labrador retriever who looked crippled with age.

Frenchie barked in his Army drill sergeant voice, "Line up for inspection! By age! Ten-hut!"

Amazingly, his siblings managed to straighten themselves out and get into a straight line in descending order by height. Once organized, they threw their oldest brother a snappy salute. The two beagles kept running in circles and leaping excitedly while the lab flopped down in front of the two smallest kids.

Frenchie resumed, with a commanding tone of voice. "You all know Cousin Jack." He was interrupted by wild cheers from the assembled throng. Jack is apparently popular with his LeBoufe kin. "And this is our friend Rob Bachmann, from Bucks County. He's a freshman at Carlisle College. Treat him with respect. And gentleness." Again, the kids broke into a cheer – for me! I've never had such a welcome.

Frenchie resumed, "First we have Mickey, age seventeen," he pointed to a tall gangly lad with an acne problem. "Next is Megan - she is fourteen." They both had the jet black hair and bright blue eyes of the Black Irish, maybe from Jack's side of the family.

Frenchie moved on down the line. "This husky young man is Martin, goes by Marty. He's twelve." Marty looked like a younger version of Frenchie. Strawberry blond red hair, lots of freckles, a big smile, somewhat stocky. "And the twins, Mark and Marley, are nine." Of all the kids, Mark's hair was the reddest – almost fire engine red. Marley's curly locks were strawberry blond. "The beagles are Duke and Dixie. This tired old lab, Murphy, is twelve years old, which is eighty four in dog years. Much like his master," Frenchie said, running his hand over his own thinning hair, "he is starting to show his age."

We all laughed and then our little troop stiffened to attention as Frenchie's mother stepped out of the side door of the house. Mrs. LeBoufe was short, not much more than 5'2". She was round, almost as wide as she was high. She had an oval face glowing with a smile of welcome. Mrs. LeBoufe hurried up to her oldest son and buried him in a long hug. "Matthew," she exclaimed, as he bent over to embrace his mother. "It is so good to see you!"

"It's only been ten weeks, Mom" protested Frenchie. "You act like I've been gone for years."

"Ever since you went off to Vietnam, I have been so grateful to have you back from that jungle. I'm thankful each time you show up in one piece. I love you, boy." Both mother and son were beaming at each other in spite of their protests.

"Mom," said Frenchie, "this is Rob Bachmann. He's from Doylestown."

Mrs. LeBoufe was wearing a blue patterned house dress. Over top was a long eggshell white apron. She reached out and enveloped me in a hug. I could smell apples, cinnamon, flour, sugar and yeast – a cloud of kitchen fragrances arose from her as she hugged me. "Welcome, Rob. I'm so glad you could come home and join our family for a few days. We are glad to have you with us."

She turned to her nephew. "Mr. Flynn, I see you still retain your unique fashion sense. I hope it won't scare the chickens!" At that she let out a hearty chopping laugh, "Ahhahahaha!" at her own little joke. We all joined in. Her laugher and affection were simply contagious. She gave Jack a terrific hug and a kiss on the cheek. When she stepped back you could see a ghostly print of flour dust on his black shirt. "You are also welcome, you strange and wonderful boy. You and Rob may both call me Aunt Maddie."

"Gee wiz Aunt Maddie," protested Jack. "I saw you at the end of August. You act like I just got off the ocean liner from the Great Potato Famine after an absence of decades."

"Glory be, boy! Don't you mock your family's sainted history in the old country. You were away from me in New Hampshire for so many years, I feel like I need to make it up to you now. I've only seen you to hug a couple times since you turned twelve, so don't deprive a foolish old woman of her small pleasures!" With that, she reached out and drew him in for another long hug. This time she pulled his head down and smothered his hair, forehead, cheeks, and even his ears with kisses. At the same time she made wet smooching noises until he collapsed in laugher and rolled on the ground.

"I surrender! I give up! I'm glad to see you too, Auntie!" As he rolled on the ground, the dogs and the kids all piled on to give him more love and affection. By the time we got this buzzing mass of humanity headed towards the house, Jack's neatly pressed black shirt was covered with grass, dirt, sticks and leaves. But he looked happier than I had ever seen him.

The LeBoufe's home is warm, comfortable and looks much loved. The furniture doesn't match, nor is there any apparent style to the decor. The house appears lived in, but it is clean and well organized. I guess with six kids, you need some kind of organizational strategy.

Frenchie, Jack and I were assigned to the basement family room, a cozy space with three single beds and a sofa on one wall. End tables, lamps, and easy chairs were scattered about. A full bath completed the space. Glass sliders looked out over the back yard and down to Big Spring Creek. Home sweet home!

Just before dinner, Mr. LeBoufe came home from the lumber yard. Frenchie's Dad is short, wiry and has bow legs like a sailor. While Frenchie's Mom is pleasantly plump, there is not an ounce of fat on his Dad. He gave Jack a big bear hug which elicited a short grunt. "Ouff! Thanks for rearranging my internal organs, Uncle Leroy," Jack protested.

Leroy laughed," It will be good for you, after all that studying away at college. It will straighten out your priorities." They both laughed.

"Rob, nice to meet you," he extended a hand and gave me a firm handshake. His hand was callused, and incredibly strong. Such a powerful handshake too, though I'm sure he was trying for gentle.

"Thank you for having us, Mr. LeBoufe," I replied.

"Call me Leroy, if you don't mind. If you are old enough to go to college and old enough to fight our country's wars, you are old enough to call me Leroy."

Jack injected, "May I call you Leroy, too?"

Mr. LeBoufe reached over and grabbed Jack in a faux strangle hold around the neck. LeBoufe started rubbing his bunched up knuckles in Jack's hair. "No, you may not!" He exclaimed. "There are very few people in this world who can call me Uncle Leroy and you are one of the lucky ones. So don't stop now."   He kept rubbing knuckle noogies into Jack's scalp, until Jack hollered, "Uncle, uncle! Ok, ok, I give up, I'll call you Uncle." The two of them had everyone else in stitches laughing as they goofed around.

At dinner time, each of the LeBoufe kids had an assigned duty to help prepare our meal. Ten chairs were put around the table, places set, dishes brought from the kitchen and in less than five minutes we were all sitting down to a great looking feast. We held hands and Mr. LeBoufe offered a short prayer, "Dear Lord, Thank you for this family which you have given to each of us. Thank you for our guests, Rob and Jack. Thank you for this excellent food. Amen." This was an organized family!

Dinner consisted of three kinds of pasta: spaghetti, penne, and shells, with steaming marinara sauce, and a choice of meat balls, Italian sausage, or mushrooms. Fresh peas, broccoli, and cauliflower were passed. These were followed by Parmesan cheese, dinner rolls and garlic Italian bread.

"Wow!" I exclaimed. "This is fabulous! I've never seen such great food organized with so little effort. You are amazing, Aunt Maddy!"

She simply smiled at me, but Leroy injected, "This is nothing. My wife is a miracle worker in the kitchen. Did you know we met at a logging camp in northern Maine? That's right. When Maddy was seventeen she went to work as a cook for a lumber camp above the Forks of the Dead River in Aroostook County. She had to feed fifty of the hungriest loggers you ever saw, and do it twice a day."

"And now we have our own little lumber crew," beamed Maddy, looking around the table at her family and guests. "Actually, after the lumber camp, taking care of this gang is relatively easy." Everyone enjoyed the joke and the three kinds of pie passed around after dinner. Apple crumb pie, blueberry pie and lemon meringue provided an appropriate finish to a great meal.

After dinner everyone gathered in the living room. The kids played board games. Aunt Maddy worked on a sewing project. Jack and Frenchie got sucked into a competitive game of Monopoly with the twins. Leroy and I sat in a couple of easy chairs and watched the different games being played.

Leroy asked, "Rob, what are you studying at Carlisle? Do you have a major in mind?"

"Ahh, that's a good question, and I don't have an answer," I responded. "Growing up, Dad never talked much about his work. He has a degree in electrical engineering and went back at night and got a Masters in industrial engineering. He works in manufacturing at the pretzel business my grandfather started in Doylestown. As a kid I knew so little about what my Dad did at work..." I hesitated and went on, "It's embarrassing to admit, but when I was in third grade my class had a 'show and tell' where we shared about our fathers' work. I said Dad worked in a salt mine. How was I to know? When he left the house for work in the morning, he would always say, 'Well, I'm off to the salt mine.' I just assumed that's what he did. After class, my teacher called Mom to ask her about my comment. I guess she thought it pretty unlikely. They both had a good laugh at my expense."

I continued, "We never talked much in our home. Dad and Teddy are both mechanically gifted - they would do projects in Dad's workshop and the garage. In high school, Teddy bought old cars and rebuilt them. When they were running well, he flipped them – sold them at a nice profit. I had trouble changing a bicycle tire, so I never fit in with the shop projects. I really don't know what I'm good at."

"Don't feel bad," Leroy replied. "It's not unusual for fellows your age to feel that way. I was lucky, I guess. I was always in love with wood. As a kid I wanted to build things out of wood. Wood, in all its forms, fascinated me. I started working in the woods as a lumberjack, then in a mill and finally studied forestry at night in college. Working in a lumber yard was a natural progression. And it's not nearly as dangerous as cutting or milling wood."

"Do you have any suggestions about how I might figure out what I want to do?"

Leroy responded, "You've already taken a good first step by going to college. The beauty of a liberal arts college like Carlisle, is you can try different things until you find subjects you're interested in. Read course listings and see which topics sound interesting. Try some until you find a subject that rings your inner bells. Then learn more about the area and how people work in that field."

He paused for a moment, and then added, "The process is simple, but not always easy. You want to find something you are passionate about, like I was about wood. Then you want to figure out what your unique strengths are. What are you especially good at doing? Truthfully, I was an ok lumberjack, and an ok mill operator. Not great, just ok. But I'm really good at running a business, at buying and selling product and finding the best applications for wood and building supplies. I'm good with customers and know how to help them. That's why I ended up at the retail end of the forestry supply chain as opposed to some other part of the process."

Leroy continued, "Identify your passions, find your unique strengths, and then find an economic opportunity that works for you. If you want to be a teacher or a nurse, there are lots of different kinds of jobs that let you do that. For me, owning a lumber yard was more stable and it pays better than working in the woods or buying lumber. It was much safer than other woods work, and I wanted a stable family life as well as to work with forest products."

After a moment, I replied, "Thanks so much. That's helpful. It gives me a way to think about things. I can tell you right now, the things I like the most and am the most passionate about include pole vaulting, any kind of woodcraft, hunting, fishing, and trapping."

Leroy laughed, "I have no idea what to tell you about pole vaulting, but if you're interested, I'm going to run the beagles for rabbits in the morning. You would be welcome to join us."

"That sounds great. I'd love to go. Thanks." With that we broke up the festivities and headed for bed.

Thanksgiving morning, we had a huge breakfast. Bacon and eggs, oatmeal, mincemeat, pumpkin, and apple pie, cantaloupe, milk, orange juice and coffee. Then Jack, Frenchie and I went out with Mr. LeBoufe and the beagles, Dixie and Duke, to hunt rabbits. We rode in Leroy's Ford F150 truck to a high wooded plateau above the large farms on the valley floor.

The beagles skittered and barked with excitement, and jumped a rabbit almost immediately. We spread out in hopes of being in shooting range when the cottontail came running back around. It was easy for the rabbits to outrun the beagles. The bunny's weakness is it doesn't feel threatened. It lopes in a big circle and ends up back where it was first flushed. If the shooter is lucky he will spot the rabbit before being spotted, and get off a shot. During the morning, we ran seven rabbits and managed to bag four of them. We also shot a nice cock pheasant Duke bumped out of a fence row. Frenchie collected a splendid ruffed grouse which popped out of a tangle of hawthorns.

At four pm we sat down to Thanksgiving dinner. It was an astonishing spread. The number and variety of dishes seemed endless. In addition to the eight members of the LeBoufe family, Jack and I, there were four other guests. A retired widow, a young couple new to town, and an older guy who had been homeless but now worked in the lumber yard. The LeBoufes seem very intentional about reaching out to include other people in the fabric of the warm family life they enjoy.

As we ate, Leroy engaged everyone in the conversation. He was adept at getting people to share. Each person, including the kids, had a chance to share about something they were grateful for from the past year. The time at dinner flew by and before I knew it, the party was breaking up. I was sorry to see the friendly and stimulating conversations come to an end.

The next day, Friday, Leroy went to work at the lumberyard. The three of us decided to go fly fishing on Big Spring Creek, which flows by the foot of the LeBoufe's yard. Jack and I sat on the picnic table at the bottom of Frenchie's lawn waiting for him to get organized. "Can I ask you a question, Jack?"

"Sure. Fire away," he replied.

"Is your family like Frenchie's?" I asked.

"Nope." was his short answer. "My family is intensely loyal to one another. But we are just as committed to work. It's my guess Granddad and his boys worship financial success a lot more than the faith taught in the Catholic Church. Truthfully, they are pretty passive and disengaged as Catholics. Material success is their religion. And I would be in much higher standing in their eyes if I was willing to lead the next generation in making the family business successful. Aunt Pauline, my sister Meghan, and I are all in the dog house because we don't see our future tied to the family business. You could say much of the love in our clan is conditional, like 'what have you done for our business lately?'"

Frenchie joined us at the table and I told him, "I'm just amazed at your family, Frenchie."

"Really? Why is that?"

"They are so open and supportive." I replied. "They work together, help each other, and have fun. Everybody is different, yet each feels loved and accepted. You all talk about so many personal things, but without the usual bickering and putdowns. Even strangers feel at home in your family."

"I don't know what to say. It's the only family I've belonged to and they've always been this way."

"My family is not like yours," I added. "What do you suppose makes your family the way it is?"

Frenchie thought for a minute or two. "We trust each other. We're willing to share how we feel. I think its unconditional love. Even when we're disappointed in ourselves or in each other, we are prepared to forgive. We have the same tensions as any family, but our bedrock foundation is a desire to communicate, a commitment to support, and unconditional love for each member."

After a bit, while Jack and I contemplated what Frenchie had said, he added, "Sometimes my Dad quotes a bible verse that says, 'There is no fear in love, and perfect love casts out fear,' or something like that. That kinda' captures the power of unconditional love."

"Thanks Frenchie. That will give me something to think about," I said.

Jack kicked in, "Yeah, me too. And thanks for sharing your family with us. They're really special."

We had a great day fishing, landing a number of big rainbow, brown, and brook trout from the swirling limestone waters. We released them all. We met back at the end of the day, and I said to Jack, "Do you think you could get a family experience like Frenchie's without the biological connection?"

"Do you mean could you get a similar family experience without being born into it?"

"Exactly my question." I responded.

"That's a great question," Jack answered, "and worth contemplating."

14

"A man who dies rich dies disgraced,"
~ Andrew Carnegie

Faith McFadden   Thanksgiving Break, 1966

Wednesday morning, Skeeter and I set off to his parent's house for Thanksgiving. It was a three-hour drive from the college to Lower Gwynedd, the Philadelphia suburb where the Stetsons live. He picked me up from Allison at eight am in the El Camino and we drove over to Grandpa's Grinder for breakfast.

While we waited for our food, I asked Skeeter, "What do you want to be when you grow up?"

"Hmmm…" was his reply. "You know I'm majoring in engineering? But that's not exactly what you asked. 'What do I want to be?' I like engineering. I'm pretty good at it. When I arrived at Carlisle I assumed I would study engineering and get a job in my family's business. But that's what I would do, not who I would be."

The waitress showed up with our platters and we both tucked in. "That was fast service." I said through a bite of butter and syrup engorged waffle.

"Yes." said Skeeter. "Good service and great food. Back to your question. I honestly don't know the answer right off, but maybe you will let me talk around it to see if I can get some ideas?"

"Sure. Have at it."

"You'll get to meet my Dad this weekend. He's a great guy, a loyal and faithful son, dutifully working in the family business. But I don't know if I want to be like him. I know I should be glad my family has a business which can offer me an engineering job. Most kids are not that lucky. But I'm curious and I like to learn new things. I am not sure I want to give my life to making hats."

Stetson paused and thought for a minute. "In all my engineering courses, two things really stand out as high points. The bra and the bridge."

That made me laugh. "The bra and the bridge?"

"Yes," he continued. "We had a lab project where you had to design and construct a strapless bra, the kind a woman would wear with an evening gown. I found this fascinating – and not because of what you are thinking. Ha ha! Now look who has the dirty mind!" He laughed. "Actually, this lab got me interested in civil engineering, especially structural engineering. I find I am passionate about bridges. Their beauty, functionality; their endurance, flexibility and grace. How they connect to nature and to mankind. Look at the Brooklyn Bridge. It is over 100 years old, but it's still an engineering marvel. People come from all over the world to study it. Or the Golden Gate Bridge. The world's longest suspension bridge and the most photographed man-made landmark in the world. It's famous for both beauty and science.

"I'm passionate about bridges. They're a solution to a large scale, complex problem. Here's my dilemma. My heart tells me to pursue a career in bridges. My mind tells me - take the secure path and go to work for Stetson. Only they don't build bridges. Even if I start out in engineering, I would eventually have to serve in management like my Dad. As Dad says, 'It's our family's name over the door.'"

I waited a bit and said, "That is a dilemma. You can be the loyal son, the prince who carries on the family's duties for the next generation. If you choose that, you'll have a clear picture of your path in life. You could have security, financial success, and professional success. Or you can pick Curtain Number Three, with no idea what lies ahead in the future. Two radically different choices."

After breakfast, Skeeter drove the El Camino east on the PA Turnpike while I dozed. He seems happy listening to the throb of the engine and I was glad to nap. When I am awake, the Pennsylvania countryside rolling by is breathtaking. As far as my eye can see are neat dairy farms creating a patchwork of green, yellow and brown fields. Contented herds of Holstein, Jersey, Guernsey and Brown Swiss dairy cattle graze in the pastures. Here and there are Black Angus beef cattle in happy little clusters. Cute white farm houses and big red barns complete this picture of rural contentment.

Outside Harrisburg, as we crossed the Susquehanna River, I could see miles of buildings and parking lots covered with thousands of Army vehicles. Willies jeeps, tank trucks, Sherman tanks, armored troop carriers, and other Army vehicles. Skeeter told me this massive display of military firepower is the New Cumberland Army Depot. I asked, "Have you ever thought about going into the military?"

"I registered for the draft when I turned eighteen. To be honest, I'm not crazy about the idea. The service has lots of cool equipment which might be fun, but…I don't want to get in the middle of a shooting war just to play with cool toys. Even without the little problem of Vietnam, I don't think the regimentation of military life would suit me. I ask too many questions. I'd make a lousy soldier."

"I can see you've given it some thought," I replied. "As a woman, I don't have to worry about being drafted. I admit - I'm awfully glad about that."

"How do you feel about the war in general?" Skeeter asked.

"If this was WWII where we were defending our country from an aggressor, or fighting for our freedom, I would be the first to enlist. Here, I'm not sure why we are fighting a civil war in a little banana republic half way around the world. I don't buy the idea that if South Vietnam goes Communist, the rest of the world will fall to Communism like a stack of dominos. When American colonists were fighting for freedom against the British, how would we have felt if Spain had joined the fight on behalf of the Brits?"

"Excellent point and well made," said Skeeter. "Now I'm beginning to see why you enjoy Political Science so much. You are much more than a pair of pretty dimples with a dazzling smile in between."

I had to laugh. Skeeter could say the funniest things. "I wonder if I was a guy, and I was drafted, if I would go or if I would become a draft dodger and run away to Canada to avoid serving?"

"You know my family is Quaker, right?" asked Skeeter. "Quakers are dead set against the war. They usually take a non-violent peace stand, but they don't think Vietnam is a just war. My Dad was drafted and served in WWII and he had no problem with that. But most Quakers hate this particular war with a passion. Many of the young men in our Meeting are draft protesters. Some like Jamie Paxton have burned their draft cards in anti-war demonstrations and are threatening to go to Canada as draft dodgers."

"Would you consider being a conscientious objector?" I asked Skeeter.

"I had that option when I signed up for the draft. But I'm not sure I believe there is a God. Given that, I have no idea whether or not God is in favor of war or against it. Nor what he might consider a just war or and unjust war. I have so many questions about God and my faith; I just didn't feel qualified to take a stand as a conscientious objector."

We lapsed into silence. As we drove, Skeeter popped the latest Buffalo Springfield album into his eight track tape player. It is nice to be with Skeeter. He is tall, handsome, 21 years old, funny, and he can afford all sorts of good things I have never been able to have.

Driving through mile after mile of Amish farms near Lancaster, I was struck by the contrast between their simple life and the lifestyle Skeeter enjoyed. Farmers dressed in plain black and white clothing walking behind teams of big tan draft horses hauling a single bit plow across the fields. Women outdoors hanging wash on a clothesline. Kids doing farm chores or pushing little scooters up and down the lane. Older children split firewood to heat the house or washed the family buggy parked in the yard.

Meanwhile, we cruise on down the highway in the El Camino, listening to the latest tunes playing on the eight-track. Frankly, I have no interest in living a simple life, living on the land, so I can get close to God. I'd rather live the good life. Nice house, nice neighborhood, nice vacations. Drive a new car and send my kids to a good school, eat out in nice restaurants, buy new clothes, and do what I want to do. The good life is the life I aspire to live.

We turned off the highway towards Skeeter's house in the suburbs of Philly. It is pretty country. We drove down the Stetson's road where I could see fields, old homes built out of brown fieldstone, and a scattering of newer homes. We drove by attractive houses, divided by bands of woods, open fields, and a few large woodlots. Each is set back at least 100 feet from the road, and all are comfortably nestled into the wooded landscape. "I can't wait to see your place," I exclaimed.

"Well, here we are," said Skeeter as we turned into a long paved lane, passing through wide green lawns and slowing to a stop between a big white house and a set of garage doors lining the end of a fieldstone barn.

Hard to imagine Skeeter's home as a farmhouse. It must have been a large farmhouse before the second wing was added doubling the living space. Two and a half stories tall, with wrap around porches, luxurious gardens and landscaping, the spacious white clapboard building looked like a mansion compared to my house on Fish Fever Lane. 'Wow,' I thought. 'This is so different from my home. I could never take Skeeter to visit. Not my house, not my neighborhood, especially not my family.'

"Come on, Faith." Skeeter exclaimed. "Let's go meet the family!" He led the way up the neat path through the now dormant flower gardens. The only signs of life were the two pink bikes dumped by the walk and a scattering of balls and toys around two storage boxes on the porch. Large clay pots with Christmas holly bushes bracketed the main door. Skeeter pushed open the door and we walked into a large slate floored foyer where he hung our coats.

Skeeter hollered, "Hey, is anybody home?" He laughed. "It's a big house. Sometimes it's hard to hear if anyone is at the door." He opened the door we just passed through and reached around to ring the doorbell. That provoked a response. Loud barking and the squeals of girls' voices came down the hall. A half grown St Bernard puppy, came running at Skeeter, jumped up, putting her paws on his chest and giving him big slobbery kisses. Skeeter laughed, "This is Daisy, the family dog." Daisy woofed with returned love and excitement and continued to lick Skeeter.

"Friendly dog," I laughed.

Down the hall came a matched brace of blond girls. "Skeetie! You're here!!!!" They screamed in unabashed excitement. "Skeetie, Skeetie, Skeetie," they shouted as they hugged him and Daisy.

"These are my sisters, Kit, or Kitty, officially named Katherine. She is eight. And Sunny, who is six."

"Hi Kitty, hi Sunny," I stuck out my hand to shake. The girls simply ignored my hand and reached out with raised arms to give me a hug. "You both have such pretty names!' I exclaimed.

"And you are so pretty," exclaimed Sunny. "Skeetie told us you were beautiful, but we had no idea he was telling the truth for a change!" We all had a good laugh.

"Girls, this is Faith McFadden, my friend from college. Where's Mom?"

Kitty jumped in. "She is putting four pumpkin pies in the oven and will be out in a minute. We don't have school today so we were playing Parcheesi in the family room. With Daisy."

The Stetson girls had straight blonde locks cut in a page boy haircut. They were dressed in identical blue jeans and each wore navy blue Carlisle College sweatshirts. Except for the apparent difference in height and age, they were hard to tell apart. Blue eyes, long limbs, they were just reaching that stage where the charms of childhood are apparent without any of the awkwardness of the adolescent years.

"Well, who is this we have here, girls? She looks like she could be your older sibling, and not that galloot over there." Skeeter's Mom had walked up behind us while we chattered. "You must be Faith. Welcome to our crazy family," she laughed. "Well, you already know Skeeter, so you should be forewarned. We are a wild bunch."

"Mom!" Skeeter exclaimed and turned to embrace her with an enthusiastic hug. The girls and dog danced in circles around us, while greetings and introductions were made. "Faith, this is my Mom, Sukie. Actually, she was named Susanna," Skeeter continued, "but she is from the South and somehow, by the time they got done with her, she was called Sukie."

Sukie Stetson was a willowy blonde dressed in brown corduroy slacks, a white turtleneck, and a red and green cotton sweater. She was wearing a bright red apron with her honey blonde hair twisted up on top of her head skewered in place with a pair of chopsticks. Mrs. Stetson has deep blue eyes set off by a dusting of freckles across her clear skin, a happy smile, and a cheerful disposition. Skeeter's little sisters look like miniatures of their mother.

"Faith, why don't you come into the kitchen and help me with lunch? Skeet can play Parcheesi with his sisters. Like most little sisters, they adore his attention."

I followed Sukie into the kitchen, a large, bright room, with a big wall of dazzling sun filled windows. A round kitchen table covered with a red and white checked table cloth, surrounded by high wooden Windsor chairs was in front of the windows. In the center of the space was a work island with a butcher block counter top, storage cabinets underneath and an array of copper pots hanging overhead. On the opposite wall stood the stove, a double chef sized sink and a nook filled with a desk and cookbooks. Big brass planters holding oversized Boston ferns were scattered about the edges of the room.

"Here, sit in one of these chairs," Sukie said pointing to a pair of comfortable easy chairs. "I don't really need help; I just thought it would be nice to have you to talk to while I finished lunch. We're having New England clam chowder, tuna fish sandwiches and blueberry cobbler. The cobbler goes in when we sit down. I've got the pumpkin pies for tomorrow in right now, and the sandwiches are already in the fridge, so not much to do. Would you like tea or coffee or a cold drink?"

This room is so cozy. Sukie is easy to talk to. She asks lots of questions and got me to talk about myself. We laughed and compared notes as Southern gals relocated to the Northeast. She asked me about college, what I wanted to study, and my plans for the future.

Forty minutes later the timer went off and Sukie pulled the pies out of the oven. "My husband is taking a half day off from work, so we are holding lunch till he gets here. I should tell you, Chip is an introvert in an extrovert's job. I don't know why he's an introvert," she laughed. "All the rest of us are extroverts. Skeeter, Kitty, Sunny, me. Even Daisy is an extrovert! Anyway, I tell you that so you don't think he is being unfriendly. He will be fine today. After lunch we are having a few friends and neighbors over to shoot clay pigeons. He will be fine tomorrow for Thanksgiving. But by Friday he'll need some peace and quiet to get his introverted batteries recharged. He and Casey, that's his Gordon setter, will go off hunting pheasants all day in splendid isolation. Now that I think about it, Casey must be an introvert too. He is a one-man dog. He has eyes only for my husband and pheasants. Period. No other interests in life."

"Will I get to meet Casey?" I asked.

"He lives in a kennel out in back of the barn. He's not unfriendly or anything, just a little distracted waiting for a pheasant to come along. That's one reason we got Daisy for the kids. Casey is not really a family pet. It's funny, trying to get close to Casey is like trying to get close to an engineer who is thinking about his next project. Ha ha! Always just a little distracted.," Sukie laughed.

Just then, the back door of the kitchen swung open. "Speaking of distracted engineers," Sukie chuckled, "here is my husband back from the hat wars in Philadelphia, the City of Brotherly Love."

I have to admit, I am really beginning to like Sukie. She has a great sense of humor and real perspective about people and what makes them tick.

Skeeter's dad walked into the kitchen. Mr. Stetson is handsome. He is tall, about 6' 3", lean, with salt and pepper gray hair. Stetson senior was wearing a gray herringbone sports coat over a deep blue cashmere sweater on top of a crisp white oxford cloth button down shirt. Gray wool slacks with a knife edge crease and black loafers with little tassels completed the look.

Mr. Stetson stuck out his hand, "Sam Stetson, Faith. My friends call me Chip. You may call me Chip, as I hope we will be friends before you leave this weekend." When Chip Stetson smiled, his face lit up. I can see why they would make him VP of Marketing. I can also see where Skeeter gets his charm. Chip Stetson is charming. He won me over in a heartbeat.

After lunch we bundled up in warm clothes and walked down the road for the Stetson's annual clay pigeon shoot. This loose collection of Stetson friends and neighbors gather every fall, to sharpen their wing shooting skills on clay pigeons. These round targets are thrown from mechanical contraptions and are supposed to imitate a flying pheasant, grouse, duck, or a running rabbit. Some people in the group are bonafide bird hunters like Chip Stetson. Others just like shooting targets. Many of the wives and families simply come for the socializing and have no real interest in shooting sports.

Shooting stations were set up and the kids organized to go out after each round of shooting to retrieve unbroken clays. The spectators gathered well behind the shooting stations where they sat in lawn chairs to gossip, and occasionally to cheer a good shot. Sukie sat chatting with her friends and neighbors while Chip and Skeeter both played a major role in killing a lot of clay pigeons.

I sat by Sukie watching the panorama unfold. "I've never done anything like this." I said to Sukie. "On St. Simons Island, the only community events we have like this might be the occasional shrimp boil."

Sukie laughed. "This is more of a social event than a hunting experience. Chip is an avid hunter, which makes some of our Quaker friends a little skittish. They think he should not derive so much pleasure from spilling blood, even if it belongs to a game bird and not a human."

"I didn't know Skeeter hunts," I added. "Several of our college friends are crazy about hunting, but I've never seen Skeeter go out with them."

Sukie sighed. "Good observation. Skeeter only goes hunting with his Dad. It's something they can do together. When I first arrived, Chip and Skeeter were so wounded by my sister's death, they had trouble relating to other people. Hunting gave Chip and Skeeter a way to share an experience without having to talk much. For years, they just went out and processed their feelings in silence behind a bird dog. I'm not sure Skeet likes to hunt, but he's a people pleaser. He's willing to hunt when his Dad wants to."

Sukie paused for a moment. "Candidly, I often wonder what Skeet is thinking. When he thinks something contrary to our feelings, he simply won't mention it. He avoids conflict like the plague. It makes it hard for us to be encouraging. We would support whatever he wants to do, but he won't bring it up if he thinks it clashes with what we want. It makes for very one sided conversations."

I was totally dumbfounded by this revelation. Sukie is so sensitive towards her men – both her husband and stepson. She genuinely wants to know what they are thinking and feeling so she can be supportive. This drove me to the edge of tears. I'm sure it has never crossed my parents' minds to wonder what my sisters and I feel. We've never been asked any questions trying to probe our feelings. We are just dictated to. We are told what to feel or think. Then we are criticized and judged for falling short.

All my life I've tried so hard to please my parents. I worked my heart out to do everything right. I got good grades, went to youth group, and said my prayers every night. I didn't do drugs, sleep around, or misbehave. Yet my parents always treat me like a criminal, trying my hardest to displease them. I just want to be loved. I just want my Dad to approve of me. By the end of my first day visiting with the Stetsons, I was ready to move in and join the family. That or run off into the woods so I could bawl my eyes out at never having a family like this.

After the shoot, Chip Stetson focused on cleaning up the equipment. Sukie took the girls in to prepare dinner. Skeeter said, "There's a bit of daylight left. Would you like to take a walk?"

"Sure, that would be nice." We walked down the road enjoying the crisp chill of fall. Skeeter held my hand. For the most part we were quiet. I was still struggling with my feelings about his family and my family. Skeeter led me off the road onto a faint path which winds down through a grove of oak trees. Eventually, the path came out above an old stone bridge which spanned the flow of a modest creek.

"When I was young, this was one of my favorite places." Skeeter shared. "I was four when I came down here and taught myself to fish for sunnies. When Mom died, I used to come down here for hours on end. I would sit on the bridge. Walk around. Hunt for frogs and tadpoles. Fish for sunnies, shiners, and turtles. Watch the bats whirling through the air when the sun went down. We ice skated here in the winter. I learned to trap muskrats, raccoons and mink on this creek. For me it was a safe place. I could just be myself, think my thoughts, and have space to figure things out."

We sat on the bridge dangling our legs over the water a few feet below. "I have to confess, I've never had a safe spot like you." I shared. "I just love your family! I'd be willing to marry you just so I could be part of your family."

"Wow, that's a high compliment," Skeeter laughed.

"I would come to work as Sukie's housekeeper, so I could be part of your family."

"Perhaps I could have Mom and Dad adopt you?" he volunteered.

"Yes, but only if I could be the child who never grew up, who stayed home and took care of the parents until they got old and died."

"What you are saying, is you are willing to be Cinderella to my family?" Skeeter asked. "You would trade your own life and choices in order to have some security in life?"

"Yes. Absolutely." I thought for a minute. "I honestly don't know what I think. At times I want to be daring, courageous, and try new things. I want to walk away from the miserable family and childhood I grew up with and strike out on my own. But at the same time, I'd love to go back and be adopted as Kitty and Sunny's little sister and have my childhood all over again in a family like yours. Who needs a successful adulthood; if only you can have a childhood where you are loved?"

15

"Everyone must believe in something.
I believe I'll go canoeing."
~ Henry David Thoreau

Nikki Clausen   Thanksgiving Break, 1966

Wednesday morning Gary and I met Linda Pence in the parking lot of Willis Hall. Gary is coming to my house for Thanksgiving and Linda offered to give us a ride. Linda is from Hollidaysburg, a small town near Altoona in west central Pennsylvania. Dropping us in Pleasant Gap only takes her thirty minutes out of her way. We are grateful for the ride and for the chance to get to know her better.

We piled into Linda's 1958 Rambler station wagon. It's not an elegant car. Ramblers are ugly at birth and age does nothing to improve their looks. This beater was once off white. Now it has dents in the body, and the bottom corners of all four door panels are rotting with rust. "I know the Rambler doesn't look like much, but she's dependable," said Linda. "I named her Lucky Lucy, and I'm glad to have her. Put your gear in the back, and we'll go."

I let Gary ride shotgun with Linda. He has long legs and probably needs the space. I sat in back on the second seat and stretched out. Pretty comfortable. As we drove up the Susquehanna River, the mountains unfolded on either side of the river. Views across the river detail of the landscape and showcase the immense size of the Allegheny forest. "Do you guys wonder where Snowden is?" I asked. "I do."

"Yeah, I think about her a lot," said Linda. "Did somebody pick her up in a bar in Harrisburg and kidnap her? Did she get drunk or have a drugged drink and wander off and lose her memory? Get amnesia? You hear about kids who run away to NYC or Haight-Ashbury, crash with strangers, get hooked on drugs, and become prostitutes."

"I worry she was picked up by some pervert who just wanted sex with a naïve girl," said Gary. "Took her off to some farmhouse in the country and chained her up in the basement as his sex slave."

"Maybe he will knock her over the head when he gets tired of feeding her," said Linda, "and bury her out in a field or in the woods."

"Ahh, man that's just awful to contemplate," I said. "But I find myself wondering if her disappearance was actually her own idea?"

"Why do you say that?" asked Gary.

"She told me her parents are uptight and judgmental. Do you know her old man is an IRS lawyer? It sounds like they disapprove of everything Snow does. She felt like she always fell short of their expectations. Snow talked a lot about wanting to feel loved and accepted for who she is. I can't help but wonder if it would occur to her to run off and start a new life?"

"Really?" asked Linda. "What would make her do that?"

"Didn't you ever wonder if you might enjoy life more if you could switch places with somebody else?" Gary asked. "What if you lived on an Indian reservation in Arizona instead of in Altoona, PA? Or if you were working in the movies in Hollywood? Would your life be better than it is now?"

"Gee, I honestly never thought of that," replied Linda. "I guess I'm happy to be in my family and to be from Hollidaysburg. It's a sweet little town full of good people."

"I don't know what I think." I concluded. "I wonder if she could have ridden off with some long-distance truck driver. She'll marry him and raise his kids in the sleeping compartment of the truck or in some cozy village in the country – like Hollidaysburg! And we'll never hear from her again."

"Wow! Too weird to contemplate," said Linda.

Lucky Lucy left the riverbank, drove through Lewistown and cruised up into the mountains. The two-lane road twisted and turned as we headed into steep terrain. Around each bend in the highway, the oncoming traffic coming down off the mountain hurtled towards us at a tremendous speed.

I zoned out, gazing vacantly out the front window at the highway, the traffic, and the scenery flying by. Suddenly, I realized the logging truck coming around the next curve was weaving back and forth over the centerline as if losing control. It was a big tandem log carrier loaded with saw logs on two trailers behind the cab. It seemed to be going too fast. The rig wobbled, shook, and looked unstable.

Gary bolted upright and shouted, "Look Out!"

The truck veered over the center line three feet into our lane. I was sure he was going smash into us. But the driver jerked on the wheel and pulled the cab back. His maneuver may have prevented a head on collision but it tipped the leading trailer over at a steep angle… It looked like the trailers were going to roll over in our lane and dump their load of saw logs on top of us. I would have slammed on the brakes in reaction, but Linda did just the opposite. She wrenched the wheel of the Rambler to the right while stomping her foot on the gas. The car leaped forward with a jolt and shot out from under the falling logs. I turned and looked back. The big logs came down like a waterfall inches behind the rear window of the Rambler. It was like watching a horror movie unfold in slow motion. The car behind us, a gold colored Chevy Impala Super Sport, simply disappeared in the fall of logs covering the roadway.

Linda wrestled the wheel and pumped her brakes until the Rambler skidded to a halt on the gravel shoulder of the highway. "Holy Shit!" she said. "That was close."

We sat for a minute shaken with fright as the experience washed over us. We were silent for a moment, and then Linda started to sob.

"You did great," I said rubbing her back. "I would have slammed on the brakes and we would be under that pile of logs right now. I've never seen such quick reactions. You should be a fighter pilot."

Gary said, "You were amazing! You're going into shock. Nikki, see if you can find a blanket to wrap around Linda. I'm going back to see if I can help." He hopped out and ran back down the road. I found a blanket in the back and wrapped Linda in it. I sat next to her and held her in my arms as she sat shaking. She sobbed quietly. Man that was scary! It would not surprise me if we had shit our pants.

Police and firemen came, then several ambulances. We sat waiting to give our statements to the cops. When Gary came back to the Rambler he looked white as a sheet and very sober. "The car behind us had two women in it. They're on the staff of the Penn Christian Camp up the road and came into Lewistown for an oil change. The woman driving was killed instantly. She was 38 and left a husband and two kids. The other woman was still sitting in the car when I got there. Two logs hit the driver's side of the Impala and sheered it off. It looked like a huge buzz saw cut the car in half right down the middle, from the hood ornament to the trunk. Half the car was sitting undamaged, the passenger unharmed but for a few cuts from splintered glass. The other half of the car is a big cube of smashed metal, with the driver in the middle, laying 200 yards down the road." He shook his head in pain.

"Man! One minute they're out for a joy ride. The next minute one is gone forever - leaving her entire family. The other is still here, but probably scarred forever by what happened in the wink of an eye."

"Lucky for us we were riding with Linda in Lucky Lucy or it could have been us in that cube of scrap metal sitting back there." I added. "Thanks for taking care of us, Linda."

The accident left us sober and depressed. We drove the rest of the way to State College in silence, each wrestling with our own thoughts and feelings. It's not every day something that traumatic jumps up out of the blue and bites you in the ass.

The next morning, Gary and I slept in. Mom was off from school. A little after nine she cooked us a big breakfast of waffles, butter, Vermont maple syrup, crisp bacon, and poached eggs, washed down with orange juice, fresh local milk and strong coffee. "You're lucky my Dad had a meeting at the college," I said. "He'd have made us eat Shredded Wheat for breakfast. You know the big bulky kind - looks like a couple of tan bricks in your bowl? He eats it every day and thinks it's the best breakfast ever."

My mom laughed. "That is not true, dear. Your father is quite liberal about what people eat for breakfast. He never complains about your having diet soda for breakfast every day."

"Point well made. But you have to admit, his diet can be amazingly dull and repetitive."

"That's because he cares more about history and teaching than he cares about food. He has us to keep his diet from being boring and tedious." After stuffing ourselves, Mom suggested, "Why don't you take your coffee and TAB and go sit on the porch? It's sunny out. I expect it will warm up soon, and I need you out of the kitchen so I can work on the Thanksgiving dinner."

"Anything we can do to help?" asked Gary. "Peel potatoes, mash stuffing, pluck the oysters?"

What a charming suck up that boy can be.

"No thanks, dear. You two just run along and have fun. We'll eat at four PM. If you come back at three thirty, you can set the table. If you get hungry before then, just come in and fix yourself a snack." With that, Mom shooed us out of the kitchen.

Gary and I went out onto the sun porch on the east side of our house. It is off the living room, which is dominated by a grand piano. Mom and her music hold sway at home. Except for his office in the basement, Dad has to exercise his talents at the college. The enclosed porch is one of my favorite places at home. When the sun is out it feels tropical, even in winter. In warm weather the screens are down and the breeze blows through. Gary and I settled onto the white wicker two-seater, and wiggled down into fluffy flowered cushions. I pulled a hassock over for our feet and we got comfortable.

"My brain," began Gary, "is stuck on overdrive. It keeps playing that film over and over. Those poor women. One minute they are out for a drive on a nice fall afternoon. The next minute, one is gone – forever. The other is left, but is forever damaged. Makes me think of Snow. One day she is with us and is working through college towards her future. Then gone. Poof! We've no idea where. Kidnapped? Raped? Killed? Or starting a new life with her long haul truck driver? I don't know how to think about it."

Gary paused to think, "It makes me wonder if you can ever figure out what life is about? Or is it all completely random? Are we all like a bucket of ping pong balls dumped out and going every which way with no rhyme or reason? Some bounce up and others roll under the furniture and are never seen again. Some get stepped on – crushed out existence like that poor woman yesterday. But it could have been me or you instead. Is it all just chance? Meaningless? With no purpose?"

"I try to take a scientific point of view," I replied. "The world is a big place. Humans are small fish in the universe. When I study biology and botany and ecosystems, humans are not at the top of the food chain – we're only about mid way up the ladder. A redwood tree is bigger than us, a brown bear can eat us for lunch, and a great white shark can have us as a snack. The one thing which separates us from all other creatures is the capacity to ask questions. How do I fit in? What is my purpose in living? Where do I find the people I want to belong to? We are the only beings who ask 'why' questions. Asking questions is the beginning of wisdom. Granted, yesterday was pretty jarring, but don't feel bad our experience raises questions. That's healthy. We may not know all the answers, but asking questions, seeking knowledge, wanting to understand, is at the core of the human experience."

"OK, I guess I can see that – conceptually." said Gary. "It's just so sudden!"

"What made you suddenly decide segregation was wrong?" I asked. "What made you sit up and say, everybody around me believes these values and behaves this way – but they're wrong! Dead wrong!"

"I don't know. I guess it was this gut check that said it was wrong for human beings to treat other people that way. I don't need a philosophy class to teach me it's wrong to kick a little kid or a dog. When I see a bully at work, my spirit rises up in protest at the wrong. When little boys tie two cats together by the tail and then set them on fire, I don't need a religious rule book to tell me this should not happen."

"When we ask, 'Why do bad things happen to good people?' where do we look for an answer?"

"That's exactly the question I'm asking," Gary replied. "Why do dreadful things happen to innocent people? Why did those logs fall on the Impala instead of on us? Why did they only take one of the two people in that car? The woman who survived is not married, and didn't leave a family. The one who died left the bigger hole in the world, or so you might argue."

"Don't you think this is a bit above our pay grade, Gary?" I said. "Why does this one live? Why does this one die? Why does this farm get enough rain and the next one goes out of business from drought? It's a big question, but I don't come out where Nietzsche does – all of life is meaningless, just random actions and events without any significance. The truth is there is some purpose to life. There must be some higher level design than the individual human. Nature tells me that much. Or look at human nature. Almost everyone has a clearly defined sense of right and wrong. Our conscience tells us there is a core of moral values and an ethical obligation towards others."

Gary reflected for a bit, then ventured, "You're saying that even when we can't answer the questions of why, there is a bigger plan which joins us together. You deduce the existence of this higher pattern from observation of nature, of human behavior and belief?"

"Yep, you've got it. That's what I am saying. I don't know why, but I think there's a why and I for one, want to learn about it. I think I'll find out more by observing and learning from other people."

"Interesting," said Gary. "I'm not sure what I think... I wonder what Father X would say?"

Later that afternoon, we decided to hike up Mt. Nittany. It's easy to do from my house. Walk out the door and cross the lawn. Hug the left side of the neighborhood ball field, and ease into the woods at the corner. We hiked up the trail through a big stand of maples, then through old hemlocks, fir and spruce trees. As the trail climbed higher, big white pines mix in with clumps of hardwoods. We climbed higher and the trees around us became short, stunted little things. Eventually the trees disappeared, replaced by expanses of rocks covered with moss and lichen.

We came out on a jumble of rocks sticking straight out of the mountain – Mt. Nittany. We inched out to the end of a rock, and sat on the edge with our feet dangling over the cliff. We could see all of Happy Valley spread out below. Looking from left to right, we had a view of the six other mountains which surround and protect our valley. Mt Nittany is the seventh of the 'seven sisters.' Straight ahead to the north, the sky is clear blue and the Allegheny ridges roll out one after the other, past the Finger Lakes of New York all the way to Canada. In the middle distance stretches the valley floor with farms and woods acting as a setting for the jewel of State College and its suburbs. The view is incredible.

"Wow! I'm speechless," said Gary. "Amazing! It takes my breath away."

"This is one of my favorite places to come and think. Somehow, the view puts everything in perspective." I replied. "From the time I was twelve, I would hike up here to see the world through fresh eyes. If I was having trouble, somehow, this put it in focus. It's so different from life on the valley floor."

"Ahh, I can see why you feel that way. It does give you a different outlook."

I continued, "What we were talking about this morning…making sense out of life. I have a deep love of nature. I spend as much time as I can outdoors and I've taken as many natural science classes as I can. When I observe nature, here's what I think. I honestly believe there is some higher power that's played a role in designing nature, natural systems, even life. When I look at a trout stream, a bass pond, a river, a forest, a mountain – I see patterns. These systems are intricate; interwoven, interdependent, and highly complex. There's a plan and purpose. Nothing exists by itself as a one off, free standing, independent entity. Americans are finding if you pollute the rivers, eventually there's no water to drink. If you pollute the air - no air to breath. All natural systems are interconnected and interdependent.

"I look at life around me and see design in the way things work in the natural order. I see a plan, a pattern, and a purpose. Then I ask myself: 'Could this just be random? Organized by chance?'"

"It could be," said Gary, "but it doesn't seem very likely."

"I won't go into all the scientific detail about how finely balanced are the variables are which sustain human life in this world, but let me offer this example. If I went down to the local lumber yard and buried loads of dynamite and blew the whole place sky high, what are the odds all the debris would fall back out of the sky and form a perfectly finished four bedroom colonial house? Everything from toilet paper to windows screens in place and ready to live in?"

Gary laughed. "Not very likely!"

I continued, "When I look at the natural world, ecosystems, and the human body, I conclude there must be a God who at least designed and created our world. What role does God play in sustaining life - I don't know? Can we know him - I don't know? But I'm convinced a higher power put this whole show together. Nature has a purpose – why wouldn't human life?"

Gary asked, "So how do you figure out what that is?"

"The same way you learn about anything. Observe. Take notes. Ask questions. Think about the evidence. How did Einstein figure out matter and energy are the same thing in different forms? Observation, asking questions, staying open and learning. I admit there's a great deal I don't know and don't understand, but I want to learn more."

Gary replied, "I can see what you're saying. As a scientist, you've been observing the evidence of the natural world and when you connect the dots you see there must be some kind of God or designer." Gary went on, "My experience of life led me in a different direction. From the time I was aware of my surroundings, I've been lonely. My parents ignored me. I'm an only child. Growing up, the only people to play with at my house were paid staff – and they always had work to do. I went to school but never fit in. I wasn't comfortable with my peers and they weren't comfortable with me.

"I spent summers at my grandparent's estate on Long Island. I was still lonely. Granddad was in the city making money and Grandma was hanging out with stuffy old ladies playing bridge. They're nice, but not suitable playmates for a twelve year old. Eventually, I got to know some kids on their street. Then I got into hockey. That helped, but I was still a pretty lonely guy.

"I'm afraid I decided finding happiness in life was about having girl friends. Maybe I watched too much TV. I focused on relationships with girls. Kissed my first girl when I was thirteen, lost my virginity at fourteen. By high school, I had girlfriends in regular cycles. There was the romantic wondering what they were like, the pursuit, the conquest, and then disillusionment. At first, the cycle took three months from beginning to end. By my senior year it only took three weeks to rotate through a relationship.

"After I graduated, I was at the Jersey Shore and I picked up this hot college chick who was a waitress at the Chatterbox Café. She was two years older, very cool and beautiful. I was seducing her, had her stripped down to her bikini briefs, and was set to make the conquest. Then she asked me, 'Why?' I was stumped. I couldn't answer the question. I put her clothes back on and have not had sex since. I don't know why I had sex with all those girls. I don't know why I thought sex was the answer. I can see now I was not having a relationship, but merely having sex. I suppose it was my way to address my loneliness. But that wasn't the solution. So I'm still looking. I don't know what I'm looking for." Gary concluded.

"Thanks for being honest," I replied. "I'm a virgin. I intend to stay that way until I'm married. I feel sex is such a special part of who you are as a person. I want to save it for the guy I marry and spend a lifetime with. I look at my parents' relationship. They're so different from each other, but they love and accept one another unconditionally. I want a love life like theirs – in the context of marriage."

We had a little hug and a snuggle, sitting up there on the cliff. I'm definitely sweet on Gary. I'm glad he respects me and won't push my boundaries. I find our relationship is a safe place for me.

"Hey, Science Girl, it's almost two thirty!" exclaimed Gary. "If we are going to be home in time to help your Mom set the table, we'd better get pointed downhill."

With that we slid back off the cliff, picked up the trail in reverse to Sunset Avenue, and headed for Thanksgiving dinner.

16

"No bird soars in a calm."
~ *Wilber Wright*

Jack Flynn   Thanksgiving Break, 1966

The Saturday morning after Thanksgiving we woke to a picture perfect fall day. We looked out to bright sunshine and no clouds in a bluebird sky. Outdoor activities of all sorts popped into my head.

"If its ok with you buckos, I'd like to go into Harrisburg today," suggested Frenchie over breakfast.

"Need to get a jump on your Christmas shopping?" I commented. "I'm sure Rob and I would be delighted to follow you around and carry all the purchases you make."

Rob laughed. "Sure, we're happy to be your personal elves as you play Santa Claus."

"For your information, Jack Wisenheimer Flynn and Robbie Pretzel Boy Bachmann, I'm not going shopping." Frenchie rebuked us. "There's going to be an anti-war demonstration in downtown Harrisburg today. My Army buddies are going to support the protest and I'm hoping to visit with them. Plus, I'd be happy to add my voice to the chorus against the war."

"Really?" I replied. "I'm surprised a veteran would take that position on Vietnam."

"Just because we served our country doesn't mean we're idiots," Frenchie retorted. "America and its allies have been fighting in Viet Nam since 1954. twelve years – three times longer than WWII. We're propping up a corrupt, puppet government the Vietnamese don't want. We should pull out now. The longer we stay, the more American lives, the more American families, and the more American futures are gonna get messed up. Even Martin Luther King has come out against the war. We're spending $twenty-five billion a year killing gooks half a world away and yet we don't have the money to give American kids a decent education. King says millions of Americans are suffering because of this war and its cost."

"Is that just your view or do other vets share that perspective?" I asked my cousin.

"I'd say the majority of vets I know regret the role they played in Nam, and most believe the sooner we pull out, the better." Frenchie replied. "But come to the demonstration and see for yourself."

Rob and I agreed to accompany Frenchie on his adventure. We piled into his yellow VW Bug and tooled over to Harrisburg – about a fifty minute drive. We got off the highway just after it crossed the Susquehanna River and looked for a parking space on North Front Street. We found a spot on the street and ditched the car. Then we took the long walk into the commercial district on 2nd Street. The city was mobbed with people. We wandered through the crowds enjoying the scene. People with long hair, mingled with clean cut high school kids. A group of black hipsters with big afros and funky clothing passed by. Young women with hippie blouses, long hair, Mexican vests, and tie-dyed t-shirts, brushed by a big orange clump of Hare Krishna devotes. The Krishna's heads were shaved, they wore saffron orange robes from the neck to the ground. Leather sandals and long strings of worry beads completed the outfit. They moved along singing an eastern religious chant to themselves.

. Rob spoke up, "You know this is where Snowden went missing?"

"I didn't realize that," said Frenchie.

We looked at the sea of people jostling us as we walked through the streets. I said to my pals, "This is crazy. I can see where you could get lost, or hook up with the wrong crowd, or not be able to find your way back to the shuttle stop. Pretty scary, when you think about it. Scary for Snowden."

Every other corner had a band playing cover tunes, folk music or funky original tunes of some kind. We came across a band playing what sounded like gospel music infused with a cool, boogie-woogie beat. Like New Orleans, or Tommy Dorsey, perhaps Mahalia Jackson or maybe some strain of the blues. We listened for ten minutes and someone suggested, "Come back to our church and you can hear more music for free. We have free snacks and hot coca too. It's just down this block."

Rob said, "I'd like to hear more; do you guys want to come?"

"I'd go for that," I said. We followed the rest of the audience and the band down the block to a brick church on the next corner. We trooped inside and filed around tables loaded with cookies and drinks and then into an auditorium. We sat on rows of benches facing the front and watched as the band set up their equipment and began to play more tunes. Very cool music!

After the musicians played a couple more songs with that barbequed Memphis blues flavor, a tall black-haired fellow dressed in a suit and tie came up to speak. "I'm Pastor Bob Parman and I'm the Senior Pastor of this church, the Full Gospel Fellowship of Second Birth Pentecostalism." When he spoke, his accent was thick and slurry with the twang of the Deep South.

Pastor Bob cranked up and started making his pitch. He bounced on the balls of his feet. He wandered back and forth behind the pulpit. He talked about salvation and eschatology. He proclaimed the blood of the lamb and mentioned the Ebenezer (who ever he is). Pastor Bob described the miracle of spiritual gifts and the divine authority of Scripture. He talked about evangelization and the blessed second baptism of the spirit, while holding on to the pulpit with one hand and pounding it with his big black Bible with the other. He went on and on for forty five minutes before he slowly wound down. As we slipped out of the back to leave, I could hear Pastor Bob urging the unwashed to come forward and throw their lives on the alter of God while there was yet time. "The end is coming!" Bob shouted. "The end times are here! Come now! Flee the fire that burns forever!"

By that point, we were only anxious to flee Pastor Bob, the wacko religious crowd, and the 'Full Gospel Fellowship of Second Birth Pentecostalism' as quickly as we could. We hit the street and cut back to 2nd Street. "Whew," said Rob. "OK, did anybody else find that a little bit crazy?"

Frenchie and I laughed. "Far out, man!" I chortled. "We have been rolled by the Holy Rollers! The music was cool but as soon as Pastor Bob opened his mouth and started speaking…Well, honestly, I didn't understand a single word he said."

Frenchie said, "Our family attends the Methodist Church in Newville and I thought I was ok with religion, but I have absolutely no clue what he was talking about. It was like he was speaking Greek or Arabic. Nothing! Nada! Planet Nowhere!"

Rob laughed, "Well that makes me feel better. I was raised a complete pagan and have had no religious education. I was stumped by his words. My spirit was grooving with the music they played – I thought it was the blues - but the rest of it was nuts. Let's go shopping!"

Together we had good laugh and turned onto 2nd Street grateful to have survived a wacky experience. Little did we suspect the startling and traumatic events we'd have before day's end.

In 1966 2nd Street projected the unique flavor of the growing hippy, flower power culture. A couple young entrepreneurs, who had visited Carnaby Street in London and Sansom Street in Philadelphia, decided to buy up old store fronts and turn the neighborhood into a hippy haven. By the time we got there shops featuring hip music, drug paraphernalia, hip clothing, black lights, lava lamps, psychedelic wear, jewelry, and other supplies filled the streets. The smell of incense wafted out of shop doors. The pavement was thronged with young, attractive shoppers.

Coming up the sidewalk was a long tall drink of water, a beautiful girl in an amazing short mini-skirt. The shortness of her skirt took my breath away. She definitely had the legs to wear it - legs which went all the way from her ankles to her shoulder blades. The black wool skirt might have been all of eight inches in length. She wore subtle black stockings underneath the skirt and a bright red cashmere sweater snug over her ample chest. Holy Macarolly! Long glossy black hair flowed down her shoulders. She had a light, olive skinned complexion. Large hazel eyes centered her face and she had a twinkle of a smile as if she was mildly amused at watching the male eyes bulge as she strolled by on the sidewalk. My eyes were certainly bulging. Whew!

Finally, Frenchie came to his senses. "Hey, let's get going before we get derailed by this scene. I want to get a good spot at the rally so I can look for my Army buddies," Frenchie added. "Rob, you look wasted. We need to get you some fresh air. Is it the second hand weed smoke?"

"It's not the dope, man," Rob protested. "My eye lids are still on fire from staring at all the hot chicks in mini-skirts. Yoww! How sizzling can they get?"

"Plenty hot," laughed Frenchie. "Come on Jack; let's get him out of here. We need to dip his head in a bucket of water before his eyeballs spontaneously combust."

"Kapoof!" I hooted, but grabbed Robbie by the arm and started pulling him towards a street leading off of 2nd Street. "I'm guessing Mennonite farm girls in Doylestown don't dress like these babes!"

Frenchie said, "Let's walk over to the Capital Plaza and grab lunch on the way." We dipped into a Mom & Pop hoagie shop for lunch. We sat on red stools at the counter and had cheese steaks, fries, and Cokes. Yummy good! That hit the spot. Good thing we ate when we did, given what unfolded next.

By the time we got to the Capital Plaza the space was absolutely packed with bodies. The State House building sits on one edge of a large square with other government buildings spread around the perimeter. The open space looks as if it can hold about 3,000 people. By the time we arrived, well over 10,000 packed the space to overflowing in the plaza, on the steps, porticos, and monuments. Many of these folks wielded homemade signs declaring: "Stop the War Now!" "Peace Now!" "Make Love Not War" Actually, this crowd looked more like they were on a picnic with a few peace slogans along for the fun.

We were engulfed by masses of people singing the civil rights anthem *We Shall Overcome.*

"We shall overcome, we shall overcome, we shall overcome some day.

Oh, deep in my heart, I do believe, we shall overcome, some day."

We joined in and continued to sing these verses over and over. The throng had a consciousness of its own. At this point, the three of us linked arms with strangers in the crowd around us, as had people all over the plaza. Somehow, we were no longer a collection of individuals with a common concern. Instead we had become a brotherhood of men and women, united against the tyranny of big government and the cruelty of a war forced upon innocent victims, both Vietnamese and American.

The official program kicked off twenty minutes later when Peter, Paul and Mary, the dynamic young folk trio, stepped to the microphone and began to sing. Their remarkable voices blended together in perfect harmony as they sang *If I Had A Hammer, Lemon Tree* and *Puff the Magic Dragon.* As much participants in the anti-war protest as entertainment, they finished by leading the massive crowd in several more stanzas of *We Shall Over Come.*

Several Vietnam vets spoke about their experiences in the jungles of Nam. All were articulate in their opposition to the war. Following the speakers, a draft card burning ceremony was held. A number of Quaker peace activists got the ball rolling by mounting the stage and lighting their draft cards on fire as an act of civil disobedience. Peter, Paul and Mary played quietly in the background as young men kept coming up to burn their draft cards to the cheers of the crowd. The audience chanted loudly, "No more war! No more war!" On the fringe of the crowd, a few counter protesters shouted out, "Traitors! Boo! Shame on you!"

Cassius Clay, the famous boxer, stepped to the microphone and addressed the crowd. Clay became the Heavyweight Champion of the World in 1964; then converted to Islam and changed his name to Mohammad Ali. He was a conscientious objector to the Viet Nam war and refused to be drafted. He spoke with eloquence against the war and the crowd around us roared their approval.

I felt Frenchie pulling Rob and me towards the outside of the crowd. I looked at him and he simply said, "Trouble." And pointed to the left side of the plaza. Along North Street, which formed one exterior boundary, police were forming into blue ranks. Many were mounted on horses. The cops in the front had high clear plastic riot shields and were wearing gas masks. Honestly, I didn't take it seriously. The crowd was peaceful. Citizens were exercising the right of free speech with a parade permit. Besides, there were only about 300 cops and well over 10,000 peaceful protesters in the plaza. What could go wrong?

Frenchie kept pushing us to the edge of the mob towards Third Street. Suddenly, the shouts and screams of the crowd to the left rose in pitch and volume. I looked back to see the blue line of police wade into the crowd of spectators with batons whipping through the air. The screams of those hit intensified. I heard the 'thunk' of batons cracking down on skulls. "Thwack," "crack," and shouts of "Oh my God!" rolled in our direction as the mounted police charged the crowd. These officers were swinging three foot long batons to better connect with their victims. When the police knocked a person to the ground, a cluster of cops surround them, slap on handcuffs and haul them off to the waiting paddy wagons. They were booked for resisting arrest.

Spectators scrambled to get away from the police. Whiz...whack!" went the baton. Crack went the skull. Blood sprayed onto horrified bystanders. The victims of this police brutality collapsed into a limp heap with blood spurting. The cops surrounded the victim, cuffed him, and dragged him off to the wagon. Some resisting arrest.

Frenchie kept pushing us away, shouting "Go, go, go!" Suddenly there was a 'whoosh' in the air and a clunk as a tear gas canister landed at Rob's feet. As quick as could be, Frenchie leaped forward, grabbed the can and flipped it back at the police line. I began to see the value of my cousin's military training. The police unrolled fire hoses and knocked people in the crowd off their feet with the powerful spray. Whenever a spectator went down, the cops were on them to cuff and arresting them.

The plaza started to look like a war zone. People screaming, crying, and shrieking with pain and fear. Clouds of tear gas drifted through the air. There was no defensive reaction from the crowd. They came for a peaceful protest. There were no rocks, sticks, or Molotov cocktails lying around on the plaza to use as defensive weapons. What were they going to do? Throw their homemade cardboard signs at the attacking cops? These people were defenseless lambs going to the slaughter.

Just then I heard the snarl of dogs barking over the screams of the crowd around me. "Oh, shit!" shouted Frenchie. "Attack dogs! Let's get the hell out of here!" He kept pushing us across 3rd Street. Curious, I turned to see a line of twenty German Shepherds leap into the crowd, pulling protesters to the ground and savagely biting them. Unbelievable! We ran down State Street with others trying to get away from the carnage. Frenchie hauled left onto a small side street in hopes we could shake the pursuit.

As we ran, I could hear the snarl and barks of a police dog chasing us. "Ooww…" screamed Rob who was in the back of our group. "He's got my leg!" I turned around and just stared at Rob trying to shake off the big German Shepherd biting his leg. In an instant, Frenchie whirled into action. He charged the dog and at the moment of collision, whipped his pointed cowboy boot up and connected with the dog under his chin. With a yelp and a cry the dog let go and flipped head over heels, up in the air, and then collapsed. Instantly, the dog was back on four feet, crouching and snarling to prepare for a charge.

"Get back!" Frenchie shouted at Rob and me. He ran forward pulling off his green Army fatigue jacket. As he ran, he wrapped the jacket around his left forearm and held it in front of his body. When the shepherd lunged at Frenchie he was met with the bundled up forearm, so he sank his fangs deeply into the jacket. Frenchie let the weight of the dog carry them to the ground where the dog was pinned by his jaws fixed on my cousin's arm. Frenchie leaned in with his right arm and laid it across the attacking dog's windpipe and pushed down with all of his weight and strength. For several moments, the dog struggled and then fell limp.

When the beast was dead, Frenchie got up and unwound his coat. He looked at me and said, "Jack, help me drag him into this alley." We picked him up, slid him down the side street. At the first dumpster, the two of us heaved the carcass into the container and flipped the lid.

Walking back to the car, I said "Wow! Now I see the value of training. You were all over what was going on there before I even had a clue what was happening."

"Yeah, if it was just Jack and me," said Rob, "we would be bleeding in the paddy wagon by now, or worse. Thanks for having our backs, Frenchie."

"Thank Uncle Sam," said my cousin. "They teach you all kinds of helpful stuff in the Army, like how to look out for trouble, anticipate what could go wrong, and always look for an exit strategy. I can't believe those god damn cops - turning attack dogs loose on civilians! I've heard that's what they did in the South with peaceful civil rights marchers. Bash them with batons, use tear gas, knock them down with fire hoses. But the dogs? That is crazy. These cops are at war with our citizens. They use military tactics I never saw used in the Vietnam. Thankfully, I was taught in the Army how to stop and kill attack dogs, but I never thought I'd use it in the streets of Pennsylvania."

17

"The heart has reasons which reason does not understand."

~ Blaise Pascal

Rob Bachmann   December, 1966

After Thanksgiving break, the weather in south central Pennsylvania took a turn for the worse. Day after day the sky was cloudy with long periods of wet soggy conditions. Most days the temperature hung just above freezing with nothing but a cold hard rain falling. Honestly, it was more depressing than a Bob Dylan ballad. If it wasn't for Koffee Klatch, I think I would have gone stark raving mad.

Koffee Klatch wasn't much fun either. The main topic was wondering what happened to Snow White, who remained missing. One Tuesday morning I was sitting with the usual culprits at the Klatch. Randi said, "I keep wondering if there is something we've overlooked, or failed to consider?"

"Like what? Like where?" asked Frenchie. "The Harrisburg cops combed the entire city. Carlisle police have searched in town and scoured the countryside around college. The National Guard went out looking. Her parents are offering a $10,000 reward."

Novaksky spoke up. "If she was kidnapped for ransom, we would have had a demand from the kidnappers by now. But honestly, her dad works for the IRS. I have trouble seeing her as a kidnapping target. There's just not enough money there."

"If somebody bumped her off and threw her body into a dumpster," ventured Jack, "they would have found her corpse by now." Jack, Frenchie and I exchanged knowing glances. "So it seems reasonable she left town in someone's car – either voluntarily or involuntarily." Jack concluded.

"When I was young," I added, "I used to run away a lot. I was just so damned unhappy at home. When I got older, I disappeared into the woods with my camping gear and was gone for days. After Mom died, I started to run away in earnest." I continued. "Summers, I would load up my backpack and hitch hike. I went wherever the road and the rides led me. No plan. Just away. I took the train, the bus, and hitched places. Slept in bus stations and under bridges. I was so miserable at home, living rough seemed a positive alternative to being at home."

"Robbie, why do you bring this up?" asked Randi.

"When I think about what Nikki said – about how unhappy Snow was at home, it makes me wonder if she just took off. Everybody handles pain in their life in different ways. I was so impressed by Frenchie's' family. If I was in his family and felt miserable, I would run home. But being in my family, if I was wretched, I would run away from home. I would simply make other choices. Choose a new approach to life. I don't think we're stuck with our original circumstances. We can make other choices. All I am saying, is maybe Snow was miserable and she has simply made another choice."

"OK, I get that," ventured Gary, after a pause. "When I realized I was miserable at home, I asked to go to my Lynch grandparents on Long Island for the summer. I was eight years old the first summer I went. I suppose I was an organized runaway. And I lived on an estate, not in a dirty bus depot. Ha ha!"

"Ok, Hockey Boy," I shot back. "Don't rub it in."

"Sorry, Rob. No offense meant. When I was fourteen, I realized I was not going to survive high school in Richmond, so once again, I ran away to Long Island. Fortunately, my grandparents were willing to go to bat for me, get me into Stony Brook and pay for it. I'm not sure my Grands ever understood what troubled me so much about my family. But they were able to read me as a human being. Maybe not understand my pain but to sympathize with my plight."

"My Grands took me in, but I was still lonely. I wandered around the neighborhood and met some families with kids. The Cartwright's, who live up the street, invited me to hang out at their house that summer. They have three kids - Tony, Max, and Adele. Plus two dogs and a Persian cat. Whenever I needed company, I'd go up the lane and hang out with the Cartwright's. We played games in the yard, rode bikes on the street, played board games and watched TV. It was fun to have actual humans to be with. I guess they've adopted me as an extra kid in their family."

Randi spoke up. "I think I see what you're saying. I grew up in a great family, had a secure home life. But maybe too much of a good thing…? My junior year I got bored. I've always had top grades, and been a good student, but I felt caged… in a small cage. I guess into every life, a little rain must fall. No matter how good our situation, we have some disappointments, some pain, some sorrow. Each of us has to find ways to deal with our pain. To find our way. To find purpose, connection, love.

"When I found I was shriveling up from boredom, I did some research and found an accelerated program in Israel. I tried to convince my parents to let me go study in Tel Aviv for six months, graduate in December and spend the last six months of my senior year traveling in Europe. Ultimately, my parents wouldn't let me go. They were afraid I would regret missing senior year, the prom, graduation – all the bells and whistles. I stuck it out, but it wasn't much fun."

When the Klatch broke up, I walked Randi to her next class. I've always admired Miss Fox, mostly because she is so damn good looking. Her long auburn hair and shapely figure knocks me out. She has a beautiful face, yet that dusting of freckles makes her look more real, less perfect. She dresses well in a big city girl kind of way, but she can be down to earth and comfortable too. I think if a girl is good-looking, they should look attractive in a pair of jeans and a t-shirt. I mean, why guild the lily? If you have it, it should be obvious without a lot of unnatural ornamentation. Or perhaps I just like my women to be straight forward. After that Klatch, I found myself more interested in Randi. I think I'm beginning to look beyond her good looks and see more of her heart. Randi is a 'namer.' She can put her finger on the heart of an issue and cut right through all the crap. I like that.

C.S. Lewis describes the reign of the White Witch in Narnia as being "always winter but never Christmas." This pretty well describes our first December at college. It seemed to drag on and on and on across a cold, bleak, weary landscape. The weather was rotten. Cold, damp, wet and miserable. Jack kept telling me how much better winter is in NH. "If we had some real cold and snow, we could ski, sled, snowshoe, even ice fish!" Jack said.

"Thanks, Jack. That makes me feel a lot better. I don't know what was wrong with me – for a second, I was bummed out, but now you've made me happy again."

Finally, we found an antidote to the blues. A group of freshman guys began an intermittent card game in the basement lounge of Wood Hall. Our dorm has student rooms on the top three floors. The basement contains a laundry room, a communal kitchen, the Hall Director's apartment, and the Blue Room. Named after the paint color on the walls, this was supposed to be a study lounge but had become a noisy social hub for the dorm. This is where our card game sprang into life that first ugly December.

No one remembers how it started but the card game grew into a regular presence in the back corner of the Blue Room. Like crabgrass in your lawn, one minute you hardly notice it and the next minute it has taken over. Mostly the guys played five card poker. Some fellows, like Jack, wouldn't play poker, preferring Black Jack or 21. Jack liked this card game so much it eventually produced his nickname, Black Jack Flynn. An appropriate handle.

The rolling card game appeared from time to time that winter on no predictable schedule. It was a diverse but compatible group of guys which produced growing friendships. One afternoon, Bunny Washington, Billy Harrison, Frank Spinelli, Jack, Gary and I were sitting in. Jack, Frank and Gary were playing Black Jack. "Anybody have a good class this trimester?" I asked.

After a pause, Bunny ventured, "I hope this doesn't sound funny, but I'm really enjoying *Survey of the New Testament.* My mother is a devoted Christian and she's always quoting the Bible at me, - been doing it all my life. Funny thing is the Bible always agrees with her point of view. Makes me wonder if she's giving me the straight scoop. I took this class to check it out for myself."

"So what are you finding," asked Gary. "Has she been bullshitting you?"

"The Bible is actually an amazing book. Particularly the teachings of Jesus in the Gospels. If you read what is in there, you get a different impression about God from what church, or religious people tell you.

"Like how?" asked Frank.

"If I was going to summarize, I'm learning God is love and he is actively reaching out to us, trying to connect us with his love."

"Wow!" said Frank. "Who would have thought that?" He paused, "When I go to mass at my Catholic Church, all I ever hear is how mad God is at me, how much trouble I am in, etc, etc."

Bunny laughed, "Well, in your case Spinelli, that may be true!" We chuckled at that. "Plus, the professor, Dr. Broderick is cool. I like his teaching style a lot."

"You don't think he's cool just because he's a brother?" asked Frank.

"No, even putting aside he's black. That just makes him beautiful, like me."

"Whoa, excuse me while I barf," laughed Frank.

"No, he's cool. Broderick knows how to relate what the Bible teaches to my life and concerns and he makes it accessible – puts the cookies on the bottom shelf."

"Speaking of love, how's your love life Rob?" asked Black Jack Flynn. "You found anyone who particularly interests you yet?"

"Gee wiz, I don't know," was all I could mutter. "Lots of good looking women on campus."

"Like who? Or is it whom? Who would be on your top five list?" asked Frank.

"I'll admit, Faith McFadden is the best looking woman on campus. At least in the freshman class. Fact, not opinion. Legs that just won't quit. But even if she was not joined at the hip to Skeeter, I'm not sure she is my type. She might be too southern, although I realize it's not her fault. Linda Pence is easy on the eyes. Reminds me of a beautiful Jersey cow. Big brown eyes; dark eyebrows; creamy smooth skin; honey blonde hair…Yum! She is soft spoken, gentle, kind. And she is kinda' ballsy. I like that."

"Shit, you can say that again," said Gary. "She's got bigger brass ones than any man on campus. You should have seen her react and drive when we were almost crushed by the logging truck."

"Nikki is also my type," I continued. "Interesting. Different. Maybe a bit crazy. But I don't want Hockey Boy to punch out my lights, so I count her as off limits. We are strictly friends."

"Amen to that, brother," said Gary with a big smile on his face.

I'm not sure why, but I was not ready to talk about my feelings for Randi. I find myself thinking about her. I enjoy talking to her. I love the way her mind works. She is sharp. Connects the dots faster than anybody I know. She is also compassionate and empathetic towards others. I like that a lot.

But, I worry she is a little too 'big city' for me. Her Dad is a big shot lawyer in Philadelphia and she lives on the Main Line. I'm awfully happy in the country and come from a family of Pennsylvania Dutch pretzel makers. She may be out of my league and out of my comfort zone.

"What about Delilah Brown?" asked Billy. "Any interest in her?"

"Now she is a weird one," I responded. "Very hot, very sexy. What ever happened with the two of you?" I asked Billy.

"I'm not sure. It was strange. At the first kegger she was happy to let me into her knickers. Eager in fact. But from the moment they pulled us out of that mine pit she won't talk to me."

"Seems like she has a new guy each week," ventured Bunny. "She's been rumored to be sleeping with at least five other guys this year. None of her guys seem to last long. 'Wham, bam, thank you Ma'am, and now it's over.' Like a preying mantis, it's the female who is churning and burning mates."

"Mac Graham lasted more than a week." suggested Frank.

"That's because he takes her to Dr. Long's and gets her stoned," suggested Gary. "Or because he's an upperclassman. The latest I heard is she's having an affair with Dr. Henning, the Biology prof."

"'Fuckin –A!' as Arty would say," said Frank. "I heard that too. Henning has a reputation for really 'getting into' his subject. Ha ha! Apparently, he picks out a tasty young tidbit from his classes each year for a regular dose of hanky panky. He gives them extra credit for their 'lab work,' so it pulls up their grades and their GPA. He's married, of course, but that doesn't seem to slow him down."

"That's pathetic. And disgusting," said Gary. "A college freshman. Poor form!"

"You said it," I added. "Hey it's almost five thirty. Let's go eat." With that, the players folded the cards and we trooped over to Musselman for dinner.

About two pm Friday afternoon, the skies began to darken. The thick gray clouds moved over us spitting rain which turned to snow. Falling, freezing rain coated every surface with a glaze of ice. As daylight faded and the street lights came on, the trees around campus were changed into a wondrous display of crystal lights. Bushes and trees turned into dancing ice sculptures. The student body was electrified by this unexpected blessing. For weeks we had suffered in a dreary and dull landscape. In hours, campus was transformed into a magical winter wonderland.

The following morning we woke up to an eerie silence across campus. Looking outside the dorm, the cause was instantly clear. No cars moving anywhere. Not on campus, not on the surrounding city streets. A half inch of hard ice coated the roads. Trees and bushes sparkled with the frozen rain and decorative snow clung to every branch. Snow covered the campus with a white blanket of pure beauty, which muffled any sounds. We took the treacherous walk to the Dining Hall by sliding our feet along on the slick surface never picking them up.

Fortunately, a few of the dining staff lived within walking distance and came in to provide students with breakfast. They told us campus was closed because cars could not drive on the slick roadways. The Town of Carlisle was closed as well. Most of south central PA was closed. Nothing to do but wait for the weather to warm a little. The fact it was a Saturday helped limit any inconvenience to students and faculty. We sat in the Dining Hall for the next two hours, eating breakfast, watching Nikki knock back TABS, and hanging out. Gary Rollins was able to join us because his morning hockey practice had been cancelled. I mean, why not hang out? Our cozy little club section is warm; there is a constant supply of food and drink. The dining room windows gave us a front row seat on everything going on outside.

After a couple hours, Jack and I got bored. I leaned over and asked Gary, "Hey, you have not had much time with Father X since hockey practice started. Would you like to go to town with Jack and me to see if we can look him up?"

Without hesitation, Gary said, "Count me in. Can we walk? There's no way I want to drive Doug's Hot Dog Wagon on this ice!"

As we walked into Carlisle there was almost no traffic. A few clever students strapped on ice skates and were flying down the middle of High Street with scarves flapping behind. They looked like Dutch figures skating on the frozen canals of Amsterdam. A mail truck wearing tire chains went cruising by forcing us off to the side of the street. As it passed, it let out a cheerful symphony of clattering, clunking noises, spitting out chunks of ice.

Eventually we arrived at Tuscarora Mountain Outfitters and passed though the store to Father X's cabin in the back. The walk between the cabin and the store was already shoveled and a sprinkling of black cinders had been flung on the path. The aroma of wood smoke filled the air, and a plume of white gray smoke climbed straight up from his stove pipe.

After we got settled inside, Jack asked the priest, "what is there to do around here in the winter? The weather since the beginning of December has been abysmal and seriously depressing."

"Patience, my lad," replied the Father. "It's not always this bad. The weather here is slower to cool down, but still offers winter activities. It's only the beginning and end of winter that are annoying. After Christmas, the late small game seasons open and you can work those until mid- February. But in January, you should teach yourselves to ice fish."

Jack jumped in, "I know how to ice fish! In NH you can ice fish from November until April."

"In the Valley, it takes a long deep stretch of cold to freeze the lakes. But, if you drive an hour north, you can fish Whipple Dam State Park from January until mid March. Its only 22 acres, but the lake sits high on a ridge over State College and it gets cold up there. The major game is trout, but there are pickerel, perch, and sometimes bass. Fish live three-inch minnows on tip-ups with flags." Father X explained the tackle we would need, which was good because I've never done any hard water angling. Jack had the general idea, but had to adopt his techniques for local conditions.

"Speaking of State College, Father X, can I ask you a question?" said Gary.

"Sure, fire away," said the Father.

Gary shared about his Thanksgiving trip to Nikki's and the accident with the logging truck. "I keep wondering why we didn't end up crushed under the logs and that other woman did? If the truck came around the curve a second sooner, I wouldn't be here. Why did one woman in the car end up dead and the other walk away from the accident? Was one good and the other bad? I don't believe that. I guess my question is, if there is a good and loving God, why do bad things happen to good people?"

After a pause, Father X said, "Gary that is a profound and disturbing question. Much about life is mysterious and confusing. But I can tell you what I believe. The short answer is 'free will.' But let me give you a longer version. God made us to be in relationship with him. He wants us to love him and he wants to pour his love out on us. But love is always voluntary. God doesn't force himself on anyone. Our broken relationship with God means evil men can do evil things to others and God does not step in and prevent it from happening. He does not force us to choose what is right.

"What would life be like if we had no choice? No free will? Say you had a hammer. If you went to use it for good, building a house, it would have all the properties you normally expect. But if you wanted to use it for evil, like hitting someone in the head, then God would intervene and turn it into foam rubber. Without free will, you could never make a bad choice. Or any choice at all. If you obeyed God because you had no choice, God could never have the relationship he wants with us."

After a moment, the Father continued. "Why do bad things happen to good people? We live in a fallen world. People make bad choices, drive too fast, and it hurts innocent bystanders. Or the brakes failed, and it wasn't the driver's fault. Bad things do happen to good people, and there often is no fault involved. It doesn't mean God spared you kids to take the woman behind you. Or that God took the driver and not the passenger for some reason. Bad things happen to good people, even those who know and love Jesus. And good things happen to bad people. God makes the sun shine and the rain fall on the good and the evil."

"OK, I can see that," said Jack. "Life is mysterious, and there's a lot of life we simply can't see and comprehend at this moment. But how can you believe in a God you can't see?"

"Ah, a keen question, my lad." replied Father X. "Because God does not want to force himself on us, and he wants to give us the freedom to choose or not choose a love relationship with him, we have to look for indications of his presence. Remember earlier we talked about things we see in nature, the sun rising, the tide coming in, and spring returning in April? Those are indications there is a guiding force, a controlling hand that keeps life in balance and does not let the whole world simply run amuck."

Gary leaned forward, "That's what Nikki thinks – you can see indications of God's design and intentionality in nature. They're foot prints left in the sand which indicate the existence of God."

"Exactly." said the Father. "Or here is another example which really helped the Tlingit Indians I worked with in Alaska. You can't see radio waves nor can you see TV signals. But some people say you can get audio messages, pictures, and such over these invisible waves. You could simply deny the existence of these phenomena because you can't see any waves in the air. But if you were smart, you would find some folks who have radio or TV and get to know them until you figure out how it's done. Look for people with their antennas up.

"In the same way, when you want to look for indications of God, you find people who seem to be able to read the signs and know God. Sidle up to these folks with their antennas up and get to know them. Observe their lives. Examine their relationship with God. Eventually, if God is really there, you too will begin to see him and can have a relationship with him."

"Huhh...?" Gary murmured. "In a weird way, that makes sense to me."

As this conversation unfolded, there came a rising noise from the ceiling of the cabin. It rattled and banged as if someone was raining marbles on the camp's tin roof. Jack stuck his head out the door, "Hey, come look at this." All four of us crowded out the doorway to see ice falling on the roof. The sun was bright and I could feel the heat on my skin. Huge gobs of ice were falling from the tree branches and smashing on the cabin, the ground and the TMO building next door. "I guess that's the end of skating down High Street," chortled Jack. "We should probably head back before it gets dangerous." We said our goodbyes to Father X and headed back to campus.

18

"Never surrender opportunity for security."
~ *Branch Rickey*

Faith McFadden   January, 1967

Saturday morning, Skeeter invited me to breakfast. Lately, cold January weather had put a crimp on our love life. With all the cold and snow it wasn't wise to drive down some country lane in the dark, turn off into a field, and park out of sight for a little foolin' around. It's not that I object to making love on the front seat of Skeeter's El Camino. It's just too darn cold! So we contented ourselves with staying on campus and waiting for warmer weather. Breakfast out at Grandpa's Grinder was a nice change of pace.

When Skeeter and I arrived at the Grinder, the place was hoppin.' Tables were filled with retired geezers shooting the breeze, old ladies chatting with friends, and family groups out for breakfast. As we slid into a booth, a waitress approached. She put down two mugs and asked, "Coffee for either of you?"

"Sure." said Skeeter as she poured us both coffees. He looked at me with a mischievous twinkle in his eye, like he desperately wanted to make a joke. "Give us a minute to read the menu," he added. As the waitress walked away, Skeeter laughed aloud and said, "I'll bet she used to have a cute ass."

That made me giggle. I can see what he means. She looks near thirty, with a pretty face and big brown eyes. I can imagine her at twenty being quite the looker. After ten years of marriage and a few toddlers, however, she has grown love handles, and has packed on some added weight on her butt. She looks kinda chubby on the way to fat. "Do you think that's what I'll look like when I'm thirty?" I asked.

Skeeter laughed. "Geezz, I hope not," he responded. "I never thought of that. I look at you and assume you'll look the way you do forever. But that's not realistic, is it? If you live to be 64, you could end up looking like my grandmother. Once I saw her dressing and her boobs hung down to her waist."

We laughed again, this time a little uncomfortably. "Well, that is an appetizing thought," I said. "Let's order some breakfast."

The menu was loaded with dishes featuring eggs, omelets, scrambles, pancakes and waffles. These come with your choice of breakfast meat – bacon, ham, sausage patties, sausage links and Canadian bacon. They have meats I've never even heard of – scrapple, blood pudding, Taylor Pork Roll, shad, and herring. This is a menu designed for protein loving carnivores, although there is a fruit cup and hot oatmeal for vegans. We both found a mix of items to our liking and ordered.

Since Thanksgiving at Skeeter's house, I've been thinking about how much I like his family and their way of life. At home on St. Simons for Christmas, it was hard not to make comparisons. Part of the contrast is the physical surroundings. My family: mother, father, and three teenage daughters, live crammed into a twenty-four by 30' one-story ranch house. Our house is old, leaky and falling apart. The inside of the house gets cold in winter, but thankfully, SSI winters are pretty mild affairs. The yard is full of junk. And our house is not the worst in the neighborhood. It's a hard scrabble existence at best.

The Stetsons have a large home with plenty of space for family and guests. It's bright, airy, and nicely decorated. The rooms are clean, spacious and well maintained as are the gardens and yard. A safe, attractive residential neighborhood. Anyone would be proud to own Skeeter's home.

Then there's his family. When you enter his home, you can feel the calm, the peace, the intuitive sense that whatever is wrong in the world is not coming in here. 'Once you are here, you are safe.' People in his family have different personalities. Yet each seems to feel known, loved, and accepted. His Mom and Dad make an effort to understand their kids and to offer support and encouragement. I felt that coming from them and I was simply a weekend guest.

My home has always felt like a cesspool that generates bad feelings, dissention, criticism, and judgment. Rather than a safe retreat from the world, in my home you yearn to escape to the world. Better to be alone, adrift in a hard, cruel world. Any other option is better than being in my cold heartless home.

"Skeeter," I began, "I was wowed by your family. Your parents are so caring. I see the way they focus on their kids and want to affirm and encourage them, even though you are each very different. I felt their compassion and I was only a visitor. Do you have any idea what an unusual home and family you have?"

"Well, I know we are well off compared to many others. Not many kids on my street go to private school, although the public schools are good."

"I'm not talking about your finances or how big your house is, although both are amazing." I replied.

"Our house isn't that big," Skeeter protested. "We only have five bedrooms and three bathrooms. It's only because the girls share a bedroom, that we have two guest rooms. Have you ever heard Ratso Ramsey go on about his house in Richmond? According to him, his family lives in a big mansion perched on a bluff over the James River. It has eight bedrooms and six and a half baths in the house. Plus they own a farm out in the country – a remnant of the old family plantation on the Rappahannock River. Ratso claims his family owned tens of thousands of acres of land and a thousand slaves before the Civil War. His Dad has a private jet and they own a beach house in Delaware. The family uses the jet to fly to the beach or the farm on weekends. We're not that kind of well off."

"I still don't think you hear what I am trying to say."

Skeeter added, "Mom does have a little help. Mrs. Moyer comes in five days a week to help with the cleaning, cooking, and domestic work inside the house. Pete is the hired man who takes care of everything outside the house. He lives on the property in a snug little apartment in the barn. When I was a teen, I would come home after school and shoot hoops in the barn with Pete. I guess he was my confidant and source of life wisdom. Pete and Mrs. Moyer are not like help, more like family."

"Sweetheart, I still don't think you're hearing me. I'm not talking about big houses, staff, and private school. Your home is unusual because of the people in it!" was my comeback.

"OK," said Skeeter, "Tell me more."

"When I compare your home to mine, yours is dramatically different. It feels like a place of peace. Tranquility. People feel safe there. They take time to know each other and accept the unique personality of each. Sukie is a gem – like the fairy godmother in all the children's bedtime stories. She sets the tone, but everyone is playing by the same set of rules. The outcome is incredibly positive, even for an outsider like me. Part of that is the people but part of it is also the fact your dad makes enough money to build and maintain an oasis of peace like that.

"When you think about your future, do you ever think working for your family company might not give you the pleasure of bridges, but it could give you the kind of family life you now enjoy?"

After a long moment, Skeeter replied, "Faith, to be honest, I've never thought of my family experience as special." He continued, "It's the only home I've known. I accept my mother's death, although that was hard. I accept the difference Sukie makes in our life, and I admit she is great. But my home just is. My family too. I may have been dealt a better hand than most people in life, but I've not seen enough of life to know that with assurance."

After that breakfast, I began to feel different about Skeeter. He takes his family environment for granted. Just assumes it is normal for most people. I think he's wrong. It may be the right people, but it may come from having the money to live that life. Skeeter may not be marriage material, if he's willing to throw away the benefits of wealth and position just to build bridges. What a fruitcake!

At the next Koffee Klatch I sat next to Spinelli. We got talking about Ratso Ramsey and Frank was spilling all the dirt he picked up in the dorm. "You know he never eats in the Dining Hall?" said Frank.

"Yes, I heard he eats every lunch and dinner at Mom's Hoagies or Chilly Dawgs." I ventured.

"You watch. Every day at lunch and dinner time, he drives his T-Bird up the street to eat. He eats pizza or a cheese steak and fries for almost every meal. Gross!"

"I'm amazed!" I added. "How can he do that? Won't the grease kill him? Unbelievable!"

"What amazes me is how he can think the food in here is crummy when he stuffs his face with greasy garbage twenty-one meals a week."

"Skeeter tells me his family is loaded – has a big house and servants, etc, etc. Is that true?"

"Well who the heck knows," said Frank. "According to Ramsey, his family is the cat's meow in Richmond. Big mansion on the river, servants, country club, country estate, beach house, and a personal jet plane." His older brother, Franklin Agnew Ramsey the IV, is a big deal too. His name makes you think we are talking about King Louis the 14th in France, and everyone knows where all his airs and pretensions got him. 'Off with his head!'." Frank laughed at his own joke.

"Have you ever met Franklin Ramsey?" I asked.

"No, but we can meet him soon, if you want to. He's coming to campus to visit his little brother Ratso. Yale, where Franklin goes, (here Frank pushed up his nose with his index finger indicating the snootiness of all this nonsense) has a J-term for the month of January. Franklin was too busy vacationing on St Johns in the Caribbean to take a J-Term course. He's driving up from Richmond for the beginning of the Spring Semester and stopping in to visit little brother at Carlisle."

"Well, that should be interesting." I mused.

Six days later Franklin Agnew Ramsey IV blew into Carlisle. Wednesday afternoon. I finished class early and was hanging out in Lane Student Center, pretending to study. I should have been next door in the Library, if I really wanted to study, but campus had been abuzz with anticipation of Ratso's brother's arrival. I wanted a sighting of the Ramsey boys, so I was in Lane.

Ratso is not a looker. Skinny, with a small skull, his face is pinched together in front. Two beady eyes perch on a slender pointed nose. Topped by a mop of limp brown hair in a bad haircut. I suppose I thought big brother would look the same. Not so. Franklin Ramsey ("Call me Frank," he says as he shoots his hand out towards me. "All my friends do") is 6' 3', with a powerfully built body. Ruggedly handsome, with a large square face, topped by short golden curls. He looks like Adonis, or some other Greek god. The epitome of youth and beauty. Whoa!

We stood around in a clump at Lane Hall playing 'get to know each other.' Ratso attracted a larger crowd of friends than he had in real life, at least at Carlisle. Ratso loved the attention his brother was bringing him. Students wandered over to see what the hubbub was about and Ratso introduced everyone as if we were his bosom buddies and best friends on campus. Anyone whose name Ratso could come up with, was ushered into the inner circle of his campus persona. It was so fake! If the older Ramsey suspects his brother is the least liked person on campus, he gives no indication.

Frank is warm, outgoing, and friendly. He has the gift of gab and is quick with one-liners and clever little comments which make an immediate connection with new people. Frank Ramsey was wearing neatly pressed blue jeans on top of snakeskin cowboy boots. His shirt is a tight, black turtleneck which emphasizes a buff mid-section. Over that a grey herringbone sports coat, which lay soft and supple on his frame as only really expensive clothing can. What makes Franklin Ramsey so attractive? His whole appearance, demeanor, and style shout, "I've got money!"

After an hour of meet and greet, Frank Ramsey cornered me and guided me off to the side where others could not hear our conversation. "Faith, it is so great to meet you. I've heard so much about you from Craig. I'd like to get to know you better. Craig and I are taking a couple of close friends out to dinner tonight and I would count it a privilege if you would join us. Would you do that for me?"

"Sure, Frank," I stammered. "That sounds like fun. Where are we going?"

"Craig though we might go to Grandpa's Grinder and have a Philly cheese steak."

"That would be nice," I replied, "but do you have any idea how many cheese steaks your brother eats in the average week?" I giggled.

Ramsey erupted with laughter! He roared until he got himself under control. Everyone in the lounge was staring at us. Frank leaned in and whispered, "A truth teller. I like that. I know about Craig's anti-social eating habits. I think he's just a bit shy and we hope he will outgrow it. Don't mention it to anyone." As he said this, his mouth brushes my ear, I could feel his breath tickle my ear. It was remarkably intimate. A gesture of confidence and shared camaraderie.

"How about we pick you up at six in front of your dorm?"

"That will be fine. Thank you." I replied.

At six sharp the Ramsey brothers arrived in their chariots. Ratso drove the black Thunderbird convertible. Franklin Ramsey was piloting a '48 lipstick red MG Roadster. A long, low, lean racing machine, Frank's car gleamed and, like it's driver, shouted "Money!" Frank Spinelli was riding with Ratso and the senior Ramsey leaned across and popped the passenger door of the MG for me.

On the way to Grandpa's, Franklin kept up a patter of clever stories about his experiences at Yale and what it was like to go to college with future leaders of America. The car purred with repressed power. Ramsey was a man comfortable with the notion he had been born to lead. Confidence and certain success oozed. It gave off an exhilarating aroma. A manly, sexual aroma - hard to withstand. So I didn't.

Dinner was fabulous. Frank Ramsey wined and dined us in style. He had waitresses fawning all over us. I wondered what he would think if he knew that if he was eating at Coconut Willie's, I could be his waitress. He ordered interesting dishes "for the table" and acted the congenial host. Money was obviously not an issue. Stories of Yale and his beloved Skull and Crossbones Society were interspersed with tales of cross country car rallies and competing on the amateur weekend racing circuit with celebrities like Paul Newman and Steve McQueen.

Later that evening, when Frank dropped me off at my dorm, we sat outside in his car necking and petting. Ramsey is an experienced lover; there's no doubt about that. Before the evening ended, I was completely under his spell. And he knew it.

"Faith, have you ever been to New York City?" Ramsey asked.

"No, Carlisle is the furthest north I've been."

"Let me take you to New York for the weekend. We can stay at the Plaza, I'll take you on carriage rides in Central Park, and we can view the city from the Empire State Building. I'll take you shopping and to dinner at the Four Seasons. We can leave in the morning and I'll have you back to your dorm Sunday afternoon. What do you say?"

As I said, I was already under his spell. This was the kind of guy I wanted to snag. Born to power and affluence, he would go out and conquer the world of business while I stayed at home caring for the kids and our social life. Living the good life. He would be like Chip Stetson and I could be like Sukie. He would provide the money and I would spend it.

"Well, I don't know…" I hedged. "I'm not sure I have the clothes for the Plaza and the Four Seasons. I wouldn't want to embarrass you."

"Forget about it." he said. "Just pack a little bag with a nightie, underwear and your toiletries. I'll take you shopping and buy you anything else you need. I have my own American Express card and my Dad gives me an unlimited allowance."

"You talked me into it." I gave Frank a long, wet, lingering kiss. "Come by at eight and I'll be ready," I said as I hopped out of the MG and ran into my dorm.

Thursday morning dawned bright and clear. It was one of those sunny cloudless days that made you forget it was winter. I was waiting when Frank and the red MG pulled up. He jumped out, wearing a brown Harris Tweed sports coat, gray flannel slacks, a natty tweed racing cap which matches his coat and a cream colored silk scarf wrapped around his neck. He looks good enough to eat!

He raced across the sidewalk and gave me a big hug. Then, always the perfect southern gentleman, he picked up my small bag and handed me into the passenger seat. He stowed my bag behind his seat. I found myself hoping my friends in the dorm are peaking out the window watching in envy as my knight in shining armor drives me away. Inside, I feel I'm leaving my old boring life and embarking on a new adventure with a man who is truly capable of loving me and caring for me in the future.

We cruised across the snow-covered country-side of Pennsylvania on the Turnpike. The MG was flashy but noisy inside, making conversation difficult. It was noon before we reached the city. New York, New York! My first view of this city has me in complete awe. The buildings are so high and so many packed into a block. The streets look like canyons as we cruised uptown towards the hotel. "This hotel is one of the most historic in the city and certainly the most luxurious," said Frank, sounding a bit like a tour guide. "The hotel overlooks Central Park, a spectacular sight. I booked us a suite on the Park side so you could enjoy the view. Shall we check into our room first?"

"Frank, that is so thoughtful of you. Thank you." We pulled up to the driveway entrance and a doorman in a stiff green and gold uniform rushed to open our doors.

Frank handed him my small bag and opened the trunk where the doorman picked up Frank's two hand tooled leather suitcases.

Frank flipped the keys to a valet and said, "Park it out of the way. We won't need it until Sunday morning and I don't want any dings on it." He passed the guy a folded bill as a tip.

The doorman ushered us across the ornate lobby to the impressive front desk. While Frank signed us in, I waited on a beautiful chair covered in gold brocade, like a princess on a throne. In that ornate lobby, Frank looks like he belongs; dressed like a dapper English gentleman out for a weekend jaunt. On the other hand, I feel conspicuous. I am wearing my best jeans, a mid-weight burgundy wool sweater, and my brand new sheepskin jacket. I say brand new, meaning new to me. I actually bought it at the Goodwill store in Carlisle when the weather turned cold because I've never owned a winter coat. On campus, I thought I looked pretty good in it. At the Plaza Hotel, I feel like an ugly duckling.

The suite was amazing. "Frank," I said, "this takes my breath away." Gazing out of our 10th story windows, I can see Central Park and an expanse of the city. Lawns, trees, paths, bridges, ponds, and other landscape features stretch out as far as the eye can see. The buildings surrounding the park make for a fascinating tableau. I can hardly stop staring in amazement.

"Sweetie, it's almost one." said Frank. "How about we get some lunch and then take you shopping?"

"I'm good with that," I said. "Let's not eat any place too fancy. I don't think I am dressed for it." I still feel out of place amidst all this luxury. I stopped in the bathroom in our suite. I bet it takes up more floor space than my family's entire three-bedroom home. It left me feeling like an imposter. Franklin Ramsey might belong here among all the trappings of the rich and famous, but I sure do not.

We left the Plaza and headed around the corner and down the street to Nathan's Famous Hot Dogs. "Will this work for you?" asked Frank.

"Perfect," I said and we went in. I thought it was a hot dog stand, but it was an entire sit down restaurant. The selection of hot dogs was probably twice the number in both Chilly Dawgs and Grandpa's Grinder put together! Who knew you could make 38 varieties of hot dogs? Plus they have hamburgers, chicken sandwiches, and even a few salads. Frank and I went with my old favorite – a chili dog and fries with a chocolate shake.

"So, do you do this often?" I asked Frank.

"Yale is only an hour from New York by train so my friends and I come in often. My Dad wants me to feel comfortable circulating in the highest levels of business and society, so he gave me the credit card and allowance. Many of my college chums have fathers on Wall Street or who are CEOs of big companies headquartered in New York. Dad says it's good for me to hang out with them. It may bring useful business connections now and it certainly will pay off in the future. Sometimes we stay with someone's family who lives here in town. Other times we crash at the Plaza. It's the place to see important people and it's the place to be seen."

I wonder what Frank's influential friends would think if they saw him slumming with a girl like me. 'Waitress from Coconut Willie's does NYC.'

"Ready to go shopping?" asked Frank. We left the restaurant and caught a cab and headed south on Fifth Avenue. We went to Macy's, Bloomingdales, Saks Fifth Avenue and finally Tiffany's where Frank bought me jewelry to go with each of the outfits he selected. When we arrived back at the Plaza, we were loaded with bags and boxes. My new wardrobe includes sexy underwear, a cocktail dress, formal gown, tailored pant suit, slacks, four pairs of new shoes, stockings, tops, and jewelry from Tiffany's. Frank bought me a matching pair of leather suitcases to hold the new wardrobe.

Back in the hotel, we went up to our suite with all the bundles. Frank said, "I'd like to see you try something on. How about this formal gown?"

"Sure," I said.

He came over, "I'd like to see you in all new finery – from the skin up. A totally new you. Can I help you undress?" I peeled up my old sweater while Frank unhooked my belt. He slid his fingers inside my jeans and slowly pushed them off my hips, down my legs, and onto the floor. He brought me into his warm embrace and we kissed. While I was enjoying his exploring tongue in my mouth, Frank slid his hands from my back up to my bra and unhooked it. I stepped back and dropped it on the floor while Frank cupped my breasts in his large warm hands. He quickly shed his own clothes. As we kissed and explored each other I discovered my panties were gone. Frank led me into the bedroom and peeled back the covers on the bed. "The sheets are 800-thread count Egyptian cotton," he whispered.

I had no idea what he was talking about and I didn't care. I was so turned on; I just wanted to get him between my legs. We crawled into the silky nest of Egyptian cotton and pulled up the covers. An hour later, when we were both sated, we crawled out and took a quick shower together. Frank resumed the process of dressing me in the beautiful garments he purchased for me. I don't know if it was the excellent sex, or the fine quality clothing, but by the time we were done, I did feel like a queen.

The entire weekend was a blur. Frank treated me like royalty. He took me dinner at the Four Seasons, the ultimate in luxury dining. We took long carriage rides in Central Park, enjoyed breakfast in bed, explored views of the city from the Empire State Building. We caught the Rockettes at Radio City Music Hall, and saw *Sweet Charity* on Broadway. We walked in the park and ate lunch at Tavern on the Green.

Between these delightful outings, Frank and I retreated to our cozy love nest in the suite at the Plaza and had luscious sex for hours at a time. Frank has an unbelievable appetite for physical pleasure and inexhaustible stamina. When we grew tired from love making, he ordered room service and we lounged around our suite in the hotel's big fluffy white bathrobes.

After our first long bout of love making, Franklin invited me into the bathroom. "Have you ever tried snorting coke?"

"No," was my hesitant but honest, reply.

"It's so easy. You'll like it." He pulled a flat silver canister out of a pocket and opened it to unfold a white plastic baggie. Carefully, Frank laid out two piles of white powder on the bathroom counter and used a razor blade to shift them into clean lines. He produced a cut down plastic drinking straw, leaned over and inserted the straw up one nostril. Pinching the other nostril closed with an index finger, Frank snorted the line of coke into his nose.

"Ahh, that's great! Here, now you try it," he said handing me the straw and stepping out of the way so I could lean over the counter. I sucked in the remaining line of powder and almost immediately felt a rush. It was like my whole body and mind was juiced with energy and enthusiasm and warmth. It made me happy and chatty. Horny too. We headed to bed. In the morning, my nose was bleeding, my head hurt, and I felt nauseous. But right at that moment with Franklin Agnew Ramsey, IV I was flying.

That pretty much describes our weekend. A bit of shopping and touring, a lot of boffing each other's brains out, and then some room service or a snort of coke. Once we were refreshed, we hopped back in the sack for more gratification. When we grew tired of bed, we had sex on the sofa in the living room, on the floor in the bedroom, in the shower while standing up, and in the dining alcove on top of the mahogany breakfast table. The entire weekend was a blur of luxury, new experiences, and steamy sex.

By ten Sunday morning we packed and I, for one, was grateful to climb into the MG and be able to keep my panties on for a few minutes. I needed a rest! Frank looked as fresh as can be when we headed away from New York driving south towards Carlisle College. As the car throbbed down the highway, I was happy for a chance to lean back in the seat, close my eyes, and rest.

The most memorable part of the weekend was yet to happen, although I could not have imagined it as we tooled along the PA Turnpike that afternoon. When we got to campus, Frank smoothly pulled the car up in front of Allison Hall and jumped out to open my door. Ever the gentleman. After handing me out of the MG, he pulled out my two new suitcases of clothes placing them gently on the curb.

"When will I see you again?" I asked as he embraced me and kissed me on the front steps.

"You won't. Consider this one and done. I've got to get back to Yale and my life and you have to get on with your life. It was a great weekend, but it was just a fling. I'm sure we will not see each other again." With that, Frank Ramsey walked around, jumped the MG, and roared off.

19

"A rich man is nothing but a poor man with money."

~ W. C. Fields

Jack Flynn   February, 1967

"Unbelievable!" was all I could say. I was enjoying Koffee Klatch with Nikki, Gary, and Randi on a cold February day. Randi had been updating us on the aftermath of Faith and Frank Ramsey.

"I was amazed at how easily Legs threw over Skeeter when Ramsey gave her the 'come hither.' I tried to warn her to tread carefully when Ramsey offered to carry her off to NY. I mean," added Randi, "how long had she known him? Two hours! The jerk offers to take her to New York City, stay in the most expensive hotel in town, shop high end fashion stores and dine at the Four Seasons. I suppose its possible Ramsey fell hopelessly in love with her standing in Lane Center gazing at her incredibly beautiful face and determined then and there to win her as his bride…"

"However," interjected Nikki, "given that he is the top shit from a family of known shits and whose little brother is the least liked shit on campus…how likely is that?"

"The logical conclusion is the jerk was just looking at her from the neck down, and simply wanted to take her away for the weekend to boff her brains out." I ventured. "If it was me, I'd have to be content with the Howard Johnsons in beautiful downtown Carlisle. Not exotic, but more within my price range."

"And," said Nikki with a smile, "if you'd offered me or Randi or any other half witted female such a proposition, we would have been pretty sure you were not inviting us to indulge in the HoJo hot fudge sundae while you admired our dimples."

"You got that right!" said Randi with a smile.

"Amen from me, too," said Gary looking at Nikki with a lecherous grin. We all laughed at him.

Randi continued, "When Ramsey dumped Faith off at the curb, she was stunned. She broke down, collapsed on the steps, bawling hysterically. I had to get our RA, Gail Clarkson, to come out and help me collect her. We got her back to our room, but she was like Cinderella after her coach turned into a pumpkin. Hopeless. Broken hearted. Legs was such a mess, Gail finally took her to the nurse to get meds to calm her down. Faith simply could not believe that spending all that money was not a pledge of undying love from Ramsey."

"Poor dear," commented Nikki, "She obviously doesn't know anything about love if she thinks material things are connected to love."

Randi went on, "It's more than ignorance. Faith has had so little love at home and has suffered such material deprivation, it sets her up for failure. She was easily snookered by that skunk. When she came back to school from Thanksgiving with the Stetsons she was blown away by his family. How warm, loving, accepting, and supportive they are. But somehow, she concluded material prosperity is what makes them that way. So, to her thinking, the wealthier the family, the more loving and accepting."

"You've got to be kidding!" blurted Gary. "What's money got to do with it? I bet I could make a pretty good case for just the opposite. The more money, the worse the people. I honestly think money corrupts people and relationships."

"I can see what you mean," said Randi, "but not always. I know a few people who are well off and who are kind and considerate to others. Although, I admit they are few and far between. When Legs came back from Stetsons', I explained that it's character, not money which creates people like Skeeter's family. And there's no connection between character and wealth. But I don't think she heard what I was saying."

Gary jumped in. "That's the heart of the issue, Randi! I've grown up with money. My family and their friends are wealthy and rotten to the core, just like Ramsey. But my Lynch Grands are wealthy. Yet they are kind and caring to everyone they meet. OK, they are still squares, but they are kind squares. If you took away all their money, made them live in a little bungalow, on a fixed pension, wearing clothes from a thrift store, I'll bet you wouldn't be able to see any difference in how they treat others. No matter how poor you made them, they would still be people of character. That's what I want to be like. Character has nothing to do with having money. People who don't have two nickels to click together have outstanding character. Lots of rich people, like Ramsey, have filthy souls – they are totally devoid of character."

"I think that's what hurt Faith," said Randi. "She realized Franklin bought her just like you would buy a hooker. Instead of paying a prostitute, he paid for lodging, her clothes, and her meals. But it was the same thing. She sold her body and her soul to a creep who just wanted a cheap ball. She thought it was love with her white knight who would carry her off to a better future. Instead he just wanted to get laid in a way befitting his rank and social class. She's ashamed she could be so stupid and foolish."

"Unbelievable!" I repeated, although it seemed a bit superfluous in light of the facts.

"What puzzles me," said Gary, "is why she and Skeeter are back together? After that stunt?"

"Yes," I agreed. "I find that hard to believe. Why would Skeeter take her back after she dumped him for a rich dirt bag who just wanted to get into her knickers? I heard he's taking her to Harrisburg for a special Valentine's dinner. Why would he do that? He acts like nothing ever happened."

"Hmmm…" said Nikki. "I don't actually know. What would make you forgive someone?"

Somehow, Nikki always finds a way to ask the tough, penetrating question. After I thinking for a bit I said, "Forgiveness is tough. We don't practice it much in my family. It's one of those things the priest talks about in church, but we don't do. Sure, I want God to forgive my sins. But in my family, the reality is we are better at holding grudges than we are at forgiving. If I was Skeeter, I'd have trouble forgiving someone who dumped me for another guy simply because his family has more money than mine. So what… she loves my family's money? I thought she loved me?"

Randi added, "What I hear you saying is it's not the betrayal that bothers you, it's being loved for your family's assets instead of for who you are as a person?"

"That's it exactly. What if a girl wanted to be with me because she loved ice cream and figured she could get a lot from the Flynn Family Restaurant? If she valued me for my family, that would bother me. I want to be known, accepted, and loved for myself."

"That's just what Snow said to me before she went missing," Nikki injected. "She wants to be loved for who she is not because she fulfilled someone else's expectations."

"Huh?" was my only reply. "That's a profound thought. Does anyone know me and love me for the real unvarnished me; just the way I am? Like, if I was an orphan with no family and money, with just my charming personality, would you still love me Nikki?"

"Yes, dear," Nikki replied. "Although I actually love you for your lack of fashion sense. If only you could play the banjo, you would be completely irresistible." That got a good laugh from the Klatch.

Rob and I made plans to go ice fishing the following Saturday. We invited Nikki and Doug to join us on the expedition for trout up to Whipple Dam State Park. Friday night the four of us walked into TMO to buy live bait and to have a chat with Father X. At TMO, we bought three dozen Black Nosed Dace minnows. They went into the bait bucket which we parked in the snow by X's door. Inside his cabin, Father X was sitting by his wood stove, playing checkers with a tall, lean African American. Our host introduced us, "Friends, this is my comrade in arms, Theo Broderick."

"Wait, not the Dr. Broderick who teaches at the college?" I inquired. "We've heard about you."

"Guilty as charged," announced Broderick. "I teach Old Testament and New Testament survey courses as an adjunct. Please call me Brody, it's what my friends call me. On campus or in class you should still call me Doctor or Professor. Don't want to shake up the establishment more than I have already."

"Dr. Broderick is a renowned Biblical scholar." Father X commented. "He was on the faculty at the Evangelical Lutheran Biblical Seminary in Lancaster, PA for several decades."

Doug spoke up, "Forgive my ironic sense of humor, but you two are an unlikely looking pair."

All eyes turned on Doug and he began to squirm. Theo and Father X burst into guffaws of laughter. "What, I'm black and he's white?" asked Brody, "Or the fact that he's a Roman Catholic priest and I'm a defrocked Evangelical Lutheran? Or is it that Father X has no offspring and I have six children?"

"Uhh, no. Actually, I was thinking about how you are so tall and lean and the good Father is…"

"Built like an oversized bowling ball, is that what you are implying, you young scamp?" growled the Father. Then we broke into relaxed laughter. Father passed around cookies and coffee.

"Father X," I began, "you know I was raised Roman Catholic?"

"Yes Jack, I do. I can still see our influence in your wardrobe." replied the Father. That got a chuckle out of everyone. "But forgive me; you were probably going to make a point."

"I was, thank you. Our friend Bunny Washington is taking New Testament Survey. He keeps telling us Christianity and Jesus are different. I don't get it? Isn't Christianity Jesus' religion, the one he came to start? Isn't he the first and foremost Christian? And Christianity the faith Jesus taught people to follow? I admit I don't attend mass as often as I should, and my family hasn't been too involved in church, but that's what I think the priests are teaching. Could you or Brody clarify this for me?"

"For me too," chimed in the rest of our crew.

Xavier looked at Dr. Broderick and smiled. "Care to take the first swing at this pitch?"

"Delighted, I'm sure," replied Brody. "Let me ask, have you ever read the Bible, the New Testament?"

The four of us looked at each other and embarrassment spread on our faces. "Not me."

"Not me."

"Nope" and a negative shake of the head, summed up our answers to the question.

"Well, you should," encouraged Brody, "especially the New Testament. Focus on the four Gospels - the history of Jesus' life and teachings. The Gospels of Matthew, Mark, Luke, and John. Before you decide what you believe about God, faith, and life, you should read what Jesus has to say for himself."

The Father interjected, "I think you'll find what Jesus has to say is dramatically different from what religious people have been telling you, even if they are Roman Catholic priests, Jack. Remember last fall I told you to keep your eyes open and to

137

take the time to think critically about what you decide to believe or not?" Xavier continued.

"Yes," I responded, "You said different religions make contradictory claims and we should be prepared to think for ourselves before we decide what to believe. You also demonstrated the old saw that all religions lead to God is provably false."

Father X brightened. "In the same way, you should read what Jesus says about himself and what he did here on earth, rather than simply trust others' accounts about what Jesus is up to. Jesus was quite the radical. History shows he had more in common with hippie freak folks than with the establishment."

"In fact," Brody added, "Jesus was deeply opposed to religious leaders and to the political establishment. Jesus says he came to call people into a living personal relationship with himself, not to introduce a religion, like Christianity. 'Christian' does not appear in the Gospels and it only appears twice in the New Testament. When it's used, it was a slur hurled at followers of Jesus, like Wop or Spic!"

"Jesus made some unusual claims about himself in the Gospels, claims no other religious founder or leader has made in the history of the world," added Father X. "Don't take my word for it – check it out yourself. As CS Lewis once said: 'Jesus' claims about himself proved he was either who he claimed to be, the one and only path to God, or he was a raving lunatic and a pathological liar.' The nature of his claims, says Lewis, are such they simply cannot be nice comments made by a human teacher of morality. You owe it to yourself to check out what Jesus said about himself and see what you think."

"OK" said Doug, "I'm willing to read what Jesus said about himself. I guess I never realized I could check it out for myself."

Brody took up the conversation. "Just as Father X told you last fall, you have to do your own thinking and your own research if you want to discover what life is all about and if there is a God, who he is. That's what I try to teach my New Testament classes. The Bible says if you seek God, he will find you! You can find the truth on your own. Study Jesus' life and words and decide for yourself."

"This makes sense," said Doug. "If each religion makes up rules, and can reinvent history at will, it would explain why my family's faith conflicts could never get sorted. It never occurred to me to go to the source and do my own homework. I'm willing to accept the challenge. To read Jesus' own words then decide what I think. But that's a lot of material. Could you give us a synopsis before we start?"

"A short overview," said Dr. Brody: "Jesus calls us into a relationship with himself. He says the way we get to know God is by getting to know Jesus."

"That's right," added Xavier. "It's simple. Not easy, but simple. If God wanted to be in relationship with us, why would he make it complex – like various religions do? If he really wanted to reconnect, he would make it simple. As he has. In Jesus."

Nikki got up and said, "Wow, that's a lot to think about. But I'm glad we can investigate for ourselves. I'm with Doug. I'm ready to accept the challenge and check out Jesus. I like to study, to learn, and to ask questions. Can we come back and talk more, once we've read the Gospels?"

"You bet," said Father. "Come back any time you want. Ask questions; challenge my thinking, or Brody's. God loves it when people engage in doubt and questions and research and debate."

With that, we retrieved our minnows from the snow bank and walked back to campus.

20

"Mistakes are the portals of discovery."
~ *James Joyce*

Nikki Clausen   Spring, 1967

The first week back after spring break in late March was ugly. It was cold, wet, and gray with low hanging clouds and intermittent rain. All we could do was to stew in our dull gray winter landscape and hope for spring to come soon.

Two weeks later I was astonished by the difference fourteen days can make. Amazing! By early April, the college was in the midst of a radical transformation. Fields of bright yellow daffodils filled the flower beds. The sidewalk borders burst with brilliant crocus in multiple shades. Hugh blooms of yellow forsythia were mounded around campus. Brilliant beds of red and yellow tulips burst into blossom beneath masses of silvery gray pussy willows. Azaleas, irises, pansies, and violets joined this spring extravaganza. The trees on campus were covered with a profusion of pale green baby leaves, painting a universal picture of hope and wonder. It's hard not to be exuberant and happy in the face of such optimistic displays of nature.

As I slid into Koffee Klatch that morning, I was high from my walk through the intoxicants of spring. That didn't last long. Surrounded by a half dozen kids, Faith was collapsed at the table, bawling into her handkerchief. I leaned over and asked Linda Pence, "Now what's wrong?"

Linda looked at me and said, "You haven't heard?"

"No, what? Heard what?"

"Skeeter flunked his gym class in badminton last trimester."

"Get out! Who cares?" How can you flunk badminton? Why cry – he can just retake it this term."

"Geez, Nikki, are you living on a different planet?" Linda replied. "Skeeter skipped gym class last term because he was bored playing badminton. You're allowed 6 absences. He lost count and took 7. Automatic F. Flunked the class and he gets 1 credit less for winter term. He just received a letter from the Draft Board notifying him he's lost his draft deferment and he has to report to the Army. They're going to draft Skeeter and send him to Vietnam!"

"Holy Shit!" was all I could say. I was stunned into shock. Every night on the news we heard how the Vietnam War was heating up. The TV says we are whomping the gooks and piling up bodies all over the place. Everyone knows this is just bullshit propaganda by the government to make the public feel like we are "winning" the war. Who cares about the gook body count? If your boy is shipped home in a box, the fake statistics of victory are not going to make you feel any better. At this point, it was a given that if you were unlucky enough to be drafted, it could prove to be a death sentence.

Gary said, "I'm amazed how calm Skeeter is. He knows he screwed up and was irresponsible. He doesn't blame Mr. Cash, the instructor. He just did his job. Skeet is the one who forgot Big Brother is watching and that he might lose his deferment if he missed a credit on his transcript. Skeeter says it's no one's fault but his own. He seems resigned to whatever comes next."

"Do we know what comes next?" Black Jack Flynn asked.

Rob ventured, "He has a date to report to the draft induction center. He takes a physical and a mental test. If Skeeter flunks either, he'll be classified 4-F: not fit for service, and he won't have to go. If he passes, they give him a week to get his affairs in order and then off to boot camp. When my brother Ted went into the Marines, he spent ten weeks in boot camp, then four weeks in advanced training. He had a week's leave then was shipped to Vietnam. A week after he landed in Nam, Ted was dead."

The table subsided into stony silence, except for Faith's sobbing.

"It's an incredibly dangerous place," offered Frenchie. "If you're career military or a volunteer, you get a year of training before they ship you to Nam. I got that plus a year of stateside duty before I was sent there. Draftees are young and green. Most are young, immature, and foolish. They get almost no training and then are sent to the front lines. They get chewed up and spit out before any of them can figure out what's going on. They're merely cannon fodder. Doomed before they get off the plane."

After we digested Frenchie's comments, Jack spoke up. "Well, he's not drafted yet. Let's not despair. I know some guys at Harvard SDS, you know, Students for a Democratic Society. I'll call them and see what can be done. Maybe we can do a protest like Harvard did. Get Skeeter's grade changed." Jack's idea was met with wide spread approval and we set a time and place to hold a campus organizing event after Jack found out what our alternatives might be.

Ten days later, Skeeter showed up for Koffee Klatch. "Hey everybody, I really appreciate your concern and support. Just wanted to let you know what's up. Last Tuesday, I had to report to the Montgomery County Draft Board office in Norristown. That was scary shit, man. I had no idea what was going on or if I'd ever see my family again. They don't tell you anything – just 'Get on the bus.'"

"It was typical Army crap. You pass all your tests before you take them. The mental test was so challenging a chimpanzee could have aced it. Even retards make the mental grade. I guess if you are just going to send these fools out to get shot up by gooks, what does it matter how smart they are?

"Not to give the impression you are a retarded chimpanzee," inquired Andy, "but did you pass?"

"Yup, with flying colors. Our nation's leaders have determined I am fit as a fiddle, or at least fit enough to serve Uncle Sam. I'm seriously thinking about enlisting for a four-year tour of duty."

"What?" exclaimed Rob. "Are you nuts? Why would you double your exposure to a war zone?"

"Cool your jets, it's not as crazy as it sounds. If I get drafted, I go in as a grunt. Ten weeks of boot camp, then I ship out to the front lines of a nasty shooting war. If I enlist, I can choose the area I work in. I want to join the Corps of Engineers. I'll get a lot more training, and I'll learn how to build bridges. I have 95% of a college degree in engineering, so I think they'll take me. The more training I get, the less time I'll spend getting shot at. Bridge building happens behind the front lines – to move supplies up to advanced combat troops. A much less dangerous place to serve. When I get out, I'll have a head start on a career in civil engineering. That's what I really want, to build bridges."

"What Skeeter is saying, makes sense, in a crazy sort of way, which is how the Army does things," suggested Frenchie. "Crazy, but maybe safer in the long run. They tend to take better care of troops they have made more of an investment in, by way of training. The bridge guys are not going to be running through the jungle chasing gooks and dodging land mines."

A few days latter, a small group lingered after Koffee Klatch. Jack had called his friends in Harvard SDS. Harvard and other schools had succeeded in getting their campus leaders to change course with sit- ins and protests. We thought, 'Why not Carlisle College?' By the time we finished planning we had an anti-war protest plan we hoped would get Skeeter's F turned to a D- and reinstate his deferment. We dressed it up with a bunch of other demands - no military recruiters, no funding for weapons research, no limits on freedom of speech by faculty or students, and permission for SDS to set up a campus chapter. But the real goal of the protest was to free Skeeter from the clutches of the Army. I had serious doubts this crazy idea would work, but you don't know if you don't try.

All weekend, Faith, Jack, Arty and others scuttled around campus to drumming up support for the protest. Not everyone was on board. Billy refused to get involved. "I wouldn't want to oppose the government or the administration. That's not right." But everyone else gladly pitched in to help.

Monday morning at dawn, the central administrative building was assaulted by the first wave of protesters. Students crept into Old West, hung protest banners from the second floor windows, and chained all the doors closed. Dr. Long deposited the lilac purple Cadillac hearse across the sidewalk blocking the steps to the front doors. Student protesters took up position sitting in front of the doors. A loudspeaker, mounted on the roof rack of the Caddy, blared out musical anthems in support of the revolution. Buffalo Springfield, Joan Baez, Peter, Paul, and Mary, Bob Dylan, and protest numbers like *Eve of Destruction* filled the early morning air as spring sunshine swept the scene.

When staff began to arrive their reactions were subdued, as you would expect in a mellow place like Carlisle. They stood around watching the protesters and staring with amusement. When Dr. Shockley, the college President, arrived, he asked to speak to the leaders. Jack, Gary and Dr. Long presented a written list of demands included Skeeter's grade adjustment. Shockley conferred with Dean Benchoff and simply called in the campus cops (all two of them) to keep an eye on things.

By the time Linda and Delilah showed up with dozens of handmade protest signs, the administrators had vanished. Signs blossomed throughout the growing crowd of students. "Free Speech!" "Draft Beer, Not Boys!" "Hell No, We Won't Go!" "Bring Our Boys Home!" and my favorite, "Make Love Not War!" It was like a picnic. Or a pep rally for the convictions of our generation. By noon several hundred students were blocking Old West and more were hanging around grooving on the freaky holiday scene which had descended on campus. Kids played football and tossed Frisbees in the sunshine. Others lay out sunbathing or reading. Benchoff came by to announce classes had been canceled for the day.

Tuesday morning we woke up groggy and wrinkled after spending the night sleeping on the steps, the floor and the sidewalk. At six forty five am, Dr. Long arrived in the hearse with gallons of coffee, orange juice, sticky buns, and other breakfast foods. He had Percy and Venus, the Great Danes, with him. Long let them out and they ran all over the lawn, and around the buildings. They paused to copulate in public periodically. The next day the Harrisburg paper ran a front page photo of sleep bedraggled students on the front steps of Old West watching the dogs go at it. Ahh, college life!

By mid- morning, over 400 students were sprawled across Old West. Other students had taken over Frost Hall and Reed Hall, two nearby classroom buildings. Arty Swoboda led the crowd in anti-war chants using an electronic bull horn. "One, Two, Three, Four, We don't want your fucking war!" "Bring Our Boys Home!" "Hell No, We Won't Go!" and Arty's favorite, "Fuckin' A, We Won't Go Away!" Around the fringe of the crowds, several local rock bands played protest songs and added to the party atmosphere. As on the previous day, everything was calm and mellow. Then reinforcements rolled in.

Mid morning three buses pulled up and disgorged 160 students from Penn State to join our protest. The SDS chapter at University Park had learned of our protest and came down to assist. The leaders of this unruly mob of students passed out individual signs and got new banners flying from the windows of the three buildings. Their loudspeaker soon got the crowd stirred up. Shouts of "Hey, LBJ! How many kids have you killed today?" echoed across campus. The mood began to turn ugly. By noon, over 800 young adults were actively participating in the protest.

Behind the scenes, this latest development concerned Dr. Shockley enough that he called the Governor and asked for National Guard support. Having seen what happened at Berkley and other campuses, it's hard to blame him. Several hours later dark green buses pulled up and let off several hundred National Guard troops dressed in military fatigues. Armed with military M-16 carbines held across the chest at the ready for action, the soldiers marched onto campus with grim determination. They set up about a hundred yards from the protest in a half circle. Compared to the surging masses of protestors and the sea of spectators, now numbering several thousand, the troops looked puny and insignificant.

As the Guard settled in, a scuffle broke out on the front steps. Dr. Long and his druggie disciples were going through the crowd handing out stones and bricks. When Frenchie realized what was going on, he and some guys from Adams raced into the crowd to retrieve the missiles. "No violence! Get rid of those stones!" Frenchie shouted. "This is a peaceful protest, you idiots. We want peace not war."

Unfortunately, a numbskull named Fatty Deffenbacher, picked up half a brick and hurled it straight out from behind the leaders on the Old West steps. The dull red projectile rose straight and high and looked like it might land smack on the hood of Deputy Dawg's lime green Chevy Impala. The Dawg had parked in a prominent position in front to make sure he got his fair share of fame and glory. As fate would have it, the soaring brick curved down and ricocheted off a lamppost. The block took a wicked hook to the left and sailed over the Impala to whack Deputy Dawg smack in the middle of his ugly forehead. The errant ricochet popped the Deputy, pressing a vertical dent across his chubby forehead. He went down in a heap. A hush immediately fell over the crowd.

In an instant, this put an end to our campus protest. Half of a brick and the war was over. Deputy Dawg was only knocked out, but an ambulance came and took him to the hospital. Almost as soon as the brick thunked into flesh, our activists started to drift away, either becoming spectators at a distance, or fading off the field of battle altogether. These students had come for a peaceful protest. At the first sign of violence, they vanished.

Chief Starrett arrested Fatty, put him in the cruiser and drove him downtown. The local cops booked him for felonious assault on a police officer and locked him up. In less than an hour, the buildings were vacated, and the students gone. The Penn State SDS contingent loaded up and headed home. The National Guard was gone. Nothing but litter and bottles remained to mark our experiment in civil protest.

Spring term came to a close with final exams during the third week of May. A few of us decided to drive up to Rockwell State Forest the Saturday before finals and hike up to Big Bear Mountain Lake. Our goal was to hike in early, bring a lunch and dinner, and have an end of the year campfire to celebrate the conclusion of our freshman year.

We got to the trailhead at ten am, packed our gear and headed up the trail. Rob offered the first topic of conversation. "So what did you think of our campus protest?"

Jack laughed, "OK, perhaps the whole thing was a bit lame. We're not Harvard, or Berkley, or some big school in a big city. Maybe the college and town are too small for effective protests."

"Well, our motives were not entirely pure," I added. "If Doc Shockley had offered to fix Skeeter's grade, we all would have gone to the Dining Hall for a milkshake and called it a day."

Rob laughed, "It's hard to get the world to join the revolution because our friend was dumb enough to skip badminton class seven times."

Gary added, "It didn't end too badly. No one got killed anyway. I was a little worried after the SDS and the National Guard showed up that things were about to get dicey. Poor Fatty has his butt in a sling. He's looking at a felony assault charge and expulsion from college. But I hear he is likely to get probation for braining Deputy Dawg. It was just bad luck the brick ended up where it did."

Rob speculated, "Wonder if we'll ever see Dr. Long again? I heard he got the heave ho by the Faculty Senate and the Administration for corrupting the morals of our student body. Although, I am not sure that's fair. He just hitched his wagon to our revolution and got the axe for his poor judgment in associating with us. He didn't lead us to bad decisions as much as he came along with us for the ride."

Faith added, "If you ask me, they were looking for an excuse to kick him out. They hated his influence on students out at his country house. With the free drugs and everything. Worse, I know they hated him letting the Percy and Venus do the wild thing in public. That really riled them!

"Maybe Dr. Long wanted to get kicked out." said Rob. "Perhaps he kept pushing their buttons until they fired him so he could add to his back story that he was martyred by the powers that be."

"Good point," said Jack. "I always thought he was sick of teaching anyway."

The six of us kept up a steady pace as we wove through the tall pines and eased into the alpine terrain at the top. Following the trail through boulders covered in lichens and interspersed with short stubby firs, we arrived on the shores of the lake. The sight was breath taking. Big Bear Mountain Lake is a crystalline body of water resting on one of the steep ridges of the Tuscarora Mountain chain. It is not high enough to be above tree line, but it has many of the attributes of an alpine meadow.

Jack and Rob set up a campsite on the shoreline where there was sunlight and shade from the big pines by the pond. Each of us crafted a comfortable seat from drift wood and settled in to relax. Jack and Rob had little telescoping fly rods with them and were soon engaged in catching and releasing native brook trout on hand tied flies. I curled up to read a book and Gary and Doug took Faith off on a nature walk.

After a nice lunch of TAB, hoagies and Mrs. Gibble's Potato Chips, I settled in for a nap. "You know," I commented, "This term has been exhausting. I'm so emotionally wrung out from Skeeter's crisis and the campus sit-in and everything." I curled up to sleep in the shade.

Faith agreed, "Amen to that sister. I feel like I've gone through the wringer. I need a little normal in my life. Skeeter seems to be coping well. He writes almost every week. I think he's glad to be headed towards bridge building even if it means he has to go through the service. He seems to be able to take a long-term view, which I'm not very good at."

After naptime, I borrowed a fishing rig from the boys and tried my hand at catching brookies. The trout were eager to cooperate but it was hot standing in the bright sunshine. I shucked my sneakers and sox and went wading in hopes of cooling off a little. The boys worked at collecting firewood for our evening bonfire. "How hot do you think it is?" I asked. "It's got to be 80 degrees. I'm roasting! Anyone want to go swimming? The water feels really nice."

The others looked at me in wonder. "You brought a swimming suit?" asked Rob.

"No, did you?"

"No."

"I was planning on swimming in my birthday suit." I commented. That made everyone laugh.

"I will, if you will!" said Gary.

I stood up, walked down to the shore. Turning my back to the group, I reached down, peeled up my tank top and hung it on a shore side bush. Off came my bra and, in one smooth swish, my panties and cutoffs slid down my legs joining the wardrobe on the bush. I stretched up for the sky, shook my hair in the breeze, and with a whoop, threw myself into the lake.

Gary gave a yell, "Wahoo!" He tore off his clothes and ran full speed towards the shore, then hurled himself into the water. In no time at all, the six of us were in the buff and enjoying the cool clear water of the pond. We laughed and screamed and cavorted like little kids, swimming, and splashing, and playing games. Many people misunderstand the joy of skinny dipping. It is not a sexual thing but it's all about being nude. It is a sensual experience. The idea of being in nothing but your own skin, with the cool, clear water sluicing over your body is exhilarating. To be free of all constraints. To live without falsehood or pretense. We swam, we laughed, we splashed, and giggled like children.

When we grew tired of swimming, we perched on the rocks in the sun until we were dry and then pulled on our clothes again. It's not like we were running a nudist colony, you know. The rest of the afternoon we spent taking little hikes of exploration, fly fishing, reading or napping. Just sitting by the lake breathing in the air and the scenery was enough to revive my spirits.

After dinner, Jack and Rob built a big bonfire and we moved our home-made camp chairs so we could sit around the fire and enjoy the flames. Gary and Doug helped build a huge pile of firewood so it wouldn't run low. Faith and I got out the marshmallows and carved long green sticks for roasting. It was a great end note to our first year at college. New adventures, the fellowship of good friends, a pristine natural setting, mesmerizing firelight, and the symphony of night noises coming from the forest.

"What plans do you have for the summer?" I asked.

"I'm going to Long Island for the summer." Gary ventured. "Plan to work as a lifeguard at a local pool and play a lot of ice hockey in my free time. How about you, Legs?"

Faith laughed, "How kind of you to ask. My parents never did. I've decided to stay here for the summer. I've been waitressing at Grandpa's Grinder for a few shifts a week. The owner, Larry Green, offered me a full-time job for the summer. Father X has a widow friend with a room for rent near the Grinder, so that's where

I'll live. Back on St Simons, I'd be waiting tables at Coconut Willies. This saves the long drive and having to live with my crazy parents."

Doug said, "No big surprise. I'm going to spend the summer at Johnny's Hot Dogs in Pequest, New Jersey. If you stop in, I'll give you a free frosted mug of root beer."

Jack laughed long and hard. "I too will be working the family restaurant. But this year, I want to. My goal for the summer is to save up enough money to buy something so cool, so over the top, so far out, that none of you will recognize me when I return next fall."

"Do you think he's going to buy new clothes?" I asked. "Maybe a red checked cowboy shirt? Canary yellow polo shirt?" We all had a good laugh. "I'm going home to State College," I said. "Frankly, I need to indulge in Happy Valley fishing and hiking. I have so many issues I've been too damn busy to think out. I think best on a trout stream or on a trail. How about you Rob? Do you have plans?"

"Good question. I've thought a lot about how to use my summer. Like you, I'm a pretty reflective thinker. I need some time and space to figure out what I'm even trying to think about. I don't want to go home. It's just too toxic. I'll stop in and see my little sister Molly for a couple days, but I think I'm going to travel out west. Stand out on Rt. 202, stick out my thumb and see where the road leads me. I need space. I'd like to see some new places and get some room to think."

"Wow! That's cool." I added. "I should think about doing that some summer. Maybe visit National Parks. I've always wanted to see the Grand Canyon and Yellowstone."

We sat and talked until late into the night. The next day was Sunday and our classes were over for the semester. When our chatter ran out and the fire died down, we put out the flames and headed back down. None of us got into bed much before two am but it was a day we will remember for years to come. A day which captured all the sweet essence of that first year at Carlisle.

Year Two

21

"It's not that I've got fears of settling down,
I just can't stop leaving town..."
~ Allison Krauss

Rob Bachmann   August, 1967

I spent the summer of 1967 hitchhiking out to the West Coast. By the time I arrived back at Carlisle for fall term of my sophomore year, I felt like I had gone off to spend the summer on Saturn, or some other distant planet. It was all so far out! The places, the people, the happenings...It's what I imagine tripping on LSD is like. I saw the most amazing sights, had total out of body experiences, met fascinating people, without any ability to discern illusion from reality. I was completely blown away!

After I got settled in my dorm, I drifted over to Lane Student Center to see who was around. Nikki spotted me across the Quad and let out a screech. "Robbie!" she squealed and ran across the lawn with her black hair flying and a grin spreading from ear to ear.

"Nikki!" I hollered back at her. She was dressed in a blue and white Penn State football jersey and a pair of cut-off jeans. Nikki was barefoot as she raced across the grass yelling and leaped at me throwing herself into my arms. We hugged enthusiastically for several minutes before Nikki whispered in my ear, "Hey, Bub, you do know that's my ass you're caressing, right?"

"Oops," I replied. "Sorry. Just trying to be supportive." She laughed, and I thought to myself...a*nd a mighty fine ass it is too.* If she were available, I could see myself making a play for this wild woman. Nikki kept smothering my face with kisses. "Wow," I said. "This is the best welcome I've ever had. Even my dog isn't this happy to see me when I come home. Thanks, Nik."

"I guess I missed you. Honestly, I missed everybody this summer, but I missed you too. You are a prince of a fellow, I don't care what they say in Doylestown."

"Long, lonely summer?" I asked.

"You got that right. I thought about so many things and I wanted to talk to someone about what I was wondering, but the only soul I could share with was Willy, my old broken down Bassett hound. He never has much to say, but he is a great listener. One out of two ain't bad."

"Likewise, my summer was crazy. It's going to take me a while to process everything. I think I did too much doing and not enough reflecting. Did you hear from Gary?"

"Yes, but I think he is more into doing than reflecting. He's reluctant to wander around in philosophic woulda, coulda, shouldas. More physical, less the existential writer. Being apart for the summer helped me learn a lot of new stuff about both of us. We are really different. I don't think that's bad, but in many ways we're opposites. I need to wonder and think and blue sky a lot – perhaps that's why I like Mother Nature so much. The outdoors gives me room to ruminate. Gary is a doer – a man of action. He wants to go out and attack the problem and make the world a better place. He is not content with theoretical approaches to action. He is all 'Damn the torpedoes! Full speed ahead!'"

Nikki makes me laugh. Such a funny way of phrasing things. We pulled up two Adirondack chairs and set them facing each other. We climbed in and put our feet up in each other's laps so we could enjoy seeing each other, and conversing. We nattered on for an hour, sharing snippets of what had happened during the summer. At four pm Rollins came bounding toward us shouting, "Howdy Campers! Welcome to Camp Fanny Side! Stir your stumps and let's get shaking. A new school year is upon us!"

After lots of group hugs and kisses, we settled down to talk some more. Gary was blabbering on about being sophomores – "It means, if you go back to the original Latin, we are the class of 'wise fools.' Or perhaps we are just foolish to think we are wise. Or we are foolish wise men... I don't know, I guess you could look at it several ways..."

As Gary chattered, we heard the throaty rumble of a throbbing engine. I looked around and saw a sweptback black chopper growling up the campus driveway. The bike was a sleek custom job. Black metal accented with bright silver chrome. It looked like it had been built on a British Triumph T-6 Thunderbird frame with a parallel twin 650cc engine. The body tilted up and the front wheel fork extended at a rakish steep angle. The handle bars curved up so the rider drove the chopper with arms stretched out front and lifted high. The seat laid back so you felt like you were riding along in an easy chair. Slung over the back wheels was a pair jet black saddle bags to match the black fuel tank, black wheel covers, and black accessories. A tall lanky rider, dressed in black leathers, drove the bike up to the edge of the lawn where we were hanging out and hooked over to a full stop. Putting the bike on the kickstand, the rider slowly pulled off his black helmet and shook out a shaggy mop of fluffy black hair.

While the rest of us just stared in wonder at this apparition, Nikki screamed out in recognition. "Jack! It's Jack!" she jumped up and sprinted across the lawn to hug him. He just looked at her and laughed. When Nikki finished mauling our friend, he joined our group. "I told you I would not be taking the bus here this year." He laughed again, a long hearty laugh. "When you ask 'what did I do with my summer?' I can tell you in a phrase. The Bike."

"Tell us more," encouraged Gary, pounding him on the back.

By now a small crowd had gathered to admire the bike and rider. Jack loved having an audience – it brought out the showman in him. "When I went back to New Hampshire for the summer I worked at Red Art's Service Station during the

151

day and the family restaurant at night. Almost every spare moment and every weekend I spent in Art's garage rebuilding and restoring this beauty. Practically everything I earned this summer went into customizing the bike. I guess you could say I'm broke, but I'm happy... and I'm overjoyed to be back here with you, my Carlisle family. I feel a lot different about being at Carlisle than I did last year. Last year college was like sticking a toe in the water for me. I want this year to be a rush! I want to have fun. To enjoy life. Risk, challenge, excitement – fill my life with that. This chopper is just the beginning of a great year for me."

"Well it's a great chopper, cowboy, but you can't take it to the returning students' convocation, so you'd better find a place to park it," suggested Gary. "It's almost five and we don't want to be late for Dean Benchoff." With that, we headed off to hear what the Dean will say to us to prepare us for the year.

We walked into the Main Auditorium to find a sea of people packing the seats. This assembly was for the survivors: sophomores, juniors and seniors – everyone who was not a freshman or a transfer. To be honest, I felt a little jaded. After last school year and my just finished summer, I hardly thought Benchoff could say anything that would surprise me. "Don't get lost, don't burn down any buildings, and don't start a riot, - PLEASE!" What could he possibly say?

We wandered down the aisle looking for a place to sit and Gary shouted out, "Hey, senoritas!" and headed over to where Faith and Randi were seated. Arty Swaboda, who was sitting with them, jumped up and with a fist pump shouted "Fucking A!" in friendly greeting. Billy Harrison, as always attached at the hip to Arty, ran over and hugged Nikki, Jack, and Gary.

Faith gave everyone hugs all around, even to stuffy old me. "Hey, Jack," Faith purred in Jack's ear so we could all listen. "I hear you have a treat in store for me?"

"Oh, yeah? What's that?" Jack replied with a puzzled look.

"I hear you are going to take me for a ride on your new bike! Will you? Please?"

"Wow, news travels fast," exclaimed Jack. "Sure Faith, I'll give you a ride on my chopper. Just name the time and place and I'll be happy to take you out for a spin." Randi, always the sensitive one, checked in with each person, by name, inquiring how we were doing and how our summers had been. She is such a caring and compassionate woman. And so smoking hot! I sat next to her so we could catch up.

A number of people came up to the microphone and made their little speeches. Announcements, more than anything else. Then the Dean came to the podium. The audience grew quiet out of admiration and appreciation. Here is a leader we have history with. He has been with us through the highs and lows of the previous year. This is a man who has earned a large measure of clout and respect by living life with us day in and day out

"Friends, it is a pleasure to be reunited with you for another year at Carlisle College. As we begin a new school year, we continue a rich tradition. Those of you in this audience, having survived the rigors of at least one academic year, have an excellent chance of finishing your studies and becoming part of the proud history of our college. My charge to you today is to strive to live up to your potential. If you maximize the time and extraordinary opportunities offered by your education here, you will leave with the capacity to change the world." The Dean paused.

"This year I want to challenge you to ask questions and explore your choices while you are here at the College. A Carlisle education is as much about self knowledge as it is about gathering information on new topics. While you are here you should be exploring and learning about who you are, what makes you tick. This involves your emotions, your understanding, and your worldview. I challenge you to grow intellectually and spiritually. Hopefully, as you proceed, you will gain understanding about potential career directions as well as a solid education."

The Dean waited a beat then continued. "As you accept my challenge, focus on this principle. **You are unique!** As you learn in writing class, each of you needs to find your own voice. Don't follow the crowd. Please don't let peer pressure or pressure from your family squeeze you into trying to be like someone else. To find personal success and fulfillment, we each must strive to find our unique selves. Don't fall into the trap of thinking you are pretty much like everybody else. That's what junior high kids think. You are not only unique, you are special!

"Allow me to prove my point Have you ever walked into a room full of people and found yourself staring at someone who looks just like you? No – even identical twins have physical differences which make each unique. Your fingerprints are unique. Our DNA strands are unique, our heartbeats are distinctive, and even our eye prints are one of a kind. Then there are our talents, emotions, areas of giftedness, our temperaments, our family upbringing and our experiences in life. These too contribute to making us each matchless, one of a kind, individuals.

"When you consider your future, please recognize all of these issues come together to make you special. There are a few things you can do better than everybody else. In most things, you are going to be mediocre or below average. It will be to your great benefit if you take these precious years at college to get to know yourself, to identify your personal passions, and your exceptional strengths. Learn from the people you meet. Every exposure to folks with different information, different experiences, and even different world views can lend a hand to finding your own special place in the world. Ask questions. Ask for help. Explore. And enjoy the journey as you go through this adventure we call life! Thank you." With that, Dean Benchoff left the podium and closed out the program.

Our group hung around to chat after most of our peers departed the Auditorium. "Hey, what did you think of that?" asked Gary.

"He certainly has not found a new tailor," laughed Jack. "In fact, I am pretty sure he's wearing the same suit as last year. Maybe he's been sleeping in it. He must have some secret to looking so rumpled."

We all laughed, but Randi came to the Dean's defense. "Not everyone is such a fashion plate as you are, Black Jack Flynn! You are entirely too conscious about your appearance. I'm not sure it's good for your health. Believe it or not, the clothes do not make the man!"

"Ouch!" said Nikki.

"Ahh…my bad," said Jack. "I'm sorry."

Randi continued, "You know that already. I know you're not really into appearances. You just pretend to be all about your image so you can put up a little camouflage to keep people from getting too close to you. Relax – take a chill pill. You are now among friends."

That Randi is something! She can take one look at you and gently lay her finger on the heart of the matter. It is as if she has x-ray vision and can look right into your soul. Honestly, that is one of the things that attracts me to Randi. At the same time, it is a little off putting. If she does have x-ray eyesight, when she looks in my soul, she might see a lot of things I'm not too proud of.

Billy asked, "The Dean's speech reminds me that this is the year we have to declare a major. How are you guys doing on that? Do you know what you want to study, or what you want to do for a career?"

"That, my friend is an interesting question," said Gary. "I really have no idea how to go about figuring out what I should do with my life. My parents expect me to join the family business which is the last thing on earth I want to do."

"I'm right there with you on that," said Jack. "I have no interest in the restaurant business nor do I want to live in a boring, old village in rural New England. It's not my idea of a good time. I don't know what I am looking for, but I think I want a better life than what I come from."

Faith injected a comment. "What do you mean Jack, 'a better life'?"

"Instead of doing what someone else expects of you," said Jack, "I wonder if you don't have to look inside yourself and see how you are wired. Figure out what makes you tick, what makes you happy, how you want to help others? I wonder if you just have to re-vision what you want in life?"

Nikki ventured an idea. "When I think about it, most of the people I know who are happy and fulfilled are passionate about what they do and excel at doing that thing. They might teach kids, which doesn't pay a lot, but if you love helping kids learn – you're satisfied. You make a great pizza or sub, which is not on top of the income making charts – but if you love making food and serving people – you're good to go. Finding what you are passionate about and what you are good at doing may be the beginning steps of re-visioning your life, as Jack put it."

"Besides Skeeter and Arty, do we know anyone who knows what they want to do in life?" asked Faith.

"Besides them?" asked Nikki. "The only other person I know who is really committed to a career direction is Snow White. You know she's back on campus, don't you?"

"Holy Shit!" exclaimed Billy. "No! When did that happen?"

"How did that happen?" asked Faith. "I thought she was missing and presumed dead."

"Turns out she went missing, but not dead," said Nikki. "She was sucked in by a religious cult off the streets of Harrisburg, put on a bus, and driven to Plano, Texas. She lived in a commune out in the sticks before her parents finally located her. They had a deprogrammer kidnap her back and detox her brain from what the cult did to her. She's back as a freshman and looks perfectly fine to me."

"That sounds like an amazing story," I added. "See if you can get her to come to Koffee Klatch and tell us the tale. I think we'd all be interested in what she went through." With that, we left the Auditorium and headed to Musselman for dinner.

The first full week of classes came in with cool breezes and bright sunshine. Early fall weather moved in providing comfortable days. It's hard to shut myself up in a classroom building with such perfect weather. I want to blow off class and go trout fishing, which I neglected all summer. Instead, I dutifully showed up for every class. I figure I am paying $63 for each; so I am not going to cut any.

I still live in Wood Hall, but Jack is now my roommate. Arty and Billy decided to live together, no big surprise there. They are down the hall from us. Jack and I figured rooming together will let us better coordinate hunting, fishing, and trapping adventures. Our class schedules don't overlap much, so we only see each other at Koffee Klatch a couple times a week.

The first Wednesday of the term, Nikki showed up with Snow White in tow. A good group was already gathered in the red leather chairs when they walked into Musselman. Faith, Jack, Frank Spinelli, Bunny, Gary, Billy, Arty, pulled in to listen as Snowden told of her experiences of the past ten months.

"I'm sure you know I went shopping in Harrisburg, the weekend before Thanksgiving break. Girls from Winn Hall were hanging out on 2nd Street. We ate lunch at the Persian Dragon and there was a band playing. The girls with the band, their groupies I suppose, invited me to hang out with them when the band went to play in a park. They seemed very relaxed, friendly and groovy. So I went.

"We sat around and rapped while the band played. They talked a lot about love, acceptance, how God loves us all and wants us to be free and enjoy life. They offered me some home-made brownies and pretty soon I felt warm and loved and happy all over. When they asked me if I wanted to go back to their pad for dinner, I said 'sure, why not?' At the house they introduced me to these cute guys and kept giving me food and drinks. Next thing I knew I woke up on a bus headed for Texas.

"When I came to I had no idea where I was or how I got there. I think now they may have been spiking my food and drink. They told me they were a Christian commune called the Children of Yahweh. The leader, Father Ron, was considered a prophet on the same level as Jesus. He wrote letters to the followers promoting his teaching and a lot of stuff from the Bible. Almost every waking moment was managed and controlled. We had prescribed meal times, required clothes to wear, and spent the day in study groups. Periodically they took us into the city to panhandle, sell flowers, or make new recruits.

"We lived out in the country in a compound which was actually just an old hay barn and a bunch of school buses and tents around the barn. The compound was surrounded by a high fence, and there were guards to keep people in and to keep outsiders out."

"What was it like?" asked Faith. "Did they treat you well?"

"At first it was great," explained Snowden. "They showered me with attention and acceptance. It was the first time in my life I felt like someone really knew me as I am and accepted me. No demands, just love. But then they started in on their teachings. First it was their religious beliefs. Then it was about Father Ron and how he is the messiah. They really got heavy on physical expressions of love."

"You mean sex?" gasped Nikki.

"Yes. They taught the women that Father Ron had special needs and he could have sex from any member any time he wanted. Then they taught that all the male members were special and could have sex with any female member when they wanted. This was called 'spiritual marriage.' Even married men could have sex with any female. I mean young girls, too. As young as twelve. Women were taught to use sex to evangelize new recruits for the group. When we went into town to panhandle, some of them would go 'flirty fishing' as they called it. Father Ron said it was fine to share the love of Christ through sex to bring men to our faith."

"Wait. I know about this." I injected. "It sounds absolutely crazy, but it's true. When I was hitchhiking out west this summer, I got picked up by two girls who kept talking about Jesus and how they could share him with me. We stopped in Cheyenne and they rented a motel room and offered to let me stay with them. The more we talked, it sounded like they were promising that if I had sex with either one of them, I would receive Jesus. If I was willing to have sex with both of them, together, then I would get Jesus and the Holy Spirit."

"Well," asked Jack. "What did you do?" Everyone laughed.

"What are you nuts? I figured they were both completely crazy or had blown their minds on peyote. They scared the poop out of me. I figured anyone dumb enough to get in bed with them would catch the crabs or have his you know what fall right off. I waited until they were in the bathroom, grabbed my gear and ran down the road to a truck stop. I got a ride west with a long haul trucker and never looked back!"

"Snow, go on with your story," prompted Nikki.

"My parents never gave up looking for me. I can't say Dad ever showed his affection before, and both my parents are often critical, but this brought out the best in them. Dad hired a private eye to search for me and he kept working his contacts at the FBI until they tracked me down to the commune outside Dallas. They couldn't get past the guards to see me, so they hired a deprogrammer, Ted Rousser, to rescue me. His team kidnapped me when I was on a begging trip in Dallas and hauled me off to a motel in Mississippi where they held me captive for six weeks. The deprogrammers kept me physically safe, helped wean me from the drugs the cult had given me, and got my mind straighten out."

"How do you feel now?" asked Bunny.

"I think I'm fine. I feel like I'm stable and back on track. I don't really understand what made me so vulnerable to all that crap they kept telling me – unless it was the drugs and sleep deprivation. I think at heart, like most of us, I just want to feel loved. We want to be known and accepted and if we find people who love us unconditionally, then we believe whatever philosophy or religion they promote. If they tell you the moon is made of green cheese, you go along with it, because - hey, they love you!

"Of course, the Children of Yahweh didn't love me unconditionally. They didn't really love me at all. They wanted to recruit me to panhandle for them, to be a sex slave, and to lure others into the cult. They even tried to get the inheritance I was given by my grandmother, but because I'm not 21, it's still controlled by a trust. That's how my family found me.

"My parents set me up with a counselor here in Carlisle who I see weekly. My art work is therapeutic and is helping me process a lot of the feelings I went through. Honestly, I think I'm in a much better place now than I was last November. I don't know much about genuine faith, but I am sure when I find the real deal, I'll be able to recognize it."

"Wow, Snow. That is the most amazing story. Thank you so much for sharing it." Faith commented. "You've learned a lot from your ordeal. Your story helps me get perspective on where I am and the feelings I struggle with. Thanks for being honest." We gathered around and gave Snow lots of hugs and told her how glad we were to have her back.

22

Faith McFadden   September, 1967

Later in the week, Randi and I met up on the Quad after class to get caught up.

"How was your summer? Randi inquired. "You worked at the Grinder, but what else did you do?"

"I lived with a widow named Mrs. Rose. She's very nice. Kind and caring without being nosey or pushy. If I could nominate someone to be my next Mom, I would pick her. She and Father X are old friends. Other than that, I just worked. Talked to Father X a few times. Got to know some townies, especially Spud Mueller. He hangs out at the bar. We went out a few times but, to be honest, he's pretty messed up. Always doing uppers or downers or some drug. I'm sympathetic…but…. We are all suffering with pain and hurt and anger –just seeking different ways to dull the pain or self medicate."

"What about your Christian faith," asked Randi? "Does that help you deal with any of the pain?"

"Honestly, I think religion is bullshit. It's for hypocrites who pretend they have their crap together. They are control freaks who don't want anybody else to have fun because they are not enjoying life. Maybe Spud is right – he says the answer to all of life's problems is 'sex, drugs, and rock and roll.'"

"What's Father X say about that?"

"I'm not sure what to make of him. He certainly is not religious in the way I experienced it at home. He is not like Snowden's Christian cult. Mostly he talks about Jesus and his love and grace. He's a great listener. My family and my pastor back home never stopped talking, telling, criticizing, judging. Yak, yak, yak. They rarely listen. They are harsh. I never heard any of them talk about a relationship with Jesus. Listen to the Father, and you would swear Jesus is alive today!"

"This summer, I asked Father X about Snowden, assuming she was dead and gone," I commented. "He said 'Life is bigger than you think. Bigger than what you see. It's like an iceberg – there's much more of it you can't see than the little bit protruding above the water. Always remember God is love. If Snowden is no longer with us, her life will go on in a new dimension, in a better place. Or she may still be in our world, planted in a new place where she is prospering, a place we don't see.' Sometimes he is so mysterious, I don't understand. Yet I'm attracted to it and want to think about it some more.

"I heard from Skeeter several times this summer. He seems very happy for a guy in Vietnam. He's in the Army Corps of Engineers and getting to work on bridges and canals. He says Nam is hot, hot, hot. And it's been raining every day for the past four months. Mostly his letters are about his family. I'm still amazed by his family. Sukie, Skeeter's mom, wrote to me a couple of times this summer. Very encouraging letters, considering I broke her son's heart.

"I just don't get it. Skeeter's choices puzzle me. Why would you give up the security of a good income, living in a nice house in a nice neighborhood, having a family like his, having a good job in a company where you would never have to worry about getting laid off or fired? Why would you give all of that up so you could pursue some odd passion like wanting to build bridges?"

"Honey, in my experience, it's hard to understand men," explained Randi. "People are wired the way they are wired. A square peg is just that – a square peg. It's true of women as well as men. Don't make the mistake of thinking you can fix them, round off the hard edges. So many girls marry a bad boy thinking they can love off the sharp edges, but it doesn't happen. You wake up one day and discover you're stuck with a shit heel. Period."

"I'm feeling so confused about life," I added. "Mystified and confused. I'm not sure how to make sense of today, let alone think the future."

"Be patient, sweetie," said Randi. "It's a process. Rome was not built in a day – it takes time to figure out life. It's ok to ask for help. Keep your chin up and keep asking and searching and eventually it will all sort itself into a clear picture. Let's keep talking and we'll figure it out together."

"Speaking of the future," Randi continued. "Are you going to Spinelli's cottage on the Delaware next weekend?"

"You bet," I replied. "It sounds like a blast. That will give us more time to catch up."

Friday afternoon, a bunch of our friends piled into several cars and drove two and a half hours to the Delaware Water Gap National Park, which sits on the border between Pennsylvania and New Jersey. The park was created from land on both sides of the Delaware River. Spinelli's aunt, who lives in New York City, owns a summer cottage built on the shore of the river, just below the small town of Columbia.

In addition to our host Frank Spinelli, Rob, Jack, Randi, Nikki, Gary, Bunny, Doug, and I came along for the adventure. We stopped at a farmers' market in Columbia and picked up fresh produce and groceries for the weekend. From there it was a few miles down River Road to the cottage.

The Spinelli cottage is a simple ranch house perched about thirty yards above the water. It has a big great room combining living room, dining area, and kitchen at one end. The hall leads to three bedrooms and a bathroom. Glass sliders in the living room open onto a deck which runs along the river side of the house. The river scenery is breathtaking. The deck sports a collection of wicker furniture, lawn chairs, a picnic table and a grill. I can see where I am going to spend my weekend!

As soon as the cars rolled to a stop, Rob, Jack, and Nikki rigged up fishing tackle and headed down to the river to try to catch some famous Delaware River smallmouth bass. While they waded into the shallows off shore, Frank took charge of preparing dinner. Gary volunteered as assistant chef. The menu was simple: spaghetti, meatballs, wings, salad, and garlic bread.

Frank started making his grandmother's marinara sauce while singing old Sinatra tunes at the top of his lungs. Gary cubed ripe tomatoes for the sauce and baked meatballs and garlic bread. As the sauce was heating, Frank whipped up a green salad with romaine, cukes, baby tomatoes, radishes, and shaved cheese. Gary worked on the grill, firing up buffalo wings. The rest of us enjoyed the proceedings from the porch. With soft drinks and beer in a cooler on ice, we were content to do nothing. It's lovely to watch the river flow by, listen to the fishermen scream and holler, and enjoy the singing and laughter of the guys in the kitchen.

We sat down to eat with a sense of camaraderie drawing us together. Gary jumped up, "A toast! To friends! To life! To the future!" We all cheered and then proposed our own toasts.

As we dug into the excellent food, Randi asked Rob, "Tell us about your trip this past summer? Where exactly did you go?"

"All over," replied Rob. "I traveled west to San Francisco, hitchhiking all the way. I stayed in Ohio, Iowa, Nebraska, and Colorado, went up to Yellowstone, and was in Haight – Ashbury in San Francisco for two weeks. It was amazing! I worked here and there loading and unloading boxes in various freight depots to earn spending money. They always need help and pay cash. No hassles."

I asked Rob, "What kind of people did you meet? Anybody interesting?"

"Honestly, I found most people I met interesting. It's got me considering a major in psychology or sociology. Nearly everyone who picked me up was kind. In Tennessee, this big black Cadillac slowed down, stopped, backed up, went forward, backed up again. I opened the car door and a blue cloud of reefer smoke billowed out. The two black guys in the Caddy were dressed in suits, big hats and jewelry. In hindsight, I think they were successful pimps. Both stoned. 'Can you drive?' one fellow asks.

"When I told him I could, he offered me a ride. I sat in the front and drove while they got in back. I drove all the way to Memphis, while they hung out in the back drinking and smoking dope. They had me go to the best hotel in town, bought me a room for two nights and gave me $50 in cash for food, before they went home. Crazy, but kind.

"In Iowa, I got picked up by a businessman who drove me to Lincoln, Nebraska where he lived. He took me home to meet his family, fed me giant steaks cooked on a grill, and I slept in the softest bed I've ever been in. I didn't want to leave. But I had to. It is so flat and there's no trout fishing." Robbie laughed at his own joke.

Rob thought, "When I got to Haight-Ashbury, I met kids who were traveling, runaways, whatever. Some were inspired by Jack Kerouac and Alan Ginsberg and were searching for the 'Beat Generation.' I mean the whole town was filled with like 100,000 people my age looking for something. Others were into free love, drugs and hippie music. Some cats were into this 'Jesus Freak' movement. I realized America is full of people like me out searching for something.

"In Breckinridge, I was staying at a hippie encampment and I met a folksinger from Pittsburgh, named Eric Anderson. He was on his way to San Francisco, as well. Around the campfire one night, he sang a song which has a line something like, 'Take off your thirsty boots and stay for a while, your feet are hot and weary from a dusty mile…' That line just got stuck in my head. It's like a metaphor for where I am in life right now. I've got thirsty boots…I'm searching for something, but I'm not sure what it is. There's an aching in my heart, a hollowness in my soul. There's something I need to be complete and to find my way in life, but I'm not exactly sure what it is." Rob lapsed into silence.

After a while, Jack spoke up. "It's interesting – our generation vacillates between activism and passivity. We can't decide if we want to change the world – to overthrow the existing order, have a revolution and save humanity, or if we want to retreat into sex, drugs, and rock & roll. Just go tripping, man. Drop out and live off the grid. Go to San Francisco and revel in the 'Summer of Love.' Join a commune and live off the land. When I'm honest with myself, I admit I just want to have fun. I want excitement, risk, even danger. The opposite of the safe life my family lives in New Hampshire."

Nikki piped up, "Is that why you keep jumping your bike over the Lincoln Avenue Bridge?"

Doug gasped, "He does what?"

Nikki replied with a disapproving tone in her voice, "He gets on his chopper, rides to the top of the hill by Rhodes Hall then races down the hill, past the chapel, hits the bridge over the Antietam Creek at full speed and simply flies by the stop sign and over Lincoln Avenue and lands on Cherry Street."

Frank and Gary broke out laughing. "Whoa Nelly!" shouted Gary with great amusement.

"You really are crazy," added Frank.

"You could also get killed if a car is coming or your timing is off." rebuked Nikki. "You idiot!"

"It makes me feel like I'm flying. You know, like Peter Pan." Jack smirked.

"You may want thrills and excitement," said Doug, "but I want to play in my rock band. I just love the music and being in a band and being on stage, playing a gig for an appreciative audience. My parents hate the idea. They want me to be a businessman. I don't have to run Johnny's Hot Dogs, although they would like that. I just have to wear a suit and go to Rotary Club and have a job that won't embarrass them.

"Hum, maybe that works for me," I replied. "I think I want financial security more than anything else. But it would be great to have people fawning all over you and cheering for you. Riches and fame might be what I need. I could be the next Janis Joplin."

"But better looking," laughed Doug.

"And maybe you could learn to sing, too," added Rob to appreciative laughter.

After dinner and Nikki and I washed the dishes and cleaned up while everyone else set up a campfire by the river. When we got there, Frank had dragged the drink cooler down, enough chairs for everyone to sit on and had a big fire burning inside a circle of stones. Nikki brought the marshmallows and Frank dug out nifty metal cooking sticks, complete with wooden handles, from the cottage basement.

We listened to the river whisper by. As the daylight disappeared over the opposite shoreline, the night noises began to rise. By the time it was pitch black, a racket of insects and other unidentified critters singing and chirping surrounded us. The fire kept us wrapped in a warm safe circle where we could laugh and talk and enjoy each other.

"Bunny, we've not heard much from you," opened Randi. "How is this year shaping up?"

"I like my classes, especially Old Testament survey with Dr. Brody. We should talk about Jewish stuff sometime. I'm learning about Jewish culture – it's interesting. My dorm floor is a mixed bag. Well, Frank knows this, he is in the middle of it." Bunny answered, "We have Ronnie Reynolds back on our floor, although I wonder about the wisdom of that. You'd think revisiting the scene of his dorm fire from last year might be a bit unsettling. Plus, Ronnie is still on the same floor as Ratso Ramsey."

"Who continues to torment the poor guy, just like he did last year," added Frank.

Doug asked, "Like what does he do?"

"He calls him names, runs him down in public. When we are in the lounge watching TV, Ratso chucks hunks of food at Ronnie trying to hit him in the head."

"He put a dead squirrel in Ronnie's drawer and it took two weeks for Ronnie to figure out what smelled so bad," Bunny added. "We can't prove it was Ratso, but somebody filled Ronnie's room with trash from the dumpster; I mean emptied the garbage bags all over his bed, and floor and everything."

"Sounds like a Ratso trick," affirmed Frank. "Why doesn't he bother you, Bunny? He hates blacks."

"He calls me nigger whenever he thinks no one else can hear him. I just ignore it. But you have to draw your boundaries, which Ronnie won't do. I had a chat with Ratso and told him if he ever chucked stuff at me or played dirty tricks, I would take Father X's chainsaw and cut his T-Bird into so many little pieces he would never find it again." After a moment of silence, everyone broke into laughter.

Rob asked, "Would you do that?"

Bunny smiled an evil grin. "Try me."

We enjoyed a lazily Saturday morning, some sleeping in, others on the deck enjoying the river scenery, and of course, Rob, Nikki, and Jack down in the river fishing. After a breakfast of pancakes and bacon, whipped up by Bunny and Gary, we set out for a hike in nearby Worthington State Forest. Nikki gave us a guided tour with commentary on trees, wild flowers, and woodland critters. It was great. At one o' clock we drove up River Road to the village of Pequest and enjoyed lunch at Johnny's Hot Dogs. It was everything Doug said it would be. I think he was pleased to introduce us to his family. We raved over the chili dogs, crispy French fries, and Tastykakes, as well as mug after frosty mug of root beer.

After lunch we split into two groups. Frank was anxious to canoe the Delaware and there were two 18-foot Grumman aluminum canoes at the cottage. Rob, Jack and Nikki volunteered to stay back at the cottage and fish and swim near the cabin so the rest of us could canoe. They kept catching big bass, so it was not much of a sacrifice to stay. Frank organized life vests, paddles and the cooler of drinks.

We drove five miles up River Road to a campground where the two canoes launched. Frank and Gary took the lead canoe with Randi as passenger. Doug and I paddled the second canoe with Bunny in the jump seat. Nikki, Rob and Jack drove the vehicles back to the cottage where our adventure will end.

Below the Water Gap, the Delaware is a broad stream several hundred yards wide. It rolls along between low hills of hardwoods now in a blaze of autumn color. The foliage of the North is like nothing I've seen in Georgia. The red maples, yellow birch trees, orange sugar maples, and green sassafras down by the water's edge are enchanting. Interspersed are masses of dark green hemlocks, spruce and pine. We paddled along the gentle water, enjoying the show, dragging our fingers in the cool water and passing beers back and forth between canoes.

Then we hit the islands. The river had been wide and placid. In the islands, it becomes Class 4 and 5 rapids. Take the wrong side of an island or the wrong strand of water and you can get in trouble. It helps to have someone who knows the river or has been down it recently. We didn't.

At first we did ok, selecting the correct side of the current split and racing around an island or a series of small waterfalls. It was thrilling, like riding a roller coaster at a park. Wahoo! Later, our luck held, but we went by some nasty looking pinch points, narrow funnels and a series of sharp rocks in the foam. Glad we didn't pick that one! Frank told us the white water on the Delaware is produced by big flat sheets of stone, rather than boulders and rocks typical of white water. Ledges stick out and during low water, offer few points of passage. You have to find one gap in the ledge rocks where there's a chute of water high enough to ride through. Pick the wrong spot; you end up sliding over a ledge. You might get by, only to fall over a four to six foot high waterfall. It takes more luck than skill to avoid capsizing after riding over one of these. The other alternative is your canoe bottoms out on the ledge and leaves you stranded on top of a rock with nowhere to go but down. It is hard to recover from this without a swim in the river, or losing your gear and canoe.

We made it to the last set of strands below Columbia without a hitch. Then disaster struck. Coming into the strands, we could find no passable channels. We ended in a series of islands which forced the water into a raging chute of white water five feet high. With black ledges sticking out all around us, there was nowhere to go but into the fire hose of water. Frank's canoe bounced up in the air, shuttered, and slid down torrents, bouncing off an exposed rock. They escaped with only a dent in the canoe.

Doug guided us down the funnel, but our canoe slid left and the bow hung up on a jagged rock. In the blink of an eye, the canoe wretched sideways, rolling and spilling us into the water. I couldn't see a thing; the froth and action of the waves were so violent. I came up sputtering and turned to point my feet down stream, the standard procedure for recovering from a white water spill.

"Faith!" Frank shouted from shore. "Over here! Swim this way!" I could see Frank up on a rock, so I swam his direction. When I got there, Doug, Randi and one canoe were on shore.

"Where's Bunny?" I asked. Frank pointed, and I saw Gary out on the rocks trying to work his way towards Bunny who was hanging onto a rock in the middle of the torrent of water. His look said it all. Panic, fear, even terror kept flashing across his face.

"Help!" he shouted. "I can't swim!"

Gary struggled to navigate through the raging water. Eventually, Bunny's grip slipped down the rock and he disappeared into the green foam. As Bunny floated by, face down in the water, Gary threw himself out into the raging current to go after him. They both disappeared from sight.

Frank and Doug took off at top speed along the shore looking for a way to get to our friends in the water. Randi collapsed by the canoe sobbing hysterically. I'm not an athlete, let alone a great swimmer, so I left the guys to the pursuit and tried to comfort Randi. Five minutes later, Frank came puffing up the shoreline. "We got him! Gary is giving him CPR. Get the canoe and gear and bring it down the shore." Randi and I hopped to it. By the time we got to Gary he had Bunny on shore, and his resuscitation efforts had paid off. Bunny was sputtering and coughing up green river water, but thank God, he was alive.

"Shit, man," exclaimed Frank. "You had me worried!"

"Hey, I had me worried," Bunny croaked, still trying to get his breath back. "Thank God for Gary the lifeguard! You saved me man!"

"My pleasure, friend. I knew that training would prove useful some day. It couldn't have served a better man. But I'm a little surprised your fancy prep school didn't bother teaching you to swim."

"Not their fault," Bunny gasped. "Guess I've always been afraid of water." We heard a horn honking from the road. Doug's van pulled off and Rob and Jack jumped out and came running down to the river.

"Hey, what's going on? Is everybody ok?" Jack asked.

"Bunny is in recovery, but he's going to live," said Frank. "How did you know we were in trouble?"

"Shit, that was easy," said Rob. "We were standing there fishing and around the corner comes an aluminum canoe with a foot of water in it. Nikki, a bright chick if there ever was one, shouts 'It's their canoe! I'll get it. You take the van and drive up and help them.' With that, she puts her rod on the rock she's standing by, and throws herself in to swim after the canoe. We just did what we were told, so here we are." Everyone had a good laugh picturing Nikki taking charge the way she did. There was also a sense of relief as we headed back to the cottage. We were happy for our escape from near disaster.

Sitting by the fire that evening, I reflected. "There is a certain amount of bonding that goes on when a person shares difficult experiences with others, especially friends you care about." In my mind, that weekend on the Delaware River was a turning point in our relationships.

Rob added, "I've been thinking the same thing. I can't tell you how panicked I was when I realized what that empty canoe might mean. It could have been any one of you was gone." He paused. "I remember something Ted said to me before he went off to Vietnam. 'You are my brother. No matter how painful our family history has been, we are bound together forever by our mutual history, by surviving a shared family experience.' Living life together forms a bond that cannot be broken."

Jack added, "It seems to me that sometimes, real family is bound together by something much stronger than blood." As we stared into the fire, I kept thinking how fortunate I am to have friends like these, friends who could be like a new family.

23

Jack Flynn   October, 1967

By early October, life settled into a routine. I had some interesting classes but also enjoyed an active social life. Koffee Klatch was a highlight, but so was the basement card game in Wood Hall. The Wood Hall Blue Room regulars included Billy, Arty, Frank, Doug, Gary, Bunny, and Scottie Crow. Rob occasionally dropped by to chat, but he never play cards. He hates to lose money. Occasionally Ratso shows up and plays, which creates some tension, as he is not well liked. On the other hand, you can't completely blow off a guy just because he is a jerk. That would make us as bad as him.

My favorite game is Black Jack, or 21. When I walk into the Blue Room, Arty and Billy shout together, "Hey, Fuckin' A! Its Black Jack Flynn himself come to visit the little people!" That always gets a laugh.

Mostly these guys want to play five card Poker. I prefer Black Jack, because it involves more skill rather than just luck. When I suggest, "Hey why don't we play Black Jack?" my pals all bust up laughing and tease me. One night Robbie commented, "You remind me of me of when I was a kid. I loved to fish so much, I eventually talked all the kids in my neighborhood into fishing too. Then I went to their parents, telling them there was going to be a neighborhood fishing contest. I raised a pot of money for prizes for the contest. Naturally, I was such a superior fisherman that I won all the prizes. All the prizes! First fish, longest fish, heaviest fish, the most fish. Ha, ha, I took all the money home. Well that was the end of that. None of the parents would ever put up prize money and the other kids lost interest in fishing."

"Your point?" I enquired.

Rob came back. "Ain't nobody going to play Black Jack with you because you win every hand and take everybody's money!" The guys roared with laughter.

Later, Frank spoke up. "I worry about Ronnie and his mental stability. He seems shaky as is and then Ratso keeps hacking away at the roots of his self-esteem and making him miserable. He's becoming lethargic, he sleeps a lot, and doesn't leave his room. Shorty St. Laurent, his roommate, tells me he's withdrawn and not very interested in school."

"Sounds like he's depressed," offered Bunny. "Even when I feel isolated, I can always go to the free movie up at the Lane Center. As one of nine black kids in our class, you know…, my social life isn't too hot. But there are still things you can do. And there is the Purple Dragon, the coffee house sponsored by the Methodist Church. All you have to do is cross High Street and you're there. Cheap coffee and food and often the music is pretty darn good. When I feel blue, I turn up there and almost always have a good conversation. I've tried to get Ronnie to go with me, but he just wants to sit around his room and mope."

"Ronnie needs to learn its ok to ask for help, but it seems unfair a beast like Ratso attacks him without any reason." I just shook my head with sadness.

Just then, Miss Feltgood stuck her head into the Blue Room. "How goes it, fellows?" she inquired. She walked over and stood next to Billy.

Billy blushed at her attention and mumbled, "Things are great Miss F."

Looking at me she said, "Jack, you're not letting cards interfere with your Sociology studies are you?"

I'm sure I blushed too. "No, Sir!" I blurted out. The guys laughed.

As the Dean walked out the door and back down the hall, Billy spoke quietly, "Is that a great pair of butt cheeks or what? And thighs? I bet she could ride the roller coaster all night long."

"Billy, you are disgusting!"

The other guys pitched in. "Don't get on the wrong side of Miss Feltgood or Jack, the teacher's pet," said Frank. "Oh, very touchy, is our friend Jack. Must be sweet on Miss F."

"How good does she feel? Huh Jack, tell me that," teased Arty.

"Does she feel good, Miss Good Feel?" added Billy. "I'd like to give her a good feel." The guys all laughed.

"She is awfully hot for a little Mennonite girl," suggested Scottie. "Miss Feeling Fine, Miss Felt Well, and Miss Feels Good to Me. Who wouldn't want to cop a feel from her? You'd better run along Black Jack. You don't want to miss a chance to stare at those cute dimples for a whole class period."

Everyone laughed at me as I blushed uncomfortably. Finally, I got up, grabbed my books and headed off. I didn't know what to say. Honestly, I don't even know what I am feeling.

After that night, I found myself thinking about Miss Feltgood a lot. Amy Feltgood is a tall, striking redhead with a beautiful face. Her carrot red hair drapes falls to her shoulders and cascades down her back. Her expression is usually serious but it only takes one comment for it to light up. When alone, she looks thoughtful. In conversation, her face beams with joy. Her bright blue eyes sparkle and her dimples are mesmerizing. The dimple on the left is the deepest I have ever seen, looking as if it has been cut in with a scalpel. Her dimples work their charms whenever she smiles her broad grin, with her brilliant white teeth and plush, luscious lips. A scattering of tiny freckles complete the picture of a seriously beautiful woman. OK, perhaps I have a crush. I find myself daydreaming about her.

The Saturday duck season opened, Rob and I went out and killed three blue winged teal. We knocked on Miss Feltgood's door and I asked her, "If you lend us the use of your kitchen and oven to cook our ducks tonight, Rob and I would like to invite you to join us for dinner so you can enjoy them with us. Would you be open to that?"

"Why that would be wonderful, boys. What time would you turn up?"

Later that afternoon, we knocked on Miss F's door loaded down with plucked ducks, a box of wild rice, stuffing, a pouch of glaze, bacon strips, toothpicks, fresh green beans, and a loaf of fresh crusty bread from the local bakery. Feltgood met us at the door wearing a pair of bell bottom jeans with fancy hand stitched patterns on the legs. On top, she wore a peasant blouse with puffy sleeves in a riot of colors. Her red hair was piled up on her head in a loose knot. "You look stunning." I managed to croak out.

"Jack, that's so kind. Please come in fellows." Rob and I piled all our stuff into her small kitchen and got to work whipping up dinner. The ducks were stuffed, trussed, wrapped with bacon and placed in the oven to roast. Rob made the toasted garlic bread while I cooked up wild rice and extra stuffing. When the ducks came out, Rob spooned out bacon drippings to cook the green beans. Just before the dinner was ready to serve, Miss Feltgood set the table and served drinks. We sat down to a splendid feast.

"Yum! This is really delicious," said Miss F. "Who knew you guys could cook?"

Rob laughed, "Oh, don't flatter us. We are just messing around – using you as a guinea pig so we can learn to cook the wild game we harvest."

She chuckled at that. "Well, feel free to use me for your experiments any time you like." She had a great laugh. Like Champaign bubbles tickling your nose. Mild, but very pleasant.

Rob asked, "How did you decide to study Sociology?"

"That was easy," said the Dean. "I've always enjoyed people. When I went to college at Penn State, I became an R A. I liked it so much I did it for three years and focused on the University as a career. I considered Psychology, because people interest me, but decided I like groups of people even more. I'm fascinated by how organizations behave. Thus, Sociology."

Rob talked about his travels over the summer and the kinds of people he met. "After my interactions with all these different kinds of folks, I'm thinking about majoring in Psychology or Sociology."

"That's a solid insight, Rob. Sometimes our experiences in life point us in the direction of our calling," said the Dean. "My parents grew up during the Great Depression. Times were hard. They spent almost all their time and energy putting food on the table and keeping a roof over our heads. Since the end of the War, America's enjoyed an economic boom. People in your generation, Rob, are searching for love, belonging, self-esteem, and self actualization. But have you thought about how would you earn a living with a Psych or Soc degree?"

"I hadn't thought of that. My Dad is a mechanical genius and an engineer. My brother Ted was like Dad. I was always the odd man out. More into my head than my hands."

"Was?"

"He died just before I came to Carlisle freshman year."

"Oh, how sad! You poor guy. May I ask how it happened?"

"He spent two years at Bucknell majoring in engineering. Then he decided to be a patriot, quit school, and enlisted in the Marines. He was killed in an accident the first week he arrived in Vietnam."

Feltgood reached out to hold Rob's hand. "You poor man! That is so hard. How about you Jack? Have you ever lost anyone close to you?"

"My little sister Maggie died when she was twelve; I was fifteen at the time. She caught spinal meningitis at school, came home and was gone two days later."

"Oh, that is so painful!" murmured the Dean. She got up and came around the table and put her arm around my shoulder. "How did you handle it?"

For a long moment, I couldn't say anything. "Honestly, it was devastating. Maggie was such a bright spot in our lives. It was like the light had gone out of the daytime. No joy, no pleasure, nothing left but gray, throbbing pain."

"Is that when you started to dress in black?" asked the Dean, still gently stroking my shoulder.

Startled, I asked, "How did you know?"

"I lost my Dad when I was fifteen," she replied. "He was killed in an accident on our farm. The tractor rolled over and crushed him. One day I came home from school and he was gone. I never got to say goodbye. It was if all the color had gone out of my world. For years I could not understand how the sun was able to shine when my personal world was so dark, so bleak."

By now tears were running down my cheeks and the Dean was weeping into a tissue. Robbie was just sitting there looking miserable. "I am so sorry guys," said Miss F. "I didn't mean to touch such a raw nerve. This was a great dinner. Let me help clean up. I want you both to feel free to come by anytime you need to talk – about anything. For you, my door is always open." When we left she gave us each a hug and patted us on the back.

As Rob and I walked down the hall and up the stairs to our dorm room, all I could say was, "That didn't turn out like I expected." We both turned in early.

One frosty morning in early November, I walked with Randi over to the Koffee Klatch in Musselman. Nikki was already there along with Bunny Washington. Rob and Faith walked in and joined us. "Did you tell everybody what happened?" Faith asked Randi.

Randi blushed – a very becoming rose hue on her freckled face. "No…"

"You should tell them" Faith urged. Smiling she said, "Remember what you said to Jack at the beginning of the semester: 'It's safe – you are now among friends.'"

Randi began. "OK, I hope you don't think this sounds too weird. Too crazy. It was scary enough to me. Two weeks ago I began to have trouble sleeping at night. Something was bothering me. Waking me up and keeping me from sleep. When I woke up I would hear screaming in my room and a red mist was swirling over my bed. The mist formed into a big mouth where the screaming came from. It scared the crap out of me. I had no idea what it was or what to do."

Faith picked up the tale. "When Randi told me, I didn't know what it was either, but it sounded like Pat Rouseau, my youth pastor, describing demons he encountered when he was doing beach ministry. I told Randi, 'If this is a demon, what you have to do is call on the name of Jesus to confront him and drive him off. I don't know anything about casting out demons, but I do know the name of Jesus is the most powerful name there is. Call out his name and he will protect you.'"

"A couple nights later, at two in the morning," Randi continued, "I woke and my room was full of screaming. But now there were three or four shapes made of swirling red mist and I could see faces and eyes and mouths all screaming obscenities and threats at me. They kept dive bombing right at my head and one had fists and another had hands with claws that looked like he would claw out my eyes. I was paralyzed with fear. Finally, I remembered what Faith said and I hollered out, 'Jesus! Jesus! Jesus! In the name of Jesus, be gone.' As soon as I said that, the red mist things froze in the air, the screaming stopped, then they shattered into a thousand pieces as if they were made of glass and the pieces fell out of the air, all over the floor and just vaporized."

"Holy Shit!" exclaimed Rob. "Then what happened?"

"Nothing!" laughed Randi. "They were gone and I felt safe and I went right back to sleep. I have not had anything bother me for a week. I think they are gone. Banished forever, by the name of Jesus."

Bunny spoke up. "That is so...wow! Someplace in the New Testament Jesus tells the Jews, 'The work of God is this: to believe the one he has sent.'"

"Well now I believe in the power of Jesus' name," added Randi.

"You know, I have very little interest in church," injected Rob. "It doesn't seem relevant. It's rarely helpful. It doesn't speak to my needs. But I find myself wondering if God is really real and might be nothing like what they say about him in church."

Faith jumped in, "What do you mean? I thought the only way to find God was to find him in church?"

"Honestly, I don't know what I mean," responded Rob. "It's like the fragment of a melody that floats through your mind at an odd time. You're sure you can hear it, and then it's gone. You can't quite place it – all you have is a phrase ('and it's just before dawn') or a few notes..."

Nikki spoke up, "I know exactly what you're talking about. I often feel like that!"

Rob continued, "So here is Randi. She calls on the name of Jesus and something shows up and destroys the demons. Have you ever been to church, Randi?"

"No. Well... maybe for a couple weddings."

"See," said Rob. "Randi is Jewish, does not go to church, and yet Jesus turns up when she cries out for help. What does that make you think?"

"'Once I was blind, but now I see.'" Rob went on. "That is something Father X told me. He told me Jesus said, 'I have come into this world, so that those who do not see, may see.'"

Bunny concluded, "Somewhere in the Bible, it says 'If you seek God, he will find you.' Thanks for sharing that, Randi. It is very unsettling, but offers a lot to think about." We all gathered around Randi and gave her hugs and encouragement. Then we headed off to class.

Late one night in mid-December, I woke to the sound of pebbles chinking my window. Lumbering out of bed, I opened it to see Randi below shivering in the cold. "Jack, "Sorry to wake you, but can you get Robbie and come help me?"

"Sure. We'll be right down."

"Dress warm and get Doug's van," Randi added. We joined her on the front steps of Wood Hall five minutes later. "I need your help with Faith. The Carlisle Police station called and asked her to come down. She is afraid to go alone. It would be great if you guys would come with us."

"Sure honey, whatever you need," said Rob putting his arm around Randi.

"We're here for you," I added. "Whatever, whenever." I looked at my watch. It was two fifteen in the morning. We got into Doug's blue Hot Dog bus and drove over to Allison Hall. On the way, Rob asked Randi, "Do you have any idea why the cops want to see Faith at two in the morning?"

"I can only imagine the worst," was Randi's reply. "My guess is it is Faith's townie boyfriend, a guy named Spud Mueller. Maybe he's in jail and needs to get bailed out. Faith took up with him this summer working at the Grinder. He's a local guy who hangs out at the bar. I think he is in his early twenties. He works as a mechanic at the Esso station on the other end of Hanover Street."

"His name is Spud?" Rob inquired.

"Spud." Randi responded. "And no, I have no idea how he got that name. I'm kinda surprised he got arrested. When I've met him, he seemed pleasant enough. Just a little messed up from doing too many drugs. OK, maybe he's a loser, but he appears to be a mild-mannered loser to me."

We pulled up to Allison and Randi ran in to get Faith. In a minute, they were out the front door into the van. "Thanks for coming with me," said Faith. She had obviously been crying. She held a tissue to her eyes. "I don't know what's going on, but I am too scared to find out on my own."

I asked Faith, "How well do you know this guy?"

"We hooked up this summer when I was working at Grandpa's. He's a regular at the bar. Spud is a nice guy, just a little down on his luck. Plus I think he self-medicates too much."

"What do you mean?" Randi asked.

"He drinks a lot and he smokes pot. Then he likes to do meth, bennies, and downers. He's tried LSD at Doc Long's place, and I know he's snorted cocaine and tried smack."

"Smack?" Rob asked.

"You know, heroin."

"Heroin?" Rob was incredulous.

"Oh, I don't do smack with him, or acid. But we have done cocaine, pot, and prescriptions together. It makes sex much better." Faith added. "When I think about it, I'm afraid he spends nearly every cent he earns on drugs and booze. He is skinny as a rail too."

"Does he have a family?" asked Randi.

"No." Faith said. "He lives by himself in a room out in the back of his boss' house next to the garage." Just then we pulled up in front of the Police Station. All four of us piled out and followed Randi as she led the way in through the main doors.

Faith approached the officer at the front desk. "I'm Faith McFadden and I got a call to come in about my friend Spud Mueller. Pointing back at us she said, "These are my friends."

"You mean Greg Mueller, Miss?" inquired the officer.

"Yes, that's right. Spud is not his real name. Is he is in trouble, Sir?"

"Miss, I am sorry to inform you we found Greg Mueller dead out behind Grandpa's Grinder earlier this evening. It appears he may have passed away from a drug overdose. I'm sorry to trouble you, but we need you to identify the body. We found his driver's license in his pants, but he has no family and we need a personal identification. I understand you were close to the deceased?"

By this time, the words the officer calmly spoke sank in and Faith realized what had happened. She screamed and collapsed on the floor sobbing hysterically. Randi knelt next to her and wrapped Faith in her arms trying to calm and soothe her. The desk officer helped get Faith comfortable in a chair and went for a glass of water and more tissues.

"Rob and I will go get Father X." I suggested. "He'll know what to do and how to help Faith."

Randi replied, "That's a good idea. Faith likes the Father and trusts him."

Rob and I got in the van and went to TMO to wake up Father X. He was bleary eyed at first, but eventually the adrenalin kicked in and he livened up. When we got to the police station, he was at full steam and took charge. By then, Faith had recovered enough to make the identification. The officer knew Father and let him assume duty as Greg's next of kin. We took Faith home to Allison and Randi put her to bed.

Saturday morning we attended the funeral at St Patrick's. It was a small gathering to say farewell to Spud. Twenty of us came from college to support Faith. I had never met Spud, and I suspect few of us had. There were a folks from Grandpa's including Larry Green, the owner, and his wife. Three young guys in the back were from the garage where Mueller worked. A sprinkling of older folks in suits and dresses were apparently the contingent from St Pat's that come to every funeral held at church.

Father X officiated and gave a short message. "Friends, this is a sad occasion for all of us regardless of how well we knew Greg. May I leave you with a few thoughts? We are not alone as we pass though the storms and trials of life. Death is not the end of our journey. Our God is a God of love. He overflows with grace and mercy. He can turn difficult situations into something good.

"I am reminded of Jesus when he was on the cross being crucified by the Roman authorities. One of the thieves who was crucified next to him cried out, 'Jesus remember me when you come into your kingdom.' Here was a guy who had made mistakes and had managed to come to a bad end. Was there any hope? Jesus said to him, 'Today you will be with me in paradise.'"

The Father continued, "There is a better world to come and Jesus is the one who can lead us there. The Bible teaches that God works all things for good for those who know him; if God is for us who can be against us; and nothing can separate us from the love of God. These promises you can depend on. As we go out from this sad time, turn your eyes to Jesus, the author and perfecter of our faith."

He paused a moment. "He promises to be there for any who seek him."

H he added, "He promises to lead us to a better place in this life."

He finished with, "and he promises to lead us to a better place in the next life. Amen."

24

"It is the heart always that sees,
before the head can see."
~ *Thomas Carlyle*

Nikki Clausen   January, 1968

After Christmas vacation, I was delighted to get back to college. It was nice to be with my family and friends in State College, but I missed my Carlisle friends. Winter is not my favorite season. I guess, when I think about it, it's my least favorite time. Still, there are interesting things to do all winter long in the Cumberland Valley.

My favorite activity is walking with Gary in back of campus. When the weather is mild, which it almost always is, even in winter, we can walk across the fields, through the woods, and around the pond. I especially like seeing wildlife, like pheasants, bobwhite quail, cottontail rabbits and songbirds. In the woods we see squirrels, chipmunks and the occasional ruffed grouse. The pond often holds a pair of colorful wood ducks and, occasionally, we are rewarded by the sight of a majestic Great Blue Heron. On rare occasions we might surprise a whitetail deer out feeding on fallen apples. This walk in the wild is one of our favorite dates.

When the weather turns cold enough, we take advantage of ice on the pond to hold skating parties. With at least four inches of ice the cold becomes a cause for celebration rather than gloom. Late afternoons or evenings find us out skating on the pond with friends or whoever shows up. Gary will organize a pickup hockey game on one edge of the pond. The other areas are filled with figure skaters twirling, skating backwards, spinning, or playing whip the tail of the dragon. Great laughs all around! When we get cold, a few guys will gather dry branches and start a fire on shore and pull logs over to sit on. Tired and cold skaters huddle close to get warmed by the roaring blaze.

On the rare occasions Carlisle gets a heavy snowfall, new pleasures await. Most of the snow at College is 'cosmetic snow' as Jack likes to call it. It makes everything look pretty for a few days, but it hardly ever gets in the way of doing what you want outdoors. Jack loves to tell tall tales about winter snow in New Hampshire: He describes childhood storms which left snow drifts up to the second story windows of his home. Hard to tell how much of this weather lore is just Jack's natural gift as a story teller and how much is true.

If we get a foot of snow, we break out the toboggans. Outside town stands a knob named Cemetery Hill. We drag our toboggans to the top of the Cemetery Hill then turn around and shoot down the slope screaming and yelling the whole way. The first downhill run is usually a little pokey as the snow needs to get packed down. Subsequent descents are faster and hysterical. With three or four people on a sled, the speed is exhilarating, and as people screamed and hollered the sled often careens out of control, overturns and dumps riders laughing in piles of fluffy snow. What fun we enjoyed!

Still, we are in college, and students are expected to go to classes and study. Koffee Klatch remains a favorite past time of our little band of merry miscreants. Early this winter term Frank came in to Musselman, sat down and blurted out, "You will never believe what I just heard from Scottie Crow! I've been wondering why I've not seen Ronnie Reynolds. It's because he never came back from Christmas! Mrs. Reynolds called Scottie last night and told him what happened."

Frank paused before beginning his story. "Ronnie caught a ride home for Christmas with Scottie Crow. Scottie took him to the airport in Columbus, where he was supposed to fly to his parents' home in Minneapolis. But he never got off the plane when it arrived."

Jack asked, "What happened to him?"

"Weird story," said Frank. "Scottie did notice Ronnie was quiet all the way to Columbus. But he's usually quiet. How was Scottie to know Ronnie was having a full blown mental breakdown?

"When they got to Columbus, Scottie dropped Ronnie at the terminal. What happened next is the subject of a lot of speculation, but this much is clear. Whatever was going on in Ronnie's life…at this point the shit hit the fan. All they know is Sunday afternoon, a full thirty one hours after arriving, Reynolds was reported to Security for 'disturbing behavior.'

"Apparently, Ronnie was dancing on the tops of passenger chairs singing snippets from the Rolling Stones' "Satisfaction." As Ronnie danced he kept shouting, 'I can't get no…satisfaction!' 'I can't get no…' Then he would belt out a bit of the chorus, 'Cause I try and I try and I try and I try…' When he wasn't dancing or singing he sat around lighting cigarettes with twenty dollar bills and muttering to himself. Someone called Airport Security. They asked him for identification, which he refused to produce. Finally he was taken to the mental ward of Mercy Hospital, where he spent 3 days raving.

"Eventually the authorities figured out who he was and called his older brother Rick, who flew out and brought him home. Ronnie's family promptly checked him into the County Nuthouse in Edina for a nice long involuntary stay. Mrs. Reynolds called Scottie to tell him what happened. Scottie said Ronnie's parents think he might be released into a day program fairly soon. Being at the nuthouse during the day, but come home to eat and sleep at night. They hope to get him adjusted and medicated so he can come back and live at home."

"Fuckin A,' said Arty. "Now that's what I call a shitty Christmas vacation!"

Rob asked, "Did anyone in your dorm suspect he was having a mental breakdown?"

"No," said Frank. "A lot of us know he's depressed. He always seemed like such a sensitive kid. I don't know if you are aware of this, but Ronnie's family picked up and moved him from Columbus to Minneapolis during his junior year of high school. He lost all his friends. I wonder if he ever really recovered? This fall, outside of a few signs of melancholy, he seemed perfectly normal."

"Just think about it for a minute," reflected Gary. "We all struggle with anxiety sometimes. Maybe pain, or fear. I think these are common symptoms of the human experience. The difference in outcomes depends on how you handle anxiety, pain and fear. Ronnie bottled his emotions up. He never asked for help. Never sought a listening ear. I don't know if he self medicated with booze or drugs, but lots of people I know do. None of that helps. I hope none of you will do that. Just find one of us to talk to. Father X says 'There is no wrong emotion, so long as you talk about it.' Or go get some counseling. Or bring it to the group to discuss. As Randi says, 'You are among friends now. It's safe to be real.'"

Gary and I left the Koffee Klatch considerably sobered by what we heard. "Man, my heart goes out to Ronnie." said Gary. "I know what its like to feel like the odd man out and not be able to talk about my concerns with anyone. Poor Ronnie."

"I realize it's hard for someone who's never felt the impact of segregation to understand what a disturbing experience it can be. Most of my friends are from the North. They don't get it. Most Southerners I know don't get it either. It just does not seem to penetrate their conscious mind. But for me it is so personal! The way my family treats other people is inhumane. And I think it makes them less human in the process. My family is so strange, so heartless, so unfeeling. And like Ronnie, there really is no one I can talk to about my feelings. To hear me describe my family – people will think I'm insane."

"You can talk to me, Gary." I said holding his arm as we walked the campus perimeter path.

"Yes, that's true Nikki, I can, and thank you for being such a good listener."

"I admit, I may not share all my parent's values, but I grew up in a loving home. They have always been there for me and even when they don't understand me, they trust me to find my way – even if it's not what they would do. At Christmas, Dad and I had a talk about my major and career directions. It was not very helpful. Dad says, 'You are what you do, so you should pick a career which has high esteem in the eyes of society.' He talked about growing up in rural Stow, where his dad was the local mail carrier. "If I had done what many of my peers did, I would still be living in a small, drafty, cold house on the edge of the woods in Stow, working for the Postal Service and humping mail out to itty bitty places without electricity…working in mud and rain and snow, grinding down my joints until I had to retire at age 60, like my dad. He was so crippled with arthritis from doing manual labor all those years; he could hardly hobble around when he retired.'"

"What did you say to that?" Gary inquired.

"Dad says you are what you do. I say you should do what you are." I paused and we both thought about that for a moment. "I don't know why I am the way I am. I love the outdoors, enjoy wildlife, botany and ecosystems. I'm fascinated by the planet and everything in it all the way down to how a cricket sings or how a toadstool reproduces. I've had these interests since I was a little kid. I don't know why. Nobody taught me. Dad was off with his nose in a history book, Mom was busy leading choral music. I wanted to sit and watch worms wiggling in a rain puddle or observe silkworms eating mulberry leaves.

"Dad thinks I ought to be a doctor, lawyer, dentist, successful business person or a college professor – someone others will admire. I'd rather float around in a canoe and learn about clouds and how to predict weather from cloud formations. I simply can't imagine being shut up in an office all day: drilling teeth, reading briefs or planning on taking over the world ball bearing market. I think I would hate a nine to five office job no matter what I did in the office. But how do you find a career in being outside?"

"Excellent question," replied Gary. "One of the things I learned from hockey is that what makes a great hockey player is not the ability to pass the puck to where your man is. What makes a top tier hockey player is the ability to pass the puck to where your man is going to be. The same thing is true in life. I want to learn to get out and go where my life is headed and not just sit here where it is today. Be pro-active! Be in forward motion!"

I laughed out loud. "That is so you, Gary!" I hooted some more. I hugged his arm and added, "Be pro-active! I have no idea what that means, but you always seem to be a body in motion, a man of action."

"When I worked as a lifeguard last summer, my favorite part of the job was the training. And the few times we actually got to jump in and rescue somebody. But I don't think I'd be happy as a 50-year old lifeguard. Ha ha! I'm pretty sure the reason I love hockey is that you're always in motion. Whether on defense or offense you keep skating, passing, checking, and shooting until you make something happen for the team. Unfortunately, I'll never be good enough to play professional hockey.

"I guess I don't feel I know myself very well. It's clear I'm not like my parents and I don't share their values. I like my grandparents a lot better, but I'm not like them either. I appreciate them as people and feel loved by them. They would do anything for me. But they don't understand me. I am like this cute little alien being who has landed in their midst they have adopted. They are unfailingly kind to me but I don't want to do what they do. I don't aspire to be a stockbroker or a financial wiz kid. Or a socialite like Grandma. So, I don't know…"

Gary lapsed into silence as we continued walking. "I guess I can relate to that. I often feel like I'm on the outside looking in. I don't know – its like, I'm not like other people. But Father X says that's actually good! He claims the Bible says we are each made unique. Like Benchoff said in his welcome speech last fall. Father X says so many people our age try desperately to be like others. They may be a square peg but if their friends are round pegs, they try to squeeze themselves into a different shape to fit in. Father says I should feel good about seeing myself as different. He says it is a sign of self knowledge and maturity."

After thinking about what I said, Gary observed, "When I was home with the Grands in high school, I was always pretty lonely. I went to a boarding school, so I didn't know any kids in the neighborhood. The Grands were usually off on Wall Street or socializing or something - I felt isolated. I'd walk around the neighborhood for hours on end. I met the Cartwright kids because Tony and Max used to play stick hockey in their driveway. I would stop and offer pointers or play hockey with them. Mr. and Mrs. Cartwright invited me into their family. I played board games with the kids and watched cartoons on TV. They invited me to stay for supper. Finally, they told me their house was my house, their family my family. And they meant it! I could wander in any time and get a snack, take a nap on the sofa, hang out, read or watch TV until somebody came home.

"This past summer, my job as a life-guard ran from noon until six. At ten pm our hockey team got ice time at the rink and I would go skate. I was free most days till noon and after dinner until ten. Most of that time I spent at the Cartwrights. They are such warm, compassionate, kind people. They ask me questions and listen to what I have to say. They do the same for their kids. Somehow they are able to offer advice without coming across as critical or judgmental. They have a healthier, more positive perspective on life than almost any other adults I know. When I am with them I feel loved and accepted – just the way I am. They give me hope for the future, even though I don't know what it holds."

"That's cool, Gary. It sounds like they've become a real family to you. Does it feel like that to you?"

"You know what, that's exactly how it feels! I don't know how it happened. It just kind of crept up on me. I spent a lot of time there during Christmas break. I talked to Mr. and Mrs. C about my major and career thoughts. One afternoon we were talking, and I said, 'I'm still pretty fuzzy on career direction but I do have strong feelings on one issue. I don't know what it is you have as people and a family that I don't have, but I want it.' They both looked at me and smiled.

"Mr. C told me, 'Gary, what we have you can have too. God created each of us and wants to be in a relationship with us. We can't make that happen on our own so he sent Jesus, his son, into history to reach out to us. Jesus lived and died and was resurrected from the dead. He is alive and well today. You can know him by simply inviting him into your life.'

"Mrs. C added, 'We are not talking about religion. We are talking about having a personal relationship with God through Jesus.'"

"I asked them, 'How do I know if I need that? And if I did, how do you do it?'"

"'The best way I know how to explain it, Gary, is that you hold up a mirror (metaphorically) and look at your life,' said Mrs. C. 'If you like what you see in the mirror, then you are probably not ready. But if you don't like what you see in your life, you can give your whole life to Jesus. He will keep the good parts of you. Over time, he will remove the bad parts of your life and replace them with his good.'"

"What was your reaction to that?" I asked.

"Honestly, I got up and said, 'I think I'm ok, thanks.' Then I walked out and headed home. But as I went down the street I found myself looking in the mirror, at my life, and I didn't like what I saw. So I got down on my knees, right on the sidewalk and gave my life to Jesus."

For a long minute I thought about that and asked, "And so...?"

"Well, its early days yet. I can sense something is different in my life, although I might have trouble putting it into words. I'm convinced I now have a connection with Jesus, but I don't know how it all plays out. Mr. C told me Jesus made this promise: 'Ask and it will be given to you; seek and you will find; knock and the door will be opened to you. For everyone who asks receives; he who seeks finds; and to him who knocks, the door will be opened.' For now, I'm seeking and waiting expectantly. Mr. C also encouraged me to read about the life and teachings of Jesus. He gave me a Good News Bible and told me to read the four gospels, which contain Jesus' story and teachings. I'm finding it a fascinating read. I've never read anything else like it!"

"OK, I'm impressed. You did have an eventful Christmas break! I don't know what I think about what happened to you. As you know, I'm a little reflective, so I'll have to cogitate on it for a while. In my heart I have this sense that there is a God. I see so much in nature which tells me that's true, but I can't seem to figure out how you get connected? I read a book by a guy named Blaise Pascal, a 17th century French mathematician and philosopher. He said, 'There is a God shaped hole in the heart of every man which cannot be filled by any created thing...' That really resonates with me. In nature I see the footprints of God, but I know there is much more. I'm just not sure how you get there?"

By now we had completed a full lap around the woods and pond and were on the walking path by the gym. All morning the sky had been filled with thick, low hanging gray clouds. They looked like snow, smelled like snow, and were downright depressing. As we approached the back of the gym, a brilliant golden shaft of sunlight broke through the clouds and shone down on Gary and me like a spotlight from heaven. "It's a God moment," we exclaimed, laughing. The sunbeam began to expand and the gloomy clouds rolled back. Sunshine poured all around us and lit up the day with a warm glow. It reminded of the new Joni Mitchell song which talks about 'the sun poured down like butterscotch and stuck to all my senses...' That's exactly how this sudden celestial appearance made me feel. Wow!

25

"One of the most important gifts of spiritual faith is forgiveness."
~ *Annie Lamott*

Rob Bachmann   March, 1968

When we returned from spring break, the weather was lousy. Typical of March in the Northeast, the days featured low hanging clouds, cold temperatures, and blustery winds. The wind is a bitch! Even on sunny days it sucks the life out of your bones. It is a grim time for anyone who loves the out of doors. Too warm to sled or ice fish. All the hunting seasons are closed. It will be weeks before trout season finally opens. It is too cold and wet to do much of anything.

One afternoon Jack, Gary and I took Nikki and Randi out to fly kites. We were that desperate! The five of us drove to Cemetery Hill where we had gone sledding during the winter and tried desperately to get a couple of kites in the air. The wind was strong enough, but we kept having string problems, or the tail wasn't quite right or just as we ran across the hill trying to catch the wind, the runner would get tangled in the long grass and fall. After 45 minutes, Nikki finally got her red and yellow kite up and it soared over the hill. We cheered and watched it fly for ten minutes, then realized we were frozen to bone, and beat a hasty retreat.

We shivered in Gary's Ford Galaxy, waiting for the heater to kick in. Driving back to campus Gary joked, "I have not been this cold since November when you guys made me go goose hunting with you at Waynesboro Reservoir. Man, that was cold!" By the time we reached campus, the wind was howling sideways and spitting wet snow.

I had to admit, "This is cold! It does feel like we've been off winter goose hunting. It must be blowing 25 miles per hour," I complained as we unloaded the Galaxy.

"As soon as we get squared away," suggested Nikki, "Let's meet back at Musselman and see if we can beg some hot cocoa."

"Great idea," Randi moaned. "I am frozen straight through."

Twenty minutes later we gathered in our usual corner, sipping big ceramic mugs of steaming hot chocolate. Nikki, best friends with everyone on the college staff, had gone back into the kitchen and rustled up hot cocoa and graham crackers to snack on so no one would starve until dinner.

While Randi thawed out she asked, "Well, Jack, what's going on with you and Miss Feltgood?"

Everyone had been chatting aimlessly until Randi dropped this boulder into the conversation. I told you she is a namer – knows how to put her finger on the heart of the issue. Jack froze, his mug of chocolate halfway to his mouth. He blanched and the color drained from his face. "Whatever do you mean?" he managed to croak.

"Hey, buddy," insisted Randi, "You know you are among friends, right? We're on your side! It's pretty clear to us you have a 'better than average' relationship with the divine Miss F."

Jack swiveled his gaze slowly around the circle. At Gary, Randi, Nikki, and at me. "Hey, Cowboy! It's time to fess up," laughed Gary. "It's plain something is going on with the two of you. You go to her apartment any time of day or night. The Card Club in Wood Hall sees you leaving her place late at night. You two have even been spotted taking walks...*long* walks around campus."

Nikki added, "Some kids have seen you riding your motorcycle with a mysterious woman with bright red hair. Next thing we know, we will hear reports the two of you have been spotted leaving the Howard Johnson's early on Saturday morning. So tell us *everything*! What's up with you two?"

"It's nothing" insisted Jack. "We're just friends."

"I don't know..." Randi commented. "When I see the two of you together, it looks like there might be something else going on."

"And," I added with a big grin, "Your reaction to Randi's question was ...like you had a guilty secret."

"Look here," Jack exclaimed, "we're just friends. I've been in to talk to her about the whole Ronnie Reynolds situation. She gave me advice to help me process my feelings over the loss of Maggie. She is a good listener. She's a good counselor and friend. That's all."

After a long pause with all of us staring at him, Jack continued, "We simply hang out and talk. She makes popcorn and apple cider or gives me cookies and milk. She tells me about her childhood among the Amish and Mennonites in the Big Valley. It's a valley in Mifflin County full of different Anabaptist groups. She says they all have lots of rules they have to keep as part of their faith. According to her, they have rules about everything.

"Horse and buggies vs. cars. Rubber rims on your wheels or steel? Electric to the house? Maybe only to the barn to run milking equipment? Telephones? Indoor plumbing or outdoor only? Any curtains in the house? Maybe half curtains? Men in white shirts only or the liberals in colored shirts? One suspender or two? In some groups, belts and suspenders are prohibited. What women wear, the color of the bonnet on the head, the color of the roof on the buggy. More liberal Mennonite sects allow cars but no chrome. They have to spray paint everything black. They are called Black Bumper Mennonites. Some baptize in the house, others down at the creek. Rules, rules, and more rules. If you follow all the rules faithfully, then you can become a member in good standing. If not, most sects will shun you – meaning no one in the church or your family is allowed to speak to you for the rest of your life."

"Wow!" gasped Randi, "That seems harsh."

"Amy was raised in a progressive Mennonite family." Jack continued.

"Amy?" asked Nikki.

"Amy?" queried Gary.

"Amy?" injected Randi. "You call her Amy?"

Jack, sputtering with embarrassment, said "Well, we're friends, so she lets me call her Amy in her apartment. Outside, I call her Miss Feltgood or Dean. Anyway, she was raised in a progressive Mennonite sect which is why she could go to college and not get shunned. She decided to do her doctoral dissertation in sociology because of all the feuds she saw among Anabaptist groups growing up. Group conflict, her dissertation topic, is something she has lived through."

Randi inquired sweetly of Jack, "What else do you talk about with Amy?"

He laughed at her snide tone of voice. "I talk about growing up in New Hampshire, living in Effingham, being a Flynn, living and working in a tourist economy. She laughs at my stories about living in the 'Live, Freeze, and Die' State of New Hampshire. It is a pretty quirky place. She is fascinated by my stories about working in the Master Baiter and restoring old British sports cars."

"Fascinated, is she?" laughed Nikki. "I don't know, that still sounds suspicious to me."

"Especially if she is fascinated by Mr. Monochrome from Effingham, NH." chortled Gary. We all laughed at Jack but finally let him off the hook. After a few minutes, he went slinking off to check on the card game in Wood Hall.

By the first week of April our world was transformed by the dawning of the new season. Spring arrived with a rush in the Cumberland Valley. All over campus golden forsythia bushes bloom. Bright yellow daffodils and red tulips line the sidewalks. The red bud trees explode with clouds of deep purple blossoms. Cherry trees add bright pink swatches throughout campus. Azaleas in a wide palette of colors pop out on the doorsteps of campus buildings. White and pink dogwoods burst into bloom. Willow trees bordering the Antietam Creek first turned yellow and then pale green with the earliest leaves. All over campus, trees drooped with buds waiting to burst into leaves. When those tiny green leaves began to appear, it was a sure sign trout season is near.

After waiting in a state of anxiety for two months, Jack and I were practically hyperventilating to go trout fishing by the time we flipped our calendars to April. One afternoon we had no classes, so we walked down to TMO to get set for the upcoming season.

As we walked, I asked Jack, "Really, what exactly is your status with Miss F?"

We walked in companionable silence for a few moments. Finally, he said, "To be honest, what I've been thinking is that I have a crush on Amy, sort of like the crush I had on my favorite sixth grade teacher in Effingham. I really like her a lot. But lately I've been daydreaming, and dreaming at night, about putting her on the back of my bike and running away to Mexico with her. In the dream, we camp out in the desert, sleeping in a little pup tent and I am boffing her brains out. So, if I face the facts of what I am actually feeling, I think I'm falling in love with her."

"Man, that's heavy," I responded. "How does she feel about you?"

"I think she likes me. We appreciate each other's company. We enjoy talking together. When we're alone, she is very touchy. What I mean is she is one of those women who puts her hand on your arm when she is talking and wants to make a point. She is always touching my shoulder or holding my arm. Very kinesthetic. But I have trouble remembering, was she always that way, or is it our relationship? Does she get touchy feely with other people or is it just me?"

"But you don't know if she thinks of you as a man or as a student?"

"Nope."

"Hmmm, that's kinda awkward, isn't it?"

"Honestly," Jack said as we reached the sports store, "the whole thing makes me very tense. I don't want to have her end up scorned on campus like Dr. Henning, Delilah's faculty flame."

Inside Tuscarora Mountain Outfitters we bought fishing licenses, more flies to fill in our stock, fresh line for spinning reels, hooks and split shot to use in bait fishing. Spring trout streams often run high and dirty from rain and snow melt. Fly fishing is best when the water reaches normal levels, but if you want to catch trout in early April your best choice is to roll worms or drift small minnows on spinning tackle. When we finished shopping, Jack and I were ready for anything.

"Shall we pop in and see the Father?" I asked Jack.

"Why not," he replied. "It's that or go back to campus, bite our fingernails, wait for the season."

Father X welcomed us into his cozy cabin. As usual, he had a low fire in the wood stove, the coffee pot was steaming on the stove and as soon as we got seated he handed out fresh baked cookies. "These are peanut butter cookies, which I baked myself. They are number three on my all-time favorite list – right after chocolate chip and oatmeal raisin."

I laughed. "I get it. In case we ever decide to bring you a snack instead of simply mooching off you and your kind nature."

"Just trying to cover any possibilities," replied the Father with a happy grin. "What are you fellows up to as you wait for the glorious Opening Day?"

"We're all set," I replied. "As we get closer we will probably go out and do a little scouting to figure out where we are going to fish Opening Day."

"What else is up in your world?" asked Father.

After a pause, Jack said, "I've been talking to a friend about forgiveness and moving forward in life. I feel like I've kinda been in a stuck place emotionally since Maggie died. It's been years, but I wonder if I am frozen emotionally? I loved her so much. We were nothing alike, but she was the joy of my life. When Maggie died, my joy died with her. When I think about it, which I generally try to avoid, I find I've not forgiven God for letting her die. It was not her fault. It wasn't anybody's fault. So it must be God's fault. I think I'm still angry about it. Now I find I'm afraid to develop affection for anyone for fear they too will die."

We sat for a while. Father X put a log in the stove and passed the cookies again. It surprises me how often the right thing to say turns out to be nothing at all. Somehow the space made me want to open up. "When I was twelve, my mother died," I began. "I was told it was an accident. She went downstairs late one night to check on the furnace. When she opened the door, the fire flashed back and caught her hair and night dress on fire. She had burns over 80% of her body and died before the ambulance arrived.

"Years later, just before I left to come to Carlisle, I found out the truth. My brother Ted was home from Marine boot camp. He was getting ready to ship out to Vietnam. According to Ted, my mother's death was vastly different from what I had been told. It was late at night and mother and father had been having one of their regular dustups. Ted, as he so often did, crept out of bed, and part way down the stairs so he could peer through the banisters to see what was going on. During a raging brawl in the kitchen, my father picked up my mother and heaved her down the basement steps. She landed on her head and shattered the step and her brain. When father realized what he had done, he ran downstairs, opened the furnace door and held my mother's body up to the heat until she caught on fire. After covering the evidence of his crime, he rolled her around in the dirt and put the fire out. Then he calmly went upstairs and called the ambulance. Ted had seen and heard it all. When I found out, something inside me died.

"A few days later Ted got on the bus and left for Vietnam. I never saw him again. A week later, Ted was boots on the ground in Quang Tri Province. By the end of the first week, Ted died, shot by his own M-16. We were told he tripped on a jungle trail and accidentally shot himself."

We sat in silence for a bit, then I continued. "I realize I still haven't forgiven my father for killing my mother and I have not forgiven God for letting Ted die in Vietnam. My home is gone. If someone dropped a bomb on 418 Ferry Road, it could not have obliterated my childhood home any more effectively. My childhood was lousy. I was not fond of my mother. But it was the only childhood I had and it's been taken away. Since Ted died it's as if my heart has turned to stone. I'm not sure I want to feel, so I don't. Yet this creates a wall inside me - wanting to keep people out or at a safe distance."

Father X pulled out his pipe, stuffed it with fragrant tobacco and lit it with a kitchen match. He puffed thoughtfully after I finished my story. "Forgiveness is a tricky thing," our mentor began. "When I was in the ministry at St Pat's I met people who were struggling with past harm others had done to them. One gal was an orphan adopted by a local family who could not get over feeling her birth parents had rejected her. A man in his mid - fifties was still angry at a boy who had bullied him in boarding school. Four decades later the shame and humiliation affected him every day. The worst situation was a girl who was sexually molested by a family member when she was fifteen and her parents would not believe her.

They said she was just trying to make trouble. Even as an adult, she never recovered."

X took a thoughtful draw on his pipe. "I'm not sure if this will be helpful, but I've found that forgiveness is one of the hardest things for people to deal with. Jesus taught that we should forgive other's sins or failures against us. He went on to say, to the extent we forgive others; God will forgive our personal failures. Well, we all have a lot of those, don't we? I know I do.

"I think where holding a grudge and not forgiving someone undermines us is that we mistakenly think forgiving someone gives a free pass to the culprit. The bully gets off free when the victim forgives. In truth, the one who really benefits from forgiveness is the one who does the forgiving. Holding a grudge, carrying bitterness in your heart, is like living every day with a 60 pound backpack on your shoulders. It is a lot to lug around. As you both have found, a lack of forgiveness interferes with your life and keeps you from getting beyond the hurt and moving on with your life."

We sat there and thought about what the Father had said. He passed the cookies one more time. Finally, we got up and trudged back to campus. We were both deep in thought about what the priest had said and how it might apply to our own lives.

On Friday I strolled into the Koffee Klatch to find a group gathered and buzzing. I sat down next to Nikki and her ever present TAB and she asked, "Did you hear about Martin Luther King?"

"No, what about Martin Luther King?"

"He was assassinated last night in Memphis," Nikki replied. "A sniper shot him with a rifle while he was standing on the balcony of his hotel. They rushed him to the hospital, but he died."

I was stunned. Looking around the table, I could see Bunny and Gary had been crying – they both looked awful. Frank looked worried, more about Bunny's mental state I think, than about Dr. King's. Nikki and Faith looked bewildered, which was my first reaction.

"That is so sad," I finally muttered. "I am disturbed by how people in this country can hate that much. I know there are lots of haters – every time the government takes a step forward and tries to help right a wrong, to give black people the right to go to school or to vote, the haters come flocking out of the woodwork. But to shoot somebody for speaking the truth? If everybody who disagrees with somebody else gets to shoot them, we will run out of people pretty damn quick."

Frank added, "And it's not as if shooting one person is going to change anything. Congress has already passed legislation to insure civil rights and voting rights. As long as the government enforces those laws, killing Dr. King won't change a thing."

"Except break the hearts of his wife and kids and everybody who loves him," injected Nikki.

Bunny spoke up, "My fear is this will inflame anger in the black community and inspire people to resort to violence themselves. Dr. King was such a strong voice for righting these wrongs with non-violence, but I don't know if people who follow him will be so self-controlled. Look at the last few years. There have been over a dozen riots in major cities including New York City, Watts in LA, and Newark. And whose neighborhood ends up destroyed in these riots? The black neighborhoods, of course."

Just then Bunny spotted Dr. Broderick walking through the dining hall. He jumped up and shouted, "Hey, Doc! Come over and join us!" Theo Broderick made a beeline for our table and sat down. Bunny said, "We are just trying to process the news about Dr. King. What do you think?"

"Ah, this is so sad." Brody said with real pain on his face. "The truth is we live in a broken and sinful world where bad things can happen to good people. This will not be the last horrific thing you deal with in your lifetime. Friends, if you place your hope in men, you will always be disappointed. But God is still in control. Even when bad things happen, God can bring good from it. Remember when Kennedy was killed? A terrible tragedy. But President Johnson was able to lead us past that. He launched the War on Poverty, got the Voting Rights Act and the Civil Rights Act passed against strong opposition. The only person you can count on, who will never let you down is Jesus. Our world is a mess, but God is working to redeem and restore this world. Jesus is the keystone of the plan."

Brody went on, "The Bible teaches us to weep with those who weep and rejoice with those who are celebrating. Now is a time for weeping as we share the pain of Dr. King's family, of the black community, of the brokenness in our country. Put your hope in Jesus, and at some future time, we'll have reason for rejoicing." With that sobering prophecy, we packed up and headed out for class.

26

"It is a poor center of a man's life – himself."
~ *Francis Bacon*

Faith McFadden   April, 1968

Spring continued to unfold on campus with brilliant swaths of color. Spring on St. Simons is slow and subtle. New leaves appear on the live oaks; the gray Spanish moss stays the same. Marsh grasses on the bay go from dull brown to a brilliant green. Quiet. Unassuming. Spring in the Northeast is stunning. Spring bulbs, flowering trees, and as the azaleas began to fade, great swaths of white bridals' wreath, grape wisteria, and lilacs in purple, plum and white take over the campus landscape. Breathtaking!

But my world is shifting from campus, to the town of Carlisle. Since my summer working at the Grinder, I find I am spending more time in the townie world and less on campus. Every Friday and Saturday night I waitress at the restaurant. When Larry needs help mid- week, I take a shift or two. Occasionally, Randi asks me why I spend so much time at the Grinder.

"Simple, really; I need the money," is my standard reply. "My scholarship covers tuition, room and board, but nothing else. I need money for books, and supplies, and personal items. You can't expect a gal to live without a new tube of lipstick, can you? If I want to get pizza with the girls on the floor or go out for donuts and coffee, it takes cash. I don't get money from home. Whenever I can I try to send extra money back home to my sisters. They are not doing well since I left."

Even on nights I'm not working, I often spend the evening hanging out with my townie friends at the bar. It reminds me of home. Well, Coconut Willies, which is what I think of as 'home.' So maybe it's about more than the money. I 'get' the party scene. You just want to have fun and forget. That's what my townie friends are into. We drink too much, smoke reefers, snort coke and occasionally do other recreational drugs. It's a way to forget the pain, at least for a little while.

My college girl friends, Randi, Nikki, and Linda, are all so... serious. It's not that they don't know how to have fun, but they are always asking uncomfortable questions, and thinking, and wondering about the future. Honestly, I don't want to think about the future. If a white knight like Skeeter Stetson or Frank Ramsey doesn't come along and rescue me from my lonely life, I can't imagine what will become of me. What future will I have when college is done? Will I have to go crawling back to St Simons and my crummy family? Live in an old slave shack on Fish Fever Lane? I dread the thought.

This term Randi and I share a British Lit class. Walking back to our dorm after class, Randi asked, "I heard you have a new boyfriend. When are you going to tell me about him?"

I laughed nervously. Maybe I feel guilty for holding out on my best friend. "Oh, yeah, Butch. I met him at Grandpa's and we've been dating for a couple weeks. He's from Carlisle."

"Oh, that's interesting," Randi said, a sarcastic tone in her voice. "Tell me all about Butch."

"Butch is a sweet guy. He works as a pressman for the Harrisburg Patriot News, the newspaper."

"That's it? That's all you got?" Randi laughed. "He's a sweet pressman?"

"Alright, there is more to Butch than that, but he is sweet. He works on the morning edition of the paper, so he works nights. Every afternoon he hangs out at the Grinder until he goes to work at 11:30. We like to talk. Actually, he talks, and I listen. He says I'm the best listener he's ever known."

"Yes, please continue...do you know anything else about this guy?" Randi prompted.

"Butch is 6' 3". I can wear my heels and he is taller than I am. Butch has sandy hair, which is thinning. He likes to wear blue jeans, t-shirts and denim jackets. And...he is... 53 years old."

Randi stopped dead in her tracks and stood stock still in the middle of the sidewalk. "He's what?!"

"He's 53 years old."

Randi took a second to absorb this. "And you are 20 years old? Does this not strike you as odd?"

"Butch has been married and divorced twice. The first time he was nineteen and she was seventeen. They moved to Harrisburg where he worked in a printing plant while Jolene went to community college. For three years, Butch worked, she went to college, they squabbled a lot, didn't see each other enough, and things got tense. One afternoon the press broke down. He came home early and discovered somebody else's cowboy boots under their bed. That was the end of the marriage.

"Butch moved back to Carlisle, played the field, and had one-night stands with girls he met at local bars. He got careless and got a waitress pregnant. This second marriage lasted for six years and produced three kids. He really didn't know Flo when they got hitched. Just that she was cute enough to bed for one night. She couldn't cook, she was a lousy housekeeper, and she didn't like being at home with squalling little kids. She nagged him constantly. Her only homemaking talent was the one a girl does on her back. That she was good at. But good sex is not enough to hold together a bad marriage. After six years, Butch had enough and left. He's been single since he was 36. I can tell you from my own experience, he is extremely careful about using birth control."

Randi resumed walking towards our dorm. "That's a lot to take in." she said. "I hope we can talk about it more, once I get my head around it."

I've recently noticed it's harder for me to be honest with my girl friends. We talk, but I'm always shading the truth or withholding vital information. I guess I'm afraid they'll judge me for my choices. Like Butch. I told Randi about him, but not that he introduced me to the world of strip clubs. One night Butch convinced me to go to Harrisburg to a strip club called the Foxy Lady. Butch used to go there during his salad days in Harrisburg and occasionally returned. "Come on, Faith, try it! It will spice up our sex life."

The Foxy Lady looked like any other bar, but bigger. We got in a line of excited, babbling men stretching out the door. After Butch paid the $10 admission fee, we entered a vast hall with platforms scattered throughout. Each platform was surrounded by a cluster of tables and chairs. Men sat drinking over-priced drinks and hollering lewd suggestions at the dancers working the platforms. They showed approval by tossing rolled up bills at the dancer on stage. Big tippers got to reach out and tuck a five or a ten dollar bill in the g-string of the gyrating stripper.

Butch and I watched the action for a while and to be honest, he enjoyed it a lot more than I did. To me it seems the men only see these women as physical bodies. People without a soul or a personality. I'm not even sure they were driven by lust. It was if they were masturbating with a live person in front of them. The whole thing was all about them. Completely self-involved.

Later Peter, the club manager, came by our table and Butch introduced us. After chatting for a while, Peter said, "You ought to consider dancing, Faith. You are certainly pretty enough. You would make a ton of money. What kind of work do you do now?"

"I'm a waitress." I answered.

Peter asked, "How much do you make on a shift?"

"I make about $50 on a good night, maybe more."

"If you worked here as a dancer, you would make $300 a shift, maybe as much as $500 on a big night. Just think about it." Peter got up, said his goodbyes and wandered off.

I admit, Peter's attention made me feel special and pretty. I am definitely attracted by the money. I've wanted to buy a car and with the cost of booze and drugs I have trouble saving enough from my current job to get a decent set of wheels. How different is dancing from waitressing?

As this spring term wore on, I had a gnawing feeling that inside, I am tense and nervous. Growing up, I often felt stressed and under pressure, but this is a kind of free floating anxiety that just keeps chewing at me. Perhaps it has something to do with the national mood. It is grim, to say the least. In the weeks after Martin Luther King was assassinated, race riots broke out in cities all over the US. Every night on the news we saw violent demonstrations, clashes with police, and burning inner cities. We talked about the situation in Koffee Klatch and in my Poly Science class, but no one seems to know what to do.

I find it so hard to know what I'm supposed to do about anything. It feels like I'm adrift, just floating aimlessly down the river of life. How am I supposed to know how to respond to evil and brokenness in our society? I don't know how to deal with the bleakness and pain in my own inner world; how can I help anyone else? Should we be waiting for the government to figure out how to fix these problems? That doesn't seem like its ever going to happen. Should we expect someone else will come along and make things better? Or should we take to the streets and stand up for what we feel is right? So many in my generation are choosing to do this. To take action, to speak out, to raise awareness and to force our culture to face the need to change, to treat people better, to make America a better place?

Honestly, I find my loss of hope for my personal situation, translates into a lack of faith that anything good can happen for our society as a whole. When I'm honest, I realize my relationship with Butch is just a way of killing time, pretending I'm ok, and hoping something better turns up. He may be comfort food, but I also know he's empty calories. There's nothing there. If there's no hope for me, why would I believe there's any hope for anyone? My only hope is the constant wish someone like Skeeter or Franklin Ramsey will come along and rescue me - make it all better.

Easter came and went. I didn't go to church. Sure, I miss the lilies, the trumpets, the grand music, and all the people in their new Easter fashions. "He is Risen!" "He is Risen Indeed!" I might miss some of it, but I find I am still mad at God, mad at church, mad at religion. Disappointed mostly - at all the promises they made that turned out to be hollow and empty. When I think about my family and being raised in church, I just kinda slide into a slow boil of anger about how I was treated. They talk a good game, but my experience was nothing their talk. I wonder if my disillusionment is just from my family system and my church, or if it really is God who is to blame? I figured I might go see Father X. He helped me out over the summer and with Spud this past fall. I trust his advice.

We got settled in his cabin, and he passed the cookies. I asked, "Father, I have questions about faith and religion. About Jesus and Christianity. In my congregation back home, I was taught you can only find God in church – our church! But some of my friends talk about Jesus as if he were somehow different from Christianity, church, and religion. Bunny says that's what Dr. Brody thinks."

After a beat, I went on. "I think I'm confused because I really don't know myself or understand myself. I don't know what I believe. What do I know about God that's true? What have I been told about God that's false – merely man made traditions?"

"Ahh, Faith, those are good questions," the Father gently replied. "Let me see if I can give you some ideas that might make sense." After a brief pause he continued, "Humans in all societies recognize a higher power, a Creator, a divine being and seek to embrace this power. Man has a universal desire to connect with God.

Different cultures ask these questions: 'How do you get connected to God? How do you get right with God?' They answer these questions in diverse ways. But almost every culture has a religion – a man made set of rules for getting close to God.

"Yet God, who created us to have a relationship with him, has not left us on our own. In contrast to man-made religions, God reveals his plan to reconnect us to himself. The first part of that revelation was where he called Abraham, Isaac, Jacob, and Moses to create a people for God – the Jews. Into this chosen people God sent his son Jesus into history. Jesus came to offer us a living relationship with God. He did not come to offer us the church or Christianity; these are merely man made religions."

I interrupted. "Gary says Jesus offers a new life and a new relationship with God. He says the Kingdom of God, which Jesus introduces, is not only about the promise of a better life in eternity. He promises a better life today as well."

Father X responded. "That's right. The path God has revealed to a relationship with him is through Jesus. It is Jesus plus nothing. Our relationship is a gift from God – an undeserved mercy on his part."

"OK," I asked, my thoughts whirling, "but what is the difference between Christianity and following Jesus? Dr. Brody and Gary talk as if they are two separate things. Wasn't Jesus a Christian?"

"Let me see if I can clear up that common misunderstanding. There are followers of Jesus who are in the church and call themselves Christians. But there are many Christians, and many church goers, who are not followers of Jesus. And there are many followers of Jesus who are not in any church."

The Father paused to let that sink in. "Being a follower of Jesus is about putting your life in Jesus' hands. Jesus responds by giving us the Holy Spirit to guide us. He gives us his Word, the Bible, which will often tell you something very different from what the Christian religion tells you. In addition, he gives us brothers and sisters, others who follow Jesus, as new family, to provide community for us as we learn to follow him. This is what the Bible calls church – it's the people running with Jesus, not an organization, a building, or an exclusive religious club.

"Christianity developed 300 years after Christ lived on earth. When the Roman Emperor Constantine converted, he merged the movement of Jesus followers with the official Roman pagan religion and produced Christianity. It may have been done 'In Jesus' name' but the result was still a religion: a man-made set of rules which tells us what we ought to do to get close to God. Much of what the Christian church believes and practices today is in direct contradiction to what Jesus teaches."

I processed that for a minute. "So following Jesus is a relationship anyone can have, even if they don't participate in our culture's religion – Christianity?"

"Exactly," the Father smiled. "Just keep your eyes on Jesus. He will work out the details."

Father X had given me a lot to wonder about. I walked back to campus thinking it was going to take time and effort to sort through what he said. This is all so different from what I grew up with.

The week after Easter, I went over to Musselman to join the Koffee Klatch. Nikki, ever present TAB in hand, led the conversation with Rob, Billy, Gary, Arty, and Linda Pence. Rob and Gary were nattering on about their recent success in trout fishing when Frank Spinelli rushed in. Literally – he was almost running by the time he got to the table. He was panting for breath. "Holy Shit!" he exclaimed. "You will never guess what happened! I was playing cards with some fellows in Wood this morning when Ratso came in and told us his brother Franklin was killed in a car accident."

Stunned silence greeted this announcement. I couldn't believe it! Franklin Ramsey dead? No, it simply could not be. No one our age ever dies. Well, hardly ever. And Franklin Ramsey? Impossible! The group around me stared at Spinelli in stunned silence. For several moments, no one spoke. Rob finally asked, "He's dead? Franklin Agnew Ramsey, IV?"

I was staggered. It's true Ramsey was a rotten shit and treated me badly, but I wouldn't wish him dead.

"Fuckin A!" Arty let out a breath. "What the hell happened?"

Spinelli told us the story. "You know he was a senior at Yale? One of his favorite things to do was to race in road rallies with his buddies from the Skull & Crossbones Society. They all drive flashy sports cars, but Franklin's is the most expensive, best looking, and fastest car. An MG TC 1250 Roadster with a four speed, in line engine, stick shift, turbo charged. They go out in the country, race all day, stay at old inns and drink all night. Prizes are awarded, toasts are raised, and everyone goes home happy."

"Last weekend Ramsey was participating in a rally near Cheshire, Connecticut, an hour north of Yale. On Sunday, racing concluded, he was at the closing dinner at the Cheshire Inn. He was quite lubed up – you know how he liked his liquor."

"And his cocaine," I added.

"Yes, that too." Spinelli affirmed. "He got into an argument about how fast his car was and a guy bet him he could not run a loop of roads in some ridiculous time. Ramsey accepted the bet and took off to win it. Nobody really knows how it happened, but he was driving narrow two-lane country roads in the dark, at high speed. He failed to make a corner. When his friends came looking for him, his car had missed the curve, bounced through a gutter, launched itself into the air and nailed a big sugar maple five feet off the ground. Police estimate he was doing close to seventy miles per hour when he left the road.

"Apparently Frank's car hurtled through the air, cleared a stone wall and hit the tree head on. The force of the collision was so great the maple pierced the middle of his engine block and the front wheels and axel wrapped around the tree trunk. Picture a small child clinging to his Daddy's leg with outstretched arms locked around him. When they discovered the wreck, the MG was nailed to the tree, five feet off the ground, and horizontal. The back of the car was suspended over top of the stone wall but never touched it. Ramsey was ejected right over his little glass windscreen and hit the tree head first, as if he had been shot out of a cannon, at a range of ten feet. Bam! I will not replay Ratso's description of his brother's physical damage. They scraped him up in a basket. Pretty sure it's going to be a closed casket funeral. Ratso is going home to Richmond for the funeral this weekend."

After a long pause and silence, I was able to mumble, "Oh, man, that is so sad!" After more commiseration by my friends, I asked Spinelli, "How is Ratso taking it?"

"I don't know – I think he's bewildered. Here is a guy who has lived the last nineteen years in the shadow of his brother. No one in his family or circle of friends ever gave a rat's ass about him. All the attention was focused on good old Franklin. His older brother was the star of the show, the perfect child, the ideal heir, the faultless son. Ratso is an after-thought and he knows it. It's almost as if planet earth just had the sun disappear. All that is left for light is the pale moon. How do you operate? How do you compensate? Franklin was the sun. Ratso is the moon."

"Man, that is way harsh, even for a dirt bag like Ratso," said Billy.

Gary added in, "I know the world he comes from and this is going to be a tsunami and earthquake put together in Ratso's life. We really need to pray for the guy and be supportive if we can. His whole world has just been wiped out by a nuclear bomb and he will be lucky to survive the fallout."

On that sobering note, we departed the dining hall.

27

"Life is stranger than fiction."
~ *Bruce Roberts Dreisbach*

Jack Flynn   May, 1968

The first week of May continued with a stretch of breath-taking weather. The hills were alive with fabulous shades of yellow greens, what I call "spring green." Flowering trees set off waves of green, the air is warm and sweet with the fragrance of blossoms. Songbirds fill the air with their warbling as they flit back and forth to new nests, and baby birds waiting for chow. The breeze is warm; soft puffy white clouds accentuate the blue sky. In the morning, as the sun rises, the air is fresh and cool from the night's rest. By mid-afternoon, it can be eighty degrees in the shade.

New Hampshire does not have spring. Winter's frost sinks seven feet into the ground, hard ice covers the lakes well into May and no flowers appear until the middle of June. In two weeks "spring" is over. On July 4th, summer officially begins. What passes for spring is so quick, if you blink, you miss it.

Spring is a glorious time in Carlisle. Every chance we can steal away, Rob, Nikki and I go fishing on one of the local trout waters. The LeTort, Yellow Breeches, Big Spring Creek, Green Spring, Falling Springs, Carbon Creek – are on our regular must fish list. When I need time alone, I walk down the road and cut through yards into the East Branch of the Antietam. This babbling freestone trout stream, coursing down the mountain, slides along our campus boundary, then wanders through back yards into the village. I wade in the stream itself, often curtained by walls of underbrush, and roll small worms downstream with the current. Almost all the trout I catch are small native brookies, only five or six inches long. A nine-inch bruiser is practically a trophy. Once in a great while, I winkle a holdover rainbow, almost a foot long, out from under an undercut bank. All these beauties are gently released.

My other preoccupation is riding my motorcycle. The bike is a joy that fills my soul with a sense of satisfaction and well-being. To throw my leg over the saddle, crank back the clutch and turn on the sweet purr of her engine gives me a visceral connection with the machine which is hard to describe. Rolling down the highway, ratcheting up through the gears, leaves me in awe of the power of this throbbing road rocket. Even while in class, I find myself humming bits of the catchy song Arlo Guthrie sings. "I don't want a pickle. I just want to ride on my motorcycle…"

Occasionally, I give a girl a ride on my bike. Faith and Nikki are the biggest fans of bike riding. I love the feeling of a sweet woman snuggling her crotch up to my ass, while wrapping arms around me, and pressing her boobs into my back. All the while purring, gasping, and shouting encouragement in my ear. It is a bit orgasmic. Yes, I get off on it. Add in the throbbing of the engine between my legs, and it's like having sex without getting naked. More Arlo, "And I don't want a tickle, 'cause I'd rather ride on my motorcycle..." Occasionally, I get Dean Feltgood to take a ride. Because of the hassle from my friends, we ride off into the mountains where people won't see us.

One afternoon I took the chopper out Rt. 15 and headed towards Maryland. Everything was great until I looked in my rear mirror and spotted a black swarm of riders approaching on my tail at high speed. There was no place to turn off before they engulfed me with a loud roar. Arlo ran through my mind again, "And I don't want to die, I just want to ride on my motorcycle."

Swallowed alive by a gang of outlaw bikers, I tried to be cool. The jacket patches identified them as *Pagans*, an organized crime syndicate masquerading as a motorcycle club out of Maryland. Noted for violent behavior and street fights with the *Hells Angels,* these are bad dudes. I was scared shitless as these dirty, long haired, thugs wove and swirled their bikes around me at sixty miles per hour. Suddenly, one of the guys realized I was on a Triumph cycle and he hooted giving me the thumbs up of approval. With a shout and a volley of high signs, the bikers roared away. As they rode off, I realized they were all on Triumph bikes themselves. Our love of the British bike was enough to get me a free pass. Whew!

The mellow spring weather just naturally makes a young man's heart turn towards love. All over campus, men and women are pairing up and couples are frequently seen taking walks, laying on a blanket on the lawn or attending some campus function. Rob and Randi are definitely becoming an item. He often escorts her to and from class. I spot Gary and Nikki taking in the free movie at Lane Hall, or "studying" together in the student lounge. Every where they go they hold hands like a couple of love sick fourth graders on their first date. Doug has finally given up trying to get any attention from Faith and settled into a comfortable relationship with Linda Pence. What a pretty girl! They are often seen going on dates or coming home to campus in the Hot Dog Bus.

As much as I understood how foolish it is, I am infatuated with Amy Feltgood. We sit together on her sofa and talk for hours on end. I just love to look at her – so beautiful! I'm mesmerized by the cascade of brilliant red hair, her bright smile, and her deep blue eyes. She is such a good listener - warm, responsive, empathetic, and sympathetic. I confess, half the time we are talking, I have a rock hard boner.

One Saturday, we decided to go on a picnic. She packed a wicker hamper and we roared off on my bike to Carbon Creek State Park. I drove to the back of the picnic grove and we left the cycle. Together, we hiked up the banks of the creek enjoying the trout rising in rapids and pools. When we reached a secluded meadow, we laid out the blanket and picnic. We removed our shoes and socks. I rolled up my jeans. Amy was wearing cut offs. Hand in hand we went wading in the chilly waters of the brook.

After a while, we retreated to the blanket to warm up in the sun. The divine Miss F broke out lunch: cold fried chicken, green grapes, string potato sticks, a couple of bottles of Coke, and an assortment of cookies. We chatted during lunch, enjoying each other's company. Amy lay back in the sun, soaking up the rays. I watched for a while, then on impulse, leaned over and kissed her forehead. She smiled, but did not open her eyes. I kissed each of her eyelids, then her cheeks and finally her lips. She was quite responsive and returned my kisses with enthusiasm.

We ended up lying side by side on the blanket, kissing and caressing. I could not keep my hands off her face, her neck, her arms, her luscious breasts, her tight little ass and the exposed skin of her legs below her shorts. We lay locked in each other's embrace for 45 minutes before Amy broke it off by sitting up. "I think I'm over heated," she exclaimed. "Maybe I'll go wading again."

I was pretty overheated too. I can hardly believe what just happened. I guess I now know how Amy feels about me. All I can do was sit on the blanket and watch this beautiful woman cavorting in the sun-drenched stream and marvel at my good fortune.

That evening, I went to Amy's apartment. We had planned to share dinner and watch the Saturday night movie on TV. I brought a fresh loaf of Italian bread from the local bakery. Amy whipped up shells, marinara meat sauce, with grated Parmesan cheese, and a tossed salad. We sat and enjoyed a great feed. Afterwards we snuggled on the sofa chatting while waiting for the movie to come on. The lights were low and I double checked the door was locked. I didn't want anyone walking in on us.

Amy reached over and took my hand in hers. "I really enjoyed our picnic, Jack. I have to confess, I have been somewhat distant from you to this point, but I am sure you understand my internal conflict. It was such a relief to finally let my real feelings show."

"You know how I feel about you," I replied, "But I've been unsure of what you felt for me."

Amy started to kiss the back of my hand while stroking my arm. "I feel for you," she said with a sweet smile. After forty minutes of chatting, cooing (that would be Amy), and light petting, the movie came on. I have no idea what it was called or what it was about. I could only think of this beautiful woman in my arms. As the evening wore on, I don't think Amy was watching the movie either. We kept kissing; long, wet, tongue exploring kisses. I caressed every part of her I could reach. While kissing her neck and the tops of her breasts, I slowly unbuttoned her filmy, beige blouse down to her waist with no resistance. I slid my hand in along her hard, flat stomach and caressed her torso and breasts. Her lean rib cage jutted out and her back was slim and long. Sensing no reluctance, I snaked my hand around and snicked her bra clasp open. I practically came in my jeans when I fondled her naked tits for the first time. So round and firm, with small but hard nipples. I was pretty hard myself.

"Ohh, ...ahh," Amy crooned and rolled towards me so I could reach her better. She was kissing me and running her hand up under my black t-shirt stroking her fingers up and down my chest. "I love a hairy man," she murmured as she ran her fingers through the hair on my chest. Kissing me harder, she fluffed the hair on my head and laughed, "I like hair here too!"

I stood and peeled off my shirt while Amy sat up and shucked her bra and blouse. I marveled at the pale skin on her breasts and the rich brown patina of freckles everywhere else. We lay together in intimate surrender to our passion.

Eventually, I reached down and unfastened her jeans so I could run my hand down her back, under her jeans and panties and onto the silken skin of her ass. Now I was the one panting, "Ohh...Ahh." Ten minutes later, I pulled her jeans right off her backside and dropped them on the floor. I dumped my jeans and briefs onto the floor and lay back down on the couch next to Amy. We intertwined our limbs and spent pleasurable moments exploring and caressing one another. Finally, I stood Amy up between my legs and began to peel her bikini briefs off her bottom.

"Wait, Jack." She put out her hand to stop me from removing the last barrier. "Jack, I have to ask you, where does this go?" She captured my hands in hers so I couldn't continue the final step in the seduction.

"Whatever do you mean, Amy?" I whispered looking deep into her eyes. "I love you."

"I love you too, Jack, but you're 19, and I am 28. I'm a staff member of the college, and you are a student. You know this is completely against the rules. I'm your Hall Director and a Ph.D. candidate. If we do this, if we are found out, I will be guilty of professional misconduct and will probably never work in a university for the rest of my life. We just can't do this. Can you see us keeping this secret for two more years while you finish college? What kind of relationship would that be?

"But, Amy, I love you. I only want you. I always want you with me. You fulfill all the needs of my soul. I can't live without you!"

"I can't do this, Jack. I'm sorry. I didn't mean to mislead you. I let my feelings for you get carried away. This is wrong." I slumped down and put my hands up to my eyes and began to cry. Amy pulled on her jeans and her blouse and sat next to me wrapping her arms around my shoulders. "I am so sorry, Jack. Can you ever forgive me?"

"Just give me a minute." I don't how to describe the emotions raging through me at that moment – hurt, shock, disappointment...and the conviction she is right. If we have to live in secret for two years; lie, hide, cover our tracks, worry about discovery... That sort of life could never lead to a healthy relationship. Just pain, misery, and sorrow for both of us. Plus I can see the practical issues. If Amy lost her job because of our relationship, how would I support the two of us? If we were discovered, she would probably be kicked out of her doctoral program and lose any return for ten years of higher education. And was I ready to make a lifetime commitment to love and care for this woman right now? Not really.

Grudgingly, in my heart, I have to admit our relationship doesn't make sense. It isn't the age difference that makes us incompatible. The student - staff conflict and the ethical conflicts make it wrong. I didn't want to be a user like Franklin Ramsey and only consider my needs and pleasure. I have to think of what is best for Amy. I pulled on my clothes and boots. Lifting Amy up to stand in front of me, I embraced her, kissed her once on the mouth and walked out of her apartment and her life.

After breaking up with Amy Feltgood, I found myself overwhelmed by crushing feelings of pain and grief. It feels like Maggie's death, but fresh and sharp in searing intensity. My love for Amy hasn't changed, but the impossibility of our love looms large over me every day and pushes me towards despair. I struggle to get through each day while bearing this burden.

The amusing antics of my pals in the card club help me forget my pain, at least for a while. Last Thursday, I was in the Blue Room playing hearts with the boys. Billy Harrison was waxing eloquent about his new girl friend, a freshman chick named Monica Albright. Arty observed, "She has a great figure, long legs a fabulous chest, but her hair is kinda mousey, don't you think?"

Frank said, "I think she's pretty, but she may need a new hairstyle. Her current doo looks like Betty Boop, circa 1946. Her hair is ok, but her hair style is twenty years out of date. I heard she's from Long Island. What kind of family does she come from, Billy?"

"Well, that's just it." Billy laughed. "She was raised in a Plymouth Brethren home, which may account for her frumpy clothes and her hair style. I don't know if her parents got the kids' clothes from the church missionary barrel, but it sort of looks that way. I admit she needs a wardrobe update, but when she peels her frock off she is hot, hot, hot. You guys know what I always say, don't you?"

Arty laughed out loud. "To quote Billy Harrison, 'Once you get a girl in bed and turn out the lights, they all look the same.'" The guys laughed uproariously.

Gary interjected, "Plymouth Brethren don't have a church building, so they don't have a church missionary barrel. They are Low Church. Very informal – instead of meeting in a building, they meet in peoples' homes, they don't have a membership roll, and they don't have a pastor. I don't know what else they believe or practice, but they are fairly different."

"She goes to church, but she puts out?" asked Arty.

Billy laughed. "Yeah, it's kind of freaky. We make passionate love and then she talks about God and church and all that stuff. Some girls want to have a smoke after sex, but Monica wants to talk about God. I admit, even though I get drunk or toked up every weekend, by Monday morning, I feel bad and wish I had God in my life. But after all the bad things I've done, how could I go to church?"

Ratso wandered into the lounge. "You look like shit!" exclaimed Gary. "Do you want to play?"

"No, I'll just watch thanks." Gary was right. Ratso looked bad. He watched in silence. This is a different Ratso. Normally, Ramsey would spew caustic and critical comments until he made such a nuisance of himself, everybody wanted to throttle him. Not today. All the bully and bluster is gone. Like a soda with no fizz.

Gary said, "How did the funeral go?"

"OK I guess," muttered Ratso. "I've never been to a funeral before, so…who knows?"

"How are your folks doing?" Gary probed.

"Bad, I guess. They are not used to sharing their emotions, or much of anything else with me."

"How about you, Ratso? How are you holding up?" Gary continued.

"You know, I lived my whole life in the shadow of my brother. He was always the favorite, the chosen one, the sun, moon, and stars according to my parents. I don't think I hated Frank, but he was like…it was like being a smaller, younger tree living in the shadow of a big tree. He just sucked up all of the sunlight until there was scarcely enough for me to exist. Never enough for me to grow and thrive. My life was defined by his life and I counted for nothing.

"Now with Frank gone, I realize how low I am in the family pecking order. I'm lower than Zippy, our dog – who everybody ignores. I can see now, all I ever wanted was a little love and attention. I never got it. It seems to me, the opposite of love is not hatred. It's indifference." Ratso paused while we thought about what he had said. "When we were at the funeral, I watched my parents closely. It's not just that they are indifferent to me, that I'm practically invisible to them. I could see both of them thinking, 'I wish it was Craig in the casket instead of Frank.'"

The Card Club sat in silence trying to process all this. Ratso wandered towards the door, looking like a guy in a trance. Just then the door flew open and Frenchie ran into the Blue Room and shouted, "Leave the cards!' He stood waving us frantically towards the door. "You have to come right now! You won't believe this! You have to see this! Come on, with me!" And he ran to the door. Like a herd of cattle in stampede, we all jumped to our feet and tore after Frenchie.

Frenchie went ripping around several dorms and pulled up on the edge of a crowd of gawkers standing on the berm of the faculty parking lot outside the back doors of the Rector Science Building. Frenchie stopped right next to Andy Sergeant and Linda Pence.

Frenchie said, "What's going down, man?"

"Oh, baby!" Andy laughed. "The philandering professor's wife has just discovered he's been cheating on her all these years with as many nubile coeds as he could get! Apparently she uncovered his current affair with Delilah Brown; and that led to the revelation that he has been cheating on her for quite a while. I'm guessing from her reaction, Mrs. Henning was surprised."

Dr. and Mrs. Henning were standing in the parking lot by his car, screaming and shrieking at each other at the top of their lungs. Henning drives a brand new 1967 BMW 1602 sports sedan. A four speed stick shift with a 1.5 liter engine. The professor is a natural attention hound, so, of course, the car is bright fire engine red. He keeps it pristine, washing and waxing it every weekend.

Linda spoke up, "It serves the bastard right! You might not guess it from looking at her right now, but I've met Mrs. Henning at normal times and she is an attractive woman. She has a sexy figure, stays in shape, and dresses well. Very striking! Her blonde hair looks like it comes from a bottle, but even so, there is no earthly reason why that wretched man should be chasing skirts!"

As the verbal brawl on the lot continued, the jilted wife went over to her Volvo, popped the trunk and took out a sledge hammer. She walked directly to the front end of the red BMW and with a graceful swing began to knock out the headlights! Dr. Henning simply looked on in horror. The blood drained from his face as she bashed in front and rear windows, and began hammering the shiny body work. Bash! Crash! Crunch! As we watched in amazement, all four side windows crumpled to her blows. For the next ten minutes, the angry woman systematically demolished her husband's car.

Totally absorbed in this spectacle, I grew aware of fire sirens in the distance. When we left the parking lot, I could see a huge column of black smoke billowing up from a nearby residential neighborhood. Later we learned, the vindictive Mrs. Henning had set their house on fire before she left to take care of the professor's fancy sport's car. I had a casual conversation with Dean Benchoff and he mentioned Mrs. Henning had the money in the family. She had paid for the flashy BMW and their house. Both were paid for with her money and in her name. The Dean said she was within her legal rights to dispose of car and house in any way she saw fit. I don't think the Dean approves of faculty fooling around with students. Ouch! And that could have been me.

28

"The significance of a man is not in what he attains,
but rather in what he longs to attain."
~ Kahil Gibran

Nikki Clausen   May, 1968

Toward the end of spring of sophomore year, things in our campus world finally seemed to settle down. The fall had been crazy with nearly losing Bunny in the Delaware River and Spud's unexpected death. By Christmas, I think we were still a little rattled. Then, Franklin Ramsey kills himself with his sports car, Martin Luther King is assassinated, and urban street riots are burning all over America. What the hell? You can't blame us for thinking the world is self destructing! It makes me wonder if we're going to survive as a civilization. Maybe the world won't last long enough for me to graduate from college?

As spring matured, events seemed to heading in a more positive direction. I can only hope the end of this school year will be uneventful. To that end, I decided to dedicate as much time as possible enjoying the sweet, warm, May weather. Some afternoons I just lay out on the grass of the Quad, closed my eyes and dreamed of peace. Feeling the breeze, watching the clouds, and daydreaming makes me want to stay put, to sleep here all night, watch the stars, and snuggle down in the warm embrace of Mother Nature.

Another favorite activity is sitting by the pond in back of the athletic fields, and processing my thinking. I walk around the pond or sit on my favorite log inside the edge of the woods and watch nature. This gives me the mental and emotional space I need to sort things out. Sometimes I bring a journal to take notes. Writing down what I'm thinking helps me organize and analyze. One morning I listened to the call of red headed wood peckers chasing beetles in the white pines. Canadian Geese on the far end of the pond screech out mating calls as the females prepared to hatch their eggs. A cute chipmunk is playing in leaf litter six feet from my feet. What a great morning to be alive!

Gary occupies a lot of my thoughts these days. I'm grateful for the way my relationship with Gary is developing. Many of my girlfriends are involved with guys, but in relationships with heavy duty sex. My observation is that sex tends to overshadow everything else in a friendship. It may even prevent the couple from getting to know each other. Faith describes her current sex life as being hit by a tornado – yet she still knows nothing about Butch. I once heard Dr. Brody say that starting a relationship with sex is like tuning up the symphony orchestra by beginning with the kettle drums. It drowns out all the delicate instruments. Brody suggested an orchestra warms up with the subtle delicate strings and woodwinds first and saves the kettle drums for last. That's what I want to do – build a relationship and when we reach the commitment of marriage, then add in the kettle drums of sex.

Gary is an affectionate guy. He is constantly touching my arm, holding my hand, opening the car door, resting his arm on my shoulders. He makes affirming and encouraging observations. The boy communicates his love and affection without stirring up the kettle drums of sex. Our friendship is built on conversation, shared experience, and sensitivity to each other. He listens to me, asks my opinion, and is respectful of how I feel about things. He offers positive feedback when I share. He is open and honest about what he feels and thinks. I find Gary honestly wants to communicate with me. Being with Gary reminds me of a warm, gentle day in May. Sort of like a Leonard Cohen song. All these elements are building a strong and healthy relationship between us - without the need for resorting to sex.

Spring is not just a good time for me to get in touch with myself and to revel in the natural world. It's also a wonderful time to take pleasure in my friendships. One sunny afternoon I went by Allison Hall to see if Randi was interested it enjoying the balmy 80-degree afternoon. I suggested we could lie out on a blanket in the sun and catch up. When I got to Randi's room, Faith was there. "Hey, stranger! Long time, no see." I said to Faith.

Faith gave me a rueful grin. "Guess I've been working a lot, but I haven't let it interfere with classes."

"Yes, but it has interfered with your social life. We miss you, Honey Bunny. You have been way too scarce this term."

"Amen to that sister!" echoed Randi. "Would you like to come get some sun with us?"

Faith paused to consider, and said, "Sure, I'd like that. I need some sun – I look as pale as a ghost. Too much time indoors, I guess. Let me go find my beach blanket and the reading I need to work on."

We got organized and walked over to the Quad. The lawn at the center of campus is ideal for sunbathing and socializing. The grass has a great southern exposure so it gets the full rays of the sun. The three of us spread out our blankets and settled in.

Randi, always one to tread where angels fear to go, opened the conversation by asking Faith, "Tell us more about your relationship with Butch? Have you met his family or friends?"

After a long silence, Faith answered, "Well, no... not exactly. Butch is not on speaking terms with his ex-wives or his kids. I think he's written off that period of his life and is trying to forget. I know he's from Carlisle, but he never talks about parents or siblings or any other family."

"Ever meet his friends?" I asked. "What are they like?"

"I can't say I've met his friends. He spends most evenings at the bar in Grandpa's so he knows the bartenders and most of the regulars by name, but I wouldn't call them friends. He doesn't play pool or shoot the shit with the other guys – in fact, he's probably twenty years older than the other barflies who are in there most nights. Most of the 'hang out, shoot pool, be buddies, and cruise for chicks' guys are in their twenties or early thirties."

"How old is Butch?" I asked.

"Fifty three," Faith answered in a very matter of fact tone.

"Jumping Jiminy!" I exclaimed. "He's old enough to be your father. What's that about?"

"Well," Faith replied, "Butch likes to talk and I like to listen – or maybe it's that I simply don't want to open up and share. He accepts me. I have taken enough psychology to understand Butch may be a substitute for my father, who has never loved me, but where I am right now, it feels OK."

Randi and I sat quietly for a bit. I had no idea what to say in response to what Faith shared. She is so brutally honest and so sad at the same time – it just makes me want to weep.

Randi asked, "Faith, what do you see as the future of your relationship with Butch?"

Faith replied, "I don't know. I guess I try not to look at the future too much. Especially in terms of our relationship. He's not a guy I would marry. I can't see him supporting me with the things I want from life on a pressman's salary. I'm certain Butch will never marry again. You could not drag him to the altar with a herd of elephants. He's a person I can be with, we are comfortable with each other, and are sexually compatible. It's what it is for today. I try not to think about tomorrow."

"It sounds like dating a married man. Its fun, but there is no risk of future entanglements," I ventured. "Do you think after what happened to Spud, this is a way to avoid being hurt in a relationship?"

Faith considered, "I think there may be some of that. Not just Spud but Frank Ramsey and Skeeter too. I had such high expectations and then the ground was ripped out from under me. I guess I've lowered my expectations. Look, I know it sounds off, but it's what I want. I am not without fears and anxiety about how this works out, but for right now – it makes me feel ok. That's enough."

As I reflected on what Faith shared, I found myself amazed at how blind and stubborn she can be. In many ways she is as willful and bullheaded as her father. She describes him as living life locked on a one-way street, yet its hard not to think Faith is doing the same thing with her choices.

After a few minutes of quiet, Randi asked, "Faith, what do you dream of for a future for yourself?"

"Wow! That's a good topic, Randi. You always ask such penetrating questions. Let me think." Faith paused to consider Randi's query for several minutes. "To be butt honest, I got nothin'… When I think about my future, I see myself staring at a blank wall. I sure as hell do not want to go back to where I'm from. Not my family, not Christianity, not even St Simons Island. If you ask me what future I hope for, I'd like to have the life Skeeter's parents live, but I don't see how I get there if

Skeeter does not want to live that life. Unless somebody comes along and rescues me, I see no hope in the future. As best I can tell, I just feel lost!" After a long minute, while her candid answer sunk in, Faith asked us, "When you gals think about the future, what do you see?"

"Gary and I have talked about it." I answered. "His folks expect him to go back to Richmond and run the family corporation. He's not interested. The other day he told me the one thing he is most passionate about is ice hockey. He's thinking he might enjoy coaching in a high school or junior college. He could never play professionally, but he could introduce other kids to the sport he loves. It's hard to get a year-round job just coaching, so Gary plans on teaching, probably Civics, Social Studies, History or something like that. I think he wants to help young people discover the kinds of things going on in our world he found out by accident from living in the South."

"What about you Nikki? Full-time job as a spokesperson for TAB?" Randi and Faith howled at Randi's jab. "No, really, do you have any ideas?"

"Gary has me thinking maybe I should go into outdoor education. There isn't such a field yet, but being outdoors and understanding nature is what I love. Right now there's been talk about starting a national Earth Day to focus on taking care of our environment. Maybe a new field will come out of that. I thought if I took Botany, Biology, Geology, and Education courses, perhaps I could end up working to introduce others to the natural world."

"What a great idea, Nikki," Randi enthused. "When it comes to picking a major and a career I'm like you Faith. I'm stumped. I enjoy my art classes, but I don't think I'm an actual artist, like Snow White. I enjoy the beautiful creations made with art. I'm especially fascinated by textile art and design. In my secret thoughts, I wonder if I might enjoy being an interior decorator? But I can just see my mother's negative reaction to that! Ka-Boom! She would blow right through the roof. My Dad doesn't think women should work – just stay home, raise babies and keep house. I don't disagree with that either. I'd like to be a wife and mother. But I'm not sure that's all I want to do."

The three of us had a great afternoon on the Quad. Sunning, sharing, laughing, and wondering about the future. We had a lot of fun, learned more about ourselves and each other, and grew in friendship. Sweet times! All in all, it was a highly successful outing.

Two months after the assassination of Martin Luther King, we learned Senator Robert Kennedy had been shot after a campaign speech in LA. The next day he died. At our morning Koffee Klatch, a somber group of friends gathered around the table. I sat nursing my third TAB of the morning. Rob and Gary looked sick and were silent. Randi, Billy, Arty just looked miserable. After 20 minutes of moping, I finally had enough. "Friends, I think the time has come for action," I blurted out.

"What do you mean Nikki?" asked Billy.

"When Dr. King was killed, Jack said our generation has a tendency to vacillate between passivity and activism? I think he's right. How can you look at what's going on in this country and do nothing?"

Rob muttered, "I remember – so what?"

"I think he's right and its time to start the revolution! We can be like an ostrich and stick our head in the sand and pretend things will get better. Or we can stand up and do something about it. In less than a decade three of our best national leaders have been murdered. Every time we try to make a change for the better, George Wallace and all the haters try to push us back into the dark ages. Our national government is run by old nitwits. Nixon tells everyone that the 'Silent Majority' support his point of view. What are we, retarded? If they are silent, who knows what they think?"

Rob jumped in. "I often think about running away and living in the woods. I could graduate from Carlisle to become the last of the mountain men. I'm sure the Alumni Association would be proud of me living off the land in the Snake River Wilderness in Idaho."

Arty laughed, "Yeah, I can see it now. Front page articles in the Alumni Newsletter about Robbie Bachmann, our own modern hermit benefiting humanity by completely withdrawing from it. Ha Ha!"

Robbie continued, "Let me finish. While I like the picture of personal peace and prosperity for me, I see two drawbacks. It leaves everybody else swirling down the shitter – especially those of you I love. The second problem is that eventually, the crap will spread to the point it invades my mountain stronghold in Idaho. Lights out, curtains for certain, for Robbie the Hermit."

"Just because you are paranoid, it doesn't mean they are not coming to get you," laughed Arty.

"Something like that," replied Rob.

"Ah, yes, I see the problem," said Billy, "but realistically, what can we do?"

Gary spoke up. "The only way 'Tricky Dick' can get away with claiming the silent people are on his side, is if we don't speak up. What if masses of young people stood up in public and said, 'This is wrong! We're not going to take it anymore. We demand change!' Who is the media going to cover? All of Nixon's silent supporters? Or the people protesting in the streets? When Walter Cronkite comes on at 6 pm and tells America we are mounting a revolution for change, people will join us. Look at what Dr. King did with the power of non-violent public protest. We could change the course of this country if we did what the blacks did over the last ten years."

"I agree," I added. "Dr. King said 'No lie can live forever.' That's true if people will speak up and call it a lie – in public. America was founded by citizens who were willing to stand up and fight for what is right. What did Dr. King say? 'We must protest, we must demonstrate, and we must resist.' Something like that. That is exactly what we have to do to change the course of this country and our history."

"Hey, you have a point," added Randi. "Look at the Democratic Party. They can't decide whether to run a party stooge like Humphrey or an agent of change like Kennedy, McCarty, or McGovern. Public pressure could help them see the light and pick a more progressive candidate for president."

"Makes sense to me." Arty spoke up. "I'll bet public protest and demonstration will have a powerful effect on Democrats in Congress. Perhaps even on the voting public. Then we could let the ballot box prove we don't want the USA to become a third rate banana republic."

"On a more practical note," asked Randi, "What precisely are you thinking we should do?"

"Frenchie says the Vietnam Vets against the War are going to go protest at the Democratic National Convention in Chicago in August. They figure with all the media coverage of the political convention, all they have to do is stand outside the door of the Amphitheater to get good TV coverage. With any luck, some people will get interviewed and the media will help spread our story to America. If college students show up and protest it will have a national impact. If we can get enough people there, the protests could be as big a story as the politicians. Who knows, if we get a really big turnout, it could influence the outcome of the nomination and the presidential election."

"So you want us to go out to Chicago, hang around the convention, stage peaceful protests and get on the news?" I asked.

"Precisely!" Gary replied. "Who wants to go?"

We hashed this proposal over and by the end of exam week, we had commitments from Frenchie, Jack, Rob, Randi, Gary, Bunny, Frank, Doug, Linda, and me to head to Chicago on Saturday August 24. The Band of Ten, we started calling ourselves. This is how the revolution begins! We plan to meet up at the end of August at Linda's grandparents' farm outside Carlisle. We will car pool together to Chicago, join the protests and come back in time for the start of fall trimester. Linda and Randi agreed to keep in touch with everyone over the summer. When we left college at the end of our sophomore year, I was really pumped. We had a committed team and a plan to make a difference in our country and own future.

Well, you know what they say about the best laid plans. If I had known the magnitude of the disaster which would come our way in August, perhaps I would not have left school on such a high.

Year Three

29

"Make voyages. Attempt them. There is nothing else."

~ *Tennessee Williams*

Nikki Clausen   August, 1968

The minute Gary laid eyes on me across the crowded bus terminal, he began hollering, skipping, and leaping towards me. "Sheeee-ooot!" He rushed across the concourse and swept me up in his arms. "Sugar Buns! It is soooo... good to see you!" We hugged, kissed and made a spectacle of ourselves in the middle of New York City's Port Authority Bus Terminal. I'm sure bystanders were barfing up lunch by the time we got done with our affectionate welcome. Honestly, who else but a couple of puppies lick each other's faces to express affection?

"Here, let me carry your bag." Gary grabbed it and headed towards the parking garage. I left State College six hours earlier and rode the Greyhound bus to New York. Gary agreed to meet me at the Port Authority and drive me up to his grandparent's place on Long Island. We had tried to set up a visit several times over the past year, but it had never worked out. We decided the week in mid - August, before our trip to protest at the Democratic National Convention might work. I quit my summer job at the Pleasant Gap Nursery a week early and hopped a bus for New York City.

When Gary talks about home, he means his Lynch grandparents' home on Long Island, NY. The Grands, as Gary calls them, are his home. Not Richmond. When asked he will say "Richmond is filled with striving, pushing, imposing, posturing. It's about appearances; it's a culture based on fear, shame, and guilt. Living in Richmond is like living with cannibals. They are so vicious, they eat their own children. Not my values; not my home."

The Lynch Grands live in Old Field, on the northern side of the Long Island. I know they live on an "estate" but I have no idea what that means. We don't have "estates" in State College. The well-heeled in my neck of the woods simply buy working farms so they can spread out a little. Estates are way too pretentious for anyone living in Centre County. As we approached his Grands' home on Evans Lane, I see large houses, set well back from the street, with expansive lawns and beautiful landscaping. Most have water views of Long Island Sound. The neighborhood smells like money.

We drove between two high brick pillars and up a long winding drive to the Lynch's home. Laid out on a ridgeline, the white brick house isn't elaborate, just spacious, with multiple additions adding to the space. Gary said it was an old house earlier owners had built onto, like sections of a telescope, to increase its capacity until it boasted six bedrooms, four and a half baths and separate servant's quarters on the far end. Opposite the driveway, near the portico, was a five-stall garage with a staff residence above.

Gary led the way to the front door, and, as we approached, it swung open and an older man with salt and pepper hair beamed at us and said, "Welcome home Mr. Gary! It's so good to see you twice in the same day. This must be the beautiful Nikki you keep talking about."

"Nikki, this is Alek Dorian who runs the house. When all else fails, he is the 'go to guy' to make anything happen around here. Of course, his boss is Karen, his wife, who is in charge of cooking, housekeeping, and making sure Alek and I don't get into too much trouble." Gary and Alek both laughed heartily at this little domestic joke.

"Are the Grands at home, Alek?"

"No, Gary. Mrs. Lynch is at a luncheon at the Yacht Club and your Grandfather is in town. Gino drove your grandmother, who said she hoped to be home by two or two thirty."

"Gino is our chauffer, car mechanic, gardener and he and his wife Susie live in the apartment over the garage. They are the reason the grounds look so good. Gino has a green thumb and knows everything about plants and things. I know the two of you will get along like gang busters. I'll have him give you a botanical tour of the grounds."

Alek dressed casually for a butler, I thought, in pressed gray flannel slacks, a white Oxford button down shirt topped with a soft blue cashmere sweater. I suppose all the butlers I've ever seen were in movies, British movies, and they always wear a tux. Mr. Dorian is my first butler in the flesh. He was very kind and not at all stuffy.

Hilltop House is pleasant, but not pretentious. Somewhat larger than normal houses, the decorating is traditional and understated, considering the multi-generational wealth of the Lynch clan. I was shown to a "guest room" which is actually a suite with a large bedroom, a private bathroom and a sitting room with comfortable easy chairs, a chaise lounge and sofa. It has a study desk, a writing table, excellent lighting and a big row of windows overlooking the back yard. I'd say the guest suite is larger than the entire first floor of my family's home in Pleasant Gap.

After I unpacked, Gary came by to check on me. "Did you get any lunch?" I shook my head no. "Neither did I. I was so excited to see you I just took off about ten thirty this morning and headed straight to 42nd Street. Let's go see if Karen will fix us something. We often don't eat dinner until late. I don't want you to starve until then." Holding my hand, we walked down the wide hallways and staircases into the sunny kitchen. The kitchen walls and woodwork were painted a rich yellow, with deep blue accents. The window ledges were stuffed with blooming plants, hanging baskets framed each window, and potted violets were scattered everywhere. The kitchen décor had a distinctly Italian flavor.

Karen Dorian, a sturdy woman in her early fifties, was glad to provide lunch. "You kids sit and I'll whip up some tomato soup and grilled cheese sandwiches.

Gary, will you fix the drinks?" I listened to them natter on about school, our drive up from the city, and the late summer weather. Gary and Karen have great rapport. Hilltop exudes a restful atmosphere. The people are welcoming, and relationships seemed to be based on abundant love and kindness. No wonder Gary prefers to call this place home.

After lunch we took a walk around the estate. "It's not very big, as North Shore estates go," he told me, "but it has some features you'll like. The views are one reason my grandparents bought this house. You can watch the sun rise over Flax Pond and you can see The Ferry Pass on Long Island Sound. Often I find the Grands gazing out the windows at the sun and wind and clouds playing on the water and trees. In nice weather they sit on the patio. They practically live out here in the summer. They appreciate nature nearly as much as you do, Nikki."

Gary led me down a walk through the trees to a private path into a wide meadow with woodlands and sand dunes. We crested the dunes, the view opened up and I was looking at a wide beach of white sand on the Sound. "This is one of my favorite spots. It's a wonderful place to sit and wool gather, watch nature or sleep in the sun." He led me to a half circle of white Adirondack chairs behind a steep sand dune. We dropped into the chairs, and spent a relaxing time enjoying each other, the conversation, the sea gulls and shore birds, the waves, the wind and the quiet.

During the week I spent with the Lynches, there was little to indicate they had wealth. Except for the servants, who they treat as members of their family. The Lynches define the word egalitarian. They are the most down to earth people I've ever met. I can see why Gary loves them dearly. They've had a remarkable influence on helping him discover himself and affirm who he is.

Friday evening, we walked up Evans Lane to meet the Cartwrights. Their home is modest compared to the neighbors. A four-bedroom, two-story colonial on a one acre lot. The kind of house you might see in any suburb in America. We had dinner with Larry and Joyce Cartwright and their three kids; Tony, Max and Adele. After dinner, we settled into the living room with desert and coffee while the kids went to watch TV in the family room. Gary asked, "Mr. and Mrs. C, could you tell Nikki about your Jesus Family? I tried to explain it, but I'm not sure I'm giving her an accurate picture."

"No problem, Gary, but don't you think you two are old enough to call us Joyce and Larry?" added Mr. Cartwright with a laugh.

"Nikki can call you Joyce and Larry. I like calling you Mr. and Mrs. C. You've become precious in my life wearing those titles. If you were my Mom and Dad, would you want me to call you Joyce and Larry?"

"Zing!" chortled Mrs. C. "Point well made. You may call us whatever pleases you, my boy."

Mr. C. proceeded with his story. "After we got married, before we had kids, we were introduced to Jesus by a friend from college. We learned early that walking with Jesus is about relationships, what our friend Jeff calls community. Jeff told me most of Jesus' commands in Scripture are about relationships. How we relate to God, how we treat each other, how we relate to those who don't know Jesus."

"When we met Jesus," Joyce continued, "we were still in college, so we joined a small group of believers who met on campus. Then we graduated, got real jobs, settled down and had kids. After a while, we just kind of fell out of the habit of being in community with others who were trying to love God and follow Jesus. When our kids were still small, a number of couples in our neighborhood had their marriages break up and end in divorce."

Larry picked up the tale, "Frankly, it scared the crap out of us, pardon my French. In self defense we decided to start a group with the Jesus followers we knew in our area and it just took off. We asked several couples with kids to join us. We meet on the first and third Tuesday each month. We just love each other, share our lives, and listen to each other. We study God's word, sing a few songs, pray together and try to care for each other. Each month we have a social outing, like a BBQ or Christmas party. Once a year we go somewhere on a retreat or vacation. We've lived these practices for many years.

"When people are sick or lose their jobs, we reach out to help. Marital conflict or problems with kids, we step in and support each other. When somebody needs aid with home repairs or moving, we all pitch in. Everyone in the family, all ages, is included. Our goal is to be like a family for each other. A community powered by Jesus. We call ourselves 'The Jesus Family.' Our core group has between six and sixteen adults plus kids. We reach out to help people in our neighborhood, at work, or anyone in our network who has needs. We're just trying to be 'Jesus with skin on' to the people in our lives. In all the high and low points of life, this group has prayed, encouraged and loved each other for decades."

"That is amazing!" I exclaimed. "I've never heard of such a thing, but it makes perfect sense. You know Gary, I think our circle of friends at college is something like that – a real family of people who care about each other. It's a budding community. I don't think we know how to tap into Jesus yet, but I can definitely see the benefits of being in community."

When I look back on my week on Long Island, I think the time with the Cartwrights had the most impact. As we drove to Grantham to meet our friends and head out to the protest in Chicago, I kept thinking about their description of the Jesus Family and wishing I was in a group like that. We talked about it a lot and I kept asking Gary questions about Jesus. This is all new to me, but I'm fascinated.

Over the summer, we decided to meet up at Willow Bend Farm in Grantham, outside Carlisle. Linda's grandparents live on a lovely dairy farm on the banks of Yellow Breeches Creek. They retired from farming, but minus the cows, the farm was everything an old-fashioned farm should be. The Band of Ten: Frenchie, Jack, Rob, Randi, Gary, Bunny, Frank, Doug, Linda, and I pulled into Linda's grandparent's farm at high noon. The property looks loved and well cared for. The girls got to sleep in two guest bedrooms in the house. The guys were assigned to the Bunk House. This converted tack room in the barn has five double bunk beds set up dormitory style. It has been used for sleepovers, grandkids, and visiting church youth groups who stay at the farm. The boys also had exclusive use of the two-hole outhouse behind the barn. What a hoot!

Gandy and Mom-Mom, Linda's grandparents, could not have been more hospitable. They let us get organized for the trek to the Windy City, helped us go shopping for food and supplies and re-pack Spinelli's Buick wagon and Doug's Hot Dog van, the two vehicles we decided to take on the trip. After we did the hard work of planning and packing, we enjoyed a wonderful dinner of burgers, hot dogs, potato salad, fresh corn on the cob, watermelon and homemade apple pie. All washed with iced tea. After the meal, we sat around the campfire, roasting marshmallows and watching shooting stars streak across the sky. Ahhh, such bliss. If we had had any inkling of what the next few days would bring, we might have just stayed on at Willow Bend Farm. But we were clueless.

The next morning, after a huge breakfast, we drove down the farm lane at eight fifteen with a cloud of dust and a hearty "Hi O' Silver!" Taking the Pennsylvania Turnpike west we headed across the state where we joined Interstate 70. We crossed through West Virginia, over the Ohio River and into Ohio. At four pm we finally pulled off the interstate in Zanesville. Doug led us down a series of narrow asphalt roads until we arrived at Spring Valley Campground, a quiet little family campground on the banks of the Muskingum River.

Everyone piled out of the vehicles, just glad to get out and stretch our legs. "Are we there yet?" had been the constant refrain for the past 2 hours. Everyone helped set up camp along the fringe of trees by the river. We enjoyed shade from the western sun, a few tree limbs to help set up our tents and an ample supply of firewood for the evening. We erected a random assortment of tents and prepared dinner. Randi and I whipped up a one pot meal of ground beef, wide pasta noodles, corn, and Campbell's Cream of Mushroom soup. It was like a casserole but required no oven to cook. Yummy!

After dinner, we settled around a blazing campfire Jack and Rob had built in the middle of our site. As dusk crept over the scene, a VW bus pulled into the campsite across the lane. Big and fat, like most VW buses, this was also a rolling work of art. The exterior featured a mural of the countryside. Green grass wrapped around the bottom. Above was a brilliant sunrise. The top was a blue sky filled with big white stars. Layered on top of this montage were small pictures of cows, trees, cars, and barns.

The doors of this rolling work of art popped open and four long hairs got out laughing. Probably glad to be off the road for the evening. They pulled out a pair of light green canvas tarps, attached them to the roof racks of the bus, and then staked the bottom corners to the ground. These additions made the bus look like it had wings. In five minutes they had two tents set up, the back of the bus was open, and all four were laughing and enjoying a stand up diner of sandwiches out of the kitchen kit in the back.

Wryly, Rob observed, "Whew! They know how to travel. Makes us look like a bunch of idiots."

Doug just laughed. "Experience is a great teacher, my son. If the mural on the bus is any clue, those dudes are traveling the country. And, as you should know, it's a big country!"

The hippies all had long hair. The pretty blonde one was definitely a woman. Two of the guys had full beards, which helped in gender identification. After eating dinner, the hippies pulled out a couple guitars and started singing folk songs. That was enough for Frenchie. He crossed the lane and invited the hippies to join our circle. When they did, Frenchie made the introductions. "Hey everyone, meet our new neighbors." This merry band consisted of a married couple and two young single guys. Cindy and Virgil, the couple. Fitz and Swope; the single cats.

Doug asked, "Not to be forward, but are you hippies?"

"No," they laughed.

"We're Jesus Freaks!" said Cindy, the cute blonde.

Virgil, her husband, added, "We're a lot like hippies, in fact, we were all hippies before we met Jesus. But we've sworn off drugs and now we get high on God's love. When we met Jesus and he gave us the Holy Spirit, we found we didn't need all those crutches we used to be addicted to."

Rob spoke up, "We're headed to Chicago to protest at the Convention. Where are you off to?"

Swope jumped in. "That's where we're going, too! We're going to share the love of Jesus, because we heard there would be a lot of people out there. Fitz and I used to live on the streets of San Francisco, peddling drugs and stuff. until we met Jesus. He totally turned our lives around. In the Bible, Jesus says you will be forgiven in the same measure you forgive others. My life was really a mess. I had a lot for God to forgive. I'm so grateful and that's what makes me want to share with others. Now we travel and share God's love with anyone we meet."

"Wow! That is so cool," Gary exclaimed. "I've heard of Jesus Freaks but I've never met any til now. I met Jesus last year when some good friends told me about him."

After a quiet pause, Doug spoke again. "I probably know less about religion than anybody here although I have been to a few churches. It appears to me that Christians are all about morality. They have certain rules about what you should do and what to avoid. What I don't get is why each church or group has a different set of rules on their list?"

"Whoa, hold on," said Virgil. "I never said we were Christians. We are followers of Jesus – something altogether different."

With a puzzled look, Jack asked, "I've heard this before, but I don't get it. Wasn't Jesus the first Christian?"

"Ahh, a common misperception," Fitz replied as he softly strummed his guitar. "Jesus is the way into a relationship with God. He said, 'I am the way and the truth and the life. No one comes to the Father except through me.' Jesus is the way to be forgiven for every wrong you have ever done, to be connected to God, and to be given a fresh start in life."

Virgil added, "Jesus said, 'If anyone is thirsty, let him come to me and drink. Whoever believes in me, streams of living water will flow from within him.' Through the Spirit, God pours his power into our lives. He heals broken places, strengthens us where we're weak, and brings new blessings into our lives."

"Jesus is not a 'Christian.'" Cindy added. "He didn't come to bring the church. If you read his teaching in the Bible, he came to introduce the Kingdom of God and to call us to follow him. Being a follower of Jesus is vastly different than being a Christian."

After a while Bunny spoke, "I grew up in the black church. I see what Doug means when he says they all seem to have long lists of rules. Most groups criticize anyone who doesn't follow their list of dos and don'ts. When I took a course on the New Testament last year, I found myself thinking what Jesus actually says in the Bible is nothing like what I hear in church. For example, he said, 'Come to me, all you who are weary and burdened, and I will give you rest. Take my yoke upon you and learn from me, for I am gentle and humble in heart, and you will find rest for your souls. For my yoke is easy and my burden is light.' That doesn't sound like the long lists of dos and don'ts."

Virgil explained. "Just because you are standing in a garage, it doesn't make you a car." Doug and Gary cracked up at that. Virgil continued. "A lot of people think if they go to church or become Christians they are right with Jesus. It's just not true. You should ignore religion, ignore Christianity. You need to focus on Jesus. Invite him into your life. Get to know him. Trust him to lead you."

Rob asked, "But how can you know if Jesus is real? If he is the way?"

"How do you know Jesus is real?" Virgil responded. "Try him! Ask him to show you if he is real. Ask him to open your eyes and your heart so you can see him. He will. Scripture says 'If you seek him, you will be found by him.'"

Oh man, that was such a cool but heavy evening. It simply blew my mind! We stayed up late and sang folk tunes with the Jesus people, rapped about God and life, laughed a lot and encouraged each other. The Jesus Freaks are the neatest people I've met in a long time. We had a wonderful time together. I found myself wondering if this is what the Cartwright's Jesus Family is like.

30

"The real voyage of discovery consists not in seeking new landscapes,
but in having new eyes."
~ Marcel Proust

Jack Flynn   August, 1968

Sunday evening we drove up the Chicago Skyway into the suburbs of the Windy City. We spent the evening camping out in the backyard of Doug's cousin Mo. Morris Novaksky lives in a spacious bungalow on the eastern edge of Oak Lawn. His roomy back yard had plenty of space for us to set up our tents. We hung out on the back porch while Mo cooked up a big pan of homemade lasagna. Randi and Nikki whipped up a fresh garden salad. Beers from our coolers circulated freely. Mo, a bachelor, seemed happy to have our company for an evening.

In the morning we loaded up, thanked Mo, and drove over to Grant Park. Lots of different groups were descending on Chicago to protest at the Democratic Convention. The Youth International Party, or Yippies, led by Jerry Rubin and Abbie Hoffman called their followers to the city for a "Festival of Life." Frenchie's Vietnam veteran buddies were marching under the banners of the National Mobilization Committee to End the War in Vietnam. Tom Hayden brought a 1,000 strong contingent from the SDS (Students for a Democratic Society). Folk singer Phil Ochs organized music to entertain the crowds of protesters. Bobby Seale brought a contingent of Black Panthers – the first I had heard of them. Many protesters are just ordinary students like us, people fed up with the status quo from our leaders, citizens demanding change. By the time the first demonstrations took place Monday evening, our ranks had swelled to close to 10,000 protesters from all over the USA. This is a far cry from our pathetic campus protest at Carlisle College. Now this is the real thing!

Protest headquarters is in Grant Park, a green space on the east edge of Chicago running from Michigan Avenue to Lake Shore Drive on Lake Michigan. Protest groups keep pouring into the park, setting up tents, and hanging out on the lawns. Hippies, straights, blacks, business types, clergy and students were making the scene. Around us bands are playing and people grooving to the music.

The place is teeming with life and activity. Our Band of Ten set up our tents in a tight circle with our camp chairs in the middle. We lounged around talking and laughing. It feels a like a festival, or a country fair. Frenchie went off to locate some Army buddies. He came back, bursting with news.

"You won't believe what I heard about the Convention! Apparently students aren't the only ones protesting. The political hacks inside the convention hall are in turmoil. Rank and file Democrats are angry because the party bosses are trying to steal the nomination for Humphrey!"

Randi asked, "How can they do that? I thought the Democrats had primaries where the people get to pick the nominee?"

"LBJ knows how unpopular he is because of the war. 80% of the primary votes went for peace candidates – Kennedy, McCarthy, or McGovern. After Kennedy was killed, his delegates were 'declared' uncommitted. Richard Daley and Johnson are rounding up delegates in back room deals so the primary votes of regular people won't count. If they succeed, Humphrey will be nominated without ever collecting a single primary vote. The arrogant prig never bothered to contest any of the state primaries."

Frank spoke up. "That stinks! But its how politics is usually played. However, we can still stand up and get media coverage for the little people of this country. Let's go over to the Yippies' headquarters and work on signs we can carry."

We abandoned our comfortable camp to roll up our sleeves and try to make a difference for America. At Yippee Central, loudspeakers were belting out the new Beatles single, *Revolution*. How ironic, yet so appropriate. Meanwhile, people are busy crafting protest signs. The signs are not revolutionary. Most have slogans like Make Peace Not War, Vets against War, Yankee Come Home, End the War Now, Make Love, Not War, and my favorite – the big peace symbol. We spent an hour creating attractive signs in hopes of getting a TV camera to focus on our message and wing it around the world. Randi, with her artistic eye, had the best sign and acted as our consultant to improve each effort.

Monday evening, we drifted with the crowds over to the International Amphitheater where the Convention was housed. Doug commented, "There are quite a few hippies, bikers and cats who look like the Jesus Freaks here, but most of these folks could be found in the audience at a Kingston Trio concert. This crowd is about 65% straight conservative Americans. Are you sure we are not at a Nixon rally or the Republican National Convention?"

"Hey, man these are Americans!" Bunny retorted. "You don't have to be a long hair to be mad at what's going on in our country. Bob Dylan and Joan Baez speak for many of us when they sing about the times they are a changing. Or that they need to change. Look at me; I don't have long hair!"

"Why you nappy haired Negro!" laughed Gary. "You only have the cutest Afro in town. Why would you need long hair?" With this Robbins piggy backed on Bunny and gave him a good knuckle rub all over his curly black head. The two of them fell to the ground slapping and pinching each other, laughing hysterically. That is pretty much how our protest began. It was more like a fun party with a few political signs thrown in. We walked and laughed and fooled around enjoying the hip music and the incredible variety of people around us at the rally.

As we approached the convention center, Rob said, "Come here and look at this!" Bachmann was standing in front of a furniture store on 42nd Street pointing at a black and white TV in the display window. We eased over to see what he was pointing at. The television was showing coverage from inside the convention. From the look of things, there is a lot more revolution inside the convention hall than out on the streets. Delegates waving signs, standing on chairs, screaming and shouting at one another. Security guards are beating up delegates and dragging them out of the hall and dumping them on the street. Mike Wallace and Dan Rather, national news reporters for CBS TV, were punched, knocked down and dragged off the floor by the Chicago cops. We watched spell bound as Walter Cronkite, the most respected journalist in America, described the brawl inside the convention in blow by blow detail. Cronkite finished his report concluding Mayor Daley's convention is being run by "a bunch of thugs."

By the time we got to the front entrance, student protesters were drifting away. Apparently, the melee inside the hall was a lot more interesting to the media than students carrying signs and making the two finger peace salute outside the hall. "I can understand that," said Rob. "After all, the protesters inside are better dressed, wearing coats and ties, shouting, smacking each other with signs, and being beaten up by cops. We're just standing out here like ninnies, singing *Kumbaya* and *We Shall Overcome*." With that snarky comment, we turned around and drifted back to our campsite.

Tuesday morning our crew was up early. We enjoyed a breakfast of hard boiled eggs, and Swiss cheese and headed off to the lakefront to enjoy the beach. We walked fourteen blocks, crossed the causeway, and arrived at the beach on Lake Michigan. We were hot and sweaty by the time we got there. Bunny and Randi were smart enough to bring swim suits. The rest of us settled for the t-shirts and cut-offs we were wearing. The water was about sixty two degrees and refreshing after the eighty five degree day. When any of us tired of swimming, and playing, we sat out and soaked up sun. Nikki never tires of splashing around. She reminds me of a wild otter cavorting on the banks of a NH trout stream.

Later, Rob and I strolled down the beach. We passed many nubile young women bathing and sunning as we walked. When we came to a stone seawall jutting out into the water, Rob and I found a comfortable place to sit. "So, Rob, how is your relationship with Randi going?"

"It's going better. I've taken Father X's advice. As best I can, I've forgiven my Dad and forgiven God. I feel I'm in a better place with God. I see how he could have created the world and set things in motion without actually being responsible for what we do with the life we've been given. Like, I don't think God sent Ted to Vietnam. The leaders of our nation sent our soldiers to Vietnam. And Ted volunteered to be a Marine, which pretty much means serving in Vietnam. Plus God did not make Ted trip and fall which resulted in his being shot by his own M-16 carbine. It doesn't seem fair to blame God for his death, when it was the result of choices he and other people made."

I asked Rob, "Do you think God sets up the scenario here on earth and we do our best, or worse, to make something out of it?"

"That's about right. Bunny was telling me stuff he learned in his Old Testament course. Brody showed the class how in Genesis God created the earth and all the

218

plants and animals and even mankind. It says he created mankind in his own image. After creating man and woman he put them in charge of the earth. God told them to be fruitful and multiply. He also told them to rule over the earth and its creatures. To me, the creation account is a metaphor to explain how we got here, where we stand in relationship to God, and our connection to the rest of creation. We are stewards of the world and the life we've been given."

Rob's comments made me pause to think. "What you say makes sense. God gave us this world and if we pollute it and wreck it, why should we blame him for the fact we now live in a cesspool? I think Nikki would buy that point of view. But what does this have to do with your relationship with Randi?"

"Just as we are stewards of the earth, we are stewards of our relationships." Rob replied. "The first year of college, I was attracted to Randi, but I wasn't willing to open myself to risk in a relationship with her. Too afraid of getting hurt, I settled for just being friends. But I love talking with her. She makes me laugh. I enjoy who she is as a person – full of surprises and the unexpected. I admire her values, her empathy, and her ethics. She is certainly a better person than I am."

"The fact that she is beautiful and sexy has no bearing on your attraction, I suppose?" I teased Rob.

"Well of course not!" Rob retorted. Then we both laughed and punched each other in boyish fun. When we stopped laughing, Rob added, "OK, maybe that explains a little of the attraction. But...I think Faith is beautiful and sexy. Personality aside, who would not want a roll in the hay with her? But she is so needy! She's kind of a mess – sad, hurt, and looking for somebody to save her. There is no way to make Randi unattractive, but I honestly think if she was average looking I would love her just as much. Or if I was blind, I think who she is as a person would attract me even without the exquisite packaging. It's who she is that turns me on.

"Since I have been working at forgiving, I find myself much more open to accepting the risk of going deeper with Randi. When I open up my heart and mind to her, she does the same for me."

After I though about it I asked, "Here's my question, Rob. Do you love her?"

"Yes."

"How do you know?"

After a minute Rob answered, "I find myself concerned about what's good for her. I don't care what I get out of the relationship, but I want to be sure she gets everything she needs to flourish. The other reason I know I love her is I simply cannot imagine living without her as a part of my daily life. Living without her would be like trying to live without air."

"Pardon my intrusive questions, you nitwit, but if your friends can't ask them who can? If that's how you feel about her, why haven't you done anything about it? I see how she looks at you and how she hangs on you. I think she's crazy about you. But she won't wait forever, you Pennsylvania Dutch slow poke! If you don't close the deal, somebody else will come along and take her off the market!"

Rob sat in silence for a moment. Then he ventured, "I know what you're saying. I've had the same thought. I guess I think she is too good for me and it will never work out. She's from a higher class background and is bright, beautiful, and sexy. Why would she settle for someone like me?"

"Who are you to decide for her? How often do we see opposites attract? Maybe she wants a goofball like you so her kids will turn out to be normal. If she married me, our kids would be so over the top gorgeous and brilliant it would make your teeth ache. They would never have any friends!"

Rob laughed and punched me in the arm. "Honestly, can't you ever be serous? I worry about the practical issues. Even if she would settle for an idiot like me, she wants to be an interior decorator which is pretty much a big city type of job. When I think past my dream of becoming the last of the mountain men and wonder what else I could do, I see myself living in a beat up old farmhouse in the country. I'd fix it up, have a big garden, hunt, fish, trap and raise six kids. For work, I'd like to teach history or sociology at a small college out in the country. The practical problem is this: how could a big city interior designer ever be married to a smalltime college prof who lives in the boondocks?"

"You remind me of the farmers I used to buy old sports cars from. One look at a wreck in a shed, viewing the rust, rot, dents and the weeds growing through the car – they concluded it was just junk. I would buy the car for $50, fix it up over the winter and sell it in the spring for thousands of dollars. In mint condition! You are so gloomy! You've decided the outcome to the problem before anyone attempts to solve it. Who are you to decide the future for Randi? What if she wants to marry an idiot like you and live in the country? Perhaps she could teach interior design at your little college? Or stay home and care for six kids and one idiot? Or commute to the suburbs to decorate houses?"

"Well," murmured Rob. "I see what you mean."

"Look man; just tell her how you feel. Tell her how you feel about her, tell her your dreams and share your fears. If she wants a career more than a relationship, she will tell you. If the fact you're a red headed moron is a deal breaker, let her tell you that. Remember what the Father says, 'There is no wrong emotion, so long as you talk about it.'"

We walked back down the lakeshore to join our friends. I could tell Rob was thinking about what I said to him. I could only hope he would act on it and not throw in his hand without trying to win the girl.

31

"Far better it is to dare mighty things, to risk glorious triumphs, though plagued by setbacks, then it is to take rank with those poor souls who neither suffer much nor enjoy much because they dwell in the gray twilight that knows neither victory nor defeat."

~ Theodore Roosevelt

Rob Bachmann   August, 1968

After talking with Jack, I had to reconsider my position on Randi. Maybe I was giving up too easily. Who knows what a woman is thinking? Why not take a chance and see? There's a lot of evidence Randi likes me. She enjoys our conversations. She likes when we toss ideas around and encourage each other's thinking. She is warm and affectionate with me and does not seem to mind kissing and making out. Normally, Randi is reserved. Around me she can be touchy feely and often holds my hand in public.

I am pretty sure her parents would not want her to marry a non- Jew. Yet, in our talks about God and spiritual things, I never get the sense Randi thinks of herself as a Jew in the traditional way her family does. She sees herself as coming from Jewish roots, just like I come from a family of Pennsylvania Dutch pretzel makers. Randi says, "Your roots have a lot to do with where you've come from, but they don't define where you're going. Nikki's dad came from Stow, rural mailman stock, but he took a different direction and became a Penn State history professor. You come from pretzel makers, but that doesn't mean that's your life. Skeeter has a great family, but he doesn't want to spend his life making hats – he's in love with bridges. It's ok to love and accept your roots but to live your life in a new direction."

As we walked back from the Lake Michigan beach with our pals, Randi strolled next to me holding my hand. "You seem pensive. Got something on your mind?"

"Hmmm…" was all I could come up with. "Jack and I had a talk about careers and the future while we walked the beach. He got me thinking. But you know I like to reflect a bit before I flap my lips. Let me have a little time to think about it. I definitely want to talk it over with you. You know how much I value your opinion and I need your insights."

"Sure honey." Randi pulled me down and kissed me on the lips. Gosh! Whenever she does that it makes me feel like I am falling down a well of sweet cream and honey. "Take your time, Robbie. If you want, maybe we could talk tonight after the protest."

"OK," was all I could get out; a surge of emotion welling up in my chest. I'm so touched by Randi's empathy and kindness. Some day, this woman is going to make me bawl my eyes out.

After a quick lunch of instant iced tea and sandwiches, we changed into long jeans and t-shirts. It was hot out, but Frenchie told us not to wear shorts. If the cops release dogs you want protection and if they chase people and club them with police batons, long jeans offer some defense against injury.

Our gang walked over to the Amphitheater, marveling at the crowds of protesters. While students gathered in the streets in front of the building to protest the war in Vietnam, the Democratic Party inside the convention hall continued to tear itself apart over America's war policy. All while being filmed and sent across the nation by TV cameras.

In front of the steps of the convention hall a thousand Chicago cops were ranked in riot gear. This wall of baby blue uniforms wrapped around the front of the building. About 100 feet away were the protesters. Thousands, perhaps tens of thousands, filled the street from side to side and as far back as the eye could see. Organizers set up a platform, off to the side, with microphones and a public address system so they could speak to crowds.

Speakers get up to the microphone and harangue against the war in Vietnam. Some, like Frenchie, are vets who served there. Others are hippies. Student leaders from colleges all across America address the throng. The SDS spoke, the Black Panthers spoke, and Jerry Rubin of the Yippies spoke. All are demanding a change in our country's foreign and domestic policies.

Between speeches, people go to the mike and share media reports about what is happening inside the convention. According to the radio, the action inside the hall continued to be far more disruptive than our peaceful demonstration outside. Inside fist fights erupted on the floor. Delegates and reporters were beaten and knocked to the ground. Others were hauled out of the Amphitheater by the pigs in blue.

There we are, ten thousand strong, filling the street and all the action is inside where we cannot even see it. The irony is not wasted on me! In truth, this second day of protest seemed more like attending a Mummers' Parade in Philadelphia. We enjoy the music and speeches from the platform. We waved our signs and the two-finger peace symbol and did a lot of people watching. Nothing much happened. The police stood passively watching us. We kept our distance and behaved with decorum. After four hours of this stand off, we drifted back to our campsite in Grant Park. Time to make dinner and relax.

By the time we arrived back at our tents, Doug had set up a card table and his two-burner Coleman stove and was busy whipping up burgers for dinner. "Hey, somebody help me get paper plates and hamburger buns ready." He yelled. Nikki, sucking down her fifth TAB of the day, pulled out cans of fruit cocktail from the van and started ladling the stuff into paper bowls.

Frank got drinks out of the cooler and Bunny fished out a box of Graham Crackers. When Jack gave him a funny look, he laughed, "Well, it is the same as bread. Or dessert." Everyone cracked up – both at Bunny and the weird menu for the dinner. Linda dug out a big bag of chips to pass around. We were all set: all of the major food groups! Burgers, beer, fruit cocktail, potato chips, and dessert-graham crackers. After we ate, Randi and I announced we were off for a stroll. We headed down to the playground on the edge of the field.

Sitting side by side on a pair of swings, we looked out over the sea of humanity in the park. "Man," exclaimed Randi, "I've never been at anything like this! All these people willing to stand up and be counted. This is so different from my time at Conestoga High. Growing up on the Main Line, my friends gave their all to fitting in. They wanted to conform, not protest! I just love all the color, the different styles, the hats and beads. Looking at this crowd is like seeing a huge painting on a museum wall, except the picture keeps on changing. It's live art!" Randi laughed with pleasure.

For a while we rocked back and forth on the swings, holding hands, enjoying the music and the captivating river of humanity sliding by. "Randi, you know I treasure our relationship."

"Yes, dear boy, and I feel the same about you."

"Just let me talk for a bit. I know this will sound disjointed, but I promise I have a point. I might need to take the long way to get there."

"OK, shoot."

"When you talk about having Jewish roots, but not having that define your direction in life, it makes me think about my family. It's in my past, but it's had a major influence in shaping who I am today. In sociology class, they talk about the three rules of the dysfunctional family: Don't talk, don't trust, and don't feel. That's my family. I'm trying to break out of that pattern, but it's hard. People change slowly. I know I'm often slow in our relationship. Please forgive me." Randi latched onto my swing and pulled me over to her and kissed me on the lips.

Once I recovered from the rush of pleasure, I continued. "When Jack was quizzing me about my plans for the future, I realized I'm in process. I'm not the person I was when I came to Carlisle, but I don't think I am yet the person I want to become. I'm a work in progress, as your artist friends would say. Here is my big ah ha. I need to plan and think about my future, but I don't want to do it alone. I want to do it with you. I want to have our future develop together. I don't know what that would look like but I would feel so much better about the future if I knew I could spend it with you."

Randi got out of the swing, and climbed into my lap. She wrapped her arms around my neck and laid her head on my shoulder. She kissed my cheek and whispered, "That is the sweetest thing you've ever said to me, my adorable friend. I want to plan my future with you, too." As the sun set on the horizon, the two of us snuggled together, savoring the moment and reveling in the safety and security of our relationship. I know we made a big step forward, but have no idea what it will mean or where it will lead.

Wednesday morning we headed out early for a rally on the edge of Grant Park. The Yippies had pulled a permit from the city and set up a platform near Michigan Avenue. When we arrived, music was playing, and the crowd continued to swell and groove to the beat. Speakers focused on the war in Vietnam and the need to bring our troops home. The crowd shouted, "Hell No, We Won't Go!" We waved signs proclaiming, 'Peace! Get Out Now! Make Love Not War!' Reefers were passed openly around the audience. Just as before, there were all the elements of a freaky holiday parade.

When a speaker began to share what was going on inside the Convention, you could sense the crowd getting angry. Lyndon Johnson, Richard Daley and the Democratic political bosses managed to steal the nomination from the majority point of view – those holding to a peace platform. Mayor Daley had unleashed 12,000 Chicago cops and called in 15,000 troops from the Illinois National Guard. If you looked across Michigan Avenue, you could see police and Guard troops massing on the opposite side of the street. There were so many of them and they just kept coming.

Folk singer Phil Ochs came to the microphone and made a sarcastic nomination speech putting a pig into nomination for President. The pig was dragged on stage, dressed in flowered wreaths, beads and painted with peace symbols. Everyone roared with laughter as the pig, named Pigasus, squealed and scrambled in discomfort. Political signs appeared – 'No Democracy without Free Speech, Who Elected HHH?, Voters For Peace, and End Tyranny Now!' The mood of the crowd grew ugly. Anger and frustration seemed to rise up like the tide at full moon.

I'm not sure what set off the cops, but suddenly, the sea of blue on the opposite side of Michigan Avenue erupted like hot lava flowing out of an exploding volcano. Waves of police wearing white helmets, light blue shirts, dark blue trousers, in full riot gear surged across the gap towards the protesters. The cops wore revolvers on their hips and were swinging long black clubs. The national guardsmen, dressed in green army uniforms, were carrying side arms and rifles.

This mass of aggression pushed into the crowd, knocking down anyone they came in contact with. Cops swinging and smacking their weapons was accompanied by screams as protesters backed away from these animals. The crowd began to scream and shout at the cops. The cops began to spray mace in the faces of students. The victims cried out, fell writhing to the ground, clutching their faces. The crowd reacted by pelting the police with food, then rocks, then hunks of concrete. Seeing several of their number flatted by projectiles only enraged Mayor Daley's thugs. They attacked with renewed vigor.

And it was all on the record. For a change, the media was there when the Chicago Police Riot of 1968 ignited. TV and radio began broadcasting the assault live for the entire world to see. Police and soldiers charged indiscriminately, beating up protestors and bystanders alike. So much mace was used by the cops clouds of it drifted up Michigan Avenue and began to drive Democratic officials out of the Hilton Hotel. The media caught it all on film. Our side shouting, "Pigs

Are Whores!", "Kill, Kill, Kill!" and "The Whole World Is Watching!" The 'Battle of Michigan Avenue' raged for hours as thousands of protesters ran through the streets pursued by police and soldiers. Tear gas rolled over city blocks. Paddy wagons carted hundreds of people off to the Cook County Jail.

When the cops attacked, we were well back in the crowd, 100 yards from Michigan Avenue where the melee started. Frenchie, always a fast thinker said, "Time to beat a hasty retreat. This is going to get ugly. Split up, get as far away as you can and don't do anything cops might think is threatening." Not only is Frenchie a fast thinker when the pressure is on, in spite of his roly-poly appearance, that man can run! He grabbed Linda and Gary and streaked off at an angle to the south side of the park. Jack and I grabbed Nikki and headed off on a northern slant towards the lakefront. Randi, Frank, Bunny, and Doug, burst straight out, like buckshot from a 12 gauge, scattering east in the general direction of our campsite.

Cops and Army guys waded into the crowds knocking people down, kicking them with black boots, thumping them with clubs and moving on to fresh victims. After beating a protester, a reporter, or a bystander, a gang of police descend on the victim and drag them to a paddy wagon. People around us were in a complete panic. Screaming, darting this way and that, Randi's living art had turned into a nightmare from hell.

The three of us produced kerchiefs which we tied over mouth and nose. It made the tear gas less noxious, though the stuff still made my eyes burn. As we ran by a clump of cops dragging a captive, one cop reached out and snagged Jack by the hair. "Owww…"he yelped, as the policeman yanked him off his feet and dumped him flat on his back. The other cops moved off with their original prey, but Jack's attacker started to kick him in the guts as he screamed in pain.

Nikki and I stopped in our tracks. I had no idea what to do. Nikki never hesitated. She ran up beside the cop, who was now leaning over Jack trying to put on handcuffs. Nikki gave the man a vicious knee to the kidney. Now it was his turn to scream in pain. He collapsed on the ground. As Jack rolled away from the moaning cop, Nikki calmly gave him a hell of a field goal kick right between his legs. The cop screamed without sound, grabbed his crotch, and rolled into a fetal position on the sidewalk. Together we grabbed Jack, got him on his feet and took off for the lake.

Eventually we worked our way over to Lake Shore Drive crossing underneath via a pedestrian tunnel. On the other side, all was quiet and calm. We led Jack to a bench so he could recover. "How are you doing?" I asked.

"I'm ok," he panted. "I bet I'm going to have some wicked ugly bruises, but I think tonight I will feel much better than the cop you mauled, Nikki. Remind me to treat you with a great deal more respect. I wouldn't want to piss you off or anything."

Nikki just smiled, "You have blood running down your neck. I think you may have a cut on your scalp. Scalp cuts bleed like a stuck pig. Does your head hurt?"

Jack reached up and put his fingers on the back of his head. "I think there's a cut and a lump from slamming the sidewalk."

Nikki used a tissue to part Jack's hair. "Yep, that's where the blood is coming from. When we get back to camp, let me wash it out and clean it up. It doesn't look too bad. How's your side?"

Jack yanked up his shirt and we could see black and blue welts forming on the one side of his rib cage. "I think I'm ok. The ribs protected me from worse damage. They don't feel cracked. I might need to get a bottle of aspirin tonight."

"Good thing the cop didn't take human anatomy class like Nik," I joked. "I can hardly believe how effectively you dropped him with the knee to the kidneys. How did you learn to do that?"

Nikki started to laugh. Next thing we knew she was rolling on the ground holding her sides, bellowing with loud guffaws. Finally, eyes tearing up, she sat up and caught her breath. "It wasn't anatomy class!" she exclaimed. "It was Uncle Butch! Remember I told you about Uncle Butch and how he was afraid if I went to a liberal arts college, it would be full of liberals? He's also convinced most college men are rapists. Before I came to Carlisle, Uncle Butch taught me how to defend myself against rape. I quote, 'If he's behind you, stamp on the arch of his foot. If he's in front of you, knee him in the nuts. If he's beside you, knee him or hit him in the kidney. It'll drop the bastard like a stone!' Good old Uncle Butch."

We all had a much-needed laugh at that. For an hour we sat on the bench trying to recover from the police assault and the awful things we witnessed. It's hard to think we live in a country where officials condone brutal attacks on unarmed citizens peacefully exercising First Amendment rights. The enormity of it all and the emotional turmoil of what went through put us in a state of shock.

After the melee died down, we worked our way back to the campsite. Frenchie, Gary, Linda, and Randi were already there. Randi jumped up and ran to hug me. "Oh, I was so worried about you! We were afraid the cops got you." She hugged Nikki and Jack.

"Actually, it took a while because Nikki had to stop and beat the shit out of every cop she could find," laughed Jack. With that, we gave our friends a blow by blow description of our escape from the forces of mayhem. "What do you know about Bunny, Doug and Frank?" Jack asked.

"Nada," said Frenchie.

"We were together when we started to run," said Randi. "We bolted straight for the campsite, but we got split up. I lost track of the guys - the place was crazyville for hours. I just kept running away from any cops and piles of bodies and trying to find open space. I felt like an NFL running back looking for holes in the opponent's line to help get me downfield. When I got to the lakefront, it took me a while to find my way to our camp. Frenchie, Linda, and Gary were already here."

"Randi Fox, crazy like a fox," laughed Frenchie. "That's a good tactic – stay out of trouble instead of aiming straight for home. I'm proud of you, girl! You can be on my patrol any time." Frenchie led Linda and Gary more to the south to avoid trouble. It took longer, but they missed most of the riot. After talking it over, we decided it best to give Doug, Frank, and Bunny more time to get home.

In the morning, there was still no sign of Frank, Bunny, and Doug. When we asked others in the park for news, we learned 650 demonstrators had been arrested and hauled off to the Cook County Jail. One demonstrator had been killed. 192 cops had been injured. No one knew how many demonstrators, journalists and bystanders had been injured in the police riot.

Frenchie finally said, "I think its time to take action. I'm going to the police station to see if I can find out if they're in jail. Then we should canvas the hospitals."

"Aww man, that's a bummer. To think they could be injured and in the hospital," Linda murmured.

Frenchie added, "Rob why don't you come with me? That way, if I disappear, you can tell the rest of the world."

We walked out to Michigan Avenue. The nearest police station is 26 blocks away, so we caught a cab to the precinct. The place was a mob scene. I suppose 650 folks arrested, each with two or three friends looking for them - that will generate a crowd. Frenchie and I spent two and a half hours waiting in line before we finally inched up to the booking desk inside the station. We asked the Sergeant about Frank, Bunny, and Doug and found out they were being held in the local jail, each arrested on charges of incitement to riot and disturbing the peace. "To get them out," said the cop, with a weary expression, "you'll need a local attorney and to post cash bail of $250 per person."

"How do we find a local attorney?" I asked.

"Beats me, but it's not my problem, is it?" Looking over my shoulder at the person behind me he shouted, "Next in line!"

As Frenchie and I took the long trip back to Grant Park, we talked it over. Hard for us to imagine how we could come up with $750 in cash and a local lawyer. But we sure weren't going to leave our pals in the lock up until their families can get them out. Hopefully, their families were not aware our little experiment in free speech and American political expression had landed their loved ones in jail.

When we reached the park, the rest of the demonstrators were moving out. Most of the campsites had been removed. Our forlorn tents stood practically alone in a field strewn with litter and trash. Frenchie suggested we break camp before we became the focus of any pissed off cop who wandered by. We were not abandoning our friends, but we did not want to end up in the clink with them.

We drove back to cousin Mo's place to see if we might camp there for a few days. Mo was happy to see us, but distressed to learn his cousin and two others were in jail. After setting up camp, we went to work on how to spring our comrades. Randi finally suggested, "Let me call my Dad. He went to law school at Northwestern and may have friends out here."

"I know what to do about the money," added Gary. "I'll call my Grandfather and ask him to wire it to us through Western Union. He can easily afford it and will probably be happy it is not me in the lock up."

By Saturday afternoon we had the money from Mr. Lynch and met Aaron Goldberg, a law school chum of Randi's dad, at the jail. He got the boys sprung from the pokey and by dinner time we were in Mo's back yard celebrating our near escape from disaster at the DNC demonstration. Two days later we made it back to the farm, picked up our cars and school stuff and headed to Carlisle. We were a few days late for the beginning of our junior year, but all ten of us were grateful to be back safe and sound on the campus of Carlisle College.

In the rearview mirror, our stint at political activism seemed pointless. There we stood shouting, "The whole world's watching," but in reality, no one was paying attention. We got beat up - but for what? The Democrats nominated that horse's ass, HHH and America voted for that crook, Tricky Dick Nixon. My only satisfaction was being able to say, "I told you so!"

32

"She's leaving home after living alone for so many years...
love is the one thing money can't buy."
~ *John Lennon / Paul McCartney*

Faith McFadden   September, 1968

Following my second year at Carlisle, I chose to stay in town for the summer. It didn't make my family happy, but I couldn't stomach the thought of returning to the pervasive ugly atmosphere of my family, church, and lack of friends on St. Simons. I moved back in with Mrs. Rose on Hanover Street.

By the first week of summer, I was waiting tables at Grandpa's Grinder and hanging out with Butch at the bar when I wasn't working. Thursday night, Butch said, "Peter at the Foxy Lady called to say they're holding an amateur night tomorrow. He wondered if you wanted to give dancing a try."

This issue has been on my mind. Do I really want to dance? Inside, I've been fretting about it. What does it say about me if I flaunt myself topless in front of strange men? What will my mother say? Well, I know what she and my dad will say! What will my sisters think? Why would they find out? The money is a temptation. I feel flattered Peter thinks I'm pretty enough to be a dancer. I have my doubts, 'Are my boobs too big? My ass too wide? What if all those men simply jeer at me when I get up there?'

In the end, the money won me over. There's a $300 prize for the winner. That's six times what I make in a night at Grandpa's. I put on my sexiest lingerie, a short black skirt, and a black lace top and Butch drove me over. I was incredibly nervous as I waited back stage. The other dancers were encouraging and supportive. Peter asked me what stage name I wanted to use – that's when I panicked. If I need a false name, what I am about to do is really wrong! But I felt too embarrassed to back out. I said the first thing that popped into my head. "Frisky Fanny will be fine." I'll just do it this one night and be done with it.

Three other amateurs competed against me. When it was over, I was declared the winner and Peter handed me $300 in crisp new $50 bills. Ultimately, I think it was the lure of big money that sucked me into being a stripper. All the way home, I sat next to Butch counting those six clean, crisp fifties. When I was up dancing, I felt like I was in a meat market and I was the meat on sale. Dirty old men slobbering over my outsides and seeing me as a thing. But when I had those six crisp bills, I kept thinking, "This is like acting in a play. It's like being a model or lots of other jobs where they hire pretty girls. And they think I'm pretty! Three hundred dollars, wow!" In the end, the money sealed my fate.

The first week at the Foxy Lady, Butch drove me the three nights I worked. I made $1,000 that week. The second week I worked two-week days and a Saturday night and came home with $1,300. Then I bought a 1965 Ford Mustang. This sweet little two-door sports car is the hottest ride in town. My Mustang is only three years old! It's probably the nicest set of wheels anyone in the McFadden clan has ever owned. Now, here I am tooling down the street in a pristine, royal blue two-door Mustang. This ride is a head turner! From now on I won't need to beg rides – I can drive myself in style.

When school started again, I moved back into Allison Hall and resumed being roommates with Randi. Funny, I never mentioned I'm working as a stripper. Everyone assumes the three nights a week I go to work, I'm down at Grandpa's Grinder waiting tables. It's not like I'm lying, exactly. Just something I forgot to mention. It makes me feel bad deceiving my friends. I hope my parents never find out and I suspect the college will give me the boot if they learn the truth about my off campus employment.

On the nights I work, I feel dirty. My clothes reek from smoke and beer fumes. What's worse, I feel degraded, abused, and blame myself for allowing this exploitation to happen. Each night I'm encouraged to give men lap dances and to couch dance. I make extra money for this and so does the club. But the men often hit me; slap my body, bite my private parts, and leave me covered in welts and bruises. In the dark corners of the club, cocaine is freely used and many of the girls turn tricks to increase their income. As much as I can, I try to avoid the worst aspects of the job, but… I feel so bad about myself. When I get back to the dorm I often sit in my car getting stoned until I'm numb enough to walk inside.

A few weeks into fall term, Jack came by to take me for a ride on his chopper. Now that I've stopped lusting after Jack's hot body and his cute smile, we've become good friends. Besides, when I daydream about who could take care of me in the future, Jack hardly qualifies. A guy who wants to restore battered old British sports cars for a living? How much money can that pay? I bet I make more money in a night at the Foxy Lady, than Jack will make in a week, even after he graduates from college.

So, we are just good friends. I enjoy his company. And he is not 'tall, dark, and all hands' like so many other horny guys at college. He doesn't treat me like an object to be pawed and squeezed. Instead he treats me like a trusted friend. I also get a thrill out of riding fast, the wind tearing at my face and hair, and exalting in the scenery ripping by as we ride. "Where do you want to go today?" I asked Jack.

"I thought we might ride over the ridge into Perry County to Whipple Dam. The foliage is starting to turn and we'll see some pretty color. How would that be? I could buy you an ice cream cone or a milk shake at the Whipple Dam Store."

Jack knows the most interesting, out of the way places. He's intrigued with learning new things. You can never guess what he'll talk about and he knows loads of quirky places like Whipple Dam in Rothrock State Forest. As long as you don't mention, Miss Feltgood, Jack can be counted on for a good time.

We roared up into the mountains, admiring the hardwoods changing into fall colors. The swamp maples are bright red. Norway maples and stripped maples have a spattering of red leaves but are still green. Sugar maples are turning a vibrant orange, while the willows, poplars, and sassafras turn vivid yellow. The oaks are going to brown and beginning to rattle in the breeze. Arriving at the Whipple Dam Store we sat outside on a picnic table slurping giant chocolate milkshakes and enjoying the spectacular view down the valley. Looking out over the scene, I said, "Fall always makes me feel a little nostalgic. Perhaps melancholic. Or just plain sad. I don't know…"

"In New Hampshire, I begin to feel that way in mid-August," Jack joked. "There's something about the waning light, the cooling temperatures, that tells you, 'winter is coming. It's going to be cold as hell. It's going to last forever.' That's when I get blue. But when fall actually arrives, I feel animated! Thrilled to the core of my being. It makes me aware life is full of excitement and fireworks. Heck, by the first week of October, it even looks like fireworks. Of course, in two more weeks all the leaves are gone, it's cold and gray, and the snow begins to fly in earnest."

"My point exactly, Flynn. To be honest, fall makes me afraid of growing old. I don't want to get old… baggy, saggy, and gray. I'd rather burn out than rust out. I don't know what tomorrow holds, but it worries me and makes me afraid. I want to live as much as I can today. It's all I've got, for certain."

"Man, that is a pessimistic outlook on life for somebody who is not yet 21." Jack responded. "Have you settled on a major, Faith?"

"Interesting question. At this point, I'm a Political Science major with a minor in Theater. These are the subjects I've enjoyed the most. Public policy is one way to right the wrongs in our country. Theater… I guess I am good at pretending to be somebody I am not." What I did not elaborate on was the fact that, given all the lies I've been telling about my personal life and my secret life as a stripper, Theater gives me the survival skills to keep up the fiction I've constructed around my life.

After a stretch of silence, Jack replied, "You know, Faith, when I was fifteen, I had dreams about what I wanted to do in life. Then Maggie died. That threw me off for a while. In high school, I got caught up in rebuilding British sports cars and thought that's what I might do for a career. Then my drug dealing cousin stuck his foot in the dog poop, and I was the one who came out smelling bad. I didn't even think about college, but here I am. I've had some disappointments… like Miss F. But I keep thinking, 'As long as there's life, there's hope.'

"The best thing about my future is I have friends to share it with. I'm not as sure as Gary is about God, …but I'm sure as long as I wake up tomorrow, there will be interesting things to learn and explore. Life is going to hand you defeat and discouragement at times, but don't let it lead you to despair."

"Geez, I wish I could feel like you. I always expect the worst. Generally, I get what I expect. It's hard to be excited about making the next choice, when I seem to make so many bad choices for myself."

We sat soaking up the pristine fall weather, listening to the rustle of leaves, and watching spent foliage flutter to the ground. Eventually, time moved on and so did we. Climbing aboard the sleek black and sliver Triumph, we headed back to campus.

One Friday evening, Nikki came by my room. "Hey, I'm going to the Purple Dragon tonight. You know, the Christian coffee house over at the Methodist Church? I'm going with Bertozzi and Cassese, the Grim Twins. Do you want to come along?

I hardly hesitated "Sure, I'd love to come. Those guys are so weird, I'd like to get to know them."

Ricky Bertozzi and Bobby Cassese were sophomores from an Italian Catholic neighborhood in Pawtucket, Rhode Island. They weren't related, but growing up they lived on the same street, went to the same school, and the same Catholic church. They acted like twins, practically joined at the hip at almost all times. In high school they drove a wrecker on I-95 at night. Late in the evening in their dorm room, they would pull out a big notebook of glossy 8 x 10 color photos of wrecks they had serviced in the tow truck. Bodies smashed on the pavement, pools of blood and gore, human body parts mashed in twisted hunks of metal, flames consuming crushed vehicles. The boys so enjoyed these souvenirs of gruesome accident scenes it produced their nickname – the Grim Twins.

"Just thinking about spending the evening with those two guys sends shivers down my spine," I said, "but they are interesting. Let's do it!"

Ricky and Bobby picked us up an hour later and we drove over to the Methodist Church a few blocks west of campus. On the way, Bobby said, "I heard the Dragon is a Christian coffee house. What's that?"

Ricky chimed in, "Yeah, does that mean they serve Christian coffee?"

Bobby bounced back, "We were raised Catholic – Italian Catholic. It's the only church we've ever gone to. We are guessing 'Christian' is not the same as Catholic, but what precisely does it mean? Will they try to convert us into Methodists or something? I know you were raised fundamentalist, Faith, but …what the hell is a fundamentalist? Did you grow up in the Mudlick Bible Church or something?"

These guys make me chuckle. "Well, not quite that bad, but almost. It's true I was raised in a very conservative Christian home. But I'm not into that anymore. I don't know what I believe about God."

Nikki spoke up. "The Purple Dragon is open to anyone. No one is going to try to convert you. It's just a safe place with music, coffee, and food. A place to hang out and talk. Have conversations, meet new people. I bet we might even meet some Jesus Freaks tonight."

"What the duce is a Jesus Freak?" I asked.

"They look like hippies," Nikki replied, "but Jesus Freaks are into Jesus, not drugs. They're not like any church people you've ever met. They are far out! Spiritual, not religious. And certainly not straight. I'd guess they are groovy!"

A few minutes later Ricky pulled into the church lot and parked the car. The coffee house was in the church basement. As we went down the stairs into the low room, Bobby exclaimed, "Cool, Man!" The basement space had black lights, hip posters hung on the walls, and lava lamps on the tables. A pretty brunette sat on a bar stool on stage strumming a Martin acoustic guitar. She had flowing raven black hair held back by a beaded Indian headband. A tie died T-shirt, worn jeans and sandals completed the outfit. She was singing Judy Collins covers, but she looked and sounded a lot like Joan Baez.

"Hey, look," Nikki pointed across the room. "There's Father X and Doc Brody. Let's sit with them." So we wandered through the crowd and pulled up folding chairs at their table.

"Hi Faith, Hi Nikki," said the Father. "Who are your friends?"

"Father Xavier, meet Ricky Bertozzi and Bobby Cassese, from Pawtucket, Rhode Island. Guys, this is Father X. And Dr. Theo Broderick, who we call Doc Brody." These introductions were followed by a warm round of get to know you conversation.

A few minutes later, Doug Novaksky sidled up to our table. "Mind if I join you?"

"Pull up a pew," laughed the Father. "What have you been up to Doug?"

"I've been reading the Gospels like you suggested," Doug replied. "It is wild stuff. Not at all what I expected. You're right, Doc Brody. Jesus was not a very religious guy. In fact, he always seems to be in trouble with the religious authorities."

Nikki spoke up, "Hey, that's weird! I've been reading the Gospels too. Jesus sees things in such a different way! He says those who are blessed include the poor in spirit, those who mourn, the meek, those who hunger and thirst for more – essentially, the have-nots, the weak! Not the strong and successful. It's just the opposite of what most folks believe. He's a revolutionary! It sounds like he came to overthrow the conventional thinking of this world."

Ricky looked puzzled. "OK, I'm a little confused. Being raised Roman Catholic; I was taught we have to put our trust in the people in charge. The church, the priests, the Bishops and the Pope. Whatever rules they set out, we have to follow. Then we are good with God. Do this and you are acceptable. Don't and they will lock you up and throw away the key."

"What bothers me is there are so many different sets of rules," added Bobby. "Each religion says, 'our rules are right and the rest of you are going to hell.' Catholics claim we're going to heaven and the Protestants are going to hell. But Gary keeps telling me that Jesus, not any man-made rule system, offers the only path to God. Can you help us understand, Father?"

Xavier pulled out his briar and filled it with fragrant tobacco. After tamping it down, he struck a match and got it going. After a couple good pulls, he said, "Friends, take a look around this room. Tell me, when you look at these people, what do you see?"

Doug took the bait. "Lots of different kinds of people. Those guys over there look like Army ROTC – flat tops and straight clothes. The cats at the next table look like normal high school kids. Those people look like Nikki's Jesus Freaks, or just regular hippies. The next bunch could be folk music types, with their guitar cases and grooving to the beat. Just a wide variety of people."

"Excellent observation, Doug. A lot of people, all human beings, but each in their own set of cultural clothing. We've talked before about Jesus. He is God's only son and he came to bring us back to God. Everything rises or falls on your relationship with Jesus. He came and lived in history, died and was raised from the dead. He is alive today and offers us a restored relationship with the Father. When he went to sit at the Father's side, Jesus gave us the Holy Spirit to guide us, comfort us, and remind us of what Jesus and the Father are teaching us. Jesus said, 'I am the light of the world. Whoever follows me will never walk in the darkness but will have the light of life.'"

Brody jumped in, "But often people are too frightened to trust in a God they cannot see. So they make up rules. They create religious systems. They put a preacher or priest in charge so we don't have to learn to listen to the Spirit. Religion is like cultural clothing; like all these different people in the Dragon are wearing different clothes to say who they are. Catholics have created a set of cultural clothing they hope will protect their people. Lutherans do the same thing. Then there are the Baptists, the Pentecostals, Presbyterians, and the Plymouth Brethren – they all have cultural clothing. We end up with a sense of safety in our rules and our cultural clothing. But it's not trust in Jesus."

"What Brody and I are trying to say, is none of these religious expressions, or denominations or theologies have anything to do with getting into a relationship with God through Jesus. The only thing that matters is Jesus. Where do you stand with Jesus? What are you going to do with Jesus? You are exactly right, Nikki when you say Jesus came to upset the existing order of the world," continued the Father. "He wants to completely change our perceptions of what is and what is not. He said, 'I have come into this world, so that the blind will see and those who see will become blind.'"

"Wait," exclaimed Nikki, "You are saying I can know Jesus and love him and follow him without going to or joining any particular church?"

"That's it exactly!" exclaimed Father X. "You need to respond to the call of Jesus on your life. Just give your life to him and ask him to lead you. He will give you the Holy Spirit to teach you, guide you, and reveal to you what is true. You need to find other Jesus followers to grow with, like Gary's Jesus Family on Long Island. Together we learn to do his work and to grow more like him. It's simple. Not always easy, but simple."

We hung out at the Dragon talking and bopping to great music for several more hours. When the Grim Twins dropped us at Allison Hall, I said to Nikki, "What did you think of that whole thing?"

"Interesting. I feel like I'm starting to understand how to get connected to God in a way that makes sense. What about you? Was that hard for you?"

"Truthfully, while I'm supposed to be the Christian, I've never heard anything like this! I'm stunned. It's so different from what I was taught as a kid. But if Christianity is just a man-made religion, it explains why my parents disagree on so many points of the faith. Crazy! I hope I can get a handle on all this. Thanks for taking me tonight."

"You bet sweetie. Don't be such a stranger." Nikki gave me a hug, and we went our separate ways.

33

"Many people die with their music still in them."
~ *Oliver Wendell Holmes*

Jack Flynn   January, 1969

My third year at Carlisle is flying by. I'm not sure why, but it seems like each successive year goes by more quickly. Some quirk of time, I guess. Rob and I continue to reside in dear old Wood Hall. Neither of us feels like changing dorms, although, as upperclassmen, we could. Wood Hall, as ratty and tattered as it is, feels like home. My card guys continue to hold regular sessions in the Blue Room. The same beat up old couches and easy chairs strewn around the room. A couple tables and handful of straight chairs are there as well – for the mythical students who are supposed to use the Blue Room as a study lounge. Ha, ha! Fat chance of that happening. As far as we can tell, not one change or improvement has been made in the three years since we were freshman. Home sweet home!

The one disadvantage of living in Wood is that I often spot Amy Feltgood. When I see that tall red-haired Valkyrie, my heart beats faster and my breathing slows. In the Old Norse mythologies, the Valkyries decided which warriors are slain and which survive to become legends and heroes. Loving Amy is like a mere man falling in love with one of the immortal gods in mythology. Which I guess I did. She is ever present and eternally out of reach. When I see her, it's like I'm seeing her for the first time and falling head over heels in love - once more.

On the other hand, I get to see Amy. I've tried to forget her and date some of the other pretty girls on campus. It's just not possible. How do you forget someone you are convinced is "the one?" How do you forget her when you see her so often? Someone who walks into your life, blows all your fuses and walks out again? I've no idea how Amy feels. I've not been back inside her apartment since that fateful night our love affair - nearly consummated, withered and turned to ashes. When we meet in public, we are civil and polite. Rob, Nikki, and Gary know how I feel, but I don't think anyone else does.

Long rides on my Triumph chopper help relieve my mind. I enjoy the ride up South Mountain north of campus. The road follows the East Branch of the Antietam Creek up through groves of hemlocks, pines and interspersed maples and oaks and I sense my anxious feelings recede. Often I'll pull over to sit and watch the stream flow, in golden and silver tones, over the rocks and pebbles as it winds down the mountain. Once in a while I catch sight of the flick of a tail, or a shadow on gravel, or the flash of red fins indicating the presence of a wild brook trout. To soak in this natural setting soothes my weary heart.

Working to the top of the mountain on my bike, I focus on the sharp switchbacks which turn in and reverse direction as the road toils up the hill. Huge logging trucks hurtling down the mountain require fierce concentration so as not to have an accident. When you reach the top, there is nothing but an old tuberculosis asylum which has been closed for years. Once upon a time, the only cure for TB was fresh air, which South Mountain has in abundance. Since the asylum closed, there is nothing left but the fresh air. Remote, quiet, peaceful – these help me get my mind off unrequited love.

One afternoon, after a long solitary ride up the mountain, I bumped into Rob. "Black Jack Flynn!" he greets me. "You are just the fellow I was looking for. I want to show you something."

"Sure, Rob, whatever you want." Rob led me out behind Wood Hall. We crossed the back parking lot to where an old panel truck was parked. The truck was a bright canary yellow covered by hand painted flowers, peace symbols, wild paisley designs, hippie slogans, and other art.

Rob walked up to the back door and knocked. The door swung open to reveal a smiling face wreathed in freckles and shaggy red hair. This happy guy was wearing blue jeans with an African dashiki shirt flowing from his shoulders to below his waist.

"Hey Carl, meet my good friend Jack Flynn. Jack, this is my cousin, Carl Bachmann."

"Howdy, Jack, delighted to meet you." Carl replied.

"Hi to you too," I returned." You two are really cousins?"

"First cousins," said Carl. "Our dads are brothers. Would you like to come in?" Rob and I mounted the steps into the warm and cozy truck. Inside the vehicle had been transformed into a small but functional home. A cottage on wheels, it contained Carl's living room, bedroom, dining room, kitchen, and bathroom. Carl flipped down a narrow single bed mounted on the wall, "The couch!" He laughed. We sat and got comfortable.

"Wow, this is neat! What ever gave you the idea to rig this up?" I asked.

Carl chuckled. "I owe it all to Rob. When he told me tales about his trip across America, I realized I've never been anywhere. I decided I want to travel around to see what the rest of America is like. See the country, meet people and see what's up. Last summer we found this old panel truck rusting away in a neighbor's field. Dad hauled it home with his tractor and we spent the fall in the barn rebuilding it into home away from home. As of Christmas break, I've taken a leave of absence from Bucks County Community College. I'm headed west to see America." Carl gave a laugh and said, "The adventure begins!"

What a hoot! Rob and I talked with Carl for another hour before we had to leave. In the morning, his truck was gone. "Go west young man, go west!" was my only thought.

Meeting Rob's cousin and his bread truck got me thinking. How do you open your horizons if you can't take nine months off to wander across America? How do you consider different options and experiences when you're tied to one spot? Or you don't have the cash to take an adventure? One day, after engineering class, I walked Randi back to her dorm and asked her that question. Her answer floored me! Mostly I was shocked because the answer's so obvious and I never thought of it.

"That's easy, Jack; talk to other people!" Randi laughed. "Think about it – each of your friends has experiences unlike your own. How many people have you met at Carlisle who grew up Irish Catholic in Effingham? Right – no one. Yet you've had that experience. You can share it with others. They've lived and been to places you haven't. They can share those experiences with you. You don't have to go to Haight-Ashbury and dive into the Summer of Love. You can simply pump Rob for his experience of it."

"OK, Randi, I confess. I am officially stumpified. That is such a cool insight and it never crossed my mind. What an idiot I am."

Randi went on, "You should come to this group Gary and Nikki started on Thursday evenings. It's called the Waffle Club, but it's a way to do what you are thinking about. To expose yourself to different people, different points of view, different life experiences. And you hardly have to get off your fanny." With that comment, Randi pinched me on the butt, gave me a friendly pat and headed into Allison Hall.

Tuesday evening, I was in Conklin watching the Bruins play hockey on TV when Gary and Nikki turned up. "Hey, you two." I greeted them. "Been out necking in Gary's car?"

They laughed. "As ugly as my Galaxy is, it has better accommodations for making out than your black chopper." Gary replied.

"Plus the Ford is heated. Can't say that for your ride. Hard to get frisky with a girl wearing leather and long johns," added Nikki. "Besides, we were doing laundry, you nitwit, not making out."

I continued, "Randi mentioned you guys started a new group that has something to do with waffles. What's that all about?"

"Ah, the Waffle Club," returned Nikki. "That's an interesting story. Gary, why don't you tell it?"

"Sometime last fall, I had a conversation with Doc Brody about how Jesus encouraged the people around him to grow. I found myself wondering, 'What would it look like if Jesus came to Carlisle College? I mean, if he was living in our dorm and wanted to help us to grow, how would he do that?' So Nikki and I started hosting a Sunday brunch in Allison's kitchen. We each invite someone, and they can each invite somebody. We serve waffles, butter, syrup, OJ and coffee. We eat, then sit around and talk for about 90 minutes about one life issue; the focus of the conversation for that morning. Hence the nickname, The Waffle Club."

"What kind of life issues?"

Nikki jumped in. "You know, the kinds of questions we all wonder about. The purpose of life, what is love, how to grow friendships that matter, how to create community, career choices, death, fear, trust, what is faith, dealing with anger, forgiveness. Those kinds of things. Everybody submits ideas for discussion and we pick one topic each week. There's no right answer, no correct point of view. We want everyone to feel appreciated, respected. To be listened to and heard. We're simply friends sharing life, listening to each other, and trying to be encouraging and supportive. The Waffle Club."

"I thought you met Thursday night?"

"Yes, good point," replied Gary. "And we don't have waffles anymore. We used to meet Sunday, mid-day, which was not a great time for everybody. Plus, we only had one waffle maker. When we started with four people, it was ok, but when we had ten people – do you have any idea how long it takes to make twenty or thirty waffles with one waffle iron?"

Nikki laughed, "We decided to take our own advice- try something different. We got the event meeting room in Lane for Thursday nights. Same rules – we can invite anybody and they can invite anybody. Most weeks we have anywhere from eight to twenty five people. We provide some kind of pasta, sauce and ice water. If you want anything else, you bring it. Frank makes his grandma's marinara sauce, Randi brings crusty bread for garlic toast, someone will bring a salad, meatballs, maybe sausage, or a dessert. Nobody has to bring anything – just an open mind. Everybody gets fed, but mostly we're there for the conversation and discussions. For some reason, everyone still calls it the Waffle Club."

"It's like exploring the world, maybe even the universe, but we do it in one room. Its crazyville!" exclaimed Gary. "You know my friends the Cartwrights have this Jesus Family they belong to? It's like an intimate caring family for people who are not your relatives. I was inspired by that to start a family for our friends and other people here at school. You don't have to know Jesus; just have to be open to discussing and exploring the kinds of questions Jesus was always discussing with people. I like to think of it as a "Friends of Jesus" group. Open to everyone, open to different points of view. A safe place to have conversations about things that really matter in life."

"OK, you had me at crazyville. Can I come this Thursday?"

"You bet! We would love to have you," laughed Nikki. "It's not formal, but you should feel free to wear black. Ha ha! We'll see you then."

Toward the end of January the sun came out for a few days, the weather warmed up and the birds began to sing as if spring was on its way. Then, overnight, the front changed, and I woke on Friday morning to find a cold hard rain falling outside my window. As I went to my first class, it was spitting snow and sleet pellets without diminishing the rain. Wicked ugly weather! After class I went to Musselman where I found my friends all huddled together in our Koffee Klatch corner, sucking down hot drinks and bemoaning the foul weather.

Spinelli walked in and immediately the conversation stopped. We could all see something was wrong. He looked awful. His eyes were red and puffy, his hair was disheveled, and he was weeping into a clump of tissues. My heart jumped to my throat and I had no idea what to say. Everyone just stared. We had never seen Frank like this and no one had words to reach out to him. Nikki moved next to him. She didn't say anything, just wrapped her arms around him. He put his head on her shoulder and burst into a fresh round of tears. We sat in stunned silence.

Finally, the sobbing subsided and Frank tried to talk. "Shorty St. Laurent came and got me this morning. I'm his RA and he was worried about Ronnie Reynolds. Ronnie was his roommate last year but has a single this term. Shorty lives across the hall, but hadn't seen him for a few days. I guess we thought he might be sick, so I got the pass key and we went into Ronnie's room." Frank heaved a sigh and cried a little more before gasping out, "We found him in his closet hanging by a belt. He committed suicide."

Cries of disbelief swept the group. Nikki hugged Frank harder. "We're here for you Frank. We'll help you through this," Nikki murmured. A low buzz spread through the gathering.

Bunny said, "I can't believe it! He seemed to be doing so well this term. Whenever I saw him he was cheerful, laid back, even funny at times. He had everything going for him. He was finally headed in a good direction, adjusting to college, making some friends. Even Ratso had stopped picking on him. Ratso is a completely different guy this year. He's changed. What happened with Ronnie?"

"No one knows," answered Frank. "Shorty and I found him three hours ago. Dean Benchoff, the police, and the ambulance crew have all been in his room. They finally kicked us out. From what I can tell from their chatter, Ronnie swallowed a handful of pills and then hung himself with his belt. The pills probably made him pass out, and hanging from the belt did the rest. No note. No warning, no nothing. Shorty thought he might have stopped taking his meds. He said he's been up and down the last couple of weeks. That's probably how he saved up enough pills knock himself out. The EMT says he's been dead for a couple of days." This grim news was greeted with stunned silence. How do you process this?

"I just don't get it," pondered Gary. "I know he had lots of baggage from his parents moving in high school and he obviously had trouble adjusting at college. The fire bombing incident and his Christmas melt down are indicators of something going on under the hood. But this year, I finally thought he had his shit together. He seemed cheerful every time I saw him. Ratso hasn't bothered him: he was finally starting to make friends. What did we miss? Could we have done more?"

"I talked with him a number of times last year," offered Bunny, "and I know he struggled a lot with feeling he didn't fit in. He was a bit of an odd duck, but aren't we all? It's not like he had no prospects, no potential. I thought he was beginning to be hopeful about the future. After his stay at the Edina County Nuthouse he's been on meds, in counseling and doing well. I can't understand how he could go off the rails now, when things were all beginning to come together for him?"

"When he came back to school last fall," Frank added, "I had some conversations with him. I think he was a little twisted up because his parents and the nuns in his Catholic school laid pretty heavy guilt trips on him. He worried about all kinds of things potentially angering God. I think he viewed God as an angry, vindictive judge waiting to smite him or crush him for his failings. He was often anxious, although I admit; he didn't show that side in public this year. My sense is he struggled with guilt, fear and shame. But I can't understand why he felt that way. He was a good kid!"

Nikki spoke up, "It is so sad. He would have been fine in the long run if he had just given it time to work itself out. I had a friend in high school commit suicide. She was a girl who was smart, accomplished, pretty, and carefree, with a bright future ahead of her. Then one day she was gone. I know we all get to make choices in life, but it is so sad to see someone choose a permanent solution to what is a temporary problem. If only Ronnie had asked for help."

Suddenly, Faith, who had been sitting quietly at the table, broke out in shuddering sobs. She collapsed in a heap on the table and cried hysterically. Randi and Nikki tried to comfort her. Their efforts had little effect in soothing her racking sobs. After another five minutes of hysterical weeping, Randi and Nikki collected Faith and her things and took her back to her dorm to put her to bed.

What a strange and depressing morning. Now my mood exactly matches the grim weather outside. The rest of us remained in silence for a good while thinking about Ronnie. I feel emotionally exhausted. Gutted, empty, and hollow. No one had anything to say, so we eventually went our separate ways.

34

Rob Bachmann   May, 1969

Spring inspires hope. No matter how tough things get, in my life or that of my friends, I can't help but feel more hopeful as spring arrives. The weather shifts from snow, rain and 30-degree temperatures; before you know it, things warm up, there's more sunlight. Flowers are blooming everywhere. Crocuses, daffodils, and tulips pop up. Around campus brilliant yellow forsythia, pink cherry trees, and red bud trees glow with new hope, whispering, "Better days are soon to come!"

Hope can show up in the most unexpected places. Like at the card table in the bowels of Wood Hall, for instance. Our recent sessions have left me feeling upbeat. Tony Lavelle is a new guy in our group. At 26 he's older than the rest of us. And he talks funny, being from Framingham, Massachusetts.

Not only does Tony sound funny, he looks funny. He is short, pudgy, and his half bald, half long haired dome makes him look like Friar Tuck resurrected from the Middle Ages. Tony was a biker for years before he got his life turned around. His wardrobe still reflects his time as a Hell's Angel. He normally wears black jeans, Harley T-shirts, a pair of steel toed motorcycle boots, and each ensemble is topped off with the black leather biker vest.

One morning Tony shared his story with the guys at the table. "I was raised Italian Catholic in a blue-collar suburb of Boston. I was always rebellious and had a smart mouth, I got in so much trouble at home and school, and I ran away when I was seventeen. I excelled at being bad, so I decided to join the Hells Angels. I worked the docks, saving enough money to buy a Harley and spent the next six years smoking dope, drinking, and running with a biker crowd up and down the I-95 corridor. We sold drugs, bootleg liquor, and cigarettes from Maine to Florida. Those years are now nothing but a blur."

"Did you come to Carlisle to open a new territory?" Arty asked.

"No, man...I turned my life into a train wreck. After six years of being high, drunk, hung-over, then sick and puking my guts out, I was so wasted I had a breakdown. Mental and physical. I woke up in an alley in Jacksonville, FL. I was rescued by a bunch of Jesus people. They ran a street ministry for down and outers.

Pulled me out from behind a dumpster where my biker pals left me to die. They took me home and cared for me until I recovered. It wasn't easy.

"In fact, it was awful. I had the DTs for days as I was drying out. When I had screaming fits, the Jesus people came in and prayed for me. They laid hands on me, cast out demons, and helped me get my life back. These folks got me into AA and Narcotics Anonymous. They helped me get a GED and encouraged me to go to college. I sold my Harley and managed to get into Carlisle with help from Father Xavier. I'm excited to have a second chance. The only souvenir I have left is my Nazi motorcycle helmet."

"Wow, that's an incredible story, Tony." Frank continued, "I wonder if that's what happened to Ratso? He seems like a completely different person this year. If you told me aliens had snatched the old Ratso and replaced him with a different version – I would believe it."

Billy chimed in, "What do you mean, Frank?"

"You know what Ratso was like the first two years? The meanest shit ever to come down the pike? Always picking on people, standoffish and nothing but cruel, hurtful things coming out of his mouth."

"That's our Ratso!" laughed Billy.

"No, you don't understand!" Frank exclaimed. "You know what he's doing now? Every Tuesday and Thursday morning he volunteers at the Harrisburg Y, helping special needs kids learn to swim."

"Ratso helps retards?" was Billy's incredulous response.

"Yes! He helps the boys' swim class then goes to their classroom for the rest of the morning. The other day Ratso was bragging he nailed a sneaker to a plank to teach his kids how to tie shoe laces."

"What?" laughed Jack. "That's crazy. It sure doesn't sound like Ratso. How did that happen?"

Frank explained, "You know Melissa Tait? She's a senior Psych major. She convinced Ratso to help with her class and got him academic credit for helping the kids two mornings a week."

"Sure it's not Melissa Ratso is interested in?" asked Arty. "She is a looker."

"Nah, I've met her boyfriend" replied Frank. "Some rich kid who goes to Franklin & Marshall. The guy looks like a Greek god and drives a '63 Porsche 911 S. I don't think she's giving him up for Ratso. Besides, I get the sense Ratso enjoys the kids, likes helping, and feels he is making a positive difference. It makes me wonder if it's Franklin's death or Ronnie's suicide, or what? I don't know the why, but I admit, the change is enough to make me believe in miracles!"

Hope is always lurking around the corner. You never know when it will suddenly appear.

One Thursday evening, I came back from my shift in the campus dish room to discover Jack sitting on his bed admiring a blue gray WW II German Army helmet. "What's that?" I asked.

"A genuine Luftwaffe helmet. Tony Lavelle wore it when he was riding with the Hell's Angels. He told me he's given that up, doesn't plan to ride again, but he kept the helmet as a reminder. He thought I might like it. I said I'd give it a try. See if it can keep my hair from blowing in my eyes."

"You guys must be tight?" I said.

"We have a lot in common, with motorcycles, and being from New England. I suppose he looks up to me. I like him! He's a genuine guy and he's working hard to carve out a new path in life."

"Yes, and you both have the same exquisite fashion taste," I laughed. Little did I realize, this odd gift would save Jack's life.

Friday afternoon I took Doug's van into town to try to replace the bald rear tires. I use the van enough – it is the least I can do. I checked a number of shops in Carlisle before I found a decent set of used tires for $40 bucks. They mounted the tires and I drove back to campus a happy camper. Spring weekends bring campus visitors. The lots were packed, so I ended up in the overflow lot at the bottom of College Avenue.

After I parked the van and grabbed my gear, I heard a roar from the top of College Avenue. I've heard this sound often enough – I know exactly what it is. I looked up the Avenue to the top of the hill. The roar increased. It sounded like a fighter jet revving up to take off. Black Jack Flynn came screaming down the hill on his 650cc Triumph T-6 as he prepared to launch himself off the stone bridge and fly through the air over Lincoln Avenue on his bike. What a nut case!

I've seen him pull this stunt many times. While I marvel at the shear courage or stupidity this takes, I've watched him land the jump with competence and control. By now I guess I don't worry about my insane friend's physical safety. The roar came closer and I can see flashes of black and chrome through the poplar trees lining the drive. As Jack's bike streaked into view, I glanced down the street and spotted a tan delivery truck lumbering north up Lincoln Avenue. I can see it, but it is still hidden from Jack's view by the college chapel. Shit!

In a panic, I dropped my gear and sprinted up the driveway towards College Avenue. I ran the fifty yards as fast as I could to wave Jack off, but I'm no sprinter and he was coming fast. I was still twenty yards short when the bike came screaming by. Jack was wearing Tony's old German helmet and his jet black hair streamed out beneath the helmet. A pair of dark sunglasses were perched on his nose and a huge grin was pasted across his face. The tan truck kept lumbering up Lincoln Avenue. I was pumping my fists wildly over my head, waving, and screaming, but Jack just smiled at me. I think he had no idea I was trying to warn him – he thought I was encouraging him in his exploit!

By the time Jack hit the upslope of the stone bridge he probably could see the tan truck off to the right. It had a small cab and a flatbed on the rear, so the view he saw was of a low profile vehicle he assumed he would just fly over. No sweat. What he couldn't see was the truck was carrying two large sheets of plate glass. Each window of thick glass was eight feet wide and six feet high. The truck bed was low, no more than thirty inches off the ground. But the invisible sheets of glass stood over eight feet off the roadway – an insurmountable obstacle. I watched in horror, seeing the western sun glint on the glass as Jack launched off the bridge and flew straight into the sheets of plate glass.

The extended front fork of the Triumph cycle hit the bottom of the glass first and pitched Jack up and over his front wheel. He was flying headlong like a man shot out of a circus cannon when he pierced both sheets head first. I could not stand to watch as the horrific sound of tearing metal, breaking glass, and screeching brakes tore though the peaceful spring afternoon.

I tore down the hill and over the bridge. By the time I arrived, the truck had stopped; the driver was out and crouched over Jack's limp body. If he had fallen off a ten story building and landed on his head, it could not have been worse. Jack was pile of crumpled limbs and flesh. His face and clothes were covered in blood. His eyes were closed. The truck driver hunched over him trying to find a pulse. As I approached, he looked up and shouted, "He's still breathing! Call an ambulance!"

I ran across the road to the Carlisle Cleaners and used their phone to call the ambulance. Within minutes, medics were on the scene. They put Jack in a neck collar, rolled him onto a gurney with spine braces and strapped him down so the transport would not add to his injuries. Before they rolled him off, I asked one EMT, "Will he make it?"

He looked at me and said, "I wouldn't hold out much hope. But if you pray – pray for a miracle!" They slammed the rear door of the ambulance, jumped in, turned on the sirens and headed east to Holy Spirit Hospital in Camp Hill, the nearest hospital with a trauma unit.

A week later we sat huddled in the waiting room of the Critical Care Unit. Jack had been in and out of surgery almost every day. The doctors told us our friend had 42 broken bones and needed 126 stitches to sew up all the cuts made by the falling sheets of glass. "If not for that helmet he was wearing, he'd already be dead." said Dr. Rosenberg, the head trauma surgeon. "That boy was going sixty miles an hour when he went through the glass. Without the steel helmet, his head would have been smashed – like a ripe tomato dropped twenty feet onto concrete. I've never seen anyone with such traumatic injuries survive, but he's hanging in there. Keep praying, if that's what you're doing to help him."

Jack had been put into a medically induced coma upon arrival. No one has been able to speak to him and we have no idea how his cognitive functions might be affected. All we can do is wait to see how his body and spirit respond. The waiting room was filled, most hours of the day and night, by those who came to support Jack either through presence or prayer.

The Koffee Klatch members were first to arrive. Next came people from the Waffle Club. Every one of us waiting for news, hope, or any light about Jack's future. Gary got everyone to gather in a circle, hold hands and he led us in prayer. "Lord," Gary prayed, "when Jesus stood at the graveside of his dear friend Lazarus he said, 'I am the resurrection and the life. He who believes in me will live, even though he dies; and whoever lives and believes in me will never die.' Lord, we believe in you. We ask you, on behalf of our friend Jack, please raise him back to life, and grant him healing, wholeness, and health. Please return our dear friend to the land of the living."

The very day Jack was admitted, Frenchie and his parents showed up. All week long at least one of the LeBoufes had been with us, waiting patiently for news and praying for Jack's recovery. Guys from the Wood Hall card club appeared, looking anxious. Tony said, "We didn't feel right playing cards knowing Jack is here. So we came to support him until he can play again." Even Ratso came. He never said much, but his quiet presence said it all. Frank was right – our old Ratso has been replaced by a different man.

To no one's surprise, Father X and Doc Brody came every day. They spent many hours encouraging and supporting the other friends gathered in the waiting area. At times, they would sneak off into the corner and huddle in quiet prayer for our comrade.

The Flynns arrived from New Hampshire. Jack's Mom, Dad, his sister Meghan, and the patriarch of the Flynn clan, Patrick Flynn himself, arrived. Patrick Flynn was a tough wiry little man with a shock of snow white hair. He had to be in his seventies, but exuded the vigor of a younger man. Granddad Flynn and Father X took an immediate liking to one another. Within hours they were old friends. The senior Flynn said, "We've already lost one child from our family – far too soon. If there's anything we can do, even if it's simply to beseech heaven day and night, we're here to claim this boy back to the land of the living." The Flynns moved into a hotel and prepared for a long stay. I have no idea who was running the businesses back home, but clearly it didn't matter compared to Jack's welfare. I remember Jack explaining how tight his family is. According to him, when threatened, the clan circles the one in danger like a herd of old bison bulls. I was seeing this deep commitment to family in action.

Even Miss Feltgood came. She visited every day, sitting quietly off to the side. Mostly her head was bowed as if she was meditating or in prayer. I don't know if Mennonites pray, or how they pray, but she was pulling for our dear pal. Several times Benchoff himself came to see how Jack was doing. He would walk up to Miss F and simply put his hand on her shoulder for a moment of quiet sympathy and solidarity. You can't tell me that man doesn't know what transpired between Jack and Amy. How he knows what he does – I'll never understand! But it's obvious; he is completely on their side.

"I have to say," laughed Nikki, "at least one good thing has come from Jack's accident. Someone has finally gotten him to try a color other than black! Don't you girls think he looks cute in that tasty little blue and white gown they have him wearing? Like a fairy princess in some bedtime tale."

"Plus you can get a good look at his tail," chortled Linda. "You notice the gown has no back in it! A cute tush indeed! Right now, his ass could be his best looking feature."

It was the last week in May, and we were settled into our seats at the Koffee Klatch. Jack had regained consciousness after ten days in la la land. The docs said he hasn't suffered any mental damage, which considering what an idiot he is, is miraculous. We have all talked with him and he seems cheerful for a guy busted into so many pieces. He is black and blue from bruises on every visible part of his body. Linda is right – only his ass appears to have survived the accident unscathed. He is covered in stitches, wrapped in miles of gauze and has wires and ropes pulling on every limb. He looks like crap, but he has a big grin on his face. Why so happy?

"You don't suppose Jack is jolly because of that tall redhead sitting by his bed every day squeezing his hand and whispering sweet nothings in his ear, do you?" asked Nikki.

"Miss Feltgood is the medicine to make you feel good!" laughed Arty. "Fuckin' A!" he chortled. "It's either the presence of the divine Miss F or it's all the cool drugs they keep pumping into his system."

Gary laughed. "I am sure she is simply tutoring him in Sociology so he won't get behind in his studies while rehabilitating." We all shared Gary's sentiment. None of us had any idea what was going on between Jack and Miss F, but it was obviously the medication he needed. It was not yet clear how much of his original capacities he would eventually regain, but we were overjoyed he was alive, able to talk and we shared his joy in Amy Feltgood, whatever that meant.

I spoke up. "We know what Jack is doing this summer. Lying around in bed squeezing Amy's hand and making cow eyes at her. How about the rest of you, do you have things planned for the break?"

"Fuckin A," cackled Arty. "Same old, same old. Back to US Steel to earn my college money. But this year I have an internship in the business office, so I won't spend the summer on the plant floor!"

"I've got an internship too," said Nikki. "I've been hired to work with a group of grad students with a research grant to explore organizing a national day to focus people's attention on the environment, A National Earth Day. It should help people see how important the environment is to everyday living – you know clean water to drink and unpolluted air to breathe. I'll be the lackey, but I'll be paid and I get to work on something I love."

"That's really far out, Nikki. I'm so happy for you," added Randi. "I don't actually get this summer off. I am going to be…back in school! I'll be spending the summer taking a certificate program in Interior Design at Philadelphia College of Art. That way, when I graduate, I may be able to turn all my art courses into a paying occupation."

"I'm going to lifeguard at the Hollidaysburg public pool," Linda said. "Not very exciting, but then, my home town is not an exciting place. I like that. I find I'm content with routine and structure in my life. It makes me happy to get up and know what I have to do today. Taking the time to do each step in the process, and to do it well, always leaves me with a sense of satisfaction."

"It also leaves you with a swell tan by the end of the summer," hooted Doug, who was sitting a little too close to Linda at our table and squeezing her knee. Doug and Linda are now a public item and Doug is always teasing her and caressing her in public.

"Oh, you lustful boy!" laughed Miss Pence. "You behave! How about you, Rob, do you have plans for the summer?"

I grinned. "Well, thanks to the generosity of Frenchie's family, I'm going to spend the summer toting lumber at the Newville Building Supply. Mr. LeBoufe not only agreed to hire me, I get to have Frenchie's room for the summer. Frenchie is going off to the Poconos to lead the Firestone Explorer Canoe Base at Resica Falls Scout Reservation, so I get to sleep in the basement and eat meals with the family. Can't do better than that! Plus all the free fly-fishing I want on Big Spring Creek. It's a great deal! I'm really looking forward to this summer."

Frank spoke up. "As a self-respecting Jersey boy, I'm going to spend my summer in Ocean City, New Jersey. That's where all the cool cats go for the summer. I'm going to work at Mack & Manco Pizza on the Boardwalk, which has no redeeming value, but it pays my expenses and leaves me free to pick up cute chicks at the Chatterbox Café when I'm off. Plus I can spend a little time on the beach and ride my surfboard. I'll be sharing a house with five high school friends."

Doug Novaksky spoke up, "Much to everyone's amazement, I am not going to spend my summer slinging hot dogs. I'm going put my old band, *The Windows*, back together and go on the road."

"*The Windows*?" queried Randi.

"Yeah, we're like *The Doors*, you know, Jim Morrison, but not as big. We open musical windows to help you see the world as it really is. We've got a solid schedule of dates for teen dances, coffee house gigs, and we are even playing at the shore. We'll be at Wonderland Pier in Ocean City."

"Cool, dude," chuckled Frank. "I'll come and see you when you are in OC and bring my guys."

"That would be great, Frank. I'd love to see you there. In late August, the guys in the band and I are headed up to the Catskills to a music festival in Woodstock."

"What's a music festival?" asked Arty.

Doug laughed. "You *are* from Pittsburgh, aren't you! Have you ever listened to WMMR, the underground rock station out of Philly? That's music." Everyone around the table had a good laugh at Arty's expense. Doug continued. "If you were from Philly or anywhere in the East Coast, you would know about the Philadelphia Folk Festival. It's an annual event near Schwenksville, north of Philly. Four days of folk music on different stages. Last year they had Joni Mitchell, John Denver, John

Foley, the Satyrs, Dave Von Ronk, and Phil Ochs. About 5,000 people came, camped, and enjoyed all the music."

Doug continued explaining, "The Woodstock Music and Arts Festival is modeled on the Philly event. But with rock musicians like Jimi Hendrix, The Who, Joan Baez, Grateful Dead, and Jefferson Airplane."

"Hey, I heard Jefferson Airplane in San Francisco; they are groovy!" I added.

"Ritchie Havens, Ten Years After, Crosby Stills and Nash, Santana, Janis Joplin, and Arlo Guthrie. It's an incredible line up. Only $18 if you buy tickets in advance. That's three days of music plus you get to camp on the grounds for free."

"Sheeoot!" Frank exclaimed. "That's a lot of big name music for not much money!"

"We should all go," cried Nikki. "It would be such a cool way to begin our senior year together. Before we have to graduate and become grownups."

"Fuckin A! A three-day party with Arty!" chortled Arty. "Sounds like a gas!"

Doug ventured, "We could meet at Linda's grandparents like last August. We could car pool together, go camping, listen to great music and not get beat up! It's August 15 to 18. We can return to Willow Bend Farm and chill out and be ready for school on time, instead of sitting around in the Cook County Jail."

"This is so much better than our fiasco in Chicago last year." Randi commented. "Let's do it!"

My Koffee Klatch friends finished out our Junior year at Carlisle College making plans to reconvene at the end of summer and have a little personal music party with Doug Novaksky and the Windows in the quiet backwater town of Woodstock. We all left for the break looking forward to sharing three days of peace and music in August.

Year Four

35

"There is a time for everything,
and a season for every activity under heaven:
a time to be born and a time to die,
a time to plant and a time to uproot,
a time to kill and a time to heal,
a time to tear down and a time to build,
a time to weep and a time to laugh,
a time to mourn and a time to dance,
a time to scatter stones and a time to gather them,
a time to embrace and a time to refrain,
a time to search and a time to give up,
a time to keep and a time to throw away,
a time to tear and a time to mend,
a time to be silent and a time to speak,
a time to love and a time to hate,
a time for war and a time for peace."
~ the prophet. Eccl 3:1-8

Nikki Clausen   August, 1969

When we gathered at Willow Bend Farm, it felt like a grand family reunion. Gary and I arrived first, followed by Linda and Doug in the Old Blue Devil. The four of us sat at a picnic table under the shade of the giant willow sipping lemonade and ice tea, waiting for the others to arrive.

Linda asked, "Do you remember doing this a year ago?" "That was an adventure that began so well, yet ended so badly. To be honest, I still have occasional nightmares about it."

Doug laughed. "Me too! I can't believe I had to flee for my life - beat up by the police and arrested for peacefully expressing an opinion! Then the humiliation of being thrown in jail. That scared the poop out of me! Now I have an underlying distrust of government and authority. So much for American values and freedom…It makes me sad."

"Hey, look!" Linda exclaimed. "Here comes Frank." A cloud of dust kicked up as Spinelli's Buick cruised down the long winding lane towards the farm house. We jumped up to greet him.

"Whoa Nellie!" Gary shouted running up to Frank's car. Before he was barely out of the door, Robbins had him wrapped in a big bear hug and was planting kisses on each cheek.

"Ewwww, cupcake! That's gross. Let Nikki do the kissing for the two of you," Frank laughed. Gary ignored him and kept planting wet ones on our sober Italian friend. Frank kept pushing Gary away. "Knock it off before you give me cooties!" he exclaimed.

We gathered around Spinelli and engaged in a group bear hug. Then Linda started tickling Frank. We collapsed in a laughing, hooting pile of arms and legs. As we sat trying to catch our breath, another car came up the lane. We stared for a while without being able to recognize the vehicle buried in the cloud of dust billowing towards us.

"It's Faith!' I cried, running to the car. As I got close, I could see the sleek 1965 royal blue Mustang through the dust. Faith pulled her sports car off the lane and onto the grass where we sprawled. She stepped out wearing cut off jean shorts and a baby blue Janis Joplin t-shirt. "Honey Bunny," I shouted. "What are you doing here? I didn't know you were coming. This is so great!"

After another group squeeze, Faith brought us up to speed. "Y'all know how much I love music - some of my favorite artists are going to be at Woodstock. When Doug planned this trip at the end of school it sounded so cool. I've never actually gone to a concert, let alone a festival, so I thought 'Why not?' I worked hard all summer and I can afford to take a week off. Is it ok if I come?"

"Dearest heart," cried Linda, "you're always welcome!"

"You don't need to ask," said Doug. "Our party is your party."

Frank, always the practical one, wondered, "Do you have any gear? You can't go camping and festing with nothing but a t-shirt, short shorts, and sandals. Although, if anyone could get away with wearing so little, I imagine it would be you." He chuckled.

"Not so, bird brain Spinelli. I may be blonde, but it doesn't mean I'm a numb nut. Butch lent me a sleeping bag and an air mattress. I have long jeans, several shirts, including a flannel, a sweat shirt, and a rain jacket. Is that good?"

"It'll do. We'll put you in the tent with Nikki and she can teach you the finer points of camping." Frank directed. "That good with you, Nik?"

Passing my arm through Faith's I said, "I could not wish for a better partner! Welcome to the team." Honestly, the longer I look at Faith, the more concerned I get. She doesn't look good. Her shiny blonde hair cascades down her shoulders, and her legs are still the longest in town. But she looks too skinny, almost haggard. Hollow cheeks and I can see ribs showing. Her color is so pale she looks wan, even sickly. I worry she has not been eating right over the summer. Perhaps she neglected herself while living with Mrs. Rose? Or worse, maybe she was developing an eating disorder; bulimia or anorexia?

We got caught up standing in a shady spot, when a beat up old truck turned into the drive. A nasty looking wreck of a Ford pickup, it might be the ugliest truck ever. Painted a dark brown, with yellow paint patches peaking out in odd places. It has large areas of rust where the metal has eroded away, and is shot full of holes. Blue paint is sprayed around the rusted edges of the bed and frame. I wonder if this is some old friend of Linda's grandparents who is down on his luck.

"Holy Crap," Gary muttered as the truck pulled up behind Faith's blue Mustang and Robbie and Randi stepped out. We all stood stunned, as if a magician had pulled the two of them out of an old black top hat. "What's up campers?" Gary yelled. The rest of us gaped in silence.

"What, you haven't seen an ugly truck before?" asked Rob.

"Yeah," continued Randi. "What are you staring at? Do you clowns think the car makes the man?"

"Well, it is pretty ugly," Doug said, finding his voice. "Even compared to my ride. What happened?"

"It's is a funny story," Rob laughed. "I went to visit Randi's family in Devon last week. Leroy LeBoufe lent me his restored '57 Chevy, which was a big hit, especially with Randi's Dad. On the way back it threw a rod on the PA Turnpike. Leroy had to come and tow us back to Newville. What we didn't know was Mr. LeBoufe had taken my old Falcon into the dealer for some repairs. Sort of a going away present. The only substitute we could rustle up was this bucket of rust – the yard truck for the lumber yard. It looks like shit, but it runs pretty good."

"Ahh, you two are still the cutest – even in that bucket of bolts." said Linda as she wrapped Randi and Rob in a hug, "Status doesn't matter. You are all we want and need."

"But don't think we are taking that to Woodstock!" Frank laughed. "It is past butt ugly. We can hide it behind the barn and hopefully no one will notice. Or else they'll pile cow shit on it to hide it." We all gathered for more hugs and enjoyed our reunion after the summer apart. Half the joy of going to Woodstock is just getting uninterrupted time to catch up before our senior year at Carlisle begins.

The next morning, we headed north to the Catskill Mountains. We took Spinelli's Buick and Doug's van like we did on the expedition to Chicago. Our crew only numbered eight, so there was plenty of room for camping gear and supplies. Arty never turned up – he probably couldn't weasel out of the last week of his internship at US Steel. Ah, responsibility. Frenchie wanted to come, but he was stuck in the Poconos running the Explorer Base.

Doug had dealt with the concert details over the summer. He purchased tickets and made plans with his band. At the last minute, the Festival had been moved from Woodstock to Bethel, another dinky little town in Sullivan County. Doug said it would take three hours to get there. He led the way in his van and we followed in the Buick, driving through countryside at the peak of summer beauty. We rolled up through the Slate Belt, into the Poconos, then up the west bank of the Delaware through the Water Gap.

I found myself thinking back on our adventures on the other side of the Delaware in the fall of 1967. It seems like it was ages ago. I feel overwhelmed with gratitude and nostalgia. After the past three tumultuous years, it is amazing we are still alive and we remain friends. I miss Jack terribly and wish he was with us and not in a rehab in Harrisburg.

We crossed the Delaware on a rickety iron bridge in Hancock, New York. Traffic moving our direction began to thicken and slow. Picking up Route 17 north through Sullivan County, we hit more congestion. Seems funny all these people are going on vacation on a Thursday in August, although I know the Catskills are popular. Approaching the outskirts of Bethel, traffic slowed to a crawl. Suddenly it hit me - these people are going to Woodstock! Holy Mack-a-rolly! For the last seven miles of our trip, into Bethel and on to Max Yazger's farm in the hamlet of White Lake, we inched along a foot at a time. It took three hours to drive the 150 miles from Grantham, PA and three more hours to creep the last few miles to the Festival site. And we came a day early, to avoid the crowds!

Mercifully, our campsite is on the edge of the field, so we are not smack in the middle of the mobs setting up camp in our meadow. The higher elevation allows us to enjoy some cooling thermals which rose into the hot August afternoon. Our four tents are set up in a crescent with the kitchen and campfire front and center. Home Sweet Home, for the next three days!

Once camp was organized I suggested, "Let's go for a walk and check out the scene. I'm curious to see who all these folks are and what they are doing here."

"Great idea," answered Frank, "I want to dig these crazy cats. So many, so cool!"

"I'd like to see if we can find my buddies from *The Windows*," added Doug. "They're supposed to come up from north Jersey this morning and should be here by now."

We wandered down the hill marveling at the massive crowds of people, the human variety, the astonishing outfits they were wearing and the vehicles they're in. The kaleidoscope blew my mind. We got to the bottom of our field to find an intersection of farm lanes. It is like the crossroads of a new country – Woodstock Country.

In one corner of the crossroads, stood a pair of water tankers distributing fresh water. Opposite the tankers - a triple row of portable outhouses – if you drink enough water, I guess it has to go somewhere. On the next corner, stretching off towards the back of the stage about 100 yards away is the bus lot. Circled in neat concentric rings are gaudy converted school bus dwellings. Not one or two, but dozens – perhaps as many as thirty. Amazing colors, ingenuity, engineering, and lots of gypsy lifestyle on display. We looked in amazement at this spectacle and then chose the fourth option, walking down the lane towards a shady copse of trees.

We pass people of all ages and types. Some nearly nude girls in buckskin are busy putting on an avant-garde interpretive dance routine for a small crowd of onlookers. A lanky blonde fellow with long hair dressed in jeans leads a group practicing yoga. We see lots of teens and young cats sit in loose clumps talking and smoking reefers. Families with naked little babies playing around their campsite laugh together as we stroll by. Musicians sit in the shade playing instruments and singing. Very back to nature. It makes me think of the Garden of Eden and I wondered if that's what we are going to experience.

Groups passing us on the lane said, "There's a lake through the woods where you can go swimming. Lot's of people are cooling off."

Rob perked up at that. "That's what I need, man. I am melting in this heat."

It was cooler in the deep shade of the woods. Ahead of us on the lane, was a naked guy holding hands with a girl carrying a pile of clothes wearing only panties. He whispered in her ear and they veered off the lane, on a path through ferns and white pines. We stared in amazement as the girl carefully laid out their clothes on the ground. She peeled off her briefs, and lay on her back on the blanket of garments on the carpet of pine needles. She reached up for her man as she spread her legs to receive him. We stood astonished; the two of them humping away 30 feet from where we stood rooted to the lane. Some picnic! Frank finally broke the spell. "My bet is Arty is really gonna be mad he missed this! Who knew when Doug promised three days of peace and love that this was what he meant?"

Our crew laughed out loud at Frank and our surprise. Further along, the path opened to a meadow stretching down to the shore of a pale blue lake. The shoreline in front of us was covered by several hundred people digging the bathing scene. Many of the young people milling about, swimmers and bystanders alike, were naked. This is skinny dipping as I've never seen it. With hundreds of strangers. Most of the people in the water were nude, though a few wore panties, jeans, or a shirt. Others were sitting naked on the grass. Some were air drying after a dip in the water. People were just enjoying the feel of warm summer sun on bare skin. Observers hung out, enjoying the view of all those beautiful naked bodies or waiting to get up the courage to disrobe and join the festivities.

Honestly, I was surprised by my reaction. I'm all in favor of being natural and I love skinny dipping, but I've only done it with friends. After a long hike up to Little Black Moshannon Falls with my girl friends, a nice long soak in the invigorating water was ideal. I feel free to be naked with my friends from college. But cavorting in the nude in front of hundreds of strangers? I don't know what I think. It's not like I aspire to be a stripper.

Rob looked at the rest of us, "Anybody bring a swim suit?"

Doug laughed. "Nope, just my guitar. I thought this was supposed to be a music festival. I never realized it was also a nudist convention."

After a long silence Frank offered a practical suggestion. "Questions of modesty and nudist values aside, it's hotter than hell and I want a swim. So if you don't mind, I'm going to take a dip" With that, he stripped to the buff and waded into the lake.

"Cute butt." said Linda to Randi. "I guess I'm with Frank. One must be practical." She peeled off her shorts, T-shirt and undies, left them next to Frank's pile, and waded into the water. "Ahh, it's delicious! Come on in!" One by one we followed, took off our clothes and waded in. I thought Randi would prove the most modest and reluctant to sport in the buff, but I was wrong. She joined our little group in the water quickly, but, for some reason, Faith resisted. She sat on the log next to our clothes and refused to join us. All our cheerful attempts to encourage her in fell on deaf ears. She just smiled ruefully and waved.

After awhile, we all got comfortable. Almost everyone in the lake is naked and a great number of those on shore are nude. It creates a level playing field where each person has nakedness as a common human trait which connects us, rather than a hidden, mysterious factor that keeps us apart. Each body looks different but they all have the same basic bits and parts in a variety of forms. "I wonder if this is how Adam and Eve felt in the Garden." I commented.

The water was cool and soothing without being cold. We splashed each other, laughed and played games. I don't know what's wrong with Faith. She just sits there looking left out. To be honest, the sight of her in T-shirt and shorts concerns me. Her legs look too skinny, and her pelvic bones jut out. The skin is tight over her ribs, and her breasts look smaller. The poor child looks emaciated, like a war refugee. Her healthy glow is gone and she has a gaunt, haggard look that makes me fear for her well being. Since Ronnie Reynolds's death, I feel like I should be looking out for my friends, and offering help when I see signs they may be in trouble. The skeletal appearance of my once beautiful friend troubled me. I don't know; is it too much work or too many drugs, or her bad relationship with her family? Faith looks like a troubled person. Or, a person in trouble.

Walking back after our splendid afternoon at the lake, I had an overwhelming sense of peace. Everyone we meet is so kind and polite. Something about the setting or the weather or the nudity seems to be bringing out the best in everyone. Music fills the air with hope and idealism as we walk past campsite bands and individuals playing pick-up music in odd places. If all these different people can come together and bring out the best in each other, maybe mankind can be saved? My reaction today is the opposite of my feelings after Chicago. Our generation wants to change the world and make it a better place. Maybe, through peace and love and music, we can achieve a better world. It is certainly not going to happen through political activism. My soul overflows with hope for mankind, when I consider what could be if we just take the message of Woodstock back home and spread it to others.

36

Faith McFadden   August, 1969

After dinner we strolled through the campground. The crowd is enormous compared when we arrived. We are flowing along in a river of people as we move down the lane. To stop and see anything requires pulling out of the flow and off to the side, like a canoe coming ashore out of a strong current. The best part is listening to the musical jams going on in the bus encampment. Bluegrass players working banjos, slide guitar, the fiddle and even a washtub bass put out some great hillbilly tunes. Mississippi delta blues wailing out of a clutch of black musicians in another circle. Jamaican dudes are belting out jive jumpin' reggae on a collection of steel drums. Hippies with guitars, long hair and beads strum out folk tunes.

When it got dark, we retreated back to the relative peace and calm of our campsite. Nikki has collected a massive pile of dead wood from the fencerow for our fire. Boy Scout Rob ignited a blaze with one match and soon we were gathered around the fire. A bag of marshmallows was making the rounds. Doug's packet of Zig Zag papers and his baggie of weed were in his lap and he rolled fat reefers which also made the rounds. Soon, we were all pretty mellow.

"I got a letter from Ratso this past week," Frankie began. "You're simply not going to believe what he spent his summer doing!"

"Ratso actually wrote you a letter?" marveled Doug. "Who knew he could write?"

"I stayed in touch with him over the summer. Since Ronnie, I figure I want to stay ahead of whatever trouble is brewing with guys in my dorm. I just can't figure out what's happened to Ratso. Is it a mental illness? A brain aneurism? A blood clot? A personality disorder? I don't know how to explain it. So I've been calling him for a friendly chat every couple of weeks. Hence the letter."

"What's he say in the letter?" asked Randi.

"Ratso went home for the summer, and, like the rich kid he is, had nothing to do but hang out at the pool at his country club. Another grad of St. Chris, Jim Showalter, called Ratso and asked him to help with an outreach program for poor inner-city kids. So Ratso spent the summer in the public housing projects in Gilpin Court playing basketball and hanging out with black kids from the hood."

"Ratso did what?" exclaimed Gary. "Gilpin Court? That's one tough neighborhood!"

"Ratso and Jim played basketball on the public courts in the projects. With local black kids. Ratso spent his summer making new friends and trying to support the kids. He said his goal was to encourage them and give them hope to help them want to get out of the projects and live a better life. Ratso claims his work with the kids at the YMCA last spring inspired him to reach out and see if he could help needy kids in his hometown."

"That's amazing," I blurted out. "Who would guess our nasty, racist, overly entitled pal could turn a new leaf and do something positive and constructive? I wish I could turn a new leaf like Ratso." For some reason, this comment brought a long pause. 'Oops! I hope I didn't step in it,' I wondered to myself.

"I had a new leaf turning experience this summer," said Nikki. "You know I went work with the Penn State team trying to launch a national Earth Day. The project was challenging and inspiring, but what really made an impact were three of my teammates. Grey Barr, Candi Potts, and Edgar Lawson are environmental grad students, but that's not what blew me away. The three of them are followers of Jesus.

"Over the summer these guys became my new best friends. We talked about Jesus – all the stuff Gary has been telling me. It was great having fresh people to discuss thoughts with, people with a different point of view." Turning to Gary, she smiled warmly. "Gary and I would write and then I was able to talk with my Penn State friends, the three amigos. Grey, Candi, and Edgar let me ask questions and helped me figure out what I'm thinking and feeling.

"The three of them met as undergrads when they got involved in an outreach ministry to kids in a local high school. It sounds like what Ratso did this summer. They hung out with teens at games and stuff and made friends. The amigos say this is what Jesus did. He came into our world and hung out with ordinary people in an everyday way in order to love them and introduce them to God. So they want to do the same for teens struggling through adolescence. Candi calls it 'being Jesus-with-skin-on.' Doing Jesus' mission with people in their world has enabled the amigos to build strong friendships, what they call community, and to make a positive difference for good. So cool!"

"It is neat," Gary remarked. "Every time I connected with Nikki this summer, she talked about how following Jesus can have a dramatic impact on the world we live in. The amigos are living love in action and making a big difference."

"That's amazing," Linda commented. "The amigos sound like totally far out people."

"That's it exactly," Nikki laughed. "The more I get to know them, the more I want to become like them, to be an amigo myself. You know how I've always talked about seeing God in nature? Candi helped me study the first chapter of the Letter to the Romans, in the Bible. It talks about how God reveals himself, his very qualities, through nature. And it says he gives us our conscience, an internal sense of what is right and what is wrong, for the same reason – so we can come to know him and trust him. The more I think about it, the more I become convinced God is real. One morning at breakfast I had Candi teach me how to pray and I gave my life to Jesus."

Gary put his arm around her and gave her a hug. Nikki smiled happily. "After six weeks, I can tell you I feel at peace, not so anxious about my future, and I feel relieved to be forgiven and learning from God. Jesus is wonderful!"

Frank, who had been quiet, looked up from the fire, "Everything is wonderful?"

"No, no," Nikki responded. "That's not what I said. I'm still addicted to TAB, and my world is not sprouting roses, but I find Jesus himself wonderful. A remarkable man and a wonderful friend. Actually, the shit hit the fan with my parents when I told them I've decided to follow Jesus. You'd think I came home and said I joined the Weathermen underground and was going to blow up buildings and kill cops.

"It's ironic. Dad is a liberal, open minded, college professor and Mom leads music in the Methodist church. Their reaction to my good news was so negative! They're appalled! Like I'm having conversations with Casper the friendly ghost. They think it's 'completely inappropriate' for me to be having conversations with a historical figure like Jesus. Like I'm little a kid with an imaginary friend. 'What do you mean he is alive today, and you talk with him? Can't you just go to church and sit through the programs like normal religious people?' they ask. It makes me wonder what they are thinking every Easter in church when the congregation celebrates the resurrection of Jesus."

After Nikki shared her story, we enjoyed a quiet spell, gazing into the fire light considering our thoughts. There's something about a fire which helps you connect with your soul. As a teen on St. Simons, we used to go up to the end of East Beach in warm weather and build a campfire in the dunes. You dig a little chair out of the sand, get comfortable and watch the flickering flames for hours. The sound of the waves rolling in is soothing. Sometimes the moon appears in a clear sky and paints a silver path across the water and waves as if nature is creating a special corridor between us and the celestial sky itself. Firelight has that effect – causing me to get in touch with the inner me. At the same time, it creates an intimate bond with those sharing the fire.

In my heart, I'm wondering why someone like Nikki is having a warm and wonderful experience with Jesus and I'm on the outside looking in? I love Nikki, but she was practically raised a heathen, for pity sake. Her family never made her go to church – just let her wander around in the woods on her own. Here I am, raised a hard core Christian and I've never had any experience remotely like what she describes. You couldn't get a more religious home than mine. How come I never found Jesus? What Nikki is describing sounds so real, freeing, and positive. Me, I've got nothing. Instead, all I got was a boatload of shit - religious rules, criticism, guilt, judgment and shame. Somehow, the beautiful relationship with Jesus got left off my plate when the meals were handed out.

Rob broke the silence. "Randi, you should share about your summer," he said, holding her hand. She looked at him and smiled that shy grin she often displays when she's embarrassed.

"Come on sugar," Nikki encouraged. "Aren't you the one who keeps telling us we are among friends?"

"Well, I suppose that is a direct quote. You know how it is…when it comes to matters of the heart I'm a little shy and private."

"Private? Except for when you go swimming buck naked with hundreds of strangers," laughed Frank. We all cracked up at Frank's rude but too true comment.

"Oh, so that's how you are going to play it, Spinelli? Alright, point taken. I guess if I trust you enough to cavort in the nude, I can share about my summer. I'm just not used to talking about spiritual things."

"Honey," Rob interrupted. "Just tell the story. Like a little play about what happened to you over the summer. You can do this. We all love you."

"OK. You know I spent my summer studying at the Philadelphia College of Art. Often I went to the Museum of Art after class to study the paintings. The steps of the museum are a hang out for young people, like Rittenhouse Square. There were these people on the steps called the Jews for Jesus. They sat around and rapped with different people about Jesus, Judaism and life. I got into some interesting conversations about how Judaism is a faith in need of a Savior, who they call the Messiah. The Passover Seder is a meal, a Jewish celebration, that talks about how God brought the Jews out of slavery in Egypt and how our faith looks forward to the final Passover Lamb, the Messiah, who will set us free from sin and failure and unite us with God forever.

"Moshe Shuman, the leader of the group, never tried to sell me. He just pointed out passages in the Bible I might want to read. I read the Old Testament book of Isaiah. It's full of promises of the coming of the Messiah. It says, 'God is going to do a new thing. Look for it!' I read the Gospel of Matthew which presents a compelling case that Jesus, or Yeshua as the Jews call him, is the Messiah.

"At times I felt I was having trouble connecting the dots. Judaism has made things so complex. Since the time of Jesus, many Jewish leaders have muddied the water instead of seeking the truth. So, Mo told me just to try it. Use the experimental approach. Take God at his word that if you seek him, you will be found by him. I asked Jesus to show me if he is real and how I could know him."

When Randi paused to collect her thoughts, Linda interrupted, "What happened? Did your experiment with faith work?"

"I didn't have a great revelation. No heavens opening with angels revealing the Truth. It was more like going down to the beach to watch the sun rise. First its pitch black – looks like night to me. The sky begins to look a little less black. Eventually it's getting grey. The horizon brightens, just a smidge. Soon I can see things around me, even though all is still in shadow. Finally the pink, purple, orange, red, and the bright yellow blaze up over the edge of the earth. And its daylight! That's what it was like for me. I asked Jesus to invade my life and he has. I asked him to show me the way and he is. Each day I learn a little more and understand a bit better.

"There's so much I don't know and don't understand. That's why I'm reluctant to share, Frank. Not because I don't trust you guys. Because I'm so new to faith. I know a tiny bit and there are worlds of things I still have no clue about. The bible is practical and helpful and I learn a lot from it. I pray and God somehow guides me in my spirit, in a small still voice. In one passage I read this summer it says if you lack wisdom you can ask God and he will give it to you freely, without making you feel foolish. Mo says Jesus gives us the Holy Spirit to guide us and tell us when to turn to the left or the right. He provides practical help and power for living. The Jesus followers I know have been a big encouragement too."

We sat in companionable silence, thinking about what our friends had shared. Frank put wood more on the fire. As he skewered another marshmallow, he ask Bachmann, "Rob, what do you think of all this? What's happened to Randi and Nikki?"

I don't think Frank was challenging Rob, Nikki or Randi. But of the people in our crew, Rob is our benchmark for sanity. Gary and Nikki are optimistic, fun loving people who bounce through life with great joy. Randi is more serious, but artsy. Jack is wild and crazy. Frenchie is cynical from his time in Vietnam. Billy and Arty are just off the wall. Doug is primarily interested in making music and making out with Linda. But Rob – he's seen some of the world, been through hard things and still seems to have his head on straight. Practical and realistic. Down to earth. Not swayed by the opinions of others or by what's popular. I suspect Frank is thinking, "If Rob is considering Jesus, maybe I should too."

After a long pause, Rob replied, "Have to admit, I have mixed feelings about the whole trusting Jesus deal. I have nothing but good things to say about what I've seen in Gary's life and in his friends of Jesus group. I love that he's pulling together people who are willing to be real and discuss issues that matter. The group is transparent and accepting. I never feel peer pressure in those sessions. Randi and I talked a lot over the summer and I respect where she and Nikki have decided to put their faith. As far as I can tell, the choice to follow Jesus has done nothing but good things for each of them."

Rob paused for a moment, "But… I do have two reservations which make me hesitate to go where Randi and Nikki have gone this summer. I like what I hear about Jesus, but I have a lot of trouble with Christians and the church. Many of my friends who go to church… Well, frankly, I find them smarmy and self-centered. When I go to church, and I've tried it several times, the talk and songs seem to be all about me, me, me! How I feel. 'Make me feel better Lord.' In general, they seem narcissistic and extremely self-centered. It reminds me of the Janis Joplin tune - 'Oh, Lord won't you buy me a Mercedes Benz, All my friends they drive Porsches, I must make amends…' I get the feeling they see God as a cosmic therapist whose job is to make me happy. My acquaintances who call themselves Christians or who admit they go to church – they're quick to criticize and judge others. Often they are hung up on all the things they're against. They epitomize the 'haters' you find in different pockets across America. I just can't see myself wanting to become that kind of person.

"I'm not saying every person of faith is like that. Certainly you guys aren't like that. Father X and Doc Brody; they aren't like that. I'm not sure why you guys are so different from the rest of them? Is it following Jesus instead of being Christian, which Father X is always trying to explain to me?

"Plus, if I'm honest with myself, I'm not ready to give up control of my life. I like being a leader – at least in my own life. I'm not interested in losing me. Shoot, I actually like a lot of who I am. And I don't want to become a smarmy bun head…I'm not saying you guys are, just…"

Randi punched Rob on the arm and laughed. "Careful, bruiser!"

Nikki laughed, "You calling me a bun head, sport?"

Robbie blushed with embarrassment. "No, no. None of my friends are bun heads. Just other people I know who are hung up on church. In the end, maybe I'm just afraid to surrender control of my life."

Wow! What an interesting night of conversation. I can't tell you how deeply my friends' stories affected me. I've been struggling with a lot of things over the past few years. I honestly don't like where I am, or a lot of the choices I've made. Stripping makes me feel cheap and ashamed. My relationships with men have never been very honoring to me as a person. With the exception of Skeeter Stetson, most of the men in my life have used and abused me and treated me like crap. Maybe my self-esteem is so low I think that's all I deserve.

I have a lot of regret about medicating myself with drugs and booze to try to sooth the pain. I may have sold out what's right in order to find material security. It's like, in spite of all my good intentions, it's me who keeps on sabotaging me with pitifully poor choices. And my family background makes me weep with sadness. Many days I wake up wishing I could be somebody else. Just get up and walk off in somebody else's life and skin.

Yet hearing about Ratso turning a new leaf, becoming a different kind of person, fills me with hope. I know the relationship with Jesus that Randi and Nikki are getting into is the kind of thing that transforms a person into someone who is exceptional. It reminds me of my friends Pat and Kris Rouseau. They are the type of people who exude love and goodness, so it overflows and touches others; people who make a difference in this world, who leave others better. Sigh! On that note, we all turned in for the night.

37

"The soul should always stand ajar,
ready to welcome the ecstatic experience."
~ Emily Dickinson

Rob Bachmann   August, 1969

I woke up before daylight. I love camping. It's always been one of my favorite things. Normally, my body wakes up at first light. It doesn't matter how late I go to bed. When nature wakes, so do I. I love to lay snug in my sleeping bag, sensing the light rise, the songbirds warble and flit. Mourning doves coo. The cool morning smells heralding a beautiful summer day seep into my tent along with the tang of last night's campfire. When I hear other campers stirring, it's time to get up!

I brewed a pot of coffee on the Coleman stove. Then I laid fresh kindling on the embers of the campfire and blew until it sprang into life. Dragging my chair and cup of hot black coffee in front of the crackling fire, I relaxed as I enjoyed the beginnings of a new day, waiting for my companions to rise. Nikki was the first to join me by the fire. "Coffee?" I ask.

She smiled and lifted her left hand wrapped firmly around a TAB. "Salute, my friend. I still prefer to ingest my caffeine in the bubbly sugar water manner. But, to each his own." Soon Doug, Gary and Frank joined us at the fire. We sat sipping our beverages and ogling the interesting people.

To our left is a Cadillac Coupe Deville. Sporting a two-tone paint job of brown and tan, it was in mint condition, covered in chrome. A genuine 'duce coupe.' Waxed and gleaming, it's a pristine example of 1950's Detroit auto styling. The beast had simply been pulled head first into the fence row on arrival the previous day. "I'm thinking that's a '58 Caddy," said Doug. "One of my buddies has one just like it in his backyard. His dad is always working on it. Says he is going to restore it and put it on the road again."

"Wowie Zowie!" exclaimed Frank. "Look at the chrome on that puppy! Dual headlights, twin fins up the hood, two tone roof, fins in the back are bigger than a great white shark. Four doors, tan interior, and tan steering wheel! The front bumpers are so big they remind me of Dolly Parton's tits. Outstanding!"

We had a good laugh at Frank's flattering description. As we joked around, the rear door of the Caddy swung open. A young coffee colored dude unfolded himself off the seat and climbed out. This tall drink of water was long and lean, dressed in black jeans, a tie-dyed t-shirt, topped with a black leather vest. He wore a red kerchief around his neck and sported a ten-inch high Afro. When he looked our way and smiled, we all waved. Our neighbor wandered into the bushes to take a pee, then headed for the trunk of the Caddy. He popped the lid up and began to shout, "Drugs for Sale! All kinds. Straight from Brooklyn. Come and get them while they last."

"A drug dealer," laughed Frank. "No wonder he has an awesome car. Lots of cash, no taxes, and plenty of time on your hands. He probably washes that car everyday."

"Did you sleep alright, Nikki?" I asked. "You look...tense."

Nikki smiled ruefully "I slept ok." She added in a whisper, "I'm just worried about Faith. She doesn't look well. I don't know what's wrong; her health is bad."

"I've had the same thought," I replied. "There's something off, but I'm not sure what."

Just then Faith crawled out of the tent and joined us by the fire circle. Nikki smoothly changed the conversation, "Good morning, Sunshine! How did you sleep?"

"I'm a little bleary eyed, I guess." Faith said, washing her face and eyes with a washcloth. "I slept pretty well, just not enough. I don't think I had any idea how tired I am until I got out of my normal routine. Being here with you guys, out in nature – I'm more self-aware I guess. I'm bone weary. I feel tired all the way down to my soul."

"The coffee may not cure fatigue," Frank handed Faith a mug, "but it might rejuvenate you for a spell." As Faith joined our circle, we heard a door latch click in the camp to the right. The side door of a white VW Vanagan camper slid open and out stepped a skinny white guy with long blonde hair. He was naked. After giving us a grin, a wave and some more full-frontal nudity, he turned aside and urinated on the back tire of his bus. Then he wandered over to our ring around the fire.

"Hello," he said with a strong French Canadian accent. "My name is Pierre. Pierre Frogale. I am from Quebec City."

"Frogale?" queried Doug.

"Yes! That's it precisely. Frog like the little beastie hopping by the pond. Ale like the drink the British guzzle," he explained pantomiming a drinker chugging a beer." He laughed at his own joke.

We sat gaping at this strange Frenchman standing six feet away with his dong hanging down chatting amiably about his name and its pronunciation. Pierre casually scratched his groin, his arm pits and then his hairy chest. Faith and Nikki were bug eyed at this vision. Gary broke the silence. "Well, hey there, Pierre. Nice to meet you," he managed to croak out. "Glad to have you as a camping neighbor."

Gary's comment seemed to satisfy Pierre and he wandered back to his VW, where a lovely petite brunette was climbing out. A short slip covered her obvious nudity, and she smiled from under sleep tousled hair. "Must have been a pretty active night," Faith remarked laughing. "And leave it to a Southern gentleman like Gary to come up with something polite to say under any circumstance." She enjoyed a good belly laugh, and we all joined in.

After breakfast, we wandered around with the mobs filling the fields and roads. We could hear hammers pounding and saws ripping as they raced to finish the stage. Crews hoisted huge black amplifiers, 20-foot square, to the top of sound towers. The towers, made of metal scaffolding, were eighty feet high. The stage was at the bottom of a natural amphitheater formed by the surrounding fields which would allow spectators to have an unobstructed view wherever they sit.

At eleven am an announcement came over the public address system. "From now on, it's a free concert, man," the announcer intoned. "We are tearing down the fences and you don't need a ticket. It's a free concert. The folks putting on the music are going to take a bit of a bath, financially, but enjoy yourselves, take care of each other, and be safe."

Frank exclaimed, "Hey that's crazy! We have tickets!"

"Save them," laughed Doug. "Some day they'll be a keepsake you can look back on as a Woodstock souvenir." We watched in amazement as the crews who worked all night putting up a five-foot chain link fence around the stage and seating areas, cut the fences down with bolt cutters, then pressed them into the ground so the hordes could simply walk over them to reach the amphitheater.

We hustled to our campsite and made sandwiches for lunch, grabbed a bag of drinks and headed back to find a spot to sit. Already the hillside was covered with spectators. We found a location with room for eight a hundred yards from the stage and settled in to wait. Randi and I agreed to hold the space while the others wandered around enjoying the scene.

"Robbie, I wanted to follow up on something you said yesterday." I smiled down at her and nodded encouragement. "You were telling me about your experience this summer with Frenchie's parents and what you learned from them?"

"I am struck with what I see in their lives. Their character and wisdom. It wasn't what they said, it was how happy they are. I can see God shining out of their lives and yet they never preached at me. Leroy is so practical. He's honest to the bone. When the check out girl at the IGA gave him too much change, he got back out of the truck, walked into the store and helped her get it right. He has a forestry degree and could have made a lot more money cruising timber, but it would require plenty of time away from home. So he runs a lumber yard. More work, less money, but time for his family."

We sat in silence for a bit, and Randi said. "Do you think Leroy and Maddie regret the choices they've made?"

"No! Not at all. They are the most fulfilled people I know. I would love to live the life they are living. Who wants more money if you're miserable? And who needs more money if you're happy and making a difference in the world?"

Randi paused a beat, "Jesus said: 'The yoke I will give you is easy and the burden light.' Trusting Jesus is not just about getting fire insurance for eternity. It's about the future, but it's also about how we live today. Jesus promises a better life today and for eternity. He says those who trust in him will have rivers of water, spiritual water, thirst quenching water, flowing out and into their lives. God wants you to live your best life. He loves you like your father never loved you."

After a few moments of silence, I responded, "What if I can't do what he wants? What if I'm a failure as a follower? What if I mess up, make mistakes? You know how often I do that."

"Jesus says he won't break a bruised reed or put out a flickering lamp. God knows we're all failure prone. He promises to lead us to a better place, to free us from our own inadequate leadership and direction in our lives."

"I see that in the LeBoufes. I want to be like them. I'm just not sure I can let go of the steering wheel, crawl over the back seat and relax while Jesus drives. What gave you the courage to let go and try Jesus?"

Randi was silent for a few moments while she thought. I admire the way she actually takes time to listen to what I say and consider before she responds. She smiled up at me, her blue eye reflecting contentment. "One weekend in July, I went to New York City to visit museums. I saw Van Gogh's *Starry Night*. The original is only thirty inches high and 36 inches wide. It's a small painting compared to most other major works of art. As soon as I laid eyes on it, I knew I was looking at a work of genius. A masterpiece. Somehow the artist captured a truth bigger than life. In a mysterious way, this small picture presents an image of reality more accurate than the actual thing itself. It's as if Van Gogh was able to see into the heart of the universe and display it for others on a little bit of canvas. I was blown away.

"When I read the gospel of Matthew, and considered what Jesus said and did, I felt the same way. Watching his life, listening to his teaching – I just knew I was looking at the essence of God poured into a human being. Jesus is who he says he is and so much more. He will love me and guide me into more of life than I can possibly understand. My heart tells me he is the real deal. It will take me a lifetime to learn about him. I have to admit, my decision to trust Jesus was more of an intuitive thing rather than a rational decision. I don't think it took courage on my part. My heart told me he's true and he is the way. So I simply went with my heart. To do anything else would have been to be untrue to myself."

The music was supposed to begin at noon. After a lot of delays, announcements, and waiting, Ritchie Havens began to play. Havens knocked it out of the park. A rangy, middle age black man with an acoustic guitar, he came alone and sat on stage. Ritchie wore a long tan dashiki, black slacks and leather sandals. He half leaned, half sat on a stool and strummed out his music. It was like Randi's description of Starry Night. I have no idea how he did it, but within moments, this man's music had snaked a hand into my guts and gripped me by the heart. The words, melody, and emotions captured me and pulled me along on his journey in a powerful way. The audience was dead silent and appeared mesmerized. It was an awesome phenomenon. The Woodstock Experience was beginning.

The next set was Ravi Shankar, an Indian guru who played the sitar. Some kind of weird, Indian instrument. Very hip, very cool, very George Harrison. Not my cup of tea, but that's why you have multiple acts. Something for every musical taste.

As Shankar played, the grey skies began to weep rain. The response of the crowd around us was incredible. People with blankets invited others to climb under their shelter. Neighbors shared what they had with others. Umbrellas, rain ponchos, big coats, even pieces of plastic were shared around to care for the community around us. We had plenty of blankets but only Linda had brought any rain gear. We invited our neighbors, who had a big plastic sheet, to pile on and join us. Together we had a dry blanket underneath and rain protection overhead. The crush of flesh provided warmth to counteract the chill brought on by falling rain. Those with food shared it around. Someone cracked open a bottle of red wine and it circulated through our expanded family. Strangers no more!

The rain was not continuous. It fell off and on – all weekend long. When we had breaks from the rain, people would uncover, get up and walk around. It gave us a chance to explore, see new people and new sights. Doug kept looking for the guys from The Windows without any success. For the rest of the weekend, we lived in that field, with 500,000 of our new best friends. Our crew was fortunate. We could retreat to our campsite; grab some food, take a break or sleep in a dry tent. Most of the people around us had only the clothes on their backs, having walked in from a distant road. It was nice to go back to camp to get out of the crush, have a snack, or take a nap without people poking you.

Friday night, during Arlo Guthrie's set, Faith announced, "I'm bushed. I keep falling asleep, even when really good music is playing. Think I'll go back to camp and turn in. I need the rest."

"Want me to come with you?" Randi asked.

"No, I'm good. I'll probably be able to enjoy the music more in a nice dry tent curled up in my sleeping bag catching some zzzs."

"OK, sweetie," said Nikki. "Don't leave a light on. I've got my little pocket flash light to guide me home. Love you, babe."

"Smooches back at you – all of you." Faith gave us a wan, tired smile and began to work her way back through the crowds heading up the hill to our camp. Arlo crooned on, "Coming into Los Angeles, bringing in a couple of keys, don't touch my bags if you please, Mr. Customs Man."

"You know, for a girl barely 21, she looks exhausted," Gary commented. "Nikki, what do you think is going on? Is it too much work?"

"I don't know." Nikki replied. "She only works three nights a week. Faith doesn't go to work until four thirty in the afternoon, although she sometimes comes in pretty late, doesn't she Randi?"

"I have no idea. I go to bed by ten and I sleep like a log. I can't imagine its work. Between the dish room and cleaning the gym five nights a week, Robbie works more hours than Faith, and he looks just fine." Randi smiled at me and I grinned at my little Jewish love bunny.

"Think she might have an eating disorder?" Linda suggested. "When we first met her, she was so curvaceous! Now she looks boney. I've had friends with anorexia who were gaunt like that. Or bulimia, where you gorge on food then blow chunks and lose it all?"

Randi thought then said, "I don't think it's physical. She eats a decent diet at school, always has plenty of money since she started to waitress. I'm sure they give you free meals if you waitress at Grandpa's. I don't know how well she's been eating over the summer living at Mrs. Rose's house, but… My gut tells me it's not her physical health. Emotional or spiritual health may be at the root of what ails her."

"Can we help her get into counseling?" asked Gary. "Doesn't the Dean's office recommend local therapists for students?"

"I've suggested Faith see a counselor," said Randi. "My parents and my older brother have gone to counseling and it was super helpful. Counseling helped my folks in their marriage and parenting. My brother worked through some hang ups he had as a teen. But Faith isn't open. Not interested. I can't tell if it's from her family or if she just doesn't think she needs help."

"Or she doesn't think it will help whatever is bothering her," I offered.

"I hate to bring this up," said Frank, "but it may be crack." A stunned silence followed Frank's pronouncement. "Just saying." Spinelli paused for long minute. "I'm not trying to be malicious or anything." More silence. "This past summer I talked with a guy who grew up down the street from my parents in Ridgewood. He was 27 and a high flyer in a New York ad agency when he started using cocaine. He said it made him feel creative and gave him more energy at work. But he got addicted. After six months he crashed and burned. Lost his job, his career, his health – everything. He's moved back in with his parents. He told me he's learned the signs to look for include a lot of sniffing, red nostrils, and a drippy nose. Bright eyes. Weight loss."

We were quiet, and then Randi spoke. "I can see that. Faith does seem to have a lot of 'colds or allergies' as she calls them. And I notice the red around her nose. I guess I just thought it was a cold."

"That and her gaunt look," Nikki added. "Did you see how skinny she looks?"

We pondered what we could do to help our friend. Finally, Gary suggested. "For sure we can pray. God's power to intervene and help heal tragic circumstances is amazing. But we probably need to pray that God will move Faith to open up and want help for whatever it is."

Gary went on, "Tony Lavelle shared about his experience in AA. I wonder if a support group would help? She came to the Waffle Club once, but didn't return. I figured she was just checking us out. She never said a word. I thought she simply didn't connect with the folks there that night. What if we helped her get in a supportive group of women? Or a group of recovering Christians?"

270

"I know what you mean, Gary." commented Linda. "Faith seems locked up tight within herself. She's struggling with something inside, but she isn't able to share with anyone or ask for help."

"That's what I mean," Randi responded, "when I say there must be something emotional or spiritual at the heart of her problem."

Linda added, "A girlfriend in high school got knocked up and went to New York for an abortion. She was a mess. So afraid people would find out and judge her. She suffered from shame, guilt, and grief over the lost baby. She couldn't talk about it, because she thought she was the only one who ever experienced tragic failure. It wasn't until she found another girl who had gone through a similar experience and was willing to talk about it that my girlfriend began to heal. That's how I read Faith. She's like my friend in that hurting place. She feels all alone. Whatever is troubling her, it's locked up inside and she's afraid to share it, let alone to ask for help."

"Couldn't we do an intervention," Doug suggested, "like people do with friends or relatives who have an alcohol problem? Confront her and make her tell us what's troubling her?"

"From what Tony says," Frank replied, "the AA method doesn't work until the alcoholic realizes he is down the shitter, is a hopeless drunk, and can't do a thing to help himself. Then others can offer help and it has a chance of success." A long silence fell on the group as we considered what had been said.

"Isn't there anything we can do to save Faith?" asked Gary in a sad plaintive voice.

Nikki reached over for Gary's hand. "You are a tender and compassionate guy. But I think only Faith can save Faith at this point. It's up to her. If she decides she wants help, she'll find she's surrounded by people who love her and will assist her. If she doesn't want help, there's probably nothing we can do."

The music went on long into the night and into Saturday morning. It was fabulous and inspirational. Finally, at one thirty in the morning, as *Sly and the Family Stone* took to the stage, we gave it up. Everyone was exhausted. We abandoned the blankets on our spot and hoped our stuff would be there when we returned. We trudged up the hill to our campsite and went to bed.

It was full light when I woke at 6 Saturday morning. Still, I was the first to roll out of bed, start the coffee and light a new campfire. Shortly after seven, Nikki stumbled out of her little tent and joined me in a chair by the fire. "Howdy, camper," Nikki drawled. "You're up bright and early! Considering the nightlife you've been living."

Nikki can always make me laugh. "No credit to my self-discipline, I'm afraid," I commented, "Just the natural rhythms of my body clock. And my chronic need for coffee."

271

Nikki hoisted her first TAB of the day and laughed. "I know exactly what you mean!" After a beat, she remarked, "This whole experience reminds me of working at Camp Kehonka in New Hampshire."

"How so?" I asked.

"You come away to a strange place you've never been, have extraordinary experiences like you never have back home, and every day seems like a magical adventure. You get in touch with yourself in ways you fail to do in everyday life, and you get into conversations and go deeper than you do with friends back home. I don't know; there's just something about getting away and having a new experience that takes you to strange new places. Kinda like dropping acid, without all the bad side effects."

"OK, Nik," I murmured, not knowing where this was going.

"What I mean is, you have these days, filled with astonishing events, you hardly get any sleep, you wake up feeling like you slept in an industrial clothes drier and yet, …you want to get up and can't wait to see what the new day will bring!"

"You really should consider switching from TAB to coffee. It might help you get a little more grounded in reality." I laughed and Nikki punched me in the arm. Doug and Frank joined us at the fire while this odd conversation was taking place. As we sipped our restorative beverages, the door to Pierre's van next door popped open to reveal our naked neighbor. After a friendly wave and a public pee in the long grass, Pierre wandered to the back of the bus to dig out something to eat.

"Ahh, new experiences," laughed Frank. We laughed. A willowy redhead clambered out of the bus. This 'new experience' was dressed only in a white t-shirt which didn't quite cover a very cute ass. Plump round tits jiggled under the fabric of the t-shirt.

"Ahh, variety; the spice of life," laughed Doug.

Nikki smacked him, "You'd better hope Linda doesn't hear you talking like that!" We laughed again. Pierre, nudist extraordinaire, certainly had a flair for attracting hot women. Variety indeed!

The music that weekend was incredible. Some of the biggest names in rock and roll performed – they simply blew me away. Others, who we had never heard of, were even better. It was a profoundly moving experience for anyone who loved music. I think the organizers planned for twelve hours of music each day, but you know about the best laid plans. The rain came and went, technical glitches slowed up the process, and then there was simply the magic of wonderful music. When you give a musician a microphone and an audience, it is hard to get him off stage. It's a like giving a Baptist preacher a pulpit. Awfully hard to pry opportunity out of their hands.

The balance of the weekend was a blur of music, at all hours, in pouring rain, brilliant sunshine and lots of mud. The stand outs for me were Ritchie Havens, Santana, Jefferson Airplane, Joe Cocker, the Grateful Dead, Crosby, Stills and Nash, and Jimi Hendrix. The Who, at a peak of popularity after the release of their ground breaking rock opera, *Tommy*, performed a memorable set. The raw and edgy Scottish singer Country Joe McDonald did a fabulous cover of the Beatle's tune *I'll Get by with A Little Help from My Friends* which might have served as an anthem for our Woodstock weekend.

My favorite song of the weekend was Alvin Lee's performance of *I'm Coming Home*. The English blues rock band Ten Years After recorded and released this powerful, driving anthem of seeking and finding home the year before, but to my mind their live recording of the tune at Woodstock has never been equaled. For me, it painted a mural on my heart describing my own journey. Seeking home, longing for and searching for something that remains just out of reach but never loses its attraction. I long to find…whatever it is my soul yearns for. I left Woodstock dedicated to the hunt, with a commitment to press on until I find that place of belonging, of peace, of fulfillment.

Years later, I would hear pundits claim, "If you remember what happened at Woodstock, you were not really there." Nothing could be further from the truth. Every moment of that remarkable weekend feels as if it is permanently seared into my consciousness. In spite of the passage of time, I can recall with crystal clarity the music, the throngs of happy people, the colorful hippie culture, the bad weather and mud, our peaceful little campsite in the meadow, and most of all, my friends - as if it was still happening right now.

38

"Not until we are lost do we begin to find ourselves."
~ *Henry David Thoreau*

Jack Flynn   Early October, 1969

While most of my friends were off having the adventure of a lifetime at Woodstock, I was strapped to a damn hospital bed being tortured within an inch of my life by medical procedures. Let's see, enjoy fabulous rock and roll music, revel in nature, and experience a new community of love, peace and human harmony, or have bloody dressings torn off, accompanied by poking, prodding, and testing of healing limbs by my orthopedic surgeon? Ouch, ouch and double ouch! It's a bummer! I feel like I've been left out, maybe even left behind; although I admit it's hard to go up country to a hippie festival dragging along a guy wired up to a hospital bed.

After school started in September, I kept hearing first hand accounts of the Woodstock Experience. These tales make me regret not being able to make the scene. I know for a fact, Frenchie and Arty feel the same. It's like all of mankind made a great leap forward, turned a new page, creating a wave of optimism and hope which has spread across the country. But not us. So different from our failed experiment engaging in the political process during the summer of '68. Will there ever be another Woodstock for those of us unlucky enough to have missed it? I seriously doubt it, but you never know.

I shouldn't complain. Even though I'm wired up and stuck in bed, Dr. Mosemann says I'm healing well and should be ready to move into a rehab hospital in a couple months. There they will torture me with physical therapy and other procedures in hopes of making me well again. Or maybe make me glad when all medical attention ceases. Five months down and four more to go.

The stitches have been pulled from my smaller cuts, which are now healed over. Larger wounds have drainage tubes in them and I'm not quite ready to tap dance. I'm afraid I'll never be pretty again, but why would I need to be pretty when I can gaze into the blue eyes of Amy Feltgood every day? My spirit soars each time I see her smiling face looking at me. OK, it's true, I am gaga in love with this woman and I'm not afraid to admit it. Having her by my side, loving me with her eyes, her soft comments, holding my hand – these make my injuries a small price to pay. If I had known flying my bike headfirst through plate-glass would obtain the adoration of the divine Miss F., I'd have done it months earlier.

Actually, besides time with Amy, I'm most grateful for visits from friends. They cheer me up. Today, as soon as visiting hours started, Rob, Gary and Nikki filed into my room. They pulled three visitor chairs into a close semi-circle around my bed and smiled at me.

"We decided," began Rob, "this is like Koffee Klatch, just in a remote location. We know about the food in here, so we brought you some good stuff." He reached into the paper sack at his feet and pulled out a large steaming cup of black coffee. "From T-Bird's Coffee Shop! Nikki got you a treat as well."

Clausen pulled an aluminum foil wrapped package out of her book bag. "This is a New York style bagel, toasted and loaded with cream cheese. The cream cheese will help heal bones. Probably won't do anything for the fact you're still an idiot," she smiled, "but we love you anyway."

"Ahh, this is so kind of you, my friends," I cried. "What's going on in the real world? What are you talking about in Koffee Klatch?"

Rob jumped in. "Senior year means every conversation ends with the same question. 'What are your plans after graduation?' To which I typically reply, 'Beats me? Think I might go fishing.' That's not entirely true, but I love the effect it has on people who ask me the question. To be honest, I suspect it's true for most of the class of 1970. Who knows what tomorrow will hold? I'll be happy to graduate, then I'll worry about what's next. Only Arty is settled on a career path. He got accepted into the management training program at US Steel. When we graduate, Arty will have his coveted entry ticket into the white collar ranks of Big Steel."

Gary added, "That's no surprise. Arty's been headed that way since the first day of orientation freshman year. Do you remember the Dodge Dart? Push button transmission?"

We all laughed, and Nikki added, "What a hoot!"

"Fuckin' A!" I responded. We cracked up. Laugher is good medicine and my friends make me laugh.

"You know who does surprise me?" Gary continued. "Ratso!" He took a long pause as everybody looked at him, waiting for the Ratso punch line. "Ratso changed his major! To outdoor education."

"He what...?" asked Rob with a large dose of amazement.

"Hey, I knew that," I chuckled.

Rob looked at me in amazement. "OK, Black Jack, you obviously have sources, tell us more."

"Certainly." I laughed at Rob's look of wonder. "Ratso changed majors because he actually does have a plan for his future! I know it sounds weird, but the new Ratso is full of surprises. He's had a change of heart and is moving in a totally different direction with his life."

A silence fell on the room while I let this sink in. "The first person who came to see me when school started was Ratso. He frequently shows up bringing me food, new reading material, and just to chat. Sometimes he brings Tony Lavelle. Tony is good at food smuggling. Must have been his early training with the Hells Angels. One night he brought me a large Mr. Mom's Italian sausage piazza. You should

275

have seen the nurses shit a brick when they found the empty pizza box in the trash the next day!"

"Yow!" yelped Nikki. "The competition for your affection is much stiffer than I expected." She looked at Rob and Gary. "Fellows, we're going to have to up our game!"

After the laughter died down, I continued. "Ratso spent his summer playing basketball with his pal Jim Showalter and all the black kids in the projects in the East End of Richmond. They played ball and built friendships. Every afternoon, when it was too stinking hot to play b-ball, they took the kids to the community center and tutored them in reading and math skills. Ratso says the only way these kids are going to get out of the ghetto is to get an education. If they can learn to read well and graduate high school, they will have a shot at a better life."

After a pause, Rob said, "Wow, that's amazing! I'm speechless."

"It gets better. Ratso claims his work with the special needs kids at the 'Y' made him realize he could help poor kids get a second chance and escape poverty. He's serious about wanting to make a difference. This is what he wants to do for a career. He and Showalter are starting a non-profit organization in Richmond to go into the poor neighborhoods and build friendships with kids, mostly through sports, and then to provide educational support to help them succeed at school. After-school tutoring programs and stuff like that. Ratso is working his family's rich connections to raise funding."

There was a long pause while my friends considered this news. Rob finally spoke up. "I don't know which I find harder to believe – Tony smuggling in a pizza or Ratso starting a non-profit to help poor black kids. I'm simply blown away. But I guess everyone needs a second chance. Often, I feel like I need some kind of a do over, a fresh start. I'm happy for Ratso if he's found his way to a new beginning."

After my friends finished digesting the news about Ratso, I said, "If you can bear with me for a few minutes, I too have been doing some thinking about my future. In fact, like Ratso, Amy and I agree it is time for me to turn over a new leaf - a fresh beginning for my life and future career."

"Amy and I?" Nikki laughed, but with a kind twinkle in her mischievous eyes.

"Amy and I?" Echoed Robbins with a hoot.

"Amy and I?" Rob laughed out loud.

As they cracked up at my expense, I just enjoyed the sound as the phrase, "Amy and I," rolled off my tongue again. "Yes, Amy and I. Get used to it you heathen devils." My dear friends laughed some more. "As I was trying to say, being tied to this bed, has given me a lot of time for reflection. I too think I want a fresh start. A 'do over' as you put it, Rob."

I paused as they waited. I do love it when I have the audience's attention. "Watching the medical professionals at work over the past five months has given me a new perspective on what I want to do with my life. Frankly, without their intervention, I would not have a second chance at life. I may not come out of this process pretty, but I will be alive and functional."

"Just promise you will save the hair!" Nikki interjected. "You never were that pretty anyway, but your hair, oh how I love your hair!" Everyone in the room cracked up at Nikki's jest.

"As I was saying before being so rudely interrupted, I admire how doctors can take a wrecked body and restore it to live a new life, as they've done for me. I've decided I want to become a doctor, specifically an orthopedic surgeon." This announcement was met with stunned silence from my friends.

"OK," said Rob, "tell us more."

"You know when I was in high school I amused myself by finding abandoned or wrecked British racing machines and restoring them to live again? This pastime used my mechanical abilities and gave me the sense I was doing some good. Now what I want to do is take the problem solving techniques I learned on old Triumphs and MGs and use them to fix the puzzle of shattered bones. Instead of restoring old cars, as cool as that is, I want to find a higher purpose by restoring lives. Just like the folks here at Holy Spirit have done for me. I've had long conversations with Dr. Mosemann, my ortho surgeon and he thinks it makes perfect sense. When he was a kid, he loved to solve puzzles. That's exactly what an orthopedic surgeon does with bones. He says my talent for rebuilding cars is the same thing. Doc says I have the grades and the smarts to get into medical school. He's agreed to use his influence as a faculty member to get me accepted at the new Penn State Medical School in Hershey, once I complete my undergrad work."

"You can do that?" asked Gary. "Change your major from Engineering and go to medical school?"

"Actually, I'm not only changing my major, I'm going to transfer to Penn State's Harrisburg campus as soon as I get out of here. I'll finish my pre-med classes there and graduate from Penn State. Hopefully then, I'll enroll at the Hershey Medical School. Oh, and by the way, once I transfer from Carlisle College into Penn State at the end of this trimester, it will be perfectly appropriate for Amy and me to date.

"At that point we can have a public relationship as a couple who are dating, and seriously in love, without causing any conflicts of interest in her professional life. Amy will defend her dissertation in November and could graduate as early as December. I'll be transferring at the beginning of Winter Term in early December. Then we can come out of the closet. Right now Amy is simply a supportive Dorm Director helping the recovery of an injured student.

"I know there's a nine year difference in our ages, but we have a lot in common. We both lost someone close to us when we were teens. Father X says that can create a close bond. In other ways, we are complete opposites."

"You can say that again Buster," laughed Nikki. "One of you is very bright and the other a complete idiot. I'm not going to say I told you so, but I did!"

Pretty funny, I admit, even if the joke is at my expense. "I repent in dust and ashes, Nikki. You were right. Rest assured I am giving up bike riding for my health. From now on I'll get my thrills from gazing at Amy's gorgeous dimples. Ahhh…"

"You gotta' stop right now," Gary exclaimed. "I'm gonna' blow chunks in a second!"

"Ahh, I think it's cute," murmured Nikki, stroking Gary's forearm. She leaned over and blew in his ear. He laughed and swatted her away.

"I know some will talk and others will disapprove, but we both feel its right. Honestly, who knows why love happens? All I know is… I fell in love with her. I'm still in love with her. I will always be in love with her."

Nikki wrapped her arms around Gary and started kissing his neck. "Come on now. You have to admit that is romantic!"

"OK, Baby Cakes." Gary laughed. "Even I admit that's romantic coming from Black Jack Flynn. Does this mean she will have you dressed in pale white gowns with little blue flowers for the rest of your life? That would be a sight people would be willing to pay to see. "

"Here's what Amy told me," Jack replied. "Before the accident she was paralyzed by the thought of the damage our relationship might do to her career and reputation. When she was sitting in the waiting room praying for me the week I was in the coma, she considered the impact losing our relationship would have on her life. It hit her that our relationship is far more important than her career. She told me, 'Careers come and go. Jobs come and go. Relationships determine who you become as a person. I think I was always holding the potential for our love in reserve like a poker player with an ace up his sleeve. As long as I could look forward to renewing it someday, I was ok pretending it didn't exist today. Your accident made me see that's crazy! You really only have today. I could have lost you forever. I want to be with you, fully, every day we have together. I now recognize how precious and fleeting life is.'"

"OK, now I'm going to start weeping," muttered Rob, "and it ain't going to be pretty." Rob knows how to make me laugh and not take myself seriously, but I think he is genuinely touched.

Before Rob could break out in hysterical bawling, the door banged open and in walked Ratso and Tony. "Yo! Retardates!" shouted Tony with a big laugh. "How's my favorite dumb-ass ex-biker pal?"

What a crack up! These two guys are always up to something stupid and I love it when they come to visit. "Hey guys," I responded.

"Now, Tony, you know I hate it when you call my little kids retards," Ratso said with a smile. "You know they are not retards, they simply have developmental needs."

"Actually, I was referring to Jack, the brainless wonder and his pals, Rob and Gary, when I was addressing the retardates in the room. No offense meant to your kids."

"And none taken, I'm sure. As long as you're referring to these three guys, retard is the proper term of endearment." With that Ratso lifted the blue gym bag he had lugged into the room. "I told the nurse I'm on my way to the YMCA, which is sort of true." Leaning over he pulled out a clean t-shirt and gym shorts and unearthed a waxed paper bag from the bottom. "When Father X heard we were coming to visit Jack, he sent a gift. Three dozen fresh home baked cookies. Peanut Butter, Chocolate Chip and Oatmeal Raisin. The Father X Trifecta!" Handing me the package, Ratso smiled a happy smile.

Once the new visitors were settled, I passed the cookies. Nikki, always one to "tread where angels fear," waded right into the topic we were all wondering about. "Ratso, Jack has been telling us a little bit about your plans for after graduation. Sounds interesting. What can you tell us?"

"Man, where to start with that story?" Ratso replied. "I guess I don't need to tell you what I was like when I got to Carlisle? Self-centered, angry, full of shit and bluster. And those were just my good traits!" That made us laugh with him, not at him. When someone opens up and shares their pain in an honest and vulnerable manner, it's hard not to be sympathetic.

Ratso went on in a quiet voice. "When Franklin died, I realized I had lived my life in reaction to him. And how unfairly my family treated me. It's as if I didn't exist. So, I lived a non-life – everything I did was a negative reaction to Frank. When Ronnie died, I realized he was a guy struggling with feelings of insignificance and insecurity, living right down the hall from me. He was just like me. I never reached out to help; I went out of my way to piss on him. Then it was too much and he was gone."

Silence followed Ratso's confession. I feel really bad about Ronnie and the lost opportunity represented by his death. Sadness and remorse overwhelm me and I wish I had done more to reach out and help him. Now it's too late.

"When Melissa Tait talked me into helping with the boys at the Y, I'm not sure why I tried it. Pretty blue eyes and a beguiling smile, I guess. But when I saw how I was helping those kids, even in a small way, it made me feel better about myself. I guess I found it interesting and personally rewarding."

"One of the things I learned from AA," said Tony, "is the key to healing lies not in focusing on yourself and your need for healing, it's to go out and find someone else who needs help and give them a hand. Jesus said, 'If you try to save your life you will lose it, but if you give it away, you will find it.' I need to get outside of myself and help others, to grow as a person."

"Hold on, wait just a minute," I exclaimed. "The only reason you come visit me all the time, sit here reading to me, and smuggle in food, is because it makes you feel better?"

"Got in one!" laughed Ratso. "Say, pass me those cookies," he chuckled and we all joined him. "Last summer in Richmond, I had the same reaction to helping the kids in the projects as I did with the boys at the Y. These kids need a friend, they just need a break. I can help. All they need is a little attention, and a hand up, which I can provide."

Tony interrupted, "When I was in recovery I learned the process of healing begins with accepting your own broken, hopeless condition. We are all failures and fall short. The cure is to reach out and help each other. To share your story, your experience of failure. Not to preach at people or to judge others like so many Christians do. We all know we are failures – what's needed is hope and a way out."

Ratso picked up the story. "That's what I discovered this summer. I'm a selfish failure, but I can reach out and give somebody a hand. Not all the poverty in my town is racial, but much of it is. Jim and I went into the projects between Mosby Court and Gilpin Court in the East End of Richmond and found thousands of kids who need love and attention. We hung out, played basketball, and eventually started a tutoring program at the local community center.

"Here's what I discovered. I'm a racist. I was raised one, most of my family and our social set are racists. I was surprised to find I'm just like the rednecks up in Hanover County. I looked down on them as ignorant savages, but we rich folks are no different. Rich people put on a polite veneer to cover it up, but, in my heart, I'm no different. Hate comes from a damaged heart. When I help these kids, I feel like it's helping heal my heart. The government has spent a hundred years trying to fix racism, but you can't change hate with laws. Desegregation and busing won't ever work. What people need are changed hearts. Jesus can do that. Reaching across the divide and helping someone can do that. Nothing else can."

Ratso paused, and then said, "I think I've found my passion and my purpose in life. I want to reach out and help those who need a hand up. My friend Jim is running our program while I finish this year at Carlisle. He's recruited some ladies from the Ebenezer Baptist Church to work as volunteers for our reading and math program." Ratso laughed, "Until I graduate, I'll be working Daddy's rich friends to raise money to support the work. I figure I might as well use their guilt to redistribute some excess assets to make a positive difference in many lives. The East Street Ministry will be our full-time job in the future. Should you desire to donate funds, I will be receiving contributions in my dorm room later today."

Nikki jumped up and gave Ratso, a big hug. There's a sight I never thought I would live to see. "That is so cool, Ratso. We are proud of you," she exclaimed.

Just then the door to the room swung open. A nurse and an orderly with a wheelchair rolled into my room. "OK, folks," the nurse proclaimed. "Everybody out. It is time for Happy Jack to go off to his weekly visit with the X-ray machine." Jennifer, my favorite nurse, efficiently herded everyone out of the room, while Randy, the orderly, got me ready for transport to the fourth floor x-ray. What a bogus ending to a very happy morning with my friends.

39

*"The great spiritual law is that
one comes to resemble what one worships."*
~ *N.T. Wright*

Faith McFadden   mid-October, 1969

Even after four years at Carlisle, the beauty of fall in the Cumberland Valley leaves me speechless. It's spectacular! I love the breathtaking colors! Each leaf is a work of art. Each tree tells a story. The variety of trees on campus paint a living mural. The waves of color on the hills behind the college blow me away. Sitting at my desk, staring out the window, I find myself in a confusion of emotions.

Fall reminds me of the people I've grown to love here. Hanging out on the Quad with Randi and Nikki. What great times we enjoy together! It makes me laugh to think of Nikki dancing all over the lawn to one of her favorite tunes playing on the radio. Gary bouncing across the lawn like a kid out for a picnic. "Howdy Campers!" Jack striding across the grass; all black, all the time. Rob lounging around, enjoying the scene, smiling at the jokes. A tall quiet man, always there when you need him. Even horny Billy Harrison and crazy Arty "Fuckin' A," Swaboda. Great days with great friends!

I think of Skeeter, hanging out on the lawn on a lovely fall day. What a dear sweet man. Riding with him in the silver El Camino. His roguish charm and witty conversation. Laying on a blanket at night behind the dorm, watching the stars overhead, marveling at the size of the universe and at his gentle touch. Why did I ever hurt him like I did? I feel so guilty when I realize, to a great extent, my current circumstances are the result of stupid things I did. There's no one to blame but me.

The good times feel like a lifetime ago. Koffee Klatch, keggers, walking around the pond, hanging out with Randi in Lane, weekend movies, munching on popcorn and playing darts in Nikki's room. Chilly Dawgs, cheese steaks at the Grinder, and eating Tastykakes with Skeeter in Philly.

Ahh, Skeeter. The Stetson family...I admit, I fell in love with Sukie, Kitty, Sunny and Daisy the first time I met them. Sometimes I feel like one of the lost boys in Peter Pan who just discovered Never Land. In my dreams it looks just like the Stetson family. Everything about them and their world feels like an impossibly perfect dream come true. Suddenly, the dream world is snatched away from me! Gone. Forever. I wonder what might have been had I stuck with Skeeter? Of what will never be for me, now?

All my mistakes - it's overwhelming to think about them. Franklin Ramsey, drugs at Dr. Long's, too much drinking, Spud Mueller, too much weed, too much cocaine, Butch, the Foxy Lady.... All my choices, all my mistakes. Nobody to blame but me.

Choices. When I consider where I am today, I see for the first time in my life I've been allowed to make my own choices. And I have made them. I decide! I go where I want, I do what I want! For the first time in my life I have money to buy what I want, I can do anything I want. Nobody tells me what to do. Yet...when I'm honest with myself, I feel like all the hope has gone out of my life. I'm filled with regrets. I hate myself for the bad things I've done. I've not been honest with my friends or myself for such a long time. So many lies, for so long, to so many people. I don't think anyone knows who I really am – I certainly don't. And I dislike who I've become.

Randi thinks I'm depressed. She doesn't know the half of it. I feel like shit, almost all the time. I'm weary to the bone. Fatigue is my constant companion. I feel lonely, abandoned, isolated, anxious, and fearful of the future. I feel uncomfortable and unwanted with most of the people I know. I find it's better to just avoid people instead of facing up to what's going on in my life. I feel like I'm being erased as a human being. All I want to do is sleep. At night I have trouble going to sleep – all the bad things from the day roam through my mind and keep me awake. When I wake in the morning, I don't want to get out of bed. I'm afraid to face my life. Honestly? I think I hate my life. It is so fucked up!

Once I had hope things might get better. Even at Woodstock, I had a glimpse...of something... a possible turn around, maybe a shot at redemption...but now I feel like it's all gone, swallowed in a dense black mist. All the music has gone out of my life. It's like my life is sliding into a deep black hole and I can't seem to do anything to save myself.

All this has affected my school work. I struggle to listen in class, I'm having trouble managing my time and getting assignments done. I even have difficulty paying attention at Koffee Klatch. My mind wanders, and I am just so consumed with anxiety I can't follow the conversation. If I can't get my grades up, I'm going to lose my scholarship. On the other hand, if I have no future after college, why get my undies in a twist? To me it feels like I have no prospects, no hope of finding myself, of finding a safe place, a sweet spot. Where I can be myself, feel accepted, and make a contribution. My soul is so weary and empty. Do I matter to God? Do I matter to anyone? I just don't know anymore.

Thursday afternoon, there was a knock at my door. I rolled out of bed, opened the blinds and tried to straighten myself up, before I opened the door and found Randi and Nikki smiling on my doorstep.

"Hello, Sugar Booger!" said Nikki. Randi just laughed. "I know what you're thinking," Nikki continued, "'you spend so much time with Gary, now you are even starting to talk like him!' That's what you're thinking, isn't it?" Nikki let go a hearty cackle.

Even I had to join in with her laughter! "No you goofball. What I was thinking was, 'at least she has not started to chew tobacco like Gary.' That's what I was honestly thinking. Come on in."

The girls trooped into my room and sat on my bed, while I took the desk chair. "What are you two lovely lasses up to on a fine fall day like this?"

Randi asked, "Its Thursday. Do you have to work tonight?"

"Nope, no work for Faith today. My last class is over. I was just hanging out. Why do you ask?"

Randi giggled. "It is now 78 degrees and sunny outside. We were wondering if you would join us for a little picnic on the lawn? Nikki worked her contacts in the kitchen and scored some brownies, potato chips, chocolate chip cookies, pears, a couple of apples and a bag of sodas. We thought of going out to the Quad and set up for some sun and a little girl gabfest. You interested?"

"Wow!" I had to chuckle with my friends. They both seem so happy; it makes me feel a little better. "Sounds like a very nutritious picnic."

Nikki and Randi burst out laughing. "Yep," said Nikki. "We've got junk food, soda pop, and junk food – all the food groups! And we have enough munchies to feed a dozen! I hope you're hungry."

"Absolutely, I'd love to join you. Let me change and find my beach towel." Randi and Nikki sat around chatting happily while I put on a pair of shorts, a t-shirt and grabbed a Carlisle College sweatshirt in case it got cool. I found my blanket and sandals; we headed out to the Quad.

The Lawn was bustling with students when we arrived. Randi led us to a nice sunny spot behind some flower beds and green lilac bushes. The sun was warm as we settled onto our blankets and Nikki passed around food and drink. For a while we sat in companionable silence, enjoying the warm rays of the sun and the mild breeze while munching on tasty, fattening snacks.

"Legs…" began Randi, "I miss being your roomy. I know you feel you needed your own room this year, but I had so much fun living with you. I don't see you enough even though I live down the hall."

Nikki joined in, "I believe the rest of us don't get to see you much anymore. Your friends truly love you and miss you; you know that, don't you?"

Randi added. "It just seems like we never get a chance hang out with you, talk to you, find out how you're doing. How are you doing, Faith? Really?"

A long awkward pause followed this statement. Finally, I replied, "I don't mean to be so scarce. I guess I work a lot, sometimes I don't feel well, and I'm often tired. I was taking a nap when the two of you showed up today. I'm struggling to keep up my grades. I don't know… everything in my life seems to be a mess these days. I don't mean to avoid you. It's just such a muddle."

"Faith, we care about you. You really matter to us", added Randi. "Those of us who know you can see you are going through a hard time and we want to help. You know we are here for you, don't you? Whatever help you need, we will make sure you get it."

"Honey, you don't look well. Let me rephrase that – you look like shit!" Nikki exclaimed. "Have you lost weight? You're skin and bones. Maybe you have jaundice, or iron poor blood, or mono. It can happen. I'm sure we can find a doctor who can help. Look what miracles they've done with Jack. We want to help. We want you to get healthy. We miss the old Faith and I'm sure you do, too."

I'm touched by my friends' concern. But what can I say? 'I've become a loose immoral woman, having sex in dark corners with men I don't know. I work as a stripper and have neglected to tell y'all for more than a year. I take every kind of drug I can find to dull the pain of my life. My family rejects me, no one loves me – men just use me and toss me aside. I've become a worthless piece of trash and I'm simply waiting to float off into the gutter and disappear.' No, I don't think I can tell them the truth. Instead, I'll just roll out some more lies. It's what I'm good at.

"I'm ok, really," I fibbed. "It's just a phase I'm going through. I'm sure I'll bounce back soon. Once I get through this term, I think I'll be ok. Some of my classes are tough. My allergies are making my system act up. I'm having sinus inflammations. Once we have a hard frost, I should be fine."

Randi and Nikki looked at each other, and then back at me. A long painful silence followed. I know I was getting uncomfortable, and I guess they felt awkward. It's so hard when you have to lie to people you love and care about. Especially when they know you are lying to them.

"Honey," Nikki continued, "I want to tell you in the clearest way possible, no matter what kind of trouble you're in, we want to help. If you're sick or are having money trouble or need a shoulder to cry on, we're here for you. Feel free to ask for help, no matter what it is, or when you need help."

"Any time of the day or night, when ever, what ever you need, please ask," said Randi. "Anything! Don't be embarrassed, just ask. You know what Gary always says. 'It's not love if it doesn't cost you something.' We both love you and will do anything you need, no matter how inconvenient or difficult. Please don't fail to ask for help any time you need it."

Wow, what do you say to that? All I could muster is a weak, "OK."

The warm yellow sun drifted behind the trees and the air cooled off. We picked up our blankets and stuff and walked back to Allison. When we got to my room, Nikki tried one more time. "Would you do us a big favor? Come have dinner with us at the Waffle Club tonight. We meet in the basement of Lane. The guys put on a great feed and we always have good discussions. Tonight we're talking about community. What it is, how to find it, nurture it and share it with others. Will you come?"

"I've been to the Waffle Club before," I hedged.

"And that gives you permission to be a hermit?" Randi laughed. "Didn't you like it? Was somebody mean to you; asking personal or prying questions?"

Randi knows how to call me out. "No, silly goose, everybody was nice to me. The meal was delicious, practically home cooking. I guess the discussion was interesting, but... I don't know..."

"Did you say anything?" Nikki challenged. "Did you participate, ask a question, share anything? Or did you sit there like a big fat bump on a log and not engage?"

"Hmmm... Are you saying maybe I didn't enjoy the discussion because I didn't participate?"

Nikki wrinkled her face at me. "Earth to Faith... If you don't join in, how can you learn anything or help anybody else learn? You're like the gal who says, 'I went out and tried tennis once. It wasn't much fun.' Of course, she never hit the ball back over the net, so how much fun could it be? Please come with us tonight and give it another chance."

"Oh, alright," I groaned. "I guess it won't kill me. What time?"

Randi gave me a big hug and a kiss on the cheek. "Thanks so much, Legs! You're the best! We'll come by at ten to six and pick you up. We can walk over together."

"See you then, Honey Bunny," chortled Nikki. She gave me a hug as well.

When we walked into Lane Center, I saw the usual cast of suspects. Gary, Frank, Bunny, and Linda were busy preparing dinner. Each wore a bright red T-shirt with a picture of a pair of waffles on the front. 'Waffle Club Staff' was stenciled in white letters across the back of the shirt. "What a great shirt, Gary." I commented. "Did you have to knock somebody down in a dark alley and peel it off them?"

Frank hooted at my snarky remark. "You, dear Faith, are envious. Anyone who comes to Waffle Club often enough gets one!" He turned back to the stove to stir a large pot of marinara sauce.

Rob was lounging on a couch and kindly moved his feet when I came over and sat on the other end. "How come you don't have a staff shirt, Bachmann?" I asked. "Is it because you don't come often enough, or that you never bother to help?"

"Oh, I come often enough. I like it. But with all the super competent people here," with this he flicked a hand at the bustling folks in the kitchen and around the table, "what could I possibly contribute? My gift to this gathering is to stay out of everyone's way and enjoy the camaraderie of the scene."

The variety of people who turned up for dinner and discussion amazed me. A couple of jocks, several hippies, a greaser, a pair of nerdy physics guys, even a couple of stoners. Tony came with a guy who looked like a refugee from the Hell's Angels. Three music majors arrived with Doug. Not the popular crowd. Not folks I would have put together. Not the kind of people you would meet at church.

By the time we finished the delicious dinner of spaghetti and meatballs, there were twenty people pulling chairs into a circle in the lounge and getting comfortable. This crowd reminded me of Jesus' explanation for why he hung out with working stiffs, tax collectors, and prostitutes. He said "I have not come to call respectable people but outsiders."

Gary opened the discussion saying, "Welcome to the Waffle Club. The guidelines are simple. We're here to break bread together, and to share life. We believe life has meaning and purpose and we want to learn more about that.

Anyone is welcome, and we encourage everyone to share, discuss and ask questions. There's no right or wrong answer and we agree to treat everyone with respect. What is said here should stay here – no talking out of school. That's pretty much it, have I forgotten anything?"

Nikki smiled at him and said, "and tonight we are discussing…?"

"Oops!" Gary laughed, and we all laughed with him. "Tonight's topic is community. What is it, why would you want it, and how do you get it?"

It took me a while to catch on to how this works. It isn't like class where people hold back and wait to figure out 'the right answer.' People jumped in and let it rip.

"Community is shared experiences, shared life, like our eating together once a week."

"Frequency! When you live in proximity and see each other often, then you get community."

"Shared passions and interests might make community," ventured a music major.

"Shared experiences?"

"I don't know," commented a coed. "I have shared experiences with lots of people on my floor or in my major, but I don't feel known. Nor do I like all of them."

"Yeah," said a petite brunette across the circle. "On campus we live in proximity and we share the same kind of things but… It's more like little kids in a sandbox engaging in parallel play."

The conversation continued to evolve with people around the circle tossing out ideas, asking questions and making comments. Eventually Bunny summarized the sharing. "Community requires proximity and regular interaction between people. Also, shared experiences, meals, passions, interests, maybe values. Yet, I think there is something more. To get to community you have to have real relationships. We need friends; need to be known. I think that is part of what community does. It's a place where we can share our stories, feelings, lives. Even ask for help."

A pause followed. Finally Rob, who had been quiet, spoke up. "Not to put too fine a point on it, but this group seems to have many of the characteristics we've described for community."

Nikki shouted, "Bingo!" She chortled with laughter, "Got it in one! You've always been such a bright lad. That's exactly what I was thinking. Parts of Koffee Klatch seem like community to me, but its so loosey goosey; I'm not sure it rises to the level community. What about the rest of you?"

Frank added, "I don't feel you know someone until you've heard their story. How can you can be friends until you open up and are honest about who you are?" Ouch! That thought made me cringe.

"This summer I was part of a community in State College," Nikki offered. "It was formed by college students who are followers of Jesus and was organized around reaching out and helping kids in area high schools. They hang out with kids, make friends, mentor students and try to steer kids off the rocks. Adolescence can be tough. This community is organic, natural. There's no structure like other organizations. It's relational. Not hierarchical like the church, with people in power over others. It's not like a business or a country club, where they elect a President, Vice President and a Court Jester."

"That would be me," laughed Gary.

Nikki turned to him. "You said it! So rude, so inappropriate," punching him in the shoulder and pretending to be mad. Gary leaned in to tickle her and they both giggled.

The group picked up the thread of conversation and asked Nikki questions about the State College community. Doug asked, "Can you only do this at a college? Or in a college town? I'd like to have community that's like a family, but simple enough you can do it anywhere with anybody. Jesus says in one passage, his little band of followers is like a new family for him. 'These are my mother and my brothers.' That's the kind of community I want."

Gary shared for a few minutes about the Cartwright's Jesus Family on Long Island. He finished by saying, "Mr. C tells me the process is simple. Anybody can do it and it can be done in any setting. It works for ordinary, garden variety people. Plumbers, teachers, doctors, lawyers, accountants, mechanics, housewives, even students like me turn up and fit right in. The Cartwright group has been flourishing for twenty five years. When people leave, they start new communities wherever they move. The principles are so universal, they work in any place or population."

Doug interjected, "Principles? What are the principles for creating community?"

"OK, let me think," Gary's said. "I imagine this is what Mr. and Mrs. C would say. Community begins with a commitment to relationships. A desire to get to know others, share your stories, to hear and learn from others. Beside eating together, you need people who are open, who want to learn and grow.

"Jesus community has a focus on the person of Jesus and the recognition that he wants to teach us and lead us in life. We have to take time to learn from him, read about his life and teaching, and converse with him – that's all prayer is. Conversation with God. Finally, you have to be willing to reach out and help others. Not just the folks in your group, but people in need around us. We live in a world of hurting people. Jesus wants us to help. Find a way to heal a hurt, or offer a hand to help someone in need."

"It is simple, but not easy." Gary continued, "It can be messy and difficult at times. You won't always like everybody or agree with them. But you don't always like everyone in your family. They are still your family. Love them, forgive them, help them – put their needs ahead of your own.

"This is not fake community, like the camaraderie of Rotary Club, the Lions, or the typical church. Everyone shaking hands, slapping backs, saying howdy, but no one knows you and they really don't want to know how you are doing. In real community, you discover you have different views and opinions. We don't pick a leader who dictates one view. We don't lobby and play politics until we win people over to our point of view. We recognize we are different, we know that won't change, but we choose to love and accept each other anyway. Some kind of miracle takes place. That is the essence of the Jesus Family."

After the discussion, people drifted off in little groups, talking and chatting as they left. I was completely blown away by the stimulating conversation. Better than the topics discussed in my courses. Relevant and practical. I sat thinking while Nikki and Randi helped Gary and Rob clean up and reset the room.

Randi sat down next to me. "What are you thinking, honey? What are you feeling? Was that helpful in any way? I didn't hear you say anything during the discussion."

"Oops, my bad. Don't tell Nik. Big fat bump on the log, that's me."

Nikki slid onto the couch and gave me a warm hug. "Its ok sweetie, I already know. We love you just the way you are. Not everyone is a big lip flapper like Gary or me. Some people actually think before they shoot off their mouth. Or so I am told."

I considered before answering. "Honestly, I love what y'all were talking about. The bit of community I've seen, I've seen here through my friends on campus. Can't say I've ever noticed anything remotely like what Gary described, outside of the college. Maybe the Stetson family. It sounds...wonderful. I wish I could trade in my family and my current experience for something like that. But I don't know..."

Gary, listening in, stood next to me while Rob finished the dishes. "Faith," Gary said, "All it takes to be part of a Jesus family is a little openness on your part. We want you. We love you. The only question is, are you willing to be open with us? Jesus says he is standing at the door of your life. He's waiting, but he needs you to open the door and let him in."

All of a sudden I burst into tears. I never saw it coming. Waves of sadness rose up and overflowed before I had any idea it was happening. Randi and Nikki wrapped me in their arms and hugged me. It was a while before I could croak out, "Why should you guys care? Why should you help me? You have no idea all the wrong I've done!" The sobs kept wracking my body. I simply couldn't stop.

While Randi and Nikki held me, Gary quietly began to pray. "Lord we lift up our dear friend Faith. In Jesus' loving name, we ask you to comfort her, soothe her weary spirit, and speak to her hurts. Assure her of your forgiveness and love. You teach us that no matter what we have done, your sacrifice pays the price for our sins. All we have to do is ask for your help and forgiveness. Wrap her in your love and give her a good night's rest. We pray in Jesus' powerful name, Amen."

When I calmed down, the girls walked me back to my dorm. As I fell asleep, I had a sense I've just passed a turning point. I'm not sure what changes will come from it, but I have a conviction things will be different in the future.

40

"Well done is better than well said."
~ Ben Franklin

Nikki Clausen   **Late October, 1969**

The last week of October began much as the previous three weeks had. Drop dead gorgeous. If it was up to me, I would add two more Octobers to the calendar, another April or May and ditch January, February, and March altogether. We could go right from Christmas to the opening day of trout season! Monday, October 27th was perfect. A bluebird day, sunny, without a cloud in the sky. The temperature was in the high sixties and a light breeze was blowing. Just enough air to tingle the skin. Perfect!

Of course, I had to spend this perfect day indoors. Randi, Linda and I were planning a Halloween Party for Friday evening and the girls wanted to work on preparations. We fussed about the menu, shopping lists, and decorations in the basement of Lane while a perfect October day sailed by outside.

Randi enthused over her costume – she promised she and Rob would come dressed as Hansel and Gretel. Ha! I've got to see this! I can't believe she'll be able to get Rob into any costume let alone dressed as Hansel, the German boy who almost gets cooked by a witch. Can you see Mr. Cool dressed in lederhosen? She'll be lucky to get Rob to come. He's just not a costume sort of guy.

Tuesday morning Gary suggested we enjoy a walk to savor the bucolic conditions. "We'd better take advantage of this weather while we can." He commented, "I read there's a chance for rain coming in later in the week. There's a low off Nova Scotia which could move south, stir up a little nor'easter in New England. Or a tropical storm near Cuba might head north and bring rain."

"Are you saying we could get hit by a nor'easter or a hurricane?" I asked.

"No, no. We almost never get either of those in Pennsylvania. It's just big storms stir up clouds for hundreds of miles. A nor'easter on Cape Cod could produce rain here. So could a hurricane on the Outer Banks. I'm just thinking this fabulous weather might not survive till the weekend."

"You may be right. The first big rain - the leaves will vamoose! Bye-bye dazzling color! Good thing we have time to enjoy it today." I slipped my arm through Gary's and pulled him closer.

We sauntered around the rear of campus, through dew drenched fields, back to the woods around the pond. As we slipped along the fringe of the woods, I whispered, "I hope we don't startle any wild game." Gary looked at me quizzically. "You know, a couple of young college students lying in the grass doing the wild thing."

He snorted. "A little cool and damp for that, I would think."

I laughed back at him. "Well you know nature. Where there's a will there's a way."

Turns out, Gary was right. Other than seeing two chipmunks and a rusty fox squirrel, we didn't stumble onto any other wildlife. The deadfall pine is our favorite spot for observing the flora and fauna on the pond, in the woods and chatting together. We settled down to watch the resident pair of wood ducks swimming in the middle of the pond. As we watched them, they watched us, showing no alarm at our presence. "What I wonder, is how they know we are not Robbie, hiding in the bushes with his 12 gauge waiting to shoot them? They know we're here yet they sense we aren't armed or dangerous."

Gary gave me a squeeze, "It's a mystery, Sugar Buns. Much like the way of a man with a maid, it's just one of life's many mysteries."

"Speaking of mysteries," I added, "I just can't figure out what's going on with Faith or how to help her. What did you think after Thursday night?"

"Man, that's a tough one." Gary began. "Our discussion of community was the best. The value of community, having some help – it's clear. But I didn't sense any interest from Faith. She's locked up tight, the lights are out, and she's pretending nobody is home. No matter how long we knock, I don't think she's going to open the door. I think she's a mess inside but isn't willing to open up and receive help. How did you and Randi make out with her?"

"She didn't come clean with us, either. Just stonewalled. 'Everything is fine. It's just a tough period for me. When I get through this term, things will get better.' Too bad we can't hire a deprogrammer like the guy who rescued Snowden from the cult and have him forcibly bring her back to reality."

"I don't think that will work. Snow was tricked and lied to. They used sleep deprivation and other tactics to brainwash her. The deprogrammer simply helped her do what she really wanted to do, but was prevented from doing by the cult. Faith's problem is her own will."

Gary hesitated. "Father X says individual will is the most powerful force on earth. That's why God lets us decide if we want to love him. If we submit our will to God, together we can be a potent force for good. If we decide to resist him, there's nothing short of death that can bring resolution to the standoff. "

"It just breaks my heart," I managed after a bit. "I'm choked up and weepy."

Gary wrapped me in his strong arms. "I know, Honey Bunch. It's so damn hard watching someone you love drive their life off the cliff when there's nothing you can do. We can pray for her and ask the Spirit to open her heart, but the choice is ultimately hers. We get to choose what we do with our life. Which is great when those we love make good choices and extremely painful when they make bad choices."

Later, as we walked back to campus, I felt overwhelmed with sadness and pain for Faith. If only we could save her. If there was just some way to help.

Tuesday afternoon the weather changed. High wispy clouds rolled in, filtering out the brilliant sunlight. As the sun set, the clouds grew thick and ominous. Winds began to swirl. By seven, when Randi and I walked over to Lane for our weekly prayer session, it looked grim. There were no stars or moon in the sky. The treetops whipsawed back and forth, strong gusts tearing at their tops. It began to rain, with as many leaves in the air as falling raindrops.

Our little band of friends, Randi, Gary, Doug, Linda, Bunny, Snowden, Frenchie and I met on Tuesday evening for about ninety minutes of sharing life, building friendships, reading God's Word together and prayer. A lot of our time this evening focused on Faith and how God might intervene in her life. The Band, short for "Merry Band of Followers" is a constant source of encouragement for me.

Walking back from Lane, Randi commented, "Ahh, here comes November. Just a few days early. You can always count on a November rainstorm to wash down the leaves and put a close to fall."

Mounting the steps to the dorm, I assumed this was your average autumn rain storm. I held out my hands trying to count rain drops. "Not too bad. But it will bring down the leaves anyway. Heck, even if it doesn't rain much, these choppy winds will pull them down. I'd say we can kiss fall goodbye." With an exaggerated swirl, we each planted a kiss on our hands, turned to face into the rain, and blew the fall away with a kiss. Laughing together we entered the dorm.

By morning, rain was coming down hard. Leaves had fallen, swirling in the gutters, clogging drains as I walked to my first course. All through class it rained steadily. When I got out and headed over to the Koffee Klatch, rain was pouring down in sheets and I had to lean forward into the wind to walk.

Conversation focused on the storm pounding around us. Frank said, "The news says the nor'easter is headed for Rhode Island and we should get four or five inches of rain."

Bunny added "I heard the weather from Harrisburg before leaving Conklin. They say Hurricane Fritz is headed up the beaches of North Carolina but should veer offshore later today."

Why is it that weather forecasters are so invariably wrong? More to the point, why do we continue to believe them when they are so often wrong? Before lunch, announcements came that classes were canceled; we should batten down the hatches and prepare for bad weather. No kidding? By then it was a deluge outside. It might have been raining two inches per hour. At dinner, we tried to collect as much portable food as we could from the dining hall in case of a power outage. Then we hunkered together in the basement lounge of Lane watching the storm coverage on the Harrisburg TV station.

Carlisle College and the town of Carlisle lie in the heart of the Cumberland Valley. A basic fact of geography is that valleys are low places surrounded by higher elevations. This is true for our valley. Steep mountain ridges of the Tuscarora's lie to the northwest. The mountain chain on our east runs all the way into the Catoctin Mountains in Maryland. Our valley is a conduit for all the water running off Central Pennsylvania into the Susquehanna River, then to the Chesapeake Bay and onto the Atlantic Ocean.

Wednesday night these two late fall storms off the East Coast took an unexpected turn and became the monster storm of the century. The fall nor'easter barreled down from Canada, hugged the coast where it was able to pick up tons of water off the ocean. Hurricane Fritz avoided the inland landfall typical of tropical depressions, veered off the southern coast of Virginia, looped out to sea picking up moisture and then hooked a left and shot right back at the mainland. When these epic storms collided off the Delmarva Peninsula, they combined into a monster typhoon and sliced right up the center of the Chesapeake Bay. Running hard and fast over the warm water of the bay allowed this maelstrom to suck up moisture into its vortex while building wind speeds of 160 miles per hour - a Category 5 hurricane.

The good news - the center of the storm shot inland and neatly squeezed between Washington DC and Philadelphia without doing any significant damage to either city. The bad news - this gigantic spout of wind and water hit Harrisburg, the capital of Pennsylvania, dead center. After thrashing the city, the storm headed on, wrecking Carlisle before roaring west to spend its fury on the Appalachian Highlands.

Thursday morning the low-lying dorms along the eastern edge of campus were evacuated. North of campus, White Pine Creek, a large stream, flows towards Harrisburg into the Susquehanna. On the eastern edge of campus, the Antietam Creek drains hundreds of square miles of mountains northeast of Carlisle. The Antietam was out of its banks, spreading a hundred and fifty yards either side of its borders. Directly south of the city, the LeTort Spring Run flooded. Normally a quiet pastoral spring creek, it jumped its banks and spread into town. White Pine, the Antietam, and the LeTort generated a raging sea of mud and debris, well over historic flood stage, filling the entire valley with torrents of dirty water.

Fortunately, our college is built on a hill. Long after town is flooded, most of the campus will be ok. Emergency shelters were set up in the gymnasium and Lane Student Center to house displaced students. Most students, no matter where they lived, began a strategic retreat towards higher ground. In the face of a crisis, there's always some comfort in being with others.

Sustained winds of 75 miles an hour wreak havoc in a community not built for hurricanes. Winds twice that speed tore though town and campus. The winds declined from the 160 mph Category 5 status as the storm moved up the Bay, but were still tremendous. We could hear branches snapping like rifle reports outside Lane. We heard a loud 'crump!' and a thrashing 'boom' as another 100-year old shade tree collapsed on the lawn outside our refuge. The rain kept coming in torrents.

We were huddled in Lane when the power went out at ten am. Gary and Frank ran outside and came back in a moment drenched to the bone. "Lights are out all over campus," Gary reported. Students in the basement lounge came up to join us and share the little natural light coming through the windows.

At lunch time, the howling winds sounded worse than ever. The kitchen staff , by some miracle, managed to fight through the gale and arrived loaded with canvas sacks and coolers. With the help of flashlights, they had made peanut butter and jelly sandwiches for lunch. Other bags contained fresh fruit, cookies and, bags of chips along with an assortment of sodas.

Our group huddled on the carpet away from the windows for fear flying debris would come through the glass. We were munching away on lunch when Randi asked, "Where's Faith? Has anyone seen her?"

A long pause followed with no response. Gary jumped up and said, "Maybe she's in here but we can't see her? I'll go look." He proceeded to circle the room several times weaving through all the bodies filling the space. He disappeared for a bit and came back to report. "I don't see her anywhere and I checked downstairs too. Where could she be?"

Rob spoke up, "She could be in Musselman or in the gym."

"Or, she could still be in her room in Allison," Randi added. "She's been spending a lot of time there recently, sitting in the dark, sleeping all the time. Maybe she didn't hear about the evacuation? She lives alone, so maybe no one told her or checked on her."

"Man, that's scary," I murmured. "To be left behind in an empty building with flood water rising all around. We have to go find her!" Everyone was silent, a little in shock contemplating this idea.

Bunny objected. "You can't go out there. It's too dangerous. You'll get blown away, tossed off your feet! A falling tree will land on you and kill you. Don't even think of going until the storm lets up."

I protested, "We sat here Tuesday night saying we wanted to help Faith. Now she actually needs help and we're going to sit here until its safe?"

Gary jumped in, "Jesus says love is about actions rather than words or feelings. I can't sit here and say Faith is my friend and not lift a finger to help her. I'm going to go find her!"

As he got to his feet, I leaped up to join him. "I'm going too!"

Rob interjected, "Whoa Nellie! I admire you both, but could we have a moment of rational thought before we go running out into the hurricane willey nilley?" That stopped Gary and I in our tracks.

"Remember when Benchoff led the search for Billy and Delilah?" Rob continued. "He didn't let us run around like chickens with our heads cut off. He made a plan. So where could Faith possibly be?"

Doug spoke, "She could be in the Dining Hall or the gym safe with the rest of the campus refugees."

"She only works at night, so she didn't go to work this morning," said Frank, "but she may not have come home last night. If she's holed up on the other side of the water in town she is probably ok and we can't get to her anyway."

"If she's still on campus," Randi said, "she is most likely in her dorm room if she's not in one of the emergency shelters. That's where I would look."

Gary took charge. "Rob and Frank, you go look in Musselman and the gym. I know you can get there because the kitchen crew got through to us. Nikki and I are better water rats. We'll run down the hill to Allison and see if she is in her room."

"Lifeguard Gary to the rescue!" I shouted with a laugh. "This is the part he loves. Let's have some action!" The four of us took off for the doors and split up as soon as we stepped outside. The boys headed right, and Gary and I peeled off to the left and headed down the hill towards Lincoln Avenue.

We ran into a screaming wind. Sheets of pelting rain made it hard to see. It was difficult to run, sort of like trying to walk up a waterfall from the bottom. As we got close to the dorms, Gary hauled me into the shelter of a screen protecting trash cans behind a dorm. Squinting through the fencing made it easier to see. "Holy Crap!" Gary exclaimed. As we looked at the dorms fronting Lincoln Avenue, all we could see was water. The dorms appeared to be floating in water; the closest edge of Allison was forty yards beyond visible ground. Past the dorms, Lincoln Ave was gone - swallowed by water. As far as we could see into town, muddy brown swollen waves and whitecaps filled streets as the flood tore up Carlisle's historic downtown. Debris floated by on the other side of Allison at a fast clip. Fallen trees, floating cars, a garden shed washed by, and a barking dog swam after it, wads of trash followed down the current.

"Come on, let's go," Gary shouted over the wind. We ran down the hill and waded through the water, which was waist high by the time we got to the front door. Gary tried to pry the glass door open but there was so much pressure from the water, he couldn't get it open. "We need a rock!" he shouted.

I ran back down the short steps, and ducked under water. I came up sputtering with a round 6-inch rock from the flower bed. I waded up the steps and gave it to Gary, who hauled back and smashed it through the glass door. With a loud 'whoosh' the dirty water poured in and joined the rest swirling inside the dorm. We ripped the door open and raced down the stairs to Faith's floor.

The water in the submerged basement level was thigh deep as we waded towards her room. Gary pulled open her room door; I could see her immediately. Faith was on her bed. She had curled up in a fetal position but was upright in the corner. Wrapped in a blanket, Faith was sitting in a foot of water. The girl looked wretched like a drowned rat. Hands clenched in front of her eyes, she was sobbing.

I waded over and wrapped my arms around her. "Its ok honey, we'll take you to safety. You'll be fine." Faith just stared at me blankly. I guess she thought she was hallucinating. "Come on, we have to get out of here." Gary gently picked her up off the bed so I could put sneakers on her bare feet. It was like caring for an infant with no understanding or ability to help with the process.

Gary took charge. "I can carry her piggy back. I need you to open her dresser and get some dry clothes. Try the top of the closet. Look for something dry and warm we can get her into. See if you can find a plastic bag to put it in so we can get it to Lane dry."

I found underwear, sweats, several t-shirts, and warm socks, then wrapped them up as instructed. He leaned down and picked Faith up like he was cradling an infant. "Come on Sugar Booger, we're taking you home." With that he walked out the door and waded up the hall to the front door.

On the steps out front, Gary set Faith down on her feet. "I want you to hop up on my back and wrap your arms around my neck like I'm giving you a piggyback ride." She did as he asked, but was still not fully with us. Perhaps it was shock. Gary is so gentle. This man can rescue me any day of the week!

Gary waded into the water – at least a foot deeper by now. We pushed through the surging current; I had to hang on to Gary's belt to stay upright and not get swept away. I kept the clothes up on my head out of the water. When we reached shore, Gary stopped under an oak for a breather. As we looked back at Allison, we could see the water rising into the second floor. Beyond the dorm, where Lincoln Ave had formerly been, a pair of black and white Holstein cows floated by, mooing in panic as they washed downstream. A moment later a mobile home went by riding the same current. How would this deluge ever end? Gary got up, hoisted Faith over his shoulder and we trudged on up the hill towards Lane.

Inside Lane, Randi took over. "Linda, collect sofa cushions and make a bed in that corner. Frenchie, clear the kids out of there and make it a quiet place. I don't care how you do it. Doug, collect three warm blankets and a nice pillow. Tell people it's an emergency. Nikki, help me get her into the bathroom."

We helped Faith strip and dried her off with paper towels. Randi gently dressed her and we got her back to the lounge. "Frank, get her something to drink. Believe it or not I think she's dehydrated, although how you get dehydrated in all this water, I don't know." Frank ran off.

Randi got her to drink and led her into the back corner to the bed we had set up. We got her on the improvised bed, and covered her with warm blankets which I tucked around her. Randi sat at the top leaning up against the wall, plumped her pillow and cradled Faith's head in her lap. She continued to blubber and whimper like she had been doing since Gary and I found her. I worried her mind was gone, but hoped it was just shock. Randi held her, rocked her, singing lullaby's until she fell asleep.

After everyone got settled, Gary picked up two blankets and led me away from the lounge into a small meeting room down the hall. Somehow he produced a flashlight which he used to show me the way. "I've had seminars here. Nice and quiet - away from all those heavy breathers in the lounge."

We arranged blankets with one doubled underneath and the other wrapped around us. I snuggled into his strong arms and he pulled me close. I laid my head on his chest and whispered, "You were heroic today. Thanks for saving Faith. I couldn't have done it without you."

"Ahh, it was nothing. Just the right thing to do. Think of all the training I got to put into action. I couldn't have done it without you, Sugar Buns." As he said this, I could feel his hand gently caressing my butt cheeks. What a turn on. Sweet talk and a sweet touch. I snuggled closer.

After a bit Gary said, "You know, we might have lost her. She was frozen in fear. The simple thing for her to do would be to walk upstairs to a higher floor. But I don't think she could move. If we hadn't turned up, she would have drowned sitting on that bed."

"Man, that's a scary thought," I replied. "But I think you're right. I'm freaked out by her mental condition. I don't know what's going on inside her pretty little head, but the girl needs help."

Gary pulled me closer. I feel warm and safe in his arms. He said, "I keep seeing the replay. I'm thinking I could have lost you. If we had slipped, we would be floating down the river with the cows."

That was a sobering idea. I never gave any thought to the risks. That's me. "Ready, Fire, Aim!"

Gary continued. "Here's what I'm thinking. I'm not ready to say goodbye to you." As he whispered in my ear, it tickled. I broke out laughing.

"Come on, I'm trying to be serious."

"It tickles. When you whisper that close, it tickles." I kept laughing.

Gary paused and backed away from my ear.

"Nikki Clausen, will you marry me?"

That got my attention. I was surprised, I guess. For once, no words came to my lips.

He continued, "Nikki, I never want to lose you. I want to spend every day of my life with you. I adore you and want to share whatever life God gives us together. Will you marry me, my dear sweet friend?"

"Hmmm, let me think," I teased. After waiting a beat…"My answer is YES!"

As he hugged me tight I said, "I love you Gary!" Much hugging and kissing followed this proposal as we rejoiced together. When we both calmed down a little I asked, "When do you want to get married?"

"Right now!" Gary laughed.

"Ahh, yes, my man of action. Seriously, how about our families and friends? Don't you want to share our special day with them?"

"I suppose. If we have to. How about the first Saturday after graduation?"

"It's a deal." With that, we snuggled together and fell asleep in each other's arms.

41

Rob Bachmann   November, 1969

Saturday morning after the storm, I met the Card Club guys for breakfast in Musselman. The bottom floor of Wood Hall is flooded so cards are out of the question for a while. The power is on in the Dining Hall, so we happily tucked into our first hot meal in days. We may not be playing cards, but I'm grateful for food, hot coffee, lights and dry clothes.

Super Storm Fritz dumped nineteen inches of rain on Carlisle in 48 hours. The damage was astonishing. Trees which stood for a century lay crumpled on the ground. Roadways and lawns are littered with branches, leaves and shredded debris. Residents of flooded dorms had been warned and moved their cars to the higher parking lots behind the gym. These open lots by the athletic fields have few trees. Unfortunately, Faith's car was still in the Allison lot where a 40-foot linden tree collapsed on top of the pretty blue Mustang smashing it flat. Flood waters covered the wreck and totaled what was left.

Other than Faith's beautiful car, there were no fatalities on campus. Thirteen people died during the storm in Carlisle. Hundreds were injured. Thousands more were driven out of their homes. Tens of thousands across central Pennsylvania were without electricity. Town streets were littered with 2,500 cars which had been abandoned in the rapidly rising water and were now inoperable. Flood waters surged into the borough so quickly people had to scramble out on foot just to save their lives.

As we sat at the table stuffing food in our faces, Gary said, "It's hard to believe two days ago this was the eye of the hurricane."

Frank added, "Seeing the sunshine streaming through the windows, you'd never guess our campus looks like a war zone after a major bombing. Although the whine of chainsaws kind of gives it away."

Frank was right. As we sat in the Dining Hall that sunny November morning, the background noise consisted of the buzz of chainsaws and the grinding of wood chippers. All over campus workers cleared away damaged trees and debris from the storm. The town itself reverberated with the same chorus of saws and chippers. Power crews from as far away as Tennessee, Ohio and Connecticut had driven in overnight and were busy repairing downed power lines and restoring our electric service.

Bunny said, "I'm sad we didn't have the Halloween party. I was looking forward to it."

Gary laughed, "You know what bums me out? Not that our Halloween party got canceled. The thing that makes me sad is never getting to see Rob Bachmann dressed in lederhosen!" The guys cracked up at this thought. Even I had to admit – it's pretty funny idea.

"I hope none of you idiots bet money on the possibility I was going to turn up dressed as Hansel. Fat chance! I wasn't even going to the party. I haven't enjoyed Halloween since I was twelve and my friends made me give up Trick or Treat because it 'wasn't cool.' Who cares if it's cool? I loved the candy! If you think I'm going to get in a costume so I can bob for apples, you're nuts!"

I paused for a beat, and then went on, "Speaking of embarrassing moments, I heard a nasty little rumor our friend, Mr. Hockey Boy, got engaged."

"No!" cried the gang around the table. "Tell us it isn't so?" and other jibes sprang from the crowd as Gary grew beet red in the face.

Frenchie laughed, "Is it true? What - did you get hit in the head by a falling tree? What happened?" All of us were laughing and congratulating Robbins, who looked embarrassed.

"Yes, it's true," admitted Gary. "Nikki and I are getting married in May after graduation. I'm sure she will send each of you an invitation."

"When did it happen?" laughed Billy.

"No, how did it happen?" added Arty, with glee.

"It's hard to remember now, but it was during the storm. Nikki says it was after midnight Thursday night, so technically, I proposed on Halloween. It was really late, very dark, and there was nothing else left to do – so I popped the question." Robbins waited a beat then broke out in a big shit eating grin. "No doubt about it; best Halloween ever!"

I chuckled and smacked Gary on the shoulder. "OK, can anybody honestly say you didn't see this coming?" Everyone roared with laughter. "Nikki has been sweet on Gary since the first week of Freshman Orientation four years ago."

Frank added, "And every one of us has been sweet on Nikki since that same week!" Guilty laughter and sheepish grins spread around the table.

"Too true," I admitted. "You know, this is my first friend ever to get serious enough to propose to a girl. Unless Black Jack and Miss F are secretly engaged, and we don't know about it."

"What are you talking about?" Arty exclaimed. "Billy proposes to a different girl every weekend. He just breaks the engagement on Monday morning." Everyone laughed at Harrison's well-known antics.

Arty said, "Speaking of the divine Miss F, I bumped into her on my way over this morning and she told me the classes we missed would be rescheduled on the next two Saturdays."

"That's a bummer," added Frenchie. "I was hoping to go to an anti-war march in DC next Saturday. Some Army buddies are taking a bus of Vietnam Vets against the War from Harrisburg to Washington."

"I hate to say this Frenchie," commented Spinnelli, "but when it comes to political action, I don't think anyone in this country is listening. Voters aren't listening and its obvious politicians in Washington are not paying attention. I think these rallies are singing to the choir – nobody cares except the protesters. Look how little we got from our efforts at the DNC convention in Chicago!"

Billy, a political science major, jumped in to defend the government. "Wait a minute, Frank. That's not fair! President Nixon made a promise to end the war in Vietnam. He's not been in office for a year. Give him a chance. You know the machinery of government grinds slowly."

"Too be honest," Frenchie replied, "I don't think Nixon means to fulfill his promise. He just said it to get elected. That's why political protests are important. Remember, I was in the Army. The military power structure loves wars. It's how you advance your career. Politicians love wars. They cost money and politicians who dole out the cash amass power. War feeds the soul of the military-industrial complex."

Billy stuck to his guns. "I'm convinced Nixon will end the war. He said so, didn't he? I believe in him! In fact, I'm applying for a White House internship when I graduate. I trust Nixon!"

Five weeks later most of the original members of the Koffee Klatch gathered around the big table in Musselman. Jack was still in rehab, but the survivors of our fellowship are simply happy to be together. During the intervening weeks we recovered from the hurricane, finished our fall finals, and departed for Thanksgiving break. It's now early December and we're in the second week of winter classes.

Nikki is presiding, queen bee that she is; TAB in hand, a witty comment and a quick joke for any topic. "Friends, I'm so excited. When I was in State College for Thanksgiving, I got together with the three amigos. Our proposal for a National Earth Day has been accepted and will roll out this April! All our work is going to pay off. On April 22, 1970 people all over the US will celebrate efforts to clean up and protect our environment. If we can get people to clean up the air, clean up the water, and pick up their trash, this country could be transformed!"

Arty laughed, "Fuckin A! Who knows, when my kids grow up maybe the rivers in Pittsburgh will be clean enough they will learn to fish. I can send them off to college to fish with Rob and Jack's offspring!"

General laughter followed the notion of our offspring going to college together. Doug asked, "Did you read the news about Altamont?"

"No, what's that?" Bunny inquired.

"The Rolling Stones felt bummed they missed Woodstock," Doug continued. "So they tried to do a replay and it blew up. The Hell's Angels started to beat everybody up and were shooting at people. Spectators were killed. It's probably going to put an end to music festivals."

"Man, that's depressing," I added. "Woodstock was so cool!"

Randi, who was sitting next to me, joined in. "I'll tell you what depresses me is Faith. Before the storm I hoped she was getting better. I'm afraid the hurricane knocked her off track again."

"I agree, I think she's in serious trouble." added Nikki. "We've only been back in school for two weeks, but I feel Faith has pitched off a cliff and is in free fall. She has all the signs of chronic depression." Nikki continued, "But how do you help someone who refuses any help?"

"It's gotten worse this term." Randi said. "The girls on our floor have noticed. She is hardly ever out of her room, the door is always closed, and the lights are off. When was the last time anybody saw her here at a meal?" Nothing but silence followed this question.

"Yeah," commented Billy, "I'm in two courses with her and I don't think she's been in class once."

"Wow," Frank interrupted. "That would be bad. She's on scholarship. If she flunks her courses or doesn't take a full load, she'll lose the scholarship."

Linda Pence jumped in, "I have not seen her coming into the dorm at night. Is she still working?"

Nikki commented, "Her Mustang got smashed in the storm, but I can't believe she would give up her job. She needs the money as much as she needs the scholarship. She's on her own. Her family in Georgia sends her nothing, not even mail."

We sat around the table for a few minutes mulling over this bad news. Frank spoke, "Friends, I think it is time to take definite action. We can't just watch Faith sinking lower and lower without doing anything. I still wonder if Ronnie would be here if I had been a little more pro-active."

Man, that makes me pause and consider. It's a sobering thought. Could a little extra help on my part actually save a life? Frank went on, "Honestly, I think about it a lot. It's not that I feel it's my fault, but I wonder if I could have done something to help, to keep him from doing what he did?"

"Frank's right," Gary responded. "That Faith isn't asking for help and doesn't want help, doesn't free us from a moral obligation to try to help. It's like this: I know you're supposed to look both ways before you cross the street. That's my responsibility. But if you were next to me and saw I was about to step out in the path of a speeding truck, I hope you would yank me back. That's simply what friends do."

This statement caused us to think. Finally I spoke up. "The guys are seeing this accurately. Faith may not want help, but there are things we can do. First, we should investigate and see what the problem is. Is she just depressed? We can get the college to connect her to counseling. Is she physically ill? You have to agree, since Woodstock, Faith has looked like she is dealing with a long-term health issue.

If she is, we take her to the school nurse and get help. Is she having an academic crisis? If she is, the Dean can help. Is work a problem without her car? Or has she lost her job? Does she need help finding another job? If that's the problem, we can help."

Nikki jumped up. "To quote my fiancé, Gary Robbins, 'Let's go do it!' And, to quote another of his famous lines: 'There's no better time than now!' Randi and I will go to Faith's room, sit her down, and sort her out. We'll report back to the rest of you at lunch."

We gathered up our books and coats and took off on our mission of mercy.

When I arrived back at Musselman at twelve thirty there was no sign of Randi, Nikki or Gary. The rest of us sat around eating and cooling our heels. What else could we do? Waiting is the only option.

Finally, at ten minutes after one, Nikki, Randi and Gary showed up. They got some lunch and came to join us. Nikki, looking agitated, jumped right in. "It was a lot worse than I imagined!"

"Totally awful," added Randi.

Gary looked like he is in shock. He had no words, a big change, and I could see tears leaking out of the corners of his eyes as he fought to control his emotions. The three of them sat down looking drawn and exhausted. The account they shared about Faith was a bombshell.

"We got there," Nikki began, "to find Faith's room dark, the door locked and there was no response to our banging and shouting. Jenn, the RA, let us in. I think she was worried about Faith too."

"It's heart wrenching," Randi continued. "Faith was in there. But the room was completely dark – at 11 in the morning. She was huddled in bed, wrapped up in all her blankets, just shivering and shaking. The room smelled nasty, like old trash, as if it had not been cleaned for a long time."

Nikki picked up the tale. "Robbie, remember I told you how Gary and I found her in the flood? Curled in a fetal position and looking comatose, like a ghost had scared the wits out of her? That's exactly how she looked. Faith just stared ahead out of eyes which didn't seem to see anything."

"Or with a mind not comprehending," Randi added. "She trembled and shook when I held her. Frank, I'm so glad you urged us to intervene. I'm afraid she is having a psychotic break down."

"We questioned her and she admitted she's been feeling sick, hasn't been to class, is having trouble getting to the bathroom. She hasn't been out of bed or out to meals for days. She said she lost her job. Then she broke down in a waterfall of tears. She was bawling, and shaking, and looked crazy."

Randi went on; "We kept hugging her and trying to calm her down. Jenn went and found Gary and he brought his car. We took her to the Health Office. The nurse, Mrs. Engle, is really nice. She was great – she took Faith in hand, got her in bed, wrapped her up in warm blankets, and made her a cup of herbal tea to 'sooth her frazzled nerves.' Mrs. Engle said Faith was acting like a person in shock.

"When Faith stopped bawling, Mrs. Engle took her vital signs, and called Dr. Kidd, the local physician on call. Fifteen minutes later he arrived, and took her vitals again. He called an ambulance and had her admitted to Holy Spirit Hospital. The EMTs took her off, and Dr. Kidd went to help admit her.

"After they left, Mrs. Engle told us she and Dr. Kidd think Faith has heart arrhythmia and maybe pneumonia. Her symptoms, however, could be a sign of something much worse. They want to keep her in the hospital for a few days, do tests, and consult specialists. The Nurse asked us to go to her dorm room, get clothes and drop them at the hospital. That's what took us so long."

"Man, I am completely freaked out!" Nikki added. "Dr. Kidd and Mrs. Engle were calm and professional, but…the body language!

"They think there's something seriously wrong with Faith. As I think about it, I wonder if the vacant staring look in her eyes is fear. It seems to me she is frightened. Frightened to death. Maybe frightened of death. Faith knows she is sick and in trouble and she feels all alone. Just like when she felt trapped by the rising water in the flood."

For a long time, we sat taking in what Randi and Nikki shared. Such a painful position. What can you do in a situation like this? We each sat consumed by our own thoughts and fears.

Bunny finally opened up. "I've been through some tough experiences in my life, but I don't think I've ever had to face them alone. My family is pretty dysfunctional, but if I ended up in the hospital, there are at least a half dozen people I could call for help. If not help, at least comfort. Who does Faith have?"

"Gee, I don't know," said Linda sarcastically. "Faith has …Butch? The guy who just wants to fuck her but not be involved in her life in anyway? The guy who does all the talking and none of the listening? And where the hell has Butch been while she has been sliding down hill all fall?" Linda was angry. "Having Butch is worse than having no one at all!"

Doug asked, "Is there anybody else? If she's seriously ill, she needs someone to support her. Is there anyone else in town she is close to? How about her family? Will they come to her aid?"

Randi may be the closest to Faith. She responded, "Since I've known her, she's had a good relationship with Skeeter and after that nothing but a succession of bad guys and bad choices. Her family…I don't know, but I think they're a lost cause. She never talks about them. Once in a while, she gets a note from her sisters. When she was working, she sent Hope and Charity money, but only through Pat and Kris Rouseau. I don't think there's been any direct communication with her parents."

Nikki commented, "Faith has always preferred the company of guys. Or she likes to be alone. Of course, she spent a lot of time at work. Of all the kids on campus, I think Randi and I are the closest to her. And, actually, we are not that close. She has trouble confiding in us. The longer I've known Faith, the more I feel she is holding back, not able to be real when we talk."

"That is serious stuff," I commented after Randi and Nikki finished sharing. "What can we do to help her? She has no family, no friends, and no support system."

"Whoa Nelly!" Gary exclaimed. "Wait just a moment. I would not say she is all alone, nor would I say she has no support system. She has us. We're her friends! We love her and want what's best for her. Personally, I am willing to stand in and be her family. Whatever she needs we'll get for her. We'll find people to help her. We will help her get better."

Nikki, scooted over and wrapped her arms around Robbins. "You are the sweetest, kindest man I know! If I was not already engaged, I would ask you to marry me."

Gary laughed. "Crazy chick!" He paused, and then added, "Seriously – remember when Jack had his accident? All the people who love him came together to help pull him through? I want everyone to have a family like the Flynns and Frenchie's family."

"Don't forget the Koffee Klatch and the Card Club," injected Frank.

"And Miss F. and the Dean. Plus Father X and Doc Brody," added Bunny.

Robbins went on, "When Bunny, Doug, and Frank were in the slammer in Chicago, who came and got them out? We did. We are there for each other. Family is as family does." He paused. "My point," Gary finished, "is that we can be family, we can be those friends for Faith. If she doesn't have a support system, we can provide one for her. All this talk in the Waffle Club and on Tuesday nights about being a 'Jesus Family' is not just talk. We have to take action. I, for one, am going to walk my talk!"

"Ahh," Nikki cooed. "My man of action!"

Doug laughed. "OK, no need to make us barf! I'm in. We are Faith's family. Whatever she needs we will find a way to get."

Bunny added, "Count me in."

Randi, Nikki, and Linda raised their hands in agreement.

Frank and I looked at each other and he said, "Count on us."

Doug said, "You'd better count Frenchie in too or he will kick your butt."

I suggested we turn the Waffle Club session that evening into a discussion of how we could help Faith. We broke up after agreeing to work on our plan to help Faith recover and to meet at seven pm.

_____

That day felt like the longest day of my life. I kept thinking about how to help Faith and I am clueless. I miss Jack. He's been my best friend since we got to Carlisle. He understands how my mind works and can always help me think of better solutions. Without him, I'm lost. Finally, I decided to hell with it. I cut my afternoon classes and drove over to Jack's rehabilitation center in Camp Hill. Jack was released from the Holy Spirit Hospital in November and is continuing his recovery at Good Shepherd.

I found Jack in his room. "I'm so glad you are here. I really need to talk."

Jack hooted. "What, you thought I might be out skydiving or something? Of course, I'm here!"

Laughing myself, I replied, "No you lunatic. I just thought you might be off getting physical therapy or some medical treatment."

"You are in luck, my friend. Sit down and tell me all about it."

I brought Jack up to speed on what happened to Faith during the Halloween hurricane and a quick outline of her decline since then. I filled him in on the details of Randi and Nikki's discoveries during the morning and the medical response to Faith's condition.

"Jack, remember how you told me about the reaction of the Flynn clan to any threat of danger to one of the family? I've never forgotten what you said - because I got to see it in action after your accident. To quote you, 'When one of us is threatened, the clan circles the one in danger like a herd of old bison bulls.' I feel like we need to be that family for Faith. We need to stand with her and protect her now in her hour of need. I just don't know what to do to help!"

Jacked looked at me and his face broke out into a wicked grin. "For a smart guy, you sure can be an idiot! We already have the old bison bulls!"

"We do?"

"Yes! We have Father X, we have Doc Brody, and we have Dean Benchoff. That is a front line you don't mess with. The Father is close to Faith. He can serve as her priest and intervene with the medical people and get stuff you and I could never access. Same with Doc Brody. He's a Lutheran pastor."

"But Faith isn't Catholic or Lutheran," I protested.

"You know that and I know that, but the hospital won't know that. It's how the system works. Benchoff represents the College. The college is 'in loco parentis' over its students. The Dean can act on Faith's behalf and do what's in her best interest. Plus, he knows everybody and has been through everything and there are no strings he doesn't know how to pull. I know Amy will want to help as well."

For a moment, I sat in stunned silence. "Jack, for an imbecile, you can be awfully bright sometimes. Absolutely none of that occurred to me and I've been fretting about it for hours. You solve the problem in minutes. Thanks! You're a pal." With that I jumped up to leave.

"Wait, you're not going already are you?" Jack laughed. "You just got here!"

"Believe it or not, it's not about you, friend. I've got to go see the Father, Doc Brody, and Benchoff. Tell Amy what's up when she comes by to smother your ugly face in pity kisses. I love you, you retardo."

42

"To have faith is to be sure of the things we hope for,
To be certain of things we cannot see."
~ *Hebrews 11:1*

Nikki Clausen   **Winter, 1970**

Saturday morning Randi, Robbie, Gary, and I went to the hospital to visit Faith. Randi and I had popped in a few days earlier, to bring Faith her undies, toiletries, and personal things. She seems settled and as comfortable as you can be in a hospital bed with wires, tubes and machines hooked up to your body. The four of us pulled up chairs next to Faith's bed and she gave us a wan smile. "Hi guys. Nice to see you. Thanks for coming. Girls, thanks so much for fetching my gear. I can't tell you how nice it is to brush your teeth with your own toothbrush and toothpaste."

I took Faith's hand in mine and caressed her fingers. Her hand feels like ice, it is so cold. "Anything you need, Sweetie, you just name it and we'll get it."

"Truthfully, I'm so much better off in here than in Allison. They take great care of me and I think I smell better. I guess I was just falling apart in that room all by myself."

Randi jumped in, "You're not by yourself any more, Legs. We're going to take care of you until you get better. Then I want to be your roommate again so you don't get into trouble."

Faith beamed at us. "I don't know what happened. I took a long slide, but it happened so gradually, I never even noticed how bad it got. Even before Woodstock, I felt so tired. Always exhausted. Even with a good night's sleep, I never wake up feeling ok. Tired, tired, always so tired. Now I feel so cold inside. Like a bitter winter chill is seeping into my insides."

Robbie asked, "Do you want me to get you a warm drink? Tea, cocoa?"

Faith smiled with a shadow of her old radiant grin. "Yes, please, kind sir! Hot chocolate would be nice." Rob immediately jumped up to do her bidding.

After he left the room, Randi asked, "What do the doctors say about your condition?"

Faith sighed. "Not much. As best I can tell, I'm not pregnant, but no other possibilities have been ruled out." She laughed a little laugh, which was better than no laugh at all. "Dr. Kidd mentioned I may have heart problems. Heart Arrhythmia. I also might have a respiratory infection of some kind. They spent most of yesterday running tests. Dean Benchoff and Father X were in last evening to see me. They may have talked to the doctors or nurse, but I don't know. Medically, I'm in the dark."

Gary, looking out the room door, spoke up. "Speak of the devil, here's the Dean himself."

We laughed as Benchoff strode through the door and glowered at Gary. "Please keep your rude comments to yourself, Mr. Robbins. There is no need to verbalize every course thought running through that hockey addled brain of yours! Only students who are guilty of some crime see me as the devil!"

"Zing!" I hooted. "Don't mess with our Dean!"

After we stopped laughing and poking fun at Gary and the Dean, we settled down. Rob returned with a mug of hot chocolate. Mostly, we listened while Benchoff gently asked Faith a lot of house-keeping questions about issues in her personal life. He made it clear these were not things Faith needed to worry about while she was in the hospital. Either he or Dean Feltgood would see that all of her needs were covered. Anything she required would be worked out. In short, his pitch was for our friend not to worry, but just focus on getting better.

When we said goodbye, the Dean gave me a nod and suggested we join him in the Waiting Room where we could talk privately. With a worried look on his face, he said, "I did speak with Dr. Linear, the critical care physician treating Faith, before I joined you. The news isn't good."

Benchoff paused, and then continued. "Her heart's been seriously compromised. They've mentioned arrhythmia, but I think they are understating the problem so they don't frighten Faith. The symptoms are more like congestive heart failure. Her lungs are damaged, and it's hard to tell how much function they can recover. Faith's kidneys have been damaged. The condition is called rhabdomyolysis, and it has to do with the inability of the body to clean the blood any more. Usually these symptoms are the result of long-term drug abuse, specifically cocaine."

Randi let out a big sigh. "That's bad, but I'm not surprised. Faith has been ingesting any drug she can get for years. I think it's her way of trying to numb the pain in her life. Can the doctors help her?"

"Her vital systems – heart, lungs, and kidneys – are weakened. How much damage is permanent, they can't tell. She needs extensive medical treatment. There's no quick and easy cure."

"Shit!" Was all I could say. "I was afraid it was something serious. She's been sick for so long and sliding downhill since the beginning of the school year. But we could never get her to ask for help or even admit there was anything wrong. I hope there's not too much damage."

"I'm sure you did all you could to reach out to her. Sometimes it's hard to help someone who doesn't feel they deserve help. Speaking of help, I've called Mrs. Stetson, Skeeter's Mom."

"Skeeter's Mom?" Gary asked." I don't get it." We all gave the Dean puzzled looks.

Benchoff continued, "Faith and Father X are surprisingly close. They've had a lot of conversations over the last year. When I called him yesterday for advice, he suggested I call Sukie Stetson. Apparently, Faith shared her regrets about Skeeter and her admiration for his family with the Father.

"Skeeter's Mom has stayed in touch with Faith, even after Skeeter joined the Army and went to Vietnam. Sukie, Kitty, and Sunny keep reaching out, sending cards and notes, and phoning Faith. I called Mrs. Stetson last night. She is coming out to care for Faith."

We looked at the Dean in stunned silence. I admit; I simply can't understand what he is saying. "Pardon me?" I'm confused, and from the looks on their faces, so are my friends.

"Mrs. Stetson is coming out to care for Faith. I know, it sounds incredible, but there it is. Some people demonstrate love and compassion with actions, rather than simply offering kind words and platitudes. I spent fifteen minutes on the phone with this woman last night, and I can assure you, she is a force of nature. Mrs. Stetson's mother is coming to stay with her own family and she is going to be here as long as needed to get Faith on the mend. No way am I going to argue with her. I'd advise you to be supportive as well. Ha, ha!...if you know what's good for you!"

With a laugh, the Dean stood, and we walked out to the parking lot. Almost four years and the man still continues to surprise me! I don't know how it's possible. We were in shock as we drove back to campus trying to digest the news of the morning.

Monday morning Mrs. Stetson showed up on campus. She walked into Musselman at breakfast time, took one look around the room and made a bee line for our group at the Koffee Klatch table. "Hi," she said, "I'm Skeeter's mom. I'm guessing you are the infamous Koffee Klatch Gang, am I right?"

I couldn't keep from busting out in a laugh. "Welcome, Mrs. Stetson, we've heard about you too!" My friends around the table stared at her, not knowing what to make of this tall willowy blonde. She was dressed in neatly pressed blue jeans, a white oxford cloth button down shirt with a blue goose down vest over the shirt. She had on a blue knit cap with white reindeer around the brim. The woman looked like she was headed over to Liberty Mountain to go skiing for the day. At the same time, she vibrated with barely suppressed energy. Skeeter's mom had a look in her eyes, a flashing intensity, which made me begin to understand the Dean's "force of nature" comments.

"Please join us, Mrs. Stetson." I said, offering her a chair. "We're so glad you are here."

"Call me Sukie. We're going to be spending a good deal of time together if we are to help Faith, and I would like to do that as friends. Do y'all know Skeeter?" she asked.

We all nodded an affirmative answer with our heads and continued to stare at Sukie Stetson.

"I don't know how much you know about Skeeter's early years, but when he was eight years old, he woke up one morning to discover his mother, my older sister, was dead. Beth died of a brain aneurism in her sleep. She was fully present at bedtime and forever gone when he woke up the next day. It was a tremendous shock to Skeet and his Dad. At the time, I was ten years younger than my sister Beth and had just graduated from college. I didn't have a job, so I moved in to help out."

Sukie paused, "Frankly, Chip and Skeeter were basket cases by the time I arrived a couple months after the funeral. I only came to look after the boy and the household, but I learned a lot about healing. People can be tremendously damaged by their emotions, by relationships, or tragic things which blindside them, like my sister's death. I'm not a nurse, but I think I have a degree of sensitivity and insight into people's feelings and inner world. It was a slow process but gradually Chip and Skeeter began to come out of deep depression. My sense is Faith is suffering from similar damage. Perhaps a broken heart, a critical loss of hope, as well as the physical problems she has. Losing your spirit and the will to live will kill you a lot faster than any physical ailment.

"The first time I met Faith, my heart went out to her. I could tell she's been wounded by her family, her upbringing, and by bad religion. I'm sorry things never worked out with Faith and Skeeter – I would have loved to have her in our family. But we've remained friends over the past few years. As a family, we're committed to helping Faith get on her feet and find the good God has for her in life. She surely has not seen much of it so far."

After a long, quiet pause, I spoke. "Thank you for coming. Faith needs people who will love her and stand by her to help her through this crisis. This little group of friends is probably all the family she has right now. We're just college students, so we appreciate anything you can do to help our friend get well. Do you have a plan?"

"I spoke with Father Xavier last night when I arrived. He brought me up to speed on this band of friends, your Jesus family, and all that's gone on. We had a long chat and the Father had plenty of good things to say about y'all. The Dean and I met at seven this morning and he shared about the medical diagnosis and Faith's family situation. I'm here for the duration. I'll be staying in a local hotel and will sit with Faith, nurse her back to health, encourage her. Whatever it takes. Chip and I have agreed to pick up her medical expenses. We can afford it. I want to share this ministry with you guys. You really are her family. She loves you and needs you – even if she can't express it. Can we do this together?"

"Whoa, Nellie!" Gary exclaimed. "You are pretty cool for a Mom. Skeeter is lucky to have you! Just tell us what you need us to do and we're there. You name it; we want to help."

Sukie Stetson took charge. She established her mama bear role with the hospital and medical staff. Within days, they were dancing to her tune. She organized our friends to visit and pray for Faith. "Every day I remind her, 'you matter to God!'" Sukie explained. "I tell her 'Jesus says not a single sparrow falls to the ground without God's consent. You're much more valuable, Faith. God knows you and loves you.'"

Mrs. Stetson told me, "You and your friends coming to see her demonstrate the truth that she matters. Each of you is sharing a little of God's love wrapped in warm human skin." Sukie organized us on a schedule so we wouldn't exhaust Faith with too much love and attention. This wonder woman got the Father, Doc Brody, Benchoff and Miss Feltgood dancing to her music. She straightened out issues with the college, made long-term care arrangements for Faith and ran a tight ship. When I grow up, this is the kind of a woman I want to be!

Her only failure was with Faith's family in Georgia. Sukie and Father X both spent time on the phone trying to interest the McFaddens in their daughter's condition. They wrote letters and sent pictures. Sukie even got the president of Carlisle College, Dr. Shockley, to call. Faith's parents were completely unresponsive. One afternoon, Sukie admitted to me, "Talking to the McFadden's is like slamming your head against a brick wall. Her father said, 'She's made her bed, now she will have to lie in it. We don't want anything to do with her.' I just don't understand people like that."

All winter long, this epic battle raged. Sukie ran the world trying to heal Faith. We went back to being college students who simply dipped in to visit our friend. Sukie didn't want Faith to have Christmas alone so she convinced Chip and the girls come out from Philadelphia to celebrate the holiday with Faith in her hospital room. When the hospital decided they could do little more to help her, Mrs. Stetson had Faith transferred to a private room at Good Shepherd, Jack's rehab facility. Our role is to turn up several times a week, visit with Faith, or to simply sit in the corner and pray quietly for her.

The days and weeks passed as in a dream world – a place where you can't tell where the nightmare ends and reality begins. We sat around Koffee Klatch missing Faith. Inside, I am so wounded by feeling my friend's pain, but there is nothing more I can do to help her. So, we distract ourselves with talking about the events of the wider world. In February, the Chicago 7 went on trial for their alleged role in the riots at the 1968 DNC convention. What a pack of lies! I know – we were there.

We visit Faith at Good Shepherd. Sukie has brightened her room with flowers and balloons, get well cards and gifts. Big windows let in lots of light. It's a warm and sunny place, as much from Sukie's life force and presence as from the rays of the sun. But the medical news gets worse. Faith is visibly weaker as time goes on. She looks so pale. Her skin is translucent, like she is fading away. The doctors say her lungs are clearing up, but her kidneys and heart are gradually failing.

In early April, we rejoiced with Arty Swaboda who announced he was engaged to Monica Albright. Monica is the Plymouth Brethren chick Gary insists on calling Betty Boop. After her fling with Billy Harrison she got a new hairdo and better clothes. Arty and Monica have been an item since last fall. In July, Monica will marry Arty as he begins his job at US Steel. She keeps walking around waggling the diamond on her finger to anyone who will look. Obnoxious! I only hope she can domesticate Arty. "Fuckin' A!"

Many of my friends are making post-graduation plans. Bunny is preparing to move back to New York City and work with poor kids from his old neighborhood. Billy landed a prestigious internship in the White House. Ratso is set to return to Richmond and run his afterschool program. Gary is looking for high school coaching jobs, and I'm waiting to see where he lands. Meanwhile, Mom and I are busy planning my wedding in State College on May 23rd.

All this excitement about the future! Then we go see Faith. What a downer. I find myself wondering if she has a future at all. She just lays in bed looking miserable and forlorn. Sukie is constantly by her side, mopping her brow with a moist cloth, urging her to take a small sip of ginger ale, plumping her pillows. Each time we come to visit, there is less light in her sad blue eyes.

Gary and I often sit quietly in the corner of the room and pray silently while Sukie ministers to our friend. Honestly, it doesn't look good. I've never seen anybody die, but I can see the life seeping out of Faith's body. You didn't need a thermometer to know what's going on. Her face is the window into her being. I have no idea what the medical issues are, but her inner light is growing dim.

One afternoon in late April, Sukie asked us if we would take over the nursing so she could run an errand. Gary and I slid our chairs over to the bed and I took up sponging her fevered brow. Gary gently held Faith's hand, "How are you doing Sugar Booger?"

Faith opened her eyes and smiled at him. "Funny man," was all she could murmur.

"Honey, may I share with you?" Gary asked.

"Please do." She whispered and squeezed his hand.

"Faith, I want to you to know about eternity. You see, God made us for relationship. He lives in relationship himself. He is in a tight little community composed of the Father, Jesus the Son, and the Holy Spirit. God loves each person he has ever made and he longs to be in relationship with them. He wants to be in a personal relationship with you."

"I don't think God wants to be in a relationship with me," was Faith's response. "You don't have any idea of how bad I am and how many things I've done wrong. I know I have to get my life cleaned up before I can get right with God. Honestly, I've made such a mess of things. Even if I had a lot more time, I could never clean up all the mess I've created."

"I agree," Gary assured her. "But we are all in the same boat. We've all screwed up and fall short of God's standards. But Jesus intervenes on our behalf. The Bible says what we are powerless to do, to clean up the mess of our lives; God did for us by sending Jesus. Jesus' death and resurrection cleans up the mess and lets us start a fresh relationship with God. He offers forgiveness, grace and peace."

For a while we sat in silence while Gary stroked Faith's hand. "Tell me more." she finally said.

"What's important is it doesn't depend on what we do. It depends entirely on God's grace. Forgiveness, salvation and a new relationship with God are free gifts. You do nothing to earn them. All you have to do is repent and accept his free gift. The Bible says repenting simply means to turn around. Go in a new direction. It's like you are walking away from the sun and everything is getting dark. Turn around and begin to walk towards the sun – things immediately get lighter."

"Man, that's me," Faith commented. "Ever since I was a teen I've been moving away from God. I don't know if it was rebellion or just reacting to all the untrue things I've been told about God. Maybe I was rejecting people who claimed to be speaking for him. Now my life is almost pitch black. Can I tell you about it?" Faith held our hands and poured out her heart. She talked about her childhood, her family, the lies, the drinking, and the sex. She told us about hurting Skeeter, trusting Frank Ramsey, the cocaine and drugs, Spud, Butch and working as a stripper. She dumped out the whole sorry story. When she finished with her confession, she looked relieved.

Gary held her hand, "Can we pray with you?" Faith nodded assent. "Father, we lift our friend Faith into your gentle loving arms. We know you have always been there with her, but often your presence is like the wind. We can feel the breeze and see the influence and results, but sometimes it's hard to see it's you. Help Faith to see you right now, to know your love. Assure her of your forgiveness and help her to enter into a relationship with you."

"Yes, Lord, I want to know you." Faith said. "I trust you. Forgive me. Lead me." With these words we lapsed into silence for several moments. The look on Faith's face began to change, to soften, and relax. Gradually, a smile spread across her face. She opened her eyes, "I feel such peace. Thank you, I feel better already. He's like the wind, blowing fresh, clean air into my life. I can feel a difference." Faith closed her eyes and fell asleep. She looked like a small child; safe; resting in her mother's arms.

On April 30th, Nixon addressed Congress informing them and the American people the US military had been secretly bombing Cambodia for the previous year. Instead of ending the war as he promised, Nixon was expanding the war. College campuses all over the US erupted in demonstrations and protests against the government and the war. Across America, there was a sense of betrayal and moral indignation. Ordinary citizens expressed their outrage, both over the lies and duplicity of our political leaders and at the continued, senseless killing of American soldiers.

Honestly, I just don't care. Frenchie got into a big argument with Billy about Nixon. All I could think about was my last conversation with Sukie Stetson. "Dear, dear Nikki," she began, wrapping me in a big hug. We were in the waiting room at Good Shepherd while Faith was sleeping. "The doctors told me there's nothing more they can do but keep Faith comfortable. She is dying. Faith has lots of issues, but they expect the congestive heart failure will take her soon. In days, not weeks. I am so sorry." Sukie hugged me tight and we held each other and wept.

"I think she's at peace, now," Sukie added." I believe she is ready to go home and be with Jesus. God's Word promises when we finally go home with the Lord, we will be in a place where there is no pain and no sadness. Jesus will heal her and give her a fresh start at life. I know you love her and will miss her, but she'll be better off at home with Jesus."

I know Sukie is right, but still, I'm so sad I'm afraid my heart will break. Except for Gary and Randi, I can hardly stand to be with anybody. This grief is crushing me, and she hasn't left us yet. Our little Jesus family is praying for Faith, but I am simply overwhelmed. I just can't be with people right now.

Saturday afternoon, Gary came to my room. "Sukie called. She wants us to get Randi and Rob and come over. We need to go now. It won't be long." I pulled on a sweatshirt and we left to pick up Bachmann and Fox. The ride to Camp Hill was somber. We each sat quietly with our own thoughts.

In Faith's room, we found Jack in a wheelchair with Amy Feltgood. Sukie had gone down the hall to get them when the hospice nurse gave her the warning. The two of them insisted on coming to support Faith in this final hour. There we were, dear friends from this life gathered around Faith's bed. Seven people who love Faith enough to help her with her transition into eternity. Eternity...that sounds so final. So permanent. Eternity.

We sat surrounding Faith with our love. Each of us took turns praying and we sang songs. Jesus songs, old hymns, whatever we could remember, even lullabies to put a child to sleep. Faith looks like a child. She is now so small and pale in the bed. It is as if her life is drifting out and leaving just the husk of her old self behind. Mostly her eyes are closed, but once in a while they creep open and she gives us a lovely smile. I think she is finally at peace.

Eventually, her eyes no longer open, but she lay there taking shallow breaths. We sat and prayed and watched her breath in, breath out. Finally, a little after five pm, there simply was no more breathing. Faith lay still, like a wax mannequin of an angel at rest. Her features smoothed over, calm lay on her face, and she looks tranquil. At the same time, there is a definite sense that her person, the soul and spirit which make her Faith McFadden, has flown the nest and is no longer home. Faith is gone. All I can do is turn to Gary, who wrapped me in his arms, hugged me and let me cry. Faith is gone.

43

"Where your treasure is,
there your heart will be also."
~ Jesus

Rob Bachmann   May, 1970

Faith died Saturday, May 2nd. Sukie Stetson and Father X took care of the funeral arrangements. The service was scheduled for Wednesday morning at the Carlisle College Chapel, the small stone structure at the edge of campus where Jack had his accident. While it's convenient for people from the college, it doesn't hold many people. We didn't expect a big turnout.

While we were absorbed by our pain and sadness at Faith's death, the nation erupted in grief and anger at yet another betrayal by our leaders. Since the revelations about Nixon's military incursion into Cambodia, college campuses and communities have been exploding with anger and resentment. At a protest rally at Kent State on Monday, May 4th, National Guardsmen fired into a peaceful crowd of several thousand students, bystanders, and observers killing four and wounding 11 others. This nightmare marked the beginning of a generational loss of trust in public authority and elected leaders.

At Carlisle College, the reaction was muted. So many of us were heartbroken over Faith. We simply didn't have room to grieve for the slain students or the loss of moral bearings in our nation. Others had given political activism a shot and found it lacking. As Frank said, "Don't be such a ninny! Believing politicians is like trusting the weather forecast. There's no future, no hope in such misplaced confidence. Remember Halloween? 'A few inches of rain?' Come on, don't be so gullible. Our leaders lied to us! What did you expect? Anyone who thinks government is going to solve our problems is a fool. Elections, laws, and policies can't change the human heart. That's the root of the problem."

Wednesday arrived and all I can think about is my sorrow that Faith's journey is over. Faith was such a sweet girl. Like me, she had a tough childhood, but she too arrived at college seeking a better way. Many of us reach a point in life where we long for a fresh beginning. One moment, we're living out an exciting opportunity, looking forward to finding new answers. Then suddenly, Faith's life was snuffed out. Gone.

I dislike funerals. Who doesn't? I've not had much experience with them, but its all been bad. My Mom's funeral when I was twelve was agonizing. There she was up front in a box in the funeral parlor. People got up and said this and said that but it felt impersonal. It was so cold and remote.

Ted's funeral was totally traumatic. The revelation that my father had killed my mother, followed by Teddy's death, left me reeling. It was if every circuit breaker inside me was blown. I felt nothing. I simply went through the motions until I could get out of there and escape to Carlisle College.

The only other funeral I've attended was Spud Mueller's. I sat there wondering how a nice girl like Faith ever got mixed up with a loser like Spud. Honestly, I guess I figured his death was a consequence of choices he made in his life. Was Faith any different? Probably not. She made a string of bad choices and the natural consequence of those choices was her early exit from life. But this is different. I loved Faith in spite of all her mixed up foolish choices. I always wanted what was best for her, even when she was busy making dreadful choices for herself.

Father X is to give the message at the service. The funeral mumbo jumbo freaks me out. The music freaks me out. I guess I'm not used to church music. The people get under my skin. Why would anyone want to kiss a body in a box? Or say sweet things to someone who is no longer here? I don't know much about any of this stuff, but take one look at Faith's body, and it's obvious whatever spirit animated her life and made her Faith McFadden is long gone. Weird!

Thankfully, when Father X rose to speak, it put a stop to all the bizarre shenanigans going on. He stood behind the small lectern for a full minute before he spoke. "We gather together to remember our dear friend Faith McFadden. For a moment, I want to talk to you about her life. As much as it may surprise you, the story of Faith's life is a love story."

He paused, "Faith arrived at Carlisle on a journey, a search to find a new life, to find home. Every one of us embarks on that same journey at one time or another. In our journey we often make mistakes or are simply the innocent victim of tragic circumstances. I think of the horrific events at Kent State earlier this week. We may be affected by tragedy for which we carry no blame. Or we are suffering the consequences of our own poor choices. As we journey through life we will face broken promises, failed ambitions, broken hearts, broken dreams, and dashed hopes.

"Yet God is a God of second chances. He is relentless in his love for us and his desire to be in relationship. His mercy and grace know no limits. He sent his son Jesus to come and live in our world and history so he could reconnect with us. Jesus died on the cross to vanquish sin and offer forgiveness for all our mistakes. His resurrection broke the power of death - he is alive and available to any of us today so we can experience his love in our lives.

"Faith was on this journey, this search for home. It's important to understand home is not a building. It's not a geographic place. Nor is it a career or an accomplishment. Many invest their lives and put their hope in such things only to find themselves deeply disappointed in the end.

"Home is a people, it's a family. Many of you sitting here today became Faith's family. Your love gave her a new beginning and a place to belong. It's a love story.

When Faith put her trust in Jesus, she found her way home. Now she is with Jesus and his forever family – home without end. It's a love story.

"Death is not the enemy, nor is it the end of life. Jesus conquered death through his life, death and resurrection. He's broken the power of death forever. The passing of this body is just a way station on the journey of life. For some, like Faith, it comes early. Others will live longer but we will all pass this point on our journey. Most of life takes place after this earth and this mortal body – it goes on in eternity."

Father Xavier had my attention. The chapel was hushed as the audience hung on his every word. "God promises us, in his word, Faith is now in a better place. Those who choose God, who accept Jesus, as Faith has, will live in a place where there are no more tears, no more pain, no more suffering, and no more sorrow. It is a place full of his peace and light. We will receive new spiritual bodies, we will build houses and live in them, plant gardens and eat from them.

"Faith's journey is not over, it's just beginning. She left home looking for a new way, a better way, a home and she achieved it through her trust in Jesus. The best days of her life are in front of her. Nothing can ever take her from that good place.

"We do not weep for Faith – she's finally home. We weep for ourselves, for our loss of this dear one, for our own search and struggle through the journey of life. This is as it should be. I urge you to guard your hearts as you go on with your journey. The heart is the wellspring of life. Be careful who or what you give your heart to. God allows us the great gift of letting us choose what we give our hearts to - but those choices have consequences.

"Open your heart to God. What he offers you is much more than fire insurance for life in eternity. Jesus says those who accept him will have rivers of living water flowing out of the heart and through our lives both on this earth and for eternity. This wellspring of life is a free gift. You can't earn it. It depends on nothing you do. Jesus is standing at the door of your life knocking. Only you can let him in. If you have doubts, that's ok. Ask him to show himself to you. To prove he is real. To show you how to be in relationship with him. He will. You can count on it.

"Love is a verb. It's an action. God demonstrated his love for us by sending Jesus when we still had no clue. Jesus lived his life to show us the way back to God. He accomplished all that's needed. But we still must respond to his free gift. It requires an action on your part. Faith has taken this step of action and is now with Jesus in his forever family."

As Father X spoke, I found myself deeply moved by his words. The picture of Faith at home in a new place, where there is no pain, no sorrow, and no tears made me want to weep. A place of family, love and relationships you can always count on. In some mysterious way, I think that's what I've been looking for all my life. When I consider the world which might be, which I can almost see beyond the mist, shimmering out ahead of me, it looks a lot like what the Father described.

X continued, "If you haven't trusted Jesus, I encourage you to do so today. Don't put it off. Don't think, 'Oh, I'll get to that later.' Today is the only day we've been given. Yesterday is gone and we can only hope there will be a tomorrow. Life is precious and fleeting. Often those we love are taken without warning, in the blink of an eye. If you feel Jesus tugging at your heart, do something about it today."

Ouch! That hit home for me. Like my mom. Like Skeeter's mom. Like Ted. Life is fleeting. We can't assume we'll live to three score and ten. Many of us, like Faith, check out much sooner. Often without any warning. When we began at Carlisle College in August of 1966, who would have ever guessed Faith would be gone before we graduated? Sobering thoughts.

We filed out of the Chapel after the service, but I simply can't stand the thought of a graveside service. My mind and heart are in turmoil. How can I endure readings of the 23rd Psalm, reciting some prayer by St. Francis of Assisi? Chanting 'ashes to ashes, dust to dust' and similar religious sayings? I don't think I see the point. Tossing dirt on the coffin to say goodbye. Why not just say goodbye?

I slipped off out of the crowd and escaped around the back of the Chapel. As people got in their cars and the procession followed the hearse out College Avenue to the cemetery, I cut across the commuter lot and followed the west bank of the Antietam Creek up into the woods above campus. I just need to think, to process my feelings. My soul is tormented.

I feel emotionally constipated; if there can be such a thing. I need space to process what's gone on in the last week. I walked up the brook until I came to a large sugar maple and sat in its shade to watch the water burble by. The smooth bark of the maple tree curved up and made a comfortable backrest for my improvised seat. The leaves overhead threw dappled shade and sunlight in changing patterns all around me. I watched the water flow down over rocks and through pockets while the light danced all over the moving surface. Occasionally I can see a shadow or the bright red orange flicker of a brook trout fining below the surface.

How many years has this brook done exactly what it's doing today? Water, collecting in rivulets, freshened by springs, steadily drifting down the mountain and joining the flow rolling past my feet. Decades? Centuries? Longer? Even the 'Storm of the Century' this past fall seems to have made little impact on this display of nature's consistency. If God is faithful about little things – like the brook, the trout, the trees, and the sunlight – why would he not be faithful in his relationships with those he created?

I'm so mixed up; I wonder if I'm going crazy? Am I crazy to want to know Jesus? I trust what Father X says because I see it in his life. I see it in Randi and Nikki and Gary. Am I crazy not to accept him? It's a fearful thing to take this step. Overwhelmed by thoughts and emotions, I got up and started walking. I headed back into town, mostly to have something to do to occupy myself in hopes my mind would sort out this confusion. As I wandered down street after street, I realized I was going to TMO. When I got to the store, I took a seat on one of the benches out front. Perhaps when Father X gets back from the service, he can help me figure this out.

316

A half hour after I took up my vigil, Doc Brody pulled to the curb and dropped the Father in front of Tuscarora Mountain Outfitters. Father X saw me sitting out front, and sat down with me. For a while, we sat in companionable silence. As the good Father has taught me on many occasions, sometimes the best thing to say is nothing at all. He waited until I was ready to talk and let me take the lead.

"I was deeply touched by what you shared at the funeral. Perhaps disturbed is a better word."

"Yes, tell me more."

"I'm trying to figure out where my heart is. I think I'm good at guarding it, but I realize I've been building a fortress around my heart for years. Even before my mother died, I felt a need to protect myself. To wall the world out, to wall out feelings so I wouldn't get hurt. I'm not sure how to open my heart to the possibility of a relationship with God. That would be a big step for me."

The Father pulled out his pipe, packed it with fragrant tobacco and fired up before responding. "Genuine conversion is a matter of the heart, but it is also a matter of the mind and the hand. It begins with a willingness to release control of our life and to give it over to God. Then we need to learn to listen for his voice and to obey his leading. Obedience is the forerunner of understanding. He illumines our mind when we give him our heart and obedience."

He paused and drew on the briar. "Don't worry; it doesn't depend on you. God knows we're frail and failure prone creatures. Jesus gives us the Holy Spirit so we can live the life he calls us to. The Spirit provides wisdom and direction through life. He also puts us in a community of fellow believers to support and encourage us. He's left us his word, the Bible. These are love letters God has written to guide his children. You will never be alone in this journey with Jesus."

We sat for a while, each with our own thoughts. Then I spoke, "I have to admit, I've always been an independent cuss. What if following Jesus makes me weird?"

"Dear boy," the Father said with a smile. "God has already made you the way you are." He laughed, "The weird, twisted, wonderful guy you are is the result of God's design. Accepting Jesus will not make you into a different person. It will make you into a better person. He loves you and planned you to be you. He will get rid of the bad things in your life and replace them with good bits. God's goal is to help you become the best 'you' you can be. Think of it as an engine tune-up rather than an engine replacement."

We sat while I digested what the Father had said. "OK. That makes sense to me. I guess I need to process it some more."

"Let me know if you have more questions. I'm here for you, but you know that."

"I do. And thanks."

I got up and wandered back towards campus. Walking helps me think, I guess. I went back to the bridge over the creek. Then I took the footpath which skirts the outside edge of campus. As I walked, I found the words of an old Woody Guthrie song rattling around in my brain. "You've got to walk that lonesome valley; you've got to walk it by yourself. No, nobody else can walk it for you; you've got to walk it by yourself." Eventually I found myself in the grove of trees around the pond. At the fallen pine log in the woods, I took a seat where I could observe the water, the trees and the wildlife.

Looking at my life, at the man I am today, I see I have worked hard to protect my heart. I've constructed fences to protect myself from hurt. I'm protected, alright, but I'm alone. I'm tired of always being alone. Unless I open up and change something in my life, it's likely I'll spend my life being alone.

I don't want to live my whole life the way I am now. I want to be like Randi. And Gary and Nikki. They are open to life, to the future. None of them is living defensively, behind walls, like I am. They are excited about what tomorrow will bring. I can see Jesus is helping them to find their best self. I want to be like them. I spoke out loud, "God if you are real, help me to trust you."

More than being like them, I want to share life with them. This Jesus family is now my family. These people are my people. I don't know where life is going to take me, but I want to go there with these people and others like them. Where ever they go, I want to go with them. These people love me, believe in me and see the best in me. I want to belong to them. I want to be part of whatever Jesus is doing in the world and I want to be part of what he is doing with my friends.

I wandered out to the edge of the orchard behind the woods and pond. The trees in front of me are bursting with new blooms. White blossoms indicate apple trees, pink marks the cherry trees, and the peach trees sport a cloud of lilac and white colored flowers. The sight before me is mind blowing. It's like a massive fireworks display, bursting bombs of color spread as far as the eye can see. Unlike fireworks made by the hand of man, this display is in broad daylight. Instead of drifting clouds of smoke, lush scents waft across to my nostrils. Unlike fireworks, the burst of color doesn't quickly fade; it keeps on going – a spectacular display of nature's power and beauty with no end in sight.

I got down on my knees, bowed my head and closed my eyes. "Lord, I'm not sure how to pray, but I want to acknowledge you. If you are real, please show me who you are. I want to give my life to you. I surrender. I want what my friends have found in you. I want to join your family and have you be the leader in my life. Show me what you would have me do."

For a while, I sat on my knees. Eventually, I rolled over into a sitting position in the grass with my arms locked around my knees. Looking out at the astonishing sight of the orchard in full bloom. What a spectacle! Inside I have no overwhelming emotions. No internal fireworks. I admit, the heavens did not open up and angels did not come down singing the 'Hallelujah Chorus.' OK, that might have been a lot to expect. I don't know what I expected. But I'll tell you what I got. I felt at peace. To me it seems I've made a positive step and I'm confident it's the right step. Somehow, I just know he will prove to be true and he will show me the way. A half hour later I walked back to campus with a comfortable feeling. Now that I've accepted Jesus' offer, I find I do believe he is true. The real deal. As Father X says,

"Hope is the confidence of good things to come." For the first time in my life, I have hope.

Saturday, May 16th dawned bright and cloudless as the Class of 1970 prepared for graduation. Benchoff warned us, "We only have two kinds of graduations at Carlisle. We have 95 degrees out on the football field in the blazing hot sun. Or we have sixty degrees, humid with pouring rain - then we hold it in the gym. In either case, be prepared to sweat buckets! Ha ha!" Dear Dean Benchoff and his clever wit. The Class of '70 got the first variety; heat and scorching sunshine. Not a cloud in sight to offer relief as we sit in nature's broiler, dressed in voluminous black gowns and caps. Yowza! Am I ever melting!

After the ceremony, the college rolled out a lovely picnic luncheon for our family and friends on the lawn in front of Musselman. We escorted our loved ones to the feast and introduced them to one another. Soon the guests were busy stuffing themselves with fried chicken, barbeque, burgers and hot dogs. Our little group managed to sneak off for one last gab fest before this final day of our college experience ended. We pulled up a circle of red Adirondack chairs in the deep shade of a big striped maple.

Nikki, TAB in hand, led off the conversation. "All during graduation I had this line from a Beatle's tune stuck in my head. It goes, 'There are places I remember, all my life...' and the song made me think about you guys and all the memories I will take away from this place. Dear precious memories, which I know I will never lose."

"OK," Randi suggested, let's share one memory from our time together you are sure you'll never forget. No couples crap either," she added looking at me with an easy smile on her face.

"Hey!" I protested, while giving Randi a squeeze, "I'm not even thinking about you. Not even on my top ten list!" She cheerfully turned and punched me on the arm.

Billy said, "My most indelible memory was the first kegger of freshman year. Spending the night trapped in a mine pit with the delectable Delilah Brown."

"Nice one, Billy," said Frank with a laugh.

"Yeah, be serious," added Gary. "For me.... The most unforgettable memory would be...seeing Nikki skinny dipping for the first time!"

After the laughter died down, Randi added, "No really! I'm feeling nostalgic. Help me with this. Help me feel nostalgia. Be serious."

"The Waffle Club is my high point," said Linda. "It definitely opened up new worlds for me."

Doug joined in. "I think Woodstock was the high point for me. There's some mysterious way where God speaks to me through music. I've always been wired to connect to music. The whole Woodstock experience was some kind of a turning point for me."

"Ratso's redemption, to me, seems like a miracle," Frank shared. "After freshman year, I would have bet everything I own, no, everything I would ever own, that Ratso would leave college the biggest shit ever known to mankind. And now he is so changed... I don't know what to say. It leaves me speechless."

I can see tears forming on the corners of Frank's eyes. Wow, he really is moved. "I guess for me, seeing as we can't talk about the opposite sex, I think my big kahuna memory will be Jack. He was my best friend most of my time here. Hunting, fishing, trapping together. Hanging out with Father X. I'll never forget my horror seeing him fly his motorcycle through the plate-glass. His survival and recovery strike me as a God sized miracle. Ditto to whatever the heck happened with him and Amy. Together, with Frenchie's help, Jack and I discovered what family really looks like and got a taste of it here."

"The Jesus family does it for me," said Randi. "Coming to faith in a way so different from my family and background, our Jesus family has given me great support and helped me grow."

Bunny spoke up. "Doc Brody, his Bible Intro courses, and almost drowning in the Delaware River are high points which will change my life forever. And thanks for saving me, Gary."

"Hold it," exclaimed Spinnelli. "Flag on the play! Bunny shared three things, maybe even four. No fair!" That brought a good chuckle from the group.

"I think Gary's heart would be my number one take away," explained Nikki. "Besides putting himself at risk to save Bunny, he started the Waffle Club, went fearlessly into the hurricane to rescue Faith and tried in every way to save her. In the end, it just was not meant to be, but Gary's heart wins my vote."

Doug laughed and poked me. "Robbie, could you pass the vomit bag? I think I'm gonna blow chunks here in a minute."

"Me too, brother!" I exclaimed. Everyone proceeded to hurl insults at both Nikki and Gary for a few minutes to express our warm affection for the two of them.

Nikki pronounced the benediction. "In some ways today is bitter-sweet. It marks the end of such an important phase of our lives. But here's the heart of the matter. We came to college looking for life, for meaning, and purpose. We found home and we found family. In one sense, we are now leaving home and going our own separate ways in life. Yet we are family. We will always be a family."

"You all know how much I like to open up and share," I explained to much laughter. "But...as we prepare to leave this place, I feel like I've finally found family, but I'm not leaving it. Here's what I realize. Home is not a place and time. It's a people. It's who we've become together. That will not change. Faith is still a part of us even though she's moved on to heaven. We will always be connected, still be family, even when we are physically far apart."

Randi finished my thought. "This is not actually the end. It's a new beginning. We are launching into the adventure of adulthood, diving into life. We have Jesus and we have lifelong friends."

"Just what I said," I laughed. "I've never been hopeful before. But I am now. We may not be able to change the world, but we can change hearts and lives. One person at a time. My heart has been changed and my life will never be the same."

At this, we all shared a round of hugs with everyone. The girls were weepy, and the guys pretended to be tough. "Let me interject one more thought," I added. "We've seen the way this works. Find others who are searching. We do it together; find the new family we all want and need. Looking for home. We may not be home yet, but we're on our way."

Nikki had the last word. "Keep your eyes open, antennas up, look for God and report back on what you find."

With that thought, we rejoiced in one last family huddle, and then headed back to begin the process of moving on with life. Goodbye, Carlisle College.

Epilogue

"Unless we remember, we cannot understand."
~ E. M. Forester

Nikki Clausen and Gary Robbins got married the Saturday after graduation. In August, Gary landed a job at the Holderness School, a private college prep school in Plymouth, NH. Robbins serves as the head boys Hockey Coach and teaches several American history courses. Nikki came along for the ride and eventually founded the Squam Lakes Outdoor Center in nearby Holderness. This non-profit educational foundation works to preserve the natural resources of the Lakes Region of New Hampshire and runs outdoor education programs for students of all ages.

Arty Swaboda returned home to Pittsburgh. He and Monica Albright (nee 'Betty Boop') were married on July 4th and both claim the marriage is still producing fireworks. Arty is an up and coming junior executive in the US Steel Accounting Department. After a few years, they were able to buy a small home in Squirrel Hill, a tony suburb, where Monica is now busy pumping out babies.

Rob Bachmann and Randi Fox were married the following Valentine's Day. The date was not chosen because of romantic connections. Robbie wanted to be sure future wedding anniversaries would not conflict with any fishing or hunting season. Bachmann was admitted to a Ph.D. Sociology program at the University of Pittsburgh and is a sociology instructor at Waynesburg College, a small school 60 miles south of Pittsburgh. The Bachmanns' purchased a rundown 30-acre property on Sugar Run Road in Mingo Creek Township. Their little homestead is midway between Pittsburgh and the college, which allows Randi to do interior decorating in the suburbs while Rob teaches and finishes his degree at Pitt.

Billy Harrison fulfilled his internship at the White House and was well received. He went on to join the staff of John Ehrlichman, a chief domestic policy advisor to President Nixon. Ehrlichman was a key figure in the Watergate break-in and cover-up. Harrison, along with his boss, was convicted of conspiracy, obstruction of justice and perjury. He served eighteen months at the Federal minimum-security prison in Stafford, Arizona.

Jack Flynn graduated from Penn State, Harrisburg the following year and married Amy Feltgood. Black Jack is now finishing his MD program at Penn State's Hersey Medical School. Amy is a full-time Sociology professor at Carlisle. In July, Jack will begin his orthopedic residency at the Mount Nittany Hospital in State College. Amy has landed a tenure track faculty position at her alma mater.

Bunny Washington returned to New York City after graduation. He is the Director of the Boys and Girls Clubs of Harlem. Bunny's programs reach and support many of the children who live above 125th Street in Manhattan. Bunny works as a community organizer, mentors many young men, and continues to believe in the power of the second chance. Washington lives in the neighborhood and is a much-loved figure in his community.

Frank Spinelli landed as a researcher with the Dow Jones News Corporation. He works on a wide variety of projects, products, and services and is based in their Princeton office. He married a girl named Wanda who plays the cello in the New York Philharmonic Orchestra. Doug Novaksky knew Wanda during his graduate school days at the Berklee College of Music in Boston. When Wanda began her position in New York, Doug set the two of them up on a blind date. The Spinelli's live in a pretty white Dutch Colonial in a charming neighborhood in East Brunswick, NJ. This convenient location allows them both to commute to their respective jobs.

Ratso Ramsey returned to Richmond. Along with his pal Jim Showalter, he continues to work full-time with *East Street*. Staff and volunteers play basketball, build friendships, and run after school programs. Ratso heads up the outdoor experience classes and adventures, and continues to spearhead fundraising. Apparently, he is quite good at it. Ramsey moved into the Church Hill neighborhood. This area is seeing some gentrification, but it is in the heart of the East End community he serves. Ratso bought an old home and is in process of bringing it back to life.

Doug Novaksky went on to marry **Linda Pence**, then earned a Doctorate in Performance Music from the Berklee College of Music in Boston. They returned to Carlisle College where Doug now heads the music faculty on campus. Doug and Linda run a Friends of Jesus group, the successor to the Waffle Club. Their Jesus Family is much like the original. Various small groups grow on campus and spread through networks of relationships, interests or even academic majors. When students leave they take the Jesus group seeds and start anew where ever they relocate. In these groups everybody gets to share, everyone can tell their story. People feel heard and find they belong. Good discussions take place, folks break bread together, experience community, and reach out to care for outsiders who are less fortunate. Doug and Linda are known as the *Godfather* and *Godmother* of the Jesus Family at Carlisle.

91269028R00183

Made in the USA
Columbia, SC
15 March 2018